Y

NICOLA
CORNICK

WHISPER *of* SCANDAL

D0036724

HQN™

If you purchased this book without a cover you should be aware
that this book is stolen property. It was reported as "unsold and
destroyed" to the publisher, and neither the author nor the
publisher has received any payment for this "stripped book."

PLEASE RECYCLE • THIS PRODUCT IS RECYCLABLE •

Recycling programs
for this product may
not exist in your area.

ISBN-13: 978-0-373-77440-1

WHISPER OF SCANDAL

Copyright © 2010 by Nicola Cornick

All rights reserved. Except for use in any review, the reproduction or
utilization of this work in whole or in part in any form by any electronic,
mechanical or other means, now known or hereafter invented, including
xerography, photocopying and recording, or in any information storage
or retrieval system, is forbidden without the written permission of the
publisher, Harlequin Enterprises Limited, 225 Duncan Mill Road,
Don Mills, Ontario M3B 3K9, Canada.

This is a work of fiction. Names, characters, places and incidents are
either the product of the author's imagination or are used fictitiously, and
any resemblance to actual persons, living or dead, business
establishments, events or locales is entirely coincidental.

This edition published by arrangement with Harlequin Books S.A.

For questions and comments about the quality of this book
please contact us at Customer_eCare@Harlequin.ca.

® and TM are trademarks of the publisher. Trademarks indicated with
® are registered in the United States Patent and Trademark Office, the
Canadian Trade Marks Office and in other countries.

www.HQNBooks.com

Printed in U.S.A.

For Martha, Mary and Anne, and for all who sailed with us around Spitsbergen on the *Professor Molchanov*. Thank you for an inspirational voyage!

Praise for Nicola's previous HQN titles

"Ms. Cornick is first-class, queen of her game."
—*Romance Junkies*

"A rising star of the Regency arena."
—*Publishers Weekly*

"Nicola Cornick creates a glittering, sensual world
of historical romance that I never want to leave."
—Anna Campbell, author of *Untouched*

"A wonderfully original, sinfully amusing
and sexy Regency historical by the always
entertaining Cornick."
—*Booklist* on *The Confessions of a Duchess*

"Fast-paced, enchanting and wildly romantic!"
—*SingleTitles.com* on *The Scandals of an Innocent*

"Witty banter, lively action and sizzling passion."
—*Library Journal* on *The Undoing of a Lady*

"RITA® Award–nominated Cornick deftly steeps
her latest intriguingly complex Regency historical
in a beguiling blend of danger and desire."
—*Booklist* on *Unmasked*

"If you've liked Nicola Cornick's other books,
you are sure to like this one as well. If you've never
read one—what are you waiting for?"
—*Rakehell* on *Lord of Scandal*

"Cornick masterfully blends misconceptions,
vengeance, powerful emotions and the realization
of great love into a touching story."
—*RT Book Reviews*, 4½ stars, on *Deceived*

Author Note

A couple of years ago I went on holiday to Spitsbergen, an island within the Arctic Circle off the north coast of Norway. It was not the sort of place that I imagined would inspire a historical romance, but when I started to read about the history of Spitsbergen, I was fascinated. Not only is it a stunningly beautiful place, but it also had a hugely important role in the history of science and exploration. The result of my reading and of that memorable cruise is *Whisper of Scandal*, which I loved writing. It combines some of the elements of the history of Spitsbergen with a rich and romantic love story.

There is much more about the historical background to *Whisper of Scandal* on my Web site at www.nicolacornick.co.uk, and I hope you enjoy exploring it. In the meantime I must own up to one liberty I took with the history and the geography. There was no monastery on Spitsbergen in the early nineteenth century, nor was there any permanent, year-round settlement, because the climate is too harsh. The monastery of Bellsund in the book is modeled on the Solovetsky Monastery on an island in the White Sea.

With a host of furious fancies
Whereof I am commander,
With a burning spear and a horse of air,
To the wilderness I wander.
By a knight of ghostes and shadowes
I summon'd am to tourney
Ten leagues beyond the wild world's end.
Methinks it is no journey.

—From *Tom O'Bedlam's Song,*
anonymous, circa 1600

Part 1
The Grass Widow

Chapter 1

Definition: A Grasswidow (or Grass-widow, grass widow) is a wife whose husband will return after a limited period of time away, usually after a voyage. The "grass" refers to the mattress which used to be filled with grass. The "widow" is left back on the grass/mattress. It might express the idea that the abandoned lover has been "put out to grass." The term is applied "with a shade of malignancy," a tantalisingly opaque comment.

London—May 1811

HE WAS LATE. Eighteen months late.

Alex Grant paused on the steps of Lady Joanna Ware's London town house in Half Moon Street. If he had expected to see any signs of mourning then he was sorely disappointed. No black drapes shuttered the windows and the presence of a large silver knocker on the door indicated that visitors were welcome. Lady Joanna, it seemed, had already thrown off her widow's weeds a bare twelve months after word of her husband's death must have reached her.

Alex raised the silver knocker and the front door opened smoothly, silently. A butler, saturnine in black, stood in the aperture. It was well before the acceptable hour for calling. The butler somehow managed to convey this information—and his disapproval—with the mere twitch of an eyebrow.

"Good morning, my lord. How may I help you?"

My lord. The man did not know him and yet had managed to place his social standing with some accuracy. It was impressive. It was exactly what Alex would have expected from the butler of so prominent and celebrated a society hostess as Lady Joanna Ware. The greeting was also less than welcoming, warning him, perhaps, that Lady Joanna was not accessible to any old member of the hoi polloi who sought her company.

"I would like to see Lady Joanna, if you please," Alex said.

It was not strictly true. He had very little desire to see Lady Joanna Ware; only a strict sense of duty, the obligation owed to his dead colleague, had prompted him to come and pay his respects to the widow. And seeing the lack of mourning, barely an acknowledgment that she had lost so eminent and respected a husband as David Ware, had made Alex's hackles rise and his wish to renew his acquaintance with Lady Joanna dwindle still further.

The butler, too well trained to keeping him standing on the step like a tradesman, had stepped back to allow him access to the hall, although his expression still showed considerable doubt. The black-and-white marble-and-stone checkerboard floor stretched elegantly to a curving stair. Two liveried footmen, identical twins, Alex observed, over six feet tall, stood like statues on either side of a doorway. And from the room behind them carried the sound of a raised feminine voice that completely spoiled this scene of aristocratic elegance:

"Cousin John! Kindly stand up and cease plaguing me with these ridiculous proposals of marriage! In addition to boring me you are obscuring my new rug. I bought it to admire, not to have it knelt upon by importunate suitors."

"Lady Joanna is engaged," the butler informed Alex.

"On the contrary," Alex said. "She has just announced that she is not." He strode across the hall and threw open the door, ignoring the butler's scandalized gasp and enjoying the look of consternation on the woodenly handsome visages of the matching footmen.

The room he entered was a library, bright with sunshine and fresh with lemon and white paint. A fire burned in the grate even though the May morning was warm. A dog, small, gray and fluffy with a blue ribbon in a fetching topknot, lay on a rug before the fire. The dog was as handsome in its own way as the footmen were in theirs and it raised its head and fixed Alex with an inquisitive brown gaze. There was the scent of lilies and beeswax in the air. The room felt warm and welcoming. Alex, who had had no settled home for over seven years and who had never felt the need for one, never wanted one, was brought up short. To relax in such a room, to take a book from those shelves and a glass of brandy from the decanter, to sink into a deep armchair before the fire, suddenly seemed the greatest temptation.

But perhaps not…

The greatest temptation must surely be the woman who was standing by the long library windows with the sunlight threading her rich chestnut hair with sparks of gold and copper. Her face was oval. Her violet eyes were set wide apart above a small, straight nose and a luscious mouth that was so full it was almost indecently sensuous. She was not conventionally beautiful in any way: too tall, too slender, too angular and her face too striking, but it did not matter one whit. In a cherry-red morning gown with a matching bandeau in her hair, she was dazzling. There were no widow's weeds here, not even the lavender of half mourning, to drain the life and vibrancy from her.

Alex had little time to do more than notice just how appealing Lady Joanna Ware was, and to register that appeal at a very deep, masculine and primitive level before she had seen him and had flown across the room to his side.

"Darling! Where have you been? I've been waiting for you for hours!" She threw herself into his arms. "Was the traffic in Piccadilly *utterly* dire?"

Her body felt warm and yielding in Alex's arms, as though she had been made specifically to match him. Shock ripped through him at the sense of deep recognition. She smelled of summer flowers. For a brief moment her face was upturned to his, her violet eyes wide and surely holding fear, of all things, as well as some wordless appeal, and then she had put one hand on the nape of his neck and brought his mouth down to hers and was kissing him as though she really, *really* meant it.

It was astonishingly, instantaneously arousing. Alex's entire body responded to the impossible seduction of her lips, so cool, so soft, so tempting. On mature reflection he thought that perhaps kissing Lady Joanna Ware was a somewhat incendiary way in which to end over two years of celibacy, but in the moment he thought of nothing other than the press of her body against his and the absolute need to take her to his bed—or her bed since it was, presumably, closer.

Heat coursed through his body, and flagrant desire, wickedly strong. But already Lady Joanna was stepping back and freeing herself, leaving him with no more than a promise of heaven and an uncomfortable arousal. Her lips clung to his for a second and he almost groaned aloud. There was a spark of mischief in her violet eyes now as she cast a fleeting glance down at his trousers.

"Darling, you *are* pleased to see me!"

She was calling him darling because she had no idea who he was, Alex realized, taking strategic refuge behind a rosewood desk piled high with books in order to hide his body's all too obvious discomfort. He smiled at her, throwing down a challenge. If she could be outrageous then he could match her. She deserved it for using him when she had no idea of his identity and cared even less.

"What man would not be, my sweet?" he said. "Surely my impatience is entirely forgivable. It seems days since I left your bed rather than hours…" He ignored her audible gasp and turned to the other occupant of the room, a rather florid man of middle age who had been watching them with his eyes popping out and his mouth hanging open a full two inches.

"I am sorry that I did not catch your name, sir," Alex drawled, "but I fear you are too late with your protestations of love. Lady Joanna and I…" He let the sentence hang suggestively.

"Darling!" There was reproach in Joanna's voice now but under it Alex detected more than a spark of anger. "You are no gentleman to make our association public."

Alex crossed to her side, taking her hand in his, turning it over and pressing a kiss to her palm. "Forgive me," he murmured, "but I rather thought you had already demonstrated how intimate we are with that entirely delightful kiss?" Her skin felt deliciously soft against his lips. Hunger stirred in him, ruthless in its demand. He had never been indiscriminate in his love *affaires,* but after the death of his wife he had not lacked female companionship, pleasant, uncomplicated arrangements requiring absolutely no emotional involvement at all. This woman, though, David Ware's less-than-grieving widow, could not be one of his *amours.* She was the widow of his best friend; a wife whom Ware had warned him not to trust. Even as Alex acknowledged all the reasons why he should keep Joanna Ware a great deal farther away than arm's length, his body made it very clear that he might not like her very much but he did want her. He wanted her badly.

How inconvenient. How impossible.

It seemed that Lady Joanna liked him even less than he liked her, for she snatched her hand away from him. A hint of color touched her cheekbones and a steely light came into her eyes.

"I am not sure that I do forgive you." There was warning in her tone. "I am exceptionally angry with you, *darling.*" This last word was hissed through her teeth.

"I don't doubt that you are, *darling,*" Alex returned smoothly.

Wrapped in the intense mixture of desire and antagonism, he had almost forgotten the man, who now sketched a stiff bow. "It seems I am very much *de trop.* Madam." He glared at Joanna, nodded stiffly to Alex and stalked out, slamming the library door behind him.

There was silence, but for the fluttering of a few pages of a book that had been dislodged from the rosewood desk, and the hiss and crackle of the fire in the grate. Then Joanna turned to him and once again Alex felt her gaze search his face. Her eyes narrowed thoughtfully as she looked him up and down, appraising him, hands on hips, head tilted to one side, all pretense of pleasure in his company gone now that they were alone. Anger and awareness simmered between them so strong it was almost tangible. Then:

"Who the hell are you?" she said.

ACTUALLY, SHE KNEW perfectly well who he was. It was simply that she had been shaken out of her habitual poise by the kiss. Joanna had not kissed anyone for longer than she could remember and then it had been her husband and it had not felt anywhere near as sweet, as thrilling, as downright *wicked* as kissing this man had done. She had only intended it to be a brief peck on the lips, light and superficial, signifying nothing. Yet as soon as his lips had claimed her she had wanted to run her fingers over the hard planes and taut lines of his face and body, learning him, reveling in the texture of his skin, the scent and the taste of him. She had wanted it so much that it made her weak at the knees to think about it. A hot spiral of lust curled tight in her stomach, she who had never ever expected to feel desire in her life again.

But this was Alex Grant, her errant husband's *best*

friend—even in her mind she invested the words with scorn—and fellow explorer, who, like David, was forever sailing off around the world in search of war or glory or adventure, trying to find some obscure trade route to China or something equally pointless. She remembered him very well now. Alex Grant had been David's groomsman when they had married ten years before.

Even now it gave her a pang to remember how happy, how hopeful, she had been on that day. High expectations and bad judgment had been a recipe for an unhappy marriage. But on that sunny May morning all that disillusionment had been in the future. She remembered Alex Grant from that day. He had been as improbably handsome then as he was now, though with a softer edge to him. And he had had a wife in tow, a pretty little blonde creature, all giggles and flounces. Annabel, Amelia? Something beginning with *A*. Joanna could not quite recall her name but she had looked at Alex adoringly and had been as charming and as superficial as thistledown.

Guilt stirred within her. Generally she did not make a habit of kissing other women's husbands since she detested the fact that so many other women had kissed hers. David's infidelities had been no secret, but she had no intention of emulating him. Kissing Alex had been a mistake in more ways than one, it seemed. Already reeling from her startling physical reaction to his touch, she now felt angry with him for being just another philandering *bastard*.

Alex bowed. He did it elegantly for all that she had tried to dismiss him as no more than an uncouth sailor in his faded navy captain's uniform. No matter that the uniform suited him rather too well, fitting his broad shoulders most flatteringly and emphasizing his muscular physique. He was a man of great physical presence with strength and authority in every line of his bearing.

Just as David had been… She shivered.

"Alexander, Lord Grant, at your service, Lady Joanna," he said.

"More at my service than I require, I think," Joanna said coldly. "I have no desire for a lover, Lord Grant."

He smiled, a flash of white teeth in his tanned face. "I am desolate."

Liar. She knew that he disliked her as much as she disliked him.

"I doubt it," she said. "Whatever made you suggest such an outrageous thing?"

"Whatever made you kiss me as though you meant it if you did not?"

Once again the air between them hummed with tension as taut as a spun thread. Ah, the kiss. He had a point. She had never before kissed a stranger with such a degree of enthusiasm. She gave a little flick of her fingers, dismissing the question.

"Had you been a gentleman, you would have pretended that we were betrothed rather than lovers." She stopped, glared. "Though I suppose that having a wife already made such a course of action an impossibility for you."

For a moment he looked puzzled and then his face cleared. "I am a widower," he said.

He was succinct, Joanna conceded. Unlike David, who had always tried to buy popularity with wordy compliments, this man seemed brief to the point of abruptness. Clearly he did not care for anyone else's opinion, good or bad.

"I am sorry." She uttered the formal condolence. "I remember your wife. She was charming."

His expression snapped shut like a door slamming. Cold, forbidding… Clearly he did not wish to discuss Annabel…Amelia or whatever her name had been.

"Thank you." He sounded brusque. "But I thought that I was here to condole with you rather than the reverse."

"If you wish to be conventional." Joanna could be succinct, too, especially when she was angry.

"You do not mourn him?" His voice held both censure and anger.

"David died over a year ago," Joanna said. "As you know. You were there."

Alex Grant had written to her from the Arctic, where David's final naval mission to find a northeast trade route via the Pole had—literally—died in the endless frozen wastes. The letter had been as short and to the point as the man himself, though she had been able to discern through the words his deep sorrow at the loss of so noble a comrade. It was not a sorrow she could share and Joanna had made no pretense of it.

Alex's dark gaze flickered over her. She could feel how tightly he was holding his temper in check now. The air was alive with his contempt.

"David Ware was a great man," he said through his teeth. "He deserved more than this—" His gesture encompassed the bright room, devoid of any gesture of mourning.

He deserved better than you…

Joanna heard the words even though they were unspoken.

"We were estranged," she said, her light tone masking the pain beneath. "You were his friend. Surely you knew."

His mouth tightened to a thin line. "I knew he did not trust you."

Joanna turned a shoulder. "The feeling was mutual. Do you think, then, that I should add hypocrisy to my sins and pretend to care that he is dead?"

She saw something feral and violent flash across Alex Grant's face and almost recoiled before she realized that it was loyalty, not anger, that drove him.

"Ware was a *hero*," he said.

Oh, she had heard that so many times it made her want to scream. In the beginning she had believed it, too, plucked from an obscure vicarage in the country, swept away by David's swashbuckling spirit, betrayed by him before the ink was barely dry on the wedding register and betrayed again more deeply years later... She clenched her fists; her palms were hot and damp. Alex Grant was watching her and his dark gaze was far too perceptive. She forced her tense muscles to relax.

"Of course he was," she said lightly. "Everyone says so, so it must be true."

"Yet it seems that you are already considering replacing him," Alex said. "I hear tales in the clubs of your suitors falling over themselves to win your hand."

For a moment his outspokenness silenced Joanna, then she was furious, driven to a whole new level of anger. She wondered what David had told this man about her. Enough to make him dislike her intensely— that was for sure. His aversion to her was not overt, but she could feel it like a constant current beneath the surface, no matter how skillfully, how *wickedly,* he had kissed her.

"If you listen to gossip in the clubs you will hear all manner of lies," she said. "You mistake, Lord Grant. I have no desire to remarry."

Never.

He raised one black brow. "Merely to kiss random strangers, then?"

Oh, this man was provoking. More than that, he was infuriating. Because she knew she did not have a leg to stand on. *She* had kissed *him,* after all, not the other way about. It had been an impulse, a desperate attempt to dissuade John Hagan, her husband's cousin, who had been becoming ever more persistent and disturbingly importunate in his attentions over the past few weeks. Trust her to choose the one man in London who not only called her bluff but also raised the stakes by claiming her as his mistress.

"I think you will find," she said coldly, "that in announcing our apparent liaison you will have created quite a stir in the ton. John Hagan will waste no time in spreading the scandal. I cannot believe that was what you intended when you came to condole with me."

"I merely took my cue from you." His dark eyes studied her, again disconcertingly keen and thorough. There was no liking in them nor the admiration to which she was accustomed, nothing but cool, calculating consideration. Had he really been David's friend? It seemed extraordinary to her. He was steady where David had been quicksilver, slipping through the fingers. The set of his mouth was firm and decisive where David had been weak and easily swayed. Every angle of Alex's face looked hard, as though chiseled from the rock of his Scots heritage.

"So why *did* you kiss me then?" His voice had the faintest of Scots lilt, too. It sounded exotic. "I asked you before but it seems you have a bad habit of failing to answer those questions you dislike."

Damn him, he had noticed that as well, had he? She raised her chin.

"I needed to…persuade John Hagan to cease his attentions to me," she said. She folded her arms tightly about her body in an attempt to ward off the fear that chilled her whenever John Hagan was close by. "He is David's cousin," she explained, "and as such he claims to be the head of the family now."

"So he seeks to take his cousin's widow as well as his place?"

Joanna's eyes narrowed at his tone. "As you heard."

"You came up with a somewhat extreme solution."

Joanna's skin prickled with antagonism at the disbelief that rang clear in his voice. "He would not accept a more subtle dismissal. He has been importuning me for weeks."

"Then it is fortunate I was here. Or would you have called in one of the servants—one of your handsome matching footmen—and kissed him instead?"

Temper flickered through Joanna. She had seldom felt so discomposed. There was something about this man that cut straight through her defenses, something so provocative that got under her skin. She could not deny that he was disturbingly, fatally attractive, but she had absolutely no wish to succumb to that attraction. Men, she had discovered, were generally more trouble than they were worth. Dogs were preferable. Max, lying so sweetly on his tasseled cushion, loved her with an uncomplicated devotion that far outstripped any attentions she had ever received from fickle males.

"My footmen *are* handsome, are they not?" she said sweetly. "Although I did not expect you to admire them, too."

"You mistake." Alex sounded amused. "It was an observation only—that you surround yourself with attractive and expensive items. The footmen, the dog…" His gaze swept around the library, over the bowl of lilies that Joanna had arranged so carefully as a centerpiece on the rosewood table and the elegant china displayed on the mantelpiece and her collection of watercolors. For some reason his scrutiny made Joanna feel lacking in some way, as though she was shallow, with tastes to match. She had always been pleased with her style and her flair for design. Damn him for disparaging them.

"I also hear that you were the darling of the ton," he said. "I am sure that is no lie. I hope it pleases you."

"It is most gratifying." She had never sought to be a leader of society, but somehow popularity and prominence had come her way anyway. In truth, what had happened was that she had used her friends and acquaintances to ward off the loneliness of being abandoned by her husband for years on end and she had come to value the life she had carved out for herself. In all the nine years of their marriage she calculated that she had been with David for perhaps a fifth of the time, possibly less. In contrast, her closest friends were always there for her.

"You had a similar celebrity when you were last in London," she reminded Alex sharply. Three years before, David and Alex had returned from some naval expedition to the Soutlı Americas with tales of hacking their way through dense jungle, discovering ancient ruins and being attacked by strange and wild creatures. At least David had boasted of it, displaying the teeth marks some giant cat had made on his arm. Joanna had uncharitably wished it had eaten him rather than being shot for its pains. She had hated the way in which David had reveled in his celebrity, rolling home drunk from some brothel at dawn, reeking of perfume and with some whore's cosmetics smeared all over him. It seemed so cheap. David had bragged his way around London from the gambling tables to the ballrooms to the bawdy houses. He had been brash and vulgar, but people had excused it as part of his larger-than-life character, David Ware the hero, beloved by all men… Pain and loss twisted inside her. When she had wed she had expected her life to be so different, with a loving husband and a brood of children. She had been quite remarkably naive.

Alex, in contrast, she seemed to recall, had scorned the ton's excited fawning and had escaped to Scotland instead whilst his comrade took all the credit for their exploits and enjoyed all the fame. And now she saw Alex's firm mouth had turned down at the corners with distaste to be reminded of his illustriousness.

"I do not seek celebrity." He made it sound as though she had suggested he was engaged in some activity that was illegal or repellent or possibly both at the same time. "You will not see me courting the ton whilst I am here. Indeed, I plan to leave London as soon as I have my orders from the Admiralty."

"I will have to dismiss you from my bed first," Joanna

said waspishly, "since you have announced to all society that you occupy it."

Once again he gave her that disconcerting, wholly unexpected smile. It was the look of an adversary not an admirer. "I imagine you will enjoy that," he murmured.

"I shall."

"How will you dismiss me?"

Joanna put her head on one side and considered him thoughtfully. "I am not certain. Be assured that it will be public and humiliating, though, and you will probably be the last in society to know. It is the least that you deserve for embarrassing me so."

His smile deepened. "It was worth it."

Joanna gritted her teeth. She was known for her glacial coolness and was certainly not going to let this man change that. She knew Alex had only claimed to be her lover in order to punish her for her presumption in using him. It was a salutary lesson not to tangle with him. However far she went, he would go further.

But for now he would go out her front door and she would be glad to see him leave.

She held out her hand to him.

"Well, Lord Grant, I thank you for calling and I wish you well on your future travels."

He took her hand again. It had probably been a mistake to offer it, for the sensation of his touch rippled along her nerves, making her tremble. For one mad moment she thought that he was going to kiss her again and her heart started to race. She could almost feel the seductive warmth of his mouth against hers, breathe in the scent of his body, taste him…

"A perfectly judged dismissal, Lady Joanna," he said.

He did not release her hand. "Should you ever require a lover again…"

"Have no fear, I shall not call on you," Joanna said. "Heroes are not to my taste."

The *very last thing* she wanted was another hero. The thought turned her so cold she almost shivered. She had thought she had found a hero in David. She had idolized him. And then she had found that he was a cad, an idol with feet—and other parts—of clay.

Alex smiled at her. Warm, intimate, his smile made her dizzy. She felt feverish, unable to breathe until he had released her hand, as susceptible as a green girl.

"Then I'll bid you good day," Alex said.

He had bowed and had gone before she could pull herself together sufficiently to ring for the butler to show him out. Even after the door had closed behind him Joanna thought she could feel the air of the library burn with the intensity of his presence.

She sat down on the rug and put her arms about Max, who accepted the hug with a tolerant sigh. *I do not want another hero,* Joanna thought. *I would be an utter fool ever to marry again.* For a moment the pain hovered at the corners of her mind, but she was so adept at dismissing it now that it was gone in a trice, leaving nothing but a habitual emptiness behind. She rested her chin on Max's topknot and breathed in the smell of dog. His little body was warm and reassuring in her arms.

"We shall go shopping, Max," Joanna said. "Just like we always do."

Shopping, balls, parties, riding in the park, the repetition, the familiarity, the emptiness lulled her back into security just like it always did.

As HE TURNED THE CORNER from Half Moon Street into Curzon Street Alex thought about David Ware's delectable widow. It was no wonder that she had men beating a path to her door. She was spectacular, a striking woman with a cool confidence that hid an inner passion strong enough to kindle a man's emotions to a blaze. She was a prize, a trophy to rival the greatest conquest a man could make. Who would not wish to have such a woman adorning his home and warming his bed? Alex reflected that he must be the only man in London who did not like Lady Joanna Ware, and even that was no bar to wanting her.

He remembered Ware's last bitter words about his wife as he lay on his deathbed, the fever ravaging his body, his face white and tight with pain and bitterness:

"No need to ask you to take care of Joanna… She's always been able to do that for herself…"

Alex could see how it might appear so. There was a cool, brittle self-containment about Joanna Ware that would not appeal to those men who liked their women winsome and obedient. Yet he had also sensed vulnerability in her along with that strength. He had seen it in her eyes when she had used him as a defense against John Hagan. Or he had thought so—but he was probably mistaken. Lady Joanna was no doubt a manipulative woman who used men to her advantage. She had certainly tried to use him and as a result had got a great deal more than she had bargained for.

Lady Joanna's lover… His body tightened at the thought of it. He had never believed himself to be an imaginative man for he embraced cool reason above all things but now he discovered that he had depths of imagination he had never previously suspected. To take Joanna Ware to bed, to peel that tempting cherry-red gown from her body and expose her pale skin to his eyes and to the touch of his lips, to bury himself in her and drive them both to heights of intolerable pleasure… He almost walked into a lamppost thinking about it. He felt as primed as a callow youth. His body felt constrained with a need he had never previously experienced. A need he could never indulge. Joanna Ware was out of bounds. He did not even like her. And he was a man who had kept tight control over his physical needs and never felt any emotional ones. It had been that way since Amelia had died and he had no intention of changing that situation.

Instinctively he quickened his step although he could never outrun the memories or the guilt surrounding the death of his wife. He had never been able to lose those phantoms. Now, for some reason, he could not dismiss David Ware's final words either:

"Joanna…devil take her…"

What on earth had given Ware so strong a dislike of his wife? No, *dislike* was too mild a word to describe that venom. Such hatred… Alex shrugged, trying to shake the matter off. He had fulfilled his duty. He had called on the less-than-stricken widow and he had also delivered to Ware's lawyer a letter that his comrade had entrusted to him on his death. The matter was closed, obligations discharged. He would retire to his hotel until he had word from the Admiralty on his next posting. He hoped they would not keep him waiting long. Unlike most officers who enjoyed their shore leave he was anxious to be gone. London in May felt ripe and rich and earthy with the promise of summer and yet he did not want to linger. Perhaps London held too many memories for him. Perhaps he had been away from England too long for it to feel like home anymore. In truth he had no home. He did not want one, had not wanted one for seven years—until he had walked into Joanna Ware's library and had felt that sensation of warmth and welcome. But such domestic comforts could never be for him.

"Alex!" Someone hailed him from across the street and Alex turned to see a tall, fair, excessively handsome young man threading his way through the throng of pedestrians and carriages. Despite his relative youth he carried himself with supreme assurance and he was drawing openly admiring glances from every woman he passed, young or old, impressionable debutante or respectable matron. Heads turned, jaws dropped. The ladies fluttered and swayed in his wake like a field of poppies going under the scythe and in return he scattered on them smiles that were so wicked Alex thought that sooner or later one of the ladies would inevitably swoon and require resuscitation. As the man reached his side, grinning broadly, Alex gave a resigned sigh.

"Stopping the traffic as usual, Dev?"

"What else was I supposed to do?" his cousin said. He held out his hand to shake Alex's with enthusiasm. "You're a difficult man to catch up with, Alex. I've been hunting you all over London."

They fell into step, Dev accommodating his stride to Alex's slight limp. "I thought that you were with the East India Squadron," Alex said. "When did you get back?"

"Two weeks since," James Devlin said. "Where are

you staying? I asked after you at White's but they had no word."

"I'm at Grillon's," Alex said.

His cousin stared. "Why on earth?"

"Because it's a good hotel. And I did not want to be found."

Devlin laughed. "Now, *that* I do understand. What have you done? Ravished a few debutantes? Ransacked a Spanish merchant ship or two?"

Alex's lips twitched into a reluctant smile. "Ravishing debutantes isn't my style. Nor is piracy." He looked at his cousin thoughtfully. "I heard that you sailed into Plymouth last year with Spanish-gold candlesticks five foot tall strapped to your masthead."

"You're mistaken," Devlin said, grinning. "That was Thomas Cochrane. I had a diamond chandelier swinging from the mainsail."

"Hell's teeth," Alex said involuntarily. "Didn't that interfere with your navigation? No wonder the Admiralty thinks you are a scoundrel." He looked Devlin over. His cousin was wearing a flamboyant blue waistcoat that matched his eyes and had a pearl swinging from one ear. It should have looked effeminate but Devlin somehow managed to get away with it, possibly because he was so undeniably masculine. Alex shook his head. "And that pearl earring does not help matters," he said. "Who are you modeling yourself on? Blackbeard? For God's sake, remove it should you be planning to set foot before the board of the Admiralty."

"The ladies love it," Devlin said. He gave his cousin a sideways look. "Speaking of which, I thought you might be in town to find a bride."

"Did you?" Alex said dryly.

"No need to cut me dead," Dev said, unabashed. "Everyone knows that Alasdair's death means that Balvenie is now in need of an heir, and as you have a taste for dangerous adventure you might wish to produce one before your next expedition."

"That would be quick work," Alex said.

"I can see you do not mean to tell me your plans," Dev said.

"Well spotted." Alex shrugged his shoulders irritably. His Scottish estate of Balvenie was indeed without an heir since his young cousin Alasdair Grant had died the previous winter. The lad's death from scarlet fever, a tragedy in itself, had been a double blow since Alasdair had been the sole heir to the Grant barony. Alex, who had successfully managed to ignore the pressures on him to remarry and beget an heir whilst Alasdair was alive, was now uncomfortably aware that this was yet another responsibility, another duty he did not wish to perform. To take some simpering little debutante or some colorless widow and make her Lady Grant for the sake of a son was deeply repugnant to him. To remarry at all was the very last thing he wished to do. And yet what choice did he have if Balvenie was to be safeguarded for the future? He felt the guilt and obligation—those twin ghosts that always dogged his steps—press a little closer.

"I have no current matrimonial plans, Devlin," he said a shade wearily. "I would make the devil of a husband."

"Some might say you would be perfect," Dev said. "Since you would be absent."

Alex's lips twisted with appreciation. "There is that, I suppose."

Dev cast him another glance. "Anyway, I'm glad I found you, Alex. I could use some help from you just now."

Alex recognized that tone of voice. It was the one Dev had used since he had been a child when his wild exploits had almost always led to Alex's bailing his young cousin out of all manner of trouble. Dev was three and twenty now, but the wild exploits were the same and so, generally, were the dire consequences. His cousin, Alex thought, only escaped hanging by the skin of his teeth and by using his fabled charm.

"What is it this time, Dev?" he asked, exasperated. "You cannot possibly be strapped for cash with all your prize money. Have you seduced an admiral's daughter? If so, my advice would be to marry her. It would be good for your career advancement."

"Always your Scots Calvinist upbringing comes to the fore," Dev said cheerfully. "I have seduced an admiral's daughter, but I was neither the first nor the only one. Nor is that the problem."

"Then you find me agog," Alex said ironically.

There was a pause whilst Dev steered Alex down a side street and into a nearby coffee shop. The Turk's Head was dark, hot and smelled richly of coffee beans and spices. They slid into a booth in a quiet corner, Alex ordering coffee and Dev chocolate.

"Chocolate?" Alex asked, inhaling the sweet scent of the steaming cup as it arrived.

"Be glad I didn't order violet-flavored sherbet," Dev said, laughing. "Francesca adores it."

"How is your sister?" Alex inquired.

Dev's mouth turned down slightly at the corners. "I

don't know. She doesn't talk to me anymore. I think she's sad."

"Sad?" Alex was startled. Somewhere in the recesses of his body the guilt kicked him again. James and Francesca Devlin were his only close relatives now and he had barely seen them in the past couple of years. When their mother, his father's sister, had died, he had salved his conscience by buying Devlin his commission and finding Francesca a home with a distant aunt to chaperone her, and had promptly departed overseas. He was not a rich man; he had only his navy salary and a small income from his Scottish estates, but he took his responsibilities seriously, materially at least. Emotionally it was a different matter. He wanted no dependents, no obligations. Such relationships were a burden. They held him back, chafing like wet rope against the skin. Always he wanted to get out of London, back to sea, to find some new quest and some new adventure, to escape...

Balvenie needs an heir...

There were some responsibilities that could never be escaped. Again Alex shrugged his shoulders to sough off the unwanted responsibility. Devlin was right, but he could not contemplate remarriage. It would be another burden, another unconscionable tie.

"Is there something Chessie needs?" he asked. "You should have told me if she required more money—"

"She doesn't," Dev said, giving him a very straight look. "You are more than generous to her, Alex." He frowned. "It is company Chessie needs," he said. "Aunt Constance isn't much fun as a companion for a girl in her teens. Oh, she's a very good sort of woman," he added swiftly as Alex raised his brows, "but a bit too good, if you know what I mean. She spends half her time at prayer meetings, which is all very worthy but not very exciting for Chessie. And the poor girl wants a come-out ball next year, but I doubt Aunt Constance will agree to that. No doubt she would deem it too frivolous—" He broke off, fidgeting with his dish of chocolate, playing with the spoon. "Listen, Alex—" He looked up suddenly. "I need your help."

Alex waited. Dev, he realized, was nervous.

"It's to do with money," Dev said suddenly. His frown deepened. "Well, sort of to do with money, if you take my meaning."

"Not at all," Alex said. "What happened to the proceeds from the diamond chandelier?"

"Spent long ago." Dev looked defiant. "The thing is, I've sold out of the navy, Alex, and bought a share in a ship with Owen Purchase. Or at least I am trying to raise the funds to do so. We plan an expedition to Mexico."

Alex swore. Owen Purchase had been a colleague of his at the Battle of Trafalgar, one of the Americans who had fought with them against the French. Purchase was an inspired sea captain, almost a legend, and he had always been a hero to Dev.

"Why Mexico?" Alex asked succinctly.

"Gold." Dev matched his terseness.

"Poppycock."

Dev laughed. "You don't believe in tales of lost treasure?"

"No. And neither should you, and Purchase definitely shouldn't." Alex ran a hand through his hair. Would his cousin never grow up? He could not believe that Dev had thrown his commission away for a wild-goose chase. "For God's sake, Dev," he said with more edge than he had intended, "must you always be playing these mad, dangerous games?"

"It's better than freezing my arse off in some snow-bound wilderness searching for a trade route that isn't there," Dev said, his candor taking Alex completely by surprise. "The Admiralty are using you, Alex. They pay you some pittance to risk your life in the noble cause of empire and just because you feel guilty over Amelia's death you let them send you to one godforsaken place after another—" He broke off as Alex made an involuntary movement of fury and raised his hands in a gesture of peace. "My apologies. I overstepped the mark."

"Damn right you did." Alex growled. He clamped down on his anger. He did not discuss Amelia's death with anybody. There were no exceptions. And Dev's blistering comments were too painful, too near the bone. Amelia had died five years previously and ever since then Alex had deliberately taken postings that had been as extreme, as reckless and as dangerous as he could find. He wanted nothing else. Even sitting here now with Dev he could feel the urge to escape, the desire to turn his back on all these tedious responsibilities and family burdens. It jarred him into guilt even as he wanted simply to take ship and set sail for wherever the wind blew him. But for now he was trapped in London anyway, hog-tied by the Admiralty whilst they decided what to do with him.

"One of these days," he said, venting some of his frustrations by glaring at his cousin, "someone is going to put a bullet through you, Devlin, and it might well be me."

Dev relaxed. "I don't doubt it," he said cheerfully. "Now, about the favor I'm asking…"

"You have a damned nerve."

"Always, but…" Dev cocked a brow. "It's easy and it won't cost you a penny of your own money and after all, you owe it to me as the big brother I never had."

Alex sighed. Even as he could feel himself softening toward his cousin he wondered how Dev managed to get round him so easily. But then, Dev could charm anything that moved.

"Your logic is faulty," he snapped, "but do go ahead."

"I need you to attend Mrs. Cummings's rout this evening in Grosvenor Square," Dev said.

Alex looked at him. "You're joking."

"I am not."

"Then you do not know me very well even after twenty-three years," Alex said. "I detest balls, routs, breakfasts and parties of all kinds."

"You will love this one," Dev said, grinning. "It is in your honor."

"What?" Alex gave his young relative a withering look. "Now you have taken leave of your senses."

"And you are turning into a curmudgeon," Dev said. "You need to get out more and enjoy yourself. What did you have planned for tonight—an evening alone, reading a book in your hotel?"

That, Alex thought, was dangerously close to the mark and did make him sound like a superannuated older relative rather than a cousin with only nine years seniority.

"Nothing wrong in that," he said.

Dev laughed. "But a rout will be much more fun. And Mr. Cummings is frightfully rich and I need to persuade him to sponsor my voyage to Mexico. So I thought…"

"I see," Alex said, seeing exactly where this was going.

"Both Mr. and Mrs. Cummings are desperately keen on explorers," Dev said in a rush, suddenly sounding very young. "They think you are most dashing. So when they discovered that I was your cousin, well... They promised to help me if I could persuade you to attend the rout..."

Alex rolled his eyes. "Devlin," he said warningly.

"I know," Dev said, "but I thought you would be attending anyway, since Lady Joanna Ware will be there and she is your mistress—"

"What?" Alex brought his coffee cup down with a crack that made the table shudder.

"It's the *on dit*," Dev said. "I heard it from Lady O'Hara just before we met up. You're the talk of the town."

"Ah," Alex said. "Yes." By his calculations it had been all of an hour since John Hagan had left Half Moon Street. Evidently the man had lost no time in spreading the scandal of Lady Joanna Ware's supposed liaison. Perhaps it served to smooth over his rejection to broadcast that Joanna Ware had another lover. Contempt for Hagan seared him.

"I admire your taste," Dev was saying. He gave Alex a frank look. "I'd always heard Lady Joanna was cold as the grave—would have tried my luck if I'd thought otherwise."

"You can give that idea up, infant," Alex said very dryly. The sensation of masculine possession that gripped him when he thought about Joanna Ware was sharp and shocking. He realized that he had reacted entirely on instinct. It was an alien sensation. "And don't speak disrespectfully of Lady Joanna either," he added, wondering as he did so why on earth he felt the need to defend her.

Dev raised his brows. "Very vehement, Alex."

"And she is not my mistress," Alex finished testily.

"Then why the bad temper?" Dev grinned. "Or are you frustrated because she is not your mistress?"

"Enough," Alex snapped.

Dev shrugged elegantly. "But you will be there tonight?" He did not quite manage to erase the note of pleading from his voice.

"You should have asked Purchase," Alex said grimly. "He likes that sort of thing."

"Purchase is dining with the Prince Regent," Dev said. "An invitation which I understand you declined, Alex."

"I hate all the celebrity nonsense."

Dev laughed. "But this is different. This is for me."

Alex thought about it. He did not approve of Dev's decision to turn in his commission, but the damage was done now. He could try to dissuade his cousin from his harebrained Mexican scheme, but he doubted he would be successful; Dev had his own share of the family obstinacy. And Alex knew he ran the risk of looking a complete hypocrite if he played the role of heavy-handed older brother. It was true that he had pursued his own adventures with the approval and support of the King's Royal Navy, but what real difference was there between a man seeking adventure under his country's flag and one setting out to prove himself in a different way? Dev was motivated by courage and a quest for adventure and independence. And he was not running away from the ghosts of the past, a charge that Alex had to plead guilty to, in part at least.

Alex tapped his fingers impatiently on the table edge. As he had told Dev, he detested social events with a deep and abiding hatred. Yet if he attended the rout he could assuage a little of the guilt he felt over neglecting his family by helping Devlin.

And he would see Lady Joanna Ware again…

For a moment he felt as green as he had done as a teenager at Eton, hoping to catch sight of the housemaster's daughter. The desire to see Joanna was very strong even as he acknowledged it was the single most foolish thing that he could do. If he wanted a woman he should buy a courtesan for a night, or two nights or however many nights it took to slake his lust. That would be straightforward, uncomplicated. Desiring David Ware's tempting widow was neither of those things. The difficulty was that it was Joanna Ware he wanted, not some Covent Garden light skirt. He doubted that bedding a Cyprian would even take the edge off his hunger, for he did not want a whore. He could pretend that this lust was no more than the natural consequence of being away from female company for months on end, but if he told himself that he would know that he was a liar.

Joanna Ware. She was temptation incarnate. She was infuriating. She was forbidden to him. He disliked her.

He would go to the rout and see if she had the temerity to dismiss him as her lover to his face, in full public view.

He remembered that when David Ware had slipped the lawyer's letter into his hand on his deathbed there had been a most peculiar, triumphant smile on Ware's face and he had whispered:

"Joanna likes surprises, damn her…"

Alex doubted that Lady Joanna would be very pleased with this particular surprise. She had not expected to see him again. She disliked him equally as much as he disliked her.

Devlin was still waiting for his reply.

"Very well," he said slowly. "Yes, I will be there."

Chapter 2

"WHAT IS LORD GRANT LIKE?" Mrs. Lottie Cummings, ton hostess extraordinaire, scandalous matron and one of Lady Joanna Ware's dearest friends, ignored the guests piling into her reception rooms in favor of quizzing her friend on the shocking news of her *affaire*. "You know I have only ever heard tell of him, Jo darling, and have not even seen a portrait."

"Well," Joanna said, "he is tall."

"So is my aunt Dorothea." Lottie gave an impatient wiggle. "Dearest, you are going to have to do better than that."

He is not really my lover... Why on earth had she let this go on for as long as it had? Why not simply say: "We are not lovers. It is all a hum..."

Joanna was not sure. Anger at Alex's high-handed behavior, and what she acknowledged was a rather childish pettiness because he disapproved of her and disliked her, had made her want to punish him. It was a foolish game of tit for tat and unworthy of her. The trouble was that if she denied the liaison now it would cause almost as much of a sensation as the original announcement. Such were the rather superficial obsessions of society. And a deeper, more disturbing truth was that she actually *liked* the idea of Alex Grant as her lover, liked it all too well as she imagined what it might be like to take him to her bed, to feel his hands on her body, to give herself to him with all the abandoned desire she had never actually felt for a man before. She had loved David passionately when they had wed, but the intensity of her infatuation had never been matched by physical desire. When David had touched her she had felt vaguely anticipatory, as though something more exciting should be happening. Unfortunately it never did. And then the relationship had turned so hideously sour that she had never wanted David to touch her ever again.

In recent years—in most years, actually—her marriage bed had resembled the snowy wastes of the Arctic, pristine, empty and untouched, and having lost her illusions about David Ware, that was exactly how she had wanted it. She had been horribly lonely through the years of her marriage, a wife and yet no true wife, but even when David had died she had not trusted any man sufficiently to allow him close. And Alex Grant could not be that man. He was not for her. David had poisoned him against her, she was sure, and most importantly he was cut from the same cloth as David, an adventurer, an explorer, a man who would forsake his home and his family, and walk out into the unknown, leaving everything that should have been most precious and valuable to him behind.

"Well?" Lottie prompted impatiently.

"He is dark," Jo said.

Lottie sighed. "Again, my aunt Dorothea can give him a run for his money on that." She threw up her hands. "Darling...you know I lead such a boring life! A little more vicarious excitement, if you please."

"That's the best I can do, Lottie," Joanna said. "Lord

Grant and I are not really lovers. The gossip is not true."

Lottie was looking at her pityingly. "Jo, darling, you don't have to explain or excuse yourself to me. Nobody blames you for taking a lover! Why, it is an age since David died. And I hear that lovely Lord Grant is very, very luscious. Is it true—" Lottie's dark eyes sparkled suddenly "—that he has the most fearsome scars on his chest from wrestling a polar bear?"

"I have no notion," Joanna said. "Why would anyone want to wrestle a bear? It sounds highly dangerous." She remembered the slight limp that characterized Alex's gait. She had a vague memory that David had mentioned that Alex had been badly injured on some expedition some years before. Unlike her late husband, however, he did not seem inclined to make capital out of it.

"Lottie," she repeated, "you aren't listening to me. Lord Grant and I are no more than acquaintances and pray don't talk like this—you are shocking Merryn." She looked at her younger sister, who had been sitting quietly by whilst Lottie chattered. Merryn was as restrained as Lottie was loud, her serenity an antidote to Mrs. Cummings's staggeringly indiscreet personality. Merryn had the habit of silence, a habit she had fostered throughout their uncle's long and difficult last illness. It was bad luck for the youngest, unmarried daughter, Joanna thought, that convention dictated that nursing duties always fell to them. Sometimes she felt just a little guilty at having left Merryn to cope with their uncle alone. She had escaped the stultifying atmosphere of the vicarage years before and had never returned. As far as she knew, neither had their middle sister, Tess. Merryn was the one who had borne the brunt of the Reverend Dixon's choleric nature.

"Don't mind me," Merryn said, her pansy-blue eyes lighting with amusement. "Oh, and I think that the polar bear story was an invention, Lottie."

Lottie was pouting. "Well, if Jo has not seen Lord Grant's chest, we cannot know for sure, can we? Do you make love in the dark, Jo darling? You are even more prim and proper than I had imagined!"

"I am exceptionally straitlaced," Joanna agreed truthfully. "Lottie, I know I may seem flighty, but it is all show and no substance."

Lottie opened her dark eyes very wide. "Oh, I know *that,* darling! All the gentlemen say you have a heart of ice! So clever of you to be so beautiful and heartless and unobtainable, for it keeps them panting after you!"

"I don't do it to encourage them," Joanna said a little uncomfortably, for Lottie's words held an undercurrent of envy as well as being close to the truth. "It is simply that I do not trust men very much."

"Oh, well, darling—" Lottie planted a consoling hand on her arm "—neither do I, but what is that to the purpose? I seduce them and cast them aside and that keeps me happy."

Joanna wondered if it was true. She knew the conquest bit was—Lottie's discreet *affaires* were well-known in ton circles, but whether her infidelities made her happy or not, Joanna had never been able to tell. They both lived in a world of mirrors where artifice and superficiality were highly prized and depth and sincerity mocked to scorn. Lottie never ever broached serious subjects with her and after ten years in the ton Joanna never confided in anyone either, having discovered early on that secrets were not respected. What was meant for private discussion quickly became the *on dit*.

"Well, if you wish to set your cap for Lord Grant, pray do not worry about cutting me out," she said now. "I am not having an *affaire* with him." She sighed. "And I cannot believe that you invited him this evening, Lottie, nor laid on this rather extravagant display in his honor."

When she had arrived at Lottie's rout and discovered that Alex Grant was promised for the evening, she had been appalled and incredulous. That Alex, with his apparent contempt for the adulation of society, should be such a hypocrite as to accept this ball in his honor had disappointed Joanna in some obscure way, reinforcing as it did that he was just another self-aggrandizing adventurer after all. And there could be no mistake. Lottie had said he had sent a message to confirm his attendance and as a result the dining room was decorated with huge ice sculptures, one of which was a life-size model of a man wielding an icy sword in one hand and the British flag in the other, clearly meant to represent Alex himself as he conquered yet another swath of virgin territory. There were also drapes of white satin sheathing the staircase to imitate a frozen waterfall and green and red lanterns hung from the ballroom ceiling to emulate the northern lights. The highlight of the entire display was a rather moth-eaten stuffed polar bear standing in the corner of the entrance hall and glaring balefully at all the guests as they arrived. It was all gloriously vulgar, but somehow it worked because Lottie had such brazen style.

"Is it not marvelous?" Lottie beamed. "I excel myself."

"You certainly do," Joanna murmured.

"And you are dressed the part, too," Lottie added, casting an approving glance over Joanna's white satin evening gown and diamonds. "How inspired! I adore you in the color, Jo darling! The other ladies will all be dressing as debutantes now you have set the fashion!"

"I do not think," Merryn said unexpectedly, "that all this show will be quite to Lord Grant's taste, Lottie. He is reputed to be somewhat reserved."

"Nonsense." Lottie beamed. "He will adore it."

"Well, if he does not I am sure he will be too polite to say so," Merryn said. "I hear he is the very epitome of chivalry."

"You seem to know a great deal about him," Joanna teased gently as her sister blushed. "Who can have been singing Lord Grant's praises to you?"

"No one," Merryn said, blushing harder. "I have been reading of his exploits, that is all. Mr. Gable has been writing about him in the *Courier*. He is quite the returning hero. Apparently he turned down an invitation to dine from the Prince Regent, which only made people more determined to secure his attendance at their events. He is the toast of all the clubs."

Joanna had shuddered at the word *hero*. "I cannot see what there is to celebrate in a failed attempt to find the Northern Pole. As I understand it, David and Lord Grant set out to discover a northeast trade route via the Pole, failed to do so, became trapped in the ice, David died and Lord Grant sailed home." She raised her hands heavenward in a gesture of exasperation. "Hardly a cause for celebration. Or am I missing some essential fact here?"

Lottie tapped her wrist disapprovingly with her fan.

"Do not be so harsh, Joanna darling. It is all about excitement and danger and the adventure of exploration! Lord Grant is the very essence of the noble hero, silent, solitary and fiendishly attractive, just like David."

"David," Joanna said dryly, "was hardly silent and solitary."

Lottie fidgeted, avoiding her eyes. "I suppose David was rather more forthcoming—"

"That's one way of putting it," Joanna said even more dryly.

Lottie grabbed a glass of champagne and drained it in one gulp. "Jo darling, you know I am sorry that I let him seduce me, but he was such a hero that it seemed impolite to refuse!" She fixed Joanna with her big, dark eyes. "And it was not as though you cared!"

"No," Joanna said, turning her face away, "I did not care whom David seduced."

There had been so many women. In the months following David's death she had received visits from any number of them claiming to be her late husband's mistress, including two former servants, three publicans' daughters and one girl who worked in the milliner's where Joanna had habitually bought her hats. She had wondered why David had seemed so keen to accompany her shopping when he had last returned to London. And considering that he was barely in the country most of the time, he had a most remarkable record of debauchery. That he had been able to conduct an *affaire* with Lottie and that she and Lottie were still friends was, Joanna thought bitterly, a reflection on the emptiness of her marriage and the shallowness of her friendships.

She caught Merryn watching her and gave her sister a reassuring smile. Merryn had lived so sheltered a life in the Oxfordshire countryside. Joanna had no wish to shock her sister.

"Anyway, we were speaking of delicious Lord Grant, not of your dead, dissolute husband," Lottie said with her usual insensitivity. She seemed impervious to the atmosphere. "Does he kiss nicely, Jo darling? My advice would be to jilt him if he does not. It is appalling to be slobbered over by a man who does not understand how to kiss. Trust me, I should know."

Merryn started to laugh and Joanna's distress eased a little. At the very least, Lottie could always be relied upon to lighten the mood with some outrageous comment or exploit. Joanna spared a moment's sympathy for the luckless Mr. Cummings, a banker rich beyond the dreams of avarice whose sole purpose in life appeared to be to fund Lottie's lifestyle and be henpecked for his troubles.

"I am not going to talk about that," she said. For a moment the frenetic buzz of the ballroom disappeared and she was back in her library, held in Alex Grant's arms, and he was kissing her with explicit demand, and the warmth unfurled through her body and her toes curled within her evening slippers.

Lottie gave a little crow of pleasure. "Look at her face! He must kiss beautifully!"

"How gratifying to know that if I am to be jilted it will not be for my lack of expertise," an amused male voice drawled from beside Joanna. "Your servant—in that as in everything—Lady Joanna." His glance slid over the white satin evening gown. "How very charming and virginal you look tonight."

Joanna jumped and spun around on her rout chair. Alex Grant was standing looking down at her, his dark eyes glittering. It was difficult to see how she could have missed his arrival, since an admiring throng of guests were pushing and jostling to claim his attention. The noise in the room was rising and there was a buzz of excitement rippling through the crowd like a breeze through corn. Joanna had seen it before with the eager crowds who had flocked to greet David as a conquering hero, had seen, too, the way in which David had lapped up that attention. Once again she felt a shiver of memory and the coldness seep into her bones.

Behind Alex was a very handsome young man, as fair as Alex was dark, who was watching her with a bright and inquisitive appraisal. Joanna smiled at him and he looked gratified and blushed rather endearingly. Joanna looked at Alex, who did not blush and looked even more sardonic. Joanna had the feeling that it would take a great deal to put him out of countenance.

"So, are we still lovers?" Alex asked softly as he bent over Joanna's hand. His breath stirred the tendrils of curls about her ear, sending goose bumps skittering over her skin. She looked up into his eyes. He had eyelashes a woman would kill for, she thought, thick and dark. Nature could be very unfair. And he had eyes that she could see now were very dark gray rather than brown, but so smoky that they were unreadable.

She realized that she was staring—and that he was smiling, one eyebrow raised in quizzical challenge.

"As much as we ever were," she said tartly. "Which is to say not at all."

"A pity," Alex said. "I have seldom had so little physical pleasure from an affair."

"Well, if you would rather be in the Haymarket than

Curzon Street, pray do not let us detain you," Joanna snapped. Really, this man was beyond provocative.

Lottie gave an agonized squawk at the thought that her guest of honor might turn on his heel and leave. "No, indeed, Lord Grant will find my rout a great deal more fun than a bordello. I guarantee it!"

Joanna caught Merryn's eye. Merryn giggled.

"May I introduce my cousin Mr. James Devlin," Alex said, drawing forward the tall young man. "He is a great admirer of yours, Lady Joanna."

Introductions were exchanged. James Devlin bowed to Joanna and then to Merryn. He looked suitably dazzled, though Joanna suspected he had practiced that look quite a bit on impressionable debutantes. Merryn, she was happy to see, remained composed and seemed unimpressed, though a tiny telltale blush suggested that her sister was not indifferent to Mr. Devlin's admiration. Joanna felt a huge rush of relief and pleasure, followed by an equally strong pang of anxiety. She knew that she was protective of Merryn—as the eldest of three girls she had mothered the others, a state of affairs that had been almost inevitable given her parents' indifference to their offspring. She did hope that now Merryn had emerged from their uncle's sickroom she might have the chance to form an attachment to a nice young man. But could James Devlin be described as nice? Probably not... He looked far too dangerous to be let loose on innocent young ladies.

Alex, meanwhile, was being extremely courteous to Lottie, thanking her for hosting such an elegant event. Despite her dislike of him, Joanna was intrigued to see how easily, how seductively, he could charm.

"You do me too much honor, Mrs. Cummings," he said.

"I told her the same," Joanna said sweetly. "As you hate being lionized for your fame, my lord, I am sure you must detest all this fuss."

James Devlin smothered a laugh. "Lady Joanna has you there, Alex."

"I am sure that I can cope with it," Alex drawled, "since Lady Joanna is here to ensure that I do not become too conceited."

"Oh, but your reluctance simply makes you more desirable, Lord Grant," Lottie gushed. "Every lady here would *love* to melt that icy aloofness of yours and set your world alight!"

Joanna stifled an unladylike snort of laughter. "Pray speak only for yourself, Lottie," she said. "I have no desire to start a conflagration, though your ice sculptures may prove useful in putting out the blaze."

"Ice sculptures?" Alex said, slanting a look down at her.

"Yes, indeed," Joanna said. "If you have not already seen them, my lord, I suggest that you look at once. You will particularly admire the rendition of yourself laying waste the unresisting acres of the Arctic and planting your flag in truly phallic fashion!"

Lottie glared at her and stroked her fan suggestively down the sleeve of Alex's immaculate evening coat. "Perhaps you may settle a small matter for me, my lord?" she purred. "Is it true that you wrestled a polar bear and have the scars to prove it? Joanna absolutely refuses to tell me!"

"Because I have no notion," Joanna said, "and less interest."

Alex gave her another quizzical look. It brought the blood burning hotly into her face, which was exceptionally annoying since the last time she had blushed had probably been when she was about twelve years old.

"You disappoint me, Lady Joanna," he said.

"I am aware of that," Joanna said. "You have made your disapproval of me quite plain."

"Oh, please," Lottie fluttered, "do show us. Are they as impressive as Lord Nelson's wounds were? I hear that he, too, encountered a bear in the Arctic wastes."

"Madam—" Alex flicked Lottie's fan firmly away as the feathers tickled his wrist "—I fear I would need to know you a great deal more intimately before I strip off in your ballroom, or indeed any other room."

He turned to Joanna and offered his hand. "May I have the pleasure of this dance, Lady Joanna? I seldom dance, but I imagine I might manage the cotillion."

"Flattered as I am that you are prepared to try for me," Joanna said, smiling demurely, "I fear we cannot dance if you wish to join me in discouraging rumors of our *affaire,* my lord. Alas, my card is full anyway."

"Then discard it and start afresh," Alex said. "I wish to speak with you."

"Don't you ever say please, my lord?" Joanna asked, stung by his high-handedness. "It may be that I would have a greater desire to converse with *you* if you exercised a little courtesy."

Something wicked kindled in Alex's eyes, making Joanna catch her breath. "If you please," Alex murmured. "You see, Lady Joanna, that sometimes I will beg—if there is something I want enough."

Their gazes locked for a long moment. A smile crept into Alex's eyes. Joanna felt as though the ground was shifting slightly under her feet. But she was getting the measure of this man now and his ability to discomfit her. She allowed a cool little smile to tilt her lips in return.

"Unlike you, my lord," she said, turning to James Devlin, "your cousin had the foresight to send me a note this afternoon requesting the first dance with me." She got to her feet and offered her hand to James. "Mr. Devlin, I should be delighted. That is—" she hesitated "—if you will be happy sitting out on your own, Merryn?"

"I shall go and chat to Miss Drayton," her sister said. "Don't worry about me."

The look of chagrin on Alex's face as he realized that he had been outwitted was rewarding, Joanna thought. Dev shot him a look that was half rueful, half triumphant. "You are always impressing on me that planning is half the battle, Alex," he said. "Those are your own tactics."

"Outmaneuvered, my lord!" Lottie declared. "You will have to dance with me instead. Mr. Cummings will be delighted—once he has opened the ball with me he never dances again but retires to his study to look at those tiresome piles of money." She stood up and held out a hand imperiously to Alex and after a moment he took it. Joanna's stomach gave a little lurch. Lottie, it seemed, was indeed intent on seduction, for she was already sliding her hand through Alex's arm in a most intimate way and looking up at him with a predatory, catlike gleam in her eyes. And really, Joanna thought, it was contrary of her to be cross when not only was she *not* Alex's mistress but she had practically *told* Lottie to seduce him anyway.

The eager press of guests in Lottie's reception rooms fell back a little to allow them through the archway into the ballroom. All about her, Joanna was aware of the feverish whisper and hiss of conversation, the sycophantic smiles of the ladies as they fluttered to attract Alex's attention, the hearty greetings of the men, the whole of society angling for his attention and notice.

"I say, ma'am," Devlin said, walking beside her, "is this not extraordinary? Who would have thought that Alex, of all people, would be so in demand! It is like escorting royalty!"

"I think Lord Grant is probably more popular than the Prince Regent," Joanna said dryly. "Society is very fickle, Mr. Devlin, and very bored. We are always looking for the next sensation and at the moment that is your cousin. Explorers are all the rage. No doubt this time next year the fashion will be for Chinese wallpaper or Scottish breeds of dog."

"Alex is hardly comparable to a *dog,* ma'am," Dev protested, though with a smile. "And he is the quarry of all the matchmaking mamas, of course."

"Is he?" Joanna felt a strange dropping feeling in her stomach. "I had no notion that Lord Grant was seeking a bride."

"Oh, I do not think he *wants* a wife," Dev said candidly, "but Balvenie currently has no heir."

"I see. Of course." Joanna felt the cold gnawing inside her. David, too, had wanted a son. "Yes," she said. "Most men want an heir."

Even though she sought to keep her tone level there must have been some note in it that caught Dev's attention for he gave her a quick, puzzled look. She smiled at him blandly and saw his brow clear. *Oh, it was so easy to pretend...*

It had taken them so long to fight their way through the crowds that the cotillion was already over and the orchestra, seeing them approach, swung into a lively rendition of Thomas Arne's march from Britannia in Alex's honor. Glancing at him, Joanna saw that his face was absolutely impassive. Lottie was clinging to his arm and beaming with reflected glory and the entire ballroom broke into spontaneous applause.

"It would be more appropriate," Joanna whispered to Dev, "to have played Mr. Arne's 'Much Ado about Nothing.'"

Alex gave her an unreadable look and Joanna realized that he had heard her. Dev was looking from one to the other with a puzzled expression on his handsome face.

"I say, you really do not like one another very much, do you, Lady Joanna? When Alex told me that you were not really...um...intimate I thought that he was merely...um—" He broke off in confusion, sounding all at once a great deal less sophisticated than his appearance suggested.

"I fear I am prejudiced against explorers, Mr. Devlin," Joanna said, taking pity on him, "having been married to one."

"Oh, but surely David was the most admirable of men," Dev said, his face lighting up. "He was a hero of mine when I was only a small boy."

"I fear," Joanna said, "that heroes can be uncomfortable men to live with." She saw his look of blank astonishment and added bitterly, "It can be so hard to live up to the expectation."

The triumphal march finished on a flourish, the applause rang out again and Alex bowed acknowledgment to the crowd before Lottie positively dragged him into the next set that was forming for a country-dance.

"I hope that Alex will forgive me cutting him out," Dev said as he and Joanna moved through the opening figures. "I was surprised he asked you to dance, ma'am. A combination of an old wound and lack of inclination usually keeps him from the floor."

Joanna had been surprised as well. Whilst Alex's injured leg did not seem to hinder him unduly, she could not imagine that a half-hour country-dance would be comfortable for him. She had observed from the grim set of his mouth when Lottie had questioned him on his polar bear injuries that this was another issue he did not discuss. Like the subject of his popularity as an explorer and the death of his wife, it was not up for debate, and there was something most stern and quelling about Alex Grant when he decided a topic was not open for discussion. Joanna doubted that many people gainsaid him. He was too authoritative and too intimidating.

"Alex only accepted Mrs. Cummings's invitation tonight as a favor to me," Dev was saying. "He is nowhere near as unhelpful as he can seem, you know, ma'am."

"I will take your word for it, Mr. Devlin," Joanna said, smiling. "And as I am sure that your cousin is indifferent to whom I dance with, so you are in no imminent danger of his calling you out."

"Well, I hope not," Dev said. "He did warn me off you earlier, though." He gave her a look of frank admiration. "Can't say I blame him, ma'am."

"Your cousin is presumptuous," Joanna snapped. She shot a furious look at Alex across the floor. Since it seemed extremely unlikely that David had made Alex promise to protect her in some touching deathbed scene—she was sure that the reverse must be true— she could only assume that Alex had warned his young cousin away because he thought her dangerous to Devlin's virtue. For a moment she watched Alex dancing with Lottie. Mrs. Cummings was turning a respectable country-dance into something a great deal more tactile. She was all over Alex like ivy, Joanna thought, feeling for those polar bear scars herself. As she saw Alex pry Lottie's fingers away from his shirtfront, she decided Lottie's persistent attentions were the least penance that he deserved.

"In your note to me this afternoon you mentioned a favor, Mr. Devlin," she said, turning back to Dev. "How can I help you? Though if it is anything to do with your cousin, I should warn you that I have absolutely no influence with him at all."

"Know what you mean, ma'am," Dev said gloomily. "Alex knows his own mind too well to welcome other counsel."

"You mean that he is arrogant," Joanna said.

Dev winced. "Well, that could be one word for it, I suppose. Truth is, I am in bad odor with him at the moment for abandoning my navy commission to take part in an expedition to Mexico." He looked at her appealingly. "I wondered if you might speak with him, ma'am, and smooth matters over for me?"

"I could try," Joanna said, "but it would only make things worse for you, Mr. Devlin. I am afraid that when it comes to incurring your cousin's disapproval, I am streets ahead of you."

The figure of the dance took them past the corner

where Merryn was sitting chatting to Miss Drayton. Joanna saw that Devlin was watching her sister.

"Lady Merryn does not dance?" he said when they came back together again.

"My sister prefers more intellectual pursuits," Joanna said, smiling. Merryn was a bluestocking who was unconventional enough to make no secret of her preference for intelligent debate over dancing. It did, however, limit her circle of friends and many people in the ton, Lottie included, thought her a complete original because of her lack of interest in frivolity.

She realized that Dev was watching her with a surprisingly perceptive gaze. "A pity," he said. "Because I am sure she would be a graceful dancer. But I admire a woman who is different."

"If you can discuss naval architecture with her then you will win her approval," Joanna said lightly. The music drew to a close and she and Dev joined in the smattering of applause from the dancers. "She has been attending the lectures at the Royal Institution with some of her friends."

"Indeed?" Dev said. There was a frown between his brows. "I attended the talk last week, the one about a new design for the American frigates. I must have seen Lady Merryn at the meeting although—" he hesitated "—I thought that I had glimpsed her in quite a different place."

"Then it seems you have an interest in common," Joanna said, smiling. She put a hand on Dev's arm. "A word of advice, though, Mr. Devlin. Merryn has lived in the country for most of her life and is unused to the ways of the ton. I would be sorry to see her…disappointed in any way."

Again she saw a slight frown mar Dev's brow and saw, too, an expression in his eyes that she could not understand, but then his face cleared and he put his hand over hers and gave her gloved fingers a comforting squeeze.

"Have no fear, ma'am. I don't trifle with young ladies…" He paused. "Well, honesty compels me to admit that I *do,* but I swear I shall do nothing to upset you with regard to your sister."

"Devlin." Jo turned to see that Alex had shaken off Lottie Cummings, whom Joanna was surprised to see dancing with John Hagan, and was prowling across the floor toward them, for once ignoring the handshakes and acclaim of those trying to gain his attention. His gaze was on their clasped hands and it seemed to Joanna that Dev released her more slowly, and more provocatively, than was strictly necessary.

"Alex," Dev said, a grin curling his mouth. "Have you come to cut in on us?"

"Mr. Cummings," Alex said, his gaze riveted on Joanna's face, "wishes to discuss your Mexican expedition plan with you, Dev, so you had better unhand Lady Joanna and join him in the drawing room."

Dev's face lit up. "Did you put in a word for me, Alex? I say, you are the most splendid chap! Your servant, Lady Joanna." He sketched Joanna a bow. "Please excuse me."

"Of course," Joanna said, smiling. "Good luck."

"May I escort you to the dining room, Lady Joanna?" Alex asked. He was quite definitely not smiling. "Such energetic flirtation as you have indulged in with my cousin must lead you to require some refreshment, I think."

Joanna shot him a look of dislike. "We were merely dancing, my lord."

Alex arched a brow. "Is that what you call it?"

"I heard that you had warned Mr. Devlin to keep away from me," Joanna said as they passed through the door into the dining room, where Lottie's ice sculptures were wilting in the heat from the candles. "Being of a charitable disposition I assumed that it was because my late husband had asked you to take a brotherly interest in my welfare and you wished to protect me from young rakes."

Alex laughed. "You could not be more mistaken, Lady Joanna. Your husband intimated to me that you were well able to take care of yourself and I am inclined to believe him."

Joanna felt a stab of sensation that felt curiously like misery. So David had made her sound like a brass-faced bitch and Alex had believed him. Of course he had. Why would he not? Everyone believed David Ware to be the most complete hero, and Alex had been David's closest friend. She gave herself a little shake. What had she expected? David was never going to sing her praises; they had been estranged for years, locked in mutual loathing. How could it be otherwise when David had felt that she had failed him in the only thing he had required of her? Within five years of their marriage they had quarreled violently, terminally, and after that they had barely spoken to one another again.

Joanna drew a deep breath to compose herself. David was dead and it should not matter now. Yet Alex Grant's poor opinion of her seemed to count for more than it ought.

She stopped dead next to the life-size ice model of

Alex himself. "Indeed?" she said scathingly. "It ill becomes *you* to step in at this eleventh hour to protect your cousin from some imaginary danger, Lord Grant. You have left him to fend for himself in the past, have you not, and his sister, too, so I hear, whilst you traipse about the globe in search of glory—"

Alex's gloved hand closed about her wrist tightly enough to make her gasp and break off. The look in his eyes was feral though he kept his tone soft. "Is this your attempt to jilt me in full public view?" he asked. There was an edge of steel to his voice. "I confess I had hoped for something more original than a list of all the ways in which I had failed my family."

"Do not be so hasty," Joanna said. She held his gaze with hers. "You will not be disappointed by your dismissal, I assure you." She shook him off, rubbing her wrist where he had held her. His grip had not hurt, but there had been something in his touch and in his eyes, something primitive and fierce, that had shaken her. The tone of their encounter had shifted in the space of a second from enmity sheathed in courtesy to all-out antagonism. Joanna could see that in the heat of the moment she had invested in Alex all the faults she had detested in David, and perhaps that was unfair, but she was in no mood to be generous. He had not extended any generosity to her, after all. He had disliked her from the start.

"You may rest easy for your cousin's virtue," she said. "I am not interested in callow youths, whatever you may think." She looked him up and down. "Nor in adventurers, for that matter, however romantic and mysterious others may find them." She squared her shoulders. "Lord Grant, I do not know what my husband said about me to make you have such an aversion to me, but I do not care for either your disapproval or your judgmental attitudes."

"David never spoke of you to me," Alex said. "Other than just before he died."

Joanna was gripping her fan so tightly between her gloved hands now that she heard the struts creak. She could see a most indiscreet crowd of guests jostling in the doorway of the room, eager to witness the scene playing out between Lady Joanna and her supposed lover.

"Well," she said sarcastically, "if David was on his deathbed then whatever he said *must* be true."

"Perhaps," Alex said. His mouth was set in a thin, angry line. "You may tell me if it was true or not. David told me never to trust you, Lady Joanna. He said that you were deceitful and manipulative. Can you tell me what you had done to incur such hatred from your husband?"

Their eyes met and locked and Joanna could feel the burn all the way through her body. Alex's gaze was narrowed on her face with dark intensity and suddenly she hated him, too, for believing her faithless, feckless husband, for taking David's word without question, for damning her unheard. She wanted to explain to him; she wanted it with a passion that shocked her, that stole her breath and made her heart ache—but she knew she could not confide in Alex Grant, a man who was practically a stranger. "Trust no one" was her maxim when it came to the ton and she had held true to it ever since the day, as a new bride, she had walked into Madame Ermine's gown shop in Bond Street and had heard two women discussing her intimate affairs in exquisite scandalous detail. It was from that gossip she had first learned of David's infidelity. As a result, she trusted no one with her secrets, especially not her late husband's closest friend, colleague and ally.

"You assume that I am the one who was in the wrong," she said bitterly, now. "I am sorry you believe that."

She saw a hint of doubt in Alex's eyes; or at least she thought that she did. It was faint and fleeting like a shadow that came and went in the blink of an eye. Then he shook his head slightly.

"That is not good enough, Lady Joanna."

Joanna's temper snapped. She had been estranged from David for five long years before he had died and had nursed her grief silently through every one of them. This man was trying to force it out into the light of day and in doing so was destroying all the layers she had built up to protect herself.

"Well, Lord Grant," she said, "it will have to do. I owe you nothing, and nothing I could say would change your opinion of me anyway, so I shall save my breath." She squared her shoulders. "I recall that you wanted me to end our supposed liaison. Let me oblige you and then we need not see one another again."

She turned to the ice sculpture and broke off the sword in the man's hand. The ice gave a very satisfying crack as the sword came free. Mrs. Cummings's guests caught their collective breath on a gasp.

Joanna snapped the sword sharply in two and handed Alex the pieces.

"That is what I think of explorers and their amatory abilities," she said clearly so that the entire company could hear her. "It is to be hoped that you can navigate your way better across the frozen wastes than you can around a woman's body, or you may end in Spain rather than Spitsbergen." She smiled. "Consider yourself jilted, Lord Grant," she added sweetly. "Good night."

Chapter 3

MRS. LOTTIE CUMMINGS stood alone in her dining room surveying the detritus her guests had left behind. In a rare gesture of generosity she had given the servants what was left of the night off and told them they could finish cleaning and tidying the following day. The candles were snuffed and the air smelled faintly of smoke. What light filtered into the room came from the first rays of dawn that streaked the eastern sky over London. Her ice sculptures were melting, dripping sadly into the large cut-glass bowls beneath with a splash that sounded like tears. Lottie felt depressed and she could not, for the life of her, understand why.

The evening had been the most tremendous success, a complete crush, and she knew it would be spoken of for months to come. Even without the thrilling quarrel between Lady Joanna Ware and her alleged lover, Lord Grant, it would have been deemed vastly entertaining. The food had, as always, been exquisite, the music perfection itself and the ice sculptures were the finishing touch. So why, Lottie wondered, trailing her fingers in the remainder of a bowl of rose-petal cream and licking it off thoughtfully, did she feel as though she had lost a guinea and found a farthing? It was true that her husband, Gregory, had barely shown his face at the rout, but then he never did. They went their separate ways and had done since the beginning. She had married him for his money not his personality, which was just as well, Lottie thought, since he did not have one. No, indeed, Gregory's neglect was not the cause of her blue devils. She did not *want* his attention. But she wanted someone's attention, someone more exciting, more daring, someone altogether more *thrilling* than poor old Gregory.

It was a pity that Alex Grant had turned down her whispered offers of a liaison. Lottie had not expected to be rejected. It happened to her very seldom. She had known Alex's reputation for coldness but had thought she would be just the woman to thaw him. She had not for a moment believed the twaddle other impressionable women whispered that he was still mourning his dead wife or some such rubbish. He was a man, wasn't he, and therefore led by his lusts. She had seen the way Alex had been looking at Joanna and she knew he wanted David Ware's luscious widow. But he was wasting his time there. Lottie sucked the remaining cream from her fingers. Joanna really *was* frigid, poor girl—David had told Lottie that when they had been in bed together one day. No, indeed, far better for Lottie to be the one to show the lovely Lord Grant the comforts she could offer a dashing adventurer. Except that Alex had rejected her advances. He had done so courteously, charmingly even, but it was still a rebuff and Lottie was still offended. She had immediately sent a servant to Gregory to tell him that on no account should he fund Alex's scapegrace cousin on his ridiculous Mexican voyage. It had been a petty revenge, perhaps, but it had made her feel better…

The click of a door closing softly and the sound of

a footfall on the marble tiles of the hall made her turn swiftly. She had thought that she was alone, but now she saw that a tall shadow had fallen across the doorway.

"I thought that you had left some time ago," she said as James Devlin came forward into the room.

Dev shook his head. "Your husband and I were talking."

"And?" Lottie prompted. Had blasted Gregory defied her and offered the stupid boy his money anyway? She felt infuriated.

But Dev was shaking his head. "He won't fund me. Says the venture is too risky."

"I am *so* sorry." Lottie swam forward and laid a gentle hand on his arm. "You must be *so* disappointed, darling." He looked disappointed, she thought, all youthful spirits downcast, so sweetly handsome she wanted to kiss him better. She pressed a glass of champagne on him. It was flat from standing but he still drank it down in one go and she gave him another, picking up a glass herself and clinking it against his in salute.

"Where does that leave you now?" she said sympathetically.

"With a half share in a ship and no money to sail it anywhere." He sounded philosophical. Bless him, Lottie thought, he really was the dearest boy. Perhaps he was not as mature or as forceful as his cousin, a boy to Alex's man, but he was here and he was extremely handsome and she was bored and miserable...

She took Dev's empty glass from his hand and placed it on the table, leaning past him and brushing her breasts firmly against his arm in the process. It was a gesture that could have been entirely accidental—or not. She felt him stiffen, more so in some places than others, and smiled.

"Darling," she said, straightening up and standing close enough so that their bodies were just touching, "is there *anything* that I can do to help you feel better?"

He was, she was delighted to discover, of extremely quick intellect. She really did not have to make her meaning any plainer.

His hands came up to grasp her upper arms and draw her in for a kiss that was not the hesitant, inexperienced embrace she might have expected but something altogether more knowing. She kissed him back eagerly, almost greedily, running her hands over his back and down over his buttocks, too, in those *deliciously* fitted pantaloons, pressing herself against his aroused cock, urging him closer. He met her demands with amusement and skill and she was just beginning to think she had fundamentally underestimated him, when he lifted her up and placed her on the table, tumbling her backward amidst the half-finished meringues and leftover fruit and moving their game into another league entirely. She felt strawberries squash against the back of her bodice and their rich, sweet scent stung the air.

"My gown!" She liked this dress too much to let some impetuous lover spoil it. But it was too late.

"You're rich enough to buy another." His voice was lazy. He completed the ruin of her clothes by tugging the bodice down to her waist so that her breasts were exposed. The material of the gown ripped, but before she could complain, she felt the cold, slippery caress of strawberries rubbing against her naked skin and then his mouth, licking, sucking, tasting her. She squirmed breathless and unbelieving beneath his ministrations, feeling the lust spiral tighter and tighter within her belly, trying not to cry out in disbelief and pleasure at the expert touch of his lips and hands. The door was open, she recalled hazily. Anyone might come in. The servants... They were always listening at keyholes, bearing tales. She had taken some risks in her time—indeed, to her it was part of the fun of the game—but this man was reckless to the point of madness. She had had no idea, no suspicion... Gregory knew of her little indiscretions, but he would divorce her if the scandal were too great. His pride would demand it. She simply had to put a stop to this. But oh, it was too sweet, too pleasurable to end...

His hand was beneath her skirts, on her thigh, and she ached to feel him within her. But then something touched her slick heat, something hard, smooth and broad, sliding inside her, icy cold encased in her warmth, the hilt of the frozen sword from the ice sculpture. The shock, the sheer illicit, erotic thrill of it made her half rise from the table with a gasp that was a mixture of astonishment, disbelief and wild excitement.

"You *cannot* do that—"

"I can." He was easing her back down amongst the smashed meringues and scattered strawberries, leaning over to kiss her even as he threw up her petticoats, spread her wider and worked that wicked sword hilt inside her. He tasted of champagne and strawberries. She could feel the ice melting against her inner thighs, running in rivulets down her skin even as the heat inside her blazed to impossible levels. She arched upward and came in one huge, overwhelming roll of sensation, biting down on one of her embroidered napkins to prevent herself from screaming loud enough to wake the whole house.

When she came to her senses she realized that there was fruit in her hair and she was lying half-naked in a pool of melted ice. Dev was laughing down at her. In the half light he looked young and vital and very, very wicked. Lottie's heart skipped a beat.

"You enjoyed that?"

"Oh, you…" Lottie was disconcerted to realize that she felt rather more for him than simple gratitude. She struggled to push aside some unfamiliar emotions and achieve her customary languor.

"Well, darling," she murmured, "what a find you have proved to be!" She reached for him and was gratified to discover that he was very hard for her.

"Not here," he said, scooping her up into his arms with an ease that was very seductive. "What do you say to a tryst in the gardens?"

"The summerhouse is nice at this time of year," Lottie murmured as he strode toward the door leading out to the terrace. "Actually, I find that the summerhouse is nice at any time of year."

ALEX GRANT SAT IN THE OFFICES of Churchward and Churchward, lawyers to the aristocratic and discerning, in High Holborn, and tried not to feel too impatient. This had most decidedly not been part of his plan. Since he was still kicking his heels in London waiting for his next commission from the Admiralty, he had decided to ignore all the tempting offers from the ton to grace their social events and to spend the day visiting a former colleague at the naval hospital at Greenwich. But when he had arisen that morning, his steward, Frazer, had told him glumly that not only were there no orders but there was an urgent letter from the lawyers—and true enough, when he opened Mr. Churchward's missive that gentleman's agitation had leaped from the page, summoning him immediately to a meeting in his chambers.

Now he was here, though, Mr. Churchward was remaining obstinately silent, for Lady Joanna Ware had not yet arrived and it would be quite improper, so Mr. Churchward said, for him to acquaint Lord Grant with the nature of the problem until her ladyship was present.

Alex drummed his fingers impatiently on the table beside him. His leg was aching today, the result no doubt of his exertions in Mrs. Cummings's ballroom the previous night. It put him in an intolerant mood. There was no sound in Mr. Churchward's office but for the rustle of papers, the muted rumble of traffic in the street below and the tick of the clock as it marked just how long Lady Joanna was keeping them waiting.

Alex had not intended to see Lady Joanna Ware again before he left London and the fact that he was now obliged to do so—or would be if she ever arrived—was sufficient to annoy him intensely. It was not, he assured himself, that he could not accept his congé. It was true that Lady Joanna had dismissed him the previous night in a manner that was fully as public and embarrassing as she had promised, but he was man enough to take that. She had given him fair warning, he had underestimated her and he had been bested. No, what troubled him was the matter of David Ware's last words.

Alex had never questioned his late colleague's integrity before and it disturbed him to find himself doing so now, particularly as he had no reason to doubt Ware's embittered words about his wife. And yet… And yet Joanna Ware's pale stricken face was before his eyes and remembering her expression made him feel as though he had been kicked squarely in the gut.

"You assume that I am the one who was in the wrong… I am sorry you believe that."

He had felt her pain then. He had not wanted to; he had no desire to be moved by this woman or to feel any affinity for her and yet he had not been able to help himself.

It was easy to canonize a man after his death, especially a man like David Ware, who had already been hailed as a hero. Joanna must have been a very pretty adornment to Ware's fame, burnishing his glory with her elegance and style. But then something must have happened; everything had gone wrong between them.

"You assume that I am the one who was in the wrong…"

Somewhere in the recesses of Alex's body he felt a wayward pang of sympathy for Joanna Ware. And yet his doubts lingered. On his deathbed Ware had called his wife a deceitful, manipulative bitch, harsh words, bitterly spoken. There had to be a reason…

Impatiently Alex dismissed his thoughts. He was not at all sure why he was expending so much time in thinking about Joanna Ware. It was infuriating and completely unacceptable that he felt drawn to her in some odd way in direct contradiction to what they both wanted. Yet he could not shift the feeling. It persisted. It made him angry and uncomfortable. He also profoundly disliked being dragged into David Ware's personal affairs. When he had delivered his late colleague's letter to the lawyers, he had thought that was an end to the matter and yet here he was; against his will he had been drawn further into Ware's business.

He itched to be gone.

There was a flurry of noise outside the door and then the clerk threw it open with a somewhat theatrical flourish and Lady Joanna Ware swept into the room. Alex got to his feet. Mr Churchward leaped up, too, apparently so eager to greet his client that he managed to knock a pile of papers off his desk.

"My lady!" Churchward looked momentarily stunned and Alex knew how he felt. Joanna's entrance had brought something bright and vital into the fusty room, chasing away the cobwebs and the shadows. For a moment Alex felt dazzled, as though he was looking directly into the sun. It was odd, he thought, for his overriding impression of Joanna had from the start been one of cool superficiality and self-containment and yet now she was all warmth and charm. It was like watching a different woman. She was shaking Mr Churchward's hand and smiling in genuine pleasure to see the lawyer and her brittle façade was quite gone, replaced by a sincerity that seemed entirely genuine.

This morning Joanna was dressed in a primrose silk morning gown with a matching spencer trimmed with black lace. A delicious little hat sat on her upswept chestnut curls. She looked breathtakingly pretty, very young and disconcertingly innocent. It was a smart, stylish, expensive outfit, neat as a pin and yet somehow subtly seductive. Alex, unversed and uninterested in fashion, had not the least idea why the sight of so apparently respectable a gown should have precisely the reverse effect on him and make him feel distinctly *unrespectable*. It covered all of Joanna from neck to toe and it made him want to uncover her, preferably immediately and in intensive detail. He shifted slightly.

"I am surprised to see that your dog can move," he said as the terrier trotted into the office in Joanna's wake, the yellow ribbon in its topknot complementing her yellow silk perfectly. "I hope he has not found the exercise of walking from your carriage too onerous."

Joanna turned. Her violet-blue eyes fixed on Alex and she did not look pleased to see him. Her luscious mouth tightened into a deeply disapproving bow, which contrarily Alex found extremely attractive.

"My dog's name is Max," she said, "and he is a border terrier and as such perfectly capable of vigorous activity. He simply chooses not to exert himself." The dog, as though to make the point, graciously accepted a biscuit Mr. Churchward had taken from his drawer, curled up neatly in a patch of sunlight on the floor and went to sleep.

"Mr. Churchward did not tell me that you would be here," Joanna added. "I was not expecting to see you."

"I was not expecting to be here," Alex said as he held her chair for her. "So both of us are disappointed." He shrugged, turning to the lawyer. "As Lady Joanna has finally deigned to grace us with her presence," he said, "shall we commence?"

"Thank you, my lord," Mr. Churchward said frostily. He fidgeted a little with his papers and settled his glasses more firmly on his nose. "Madam…" His voice quivered a little and Alex realized that he was laboring under a strong emotion, "may I first say how sorry, how *very* sorry I am to be the bearer of yet more bad news in relation to your husband's death. When we met a year ago to discuss the *distressing* terms of his will—" He broke off and shook his head. "It pains me greatly," he added, "to bring yet more trouble upon you."

"Dear Mr. Churchward—" there was more warmth in Joanna's tone than Alex had ever heard from her before "—I fear you are making me nervous!" She smiled reassuringly at the lawyer though Alex thought there was an edge of anxiety beneath her assumption of ease. "You cannot be held responsible in any way for my late husband's behavior," Joanna said. "Pray do not concern yourself."

Looking from Joanna's composed features to Mr. Churchward's anguished ones, Alex wondered for the first time about the depositions of David Ware's will and about the codicil, that very document that he had carried back all the way from the Arctic at Ware's behest. He had assumed that his late comrade had left his not-inconsiderable fortune to Lady Joanna to allow her to continue to live in the lavish style to which she was clearly accustomed. That would surely have been in keeping with Ware's character, with his honor and his sense of duty. But now, looking at the lawyer's gloomy face—and remembering Ware's venom toward his wife—Alex realized that his assumption might well have been false.

"What *were* the terms of Ware's will?" he interrupted.

Both Joanna and the lawyer jumped as though they had forgotten he was there. Joanna refused to meet his eyes, smoothing the material of her skirts in a quick, fidgety gesture. Churchward flushed.

"My lord, I beg your pardon, but I am not certain that it is your business."

Joanna looked up suddenly and Alex felt the impact of her gaze like a physical blow, it was so keen and clear.

"On the contrary, Mr. Churchward," she said, "I imagine that Lord Grant is here because David has somehow embroiled him in my affairs. If that is the case then he deserves to know the truth from the beginning."

"If you wish, madam." Churchward sounded huffy. "It is most irregular, however."

"David," Joanna said gently, "*was* irregular, Mr. Churchward." She glanced back at Alex, took a deep breath and seemed to be choosing her words with some care. "My late husband," she said, "left his estate to his cousin John Hagan in his will and cut me off without a penny." She paused. "You may be aware, Lord Grant, that Maybole was bought with David's navy prize money?" She waited and Alex nodded. David Ware, as a younger son, had not inherited an entailed estate. He had bought a piece of land at Maybole in Kent and had built a gaudy mansion in which Alex had been just the once.

"His arrangements," Joanna continued, "left me somewhat financially embarrassed." Once again she dropped her gaze and smoothed some imaginary crease from the pristine folds of her skirts.

"He did not explain his actions to me," she finished, "but no doubt he had his reasons."

"No doubt he did," Alex said. He was shocked and puzzled that his late colleague had been so ungallant as to leave his wife penniless. It seemed quite out of character, but then had Ware not implied that he had good reason to mistrust his wife? Presumably he had done the minimum for her that he was required to do under the law.

"In my experience Ware was a good judge of character and never acted without just cause," he said stiffly. "The provocation must have been considerable."

He saw the angry color mantle Joanna's cheeks. "Thank you for your unsolicited opinion," she said coldly. "I might have known that you would take his part on the basis of no evidence whatsoever."

"It was unforgivable of Commodore Ware to make so little provision for Lady Joanna," Churchward muttered. The lawyer, Alex was interested to see, made no attempt at impartiality. "It was not the action of a hero."

Mr. Churchward, Alex thought, was a man who approved of things being done in the proper way and David Ware had apparently transgressed that code in failing to provide sufficiently for his wife.

"Surely you had a jointure, Lady Joanna," he said abruptly. "I cannot believe Ware left you utterly destitute."

There was a small silence. Joanna bit her lip. "David did leave me a small sum of money, it is true…"

Alex felt a rush of relief that his faith in his late friend had not been misplaced. He could see clearly enough what must have happened. Ware had left his wife a perfectly adequate settlement but she was so spendthrift and careless that it was never enough.

"I suppose that it is a sum that you easily outrun with your extravagance?" he said. He allowed his gaze to sweep over Joanna and did not hide his scorn. "I can well imagine that you are expensive to run."

"I am not a *carriage,*" Joanna said haughtily. "And

yes—" she smoothed the skirts of her yellow silk "—I appreciate fine things—"

"Then you have only yourself to blame," Alex said. "It is a simple matter of economics. If you do not possess the money in the first place, don't spend it."

"Thank you for the lesson," Joanna snapped. There was a slight flush in her cheeks now, but the sparkle in her eyes was anger not embarrassment.

"Last night," she said, "you did not scruple to point out to me that David hated me, Lord Grant." She made a slight gesture. "You will be pleased that there is evidence to support your assertion."

Alex saw Churchward stiffen with outrage. The lawyer, he thought with amusement, was looking as though he would like to run him through—if such martial thoughts ever occurred to a peaceful man of the pen.

"My lord!" Churchward sounded reproachful. "How very ungallant of you to suggest such a thing."

"But true," Joanna said smoothly. "David hated me and through various ingenious means sought to punish me, even after he was dead. Clearly he was every bit as resourceful as everyone claimed him to be." She sighed. "Anyway, we must let that go and turn to the current matter."

"A moment." Alex held up a hand. He was thinking of the beautiful house in Half Moon Street and the attractive and expensive items with which Lady Joanna Ware surrounded herself. He wondered who was paying for them if her jointure really was as minuscule as she claimed. David Ware's close relatives were dead and Alex had the impression that Joanna herself, whilst an Earl's daughter, had come from a relatively impoverished country family. If Ware had left her practically without a feather to fly then her comparative wealth was curious, to say the least.

"If you inherited little of Ware's fortune and the bulk of it went to John Hagan," he said slowly, "how are you funded?"

He heard Mr. Churchward give a snort of disgust. The lawyer, like Lady Joanna herself, had picked up on the implications of his question:

"Who is supporting you? Is it a lover?"

Lady Joanna raised her brows; a smile curved her delectable mouth.

"I thought that they taught manners at the naval academy, Lord Grant," she said. "Did you play truant for those lectures?"

"I find it easier to ask a direct question when I want a straight answer," Alex said.

"Well, you are not barking questions at your mcn now," Joanna said. She lifted one slim shoulder in an elegant shrug. "Nevertheless, I will answer your question." Her tone was cold now. "The house in Half Moon Street belongs to Mr. Hagan. As for the rest—prepare yourself for a shock." Her violet-blue eyes mocked him. "I hope that you are strong enough to withstand it, Lord Grant." She paused. "I work for my living."

"You *work?*" Alex *was* shocked. "As what?" He made no attempt to erase the incredulity from his tone.

Joanna laughed. "Certainly not as a courtesan—" her tone was derisory "—in case you thought that the only talent I might have to offer."

"As to that," Alex said, holding her eyes, "I really would not know if it is one of your talents." He paused. "Would I?"

Her eyes flashed, smoky with dislike. "Nor will you."

"My lord, my lady!" Mr. Churchward intervened. The tips of his ears glowed bright red. "If you please."

Joanna dropped her gaze. "People pay me to design the interior of their homes, Lord Grant. I am considered to have excellent taste, sufficient that people wish to buy it for themselves. They pay me well and a few years ago I was also fortunate enough to inherit a legacy from my aunt." She shifted in her seat, glancing again at Mr. Churchward, who was looking most uncomfortable. "But we wander from the point. Mr. Churchward has more bad news to impart, I believe. Let us put him out of his misery."

"Thank you, my lady," Churchward said unhappily. He placed the letter Alex had delivered two days before on the top of his desk and smoothed it as though in doing so he could somehow alter the content.

"Lord Grant delivered this letter to me on behalf of your husband," he said to Joanna. "It is a codicil to his will."

"David entrusted it to me when he was dying," Alex added.

Joanna looked at him thoughtfully. He could not read her expression now. Those violet eyes were guarded. "Another of David's melodramatic deathbed gestures," she said. "You did not mention this when you called on me, Lord Grant."

"No," Alex said, "I did not. I had no idea if the contents were relevant to you or not."

He saw her lashes come down, veiling her expression still further. Only the tattoo beaten by her fingers on the desk suggested she was in any way discomposed. He knew what she was thinking, though. He could read her as clearly as if she had spoken. She thought him David's pawn; that his loyalty to her late husband had enabled Ware to use him. Alex found that he did not like to be judged that way, as though he had no independent thought. Then he recognized with grim irony that he had judged Joanna Ware, too. Not on his experience of her but on Ware's word alone. The tension thickened, the atmosphere in the room feeling prickly with antagonism.

"Please proceed, Mr. Churchward," Joanna said politely.

Churchward cleared his throat. "'Written in my own hand, by Commodore David Ware on the seventh of November in the year nine.'" He looked at them over his glasses.

"'I have decided that I have been remiss,'" he read aloud, "'in leaving so little in my last will and testament to my wife, Lady Joanna Caroline Ware. I am aware that various parties might criticize my neglect of her, so I hereby redress the balance in this codicil to my will.'"

Alex looked at Joanna. She did not look like a woman eagerly anticipating a hitherto-unexpected windfall. Her expression was that of someone expecting a very nasty surprise.

"'I leave to Lady Joanna's care and welfare—'" Mr. Churchward paused and swallowed so hard that his Adam's apple bobbed "'—my baby daughter, Nina Tatiana Ware.'"

Alex felt a short, sharp jolt of shock. He had known that Ware had taken a Russian mistress during their last expedition to the Arctic. Ware's association with the girl had been no secret; he had boasted of it, claiming that she was Pomor nobility even if he had found her in a whorehouse. Ware's men had joked about their captain's promiscuity and the fact that even on a trip where women were few and far between, he had found both time and opportunity for his whoring. Alex had thought that the girl had left Spitsbergen for the Russian mainland. But Ware had never mentioned a child before. Alex could only assume that approaching death had shaken his colleague into taking some action toward his bastard daughter.

Churchward's words reclaimed his attention. "'Nina is currently four years old and an orphan resident in the monastery at Bellsund, in Arctic Spitsbergen.'" The lawyer's voice wobbled. "'I know my wife will be delighted at this proof of my fecundity…'" Churchward's voice dwindled and died away. Looking at Joanna, Alex could see that she had turned chalk white, her eyes vivid in a parchment-pale face. "Madam—" Churchward said helplessly.

"Pray proceed, Mr. Churchward," Joanna said again. Her voice was quite steady.

"'There are two conditions contingent on this legacy,'" Churchward read. "'Firstly that my wife must travel in person to the Bellsund Monastery in Spitsbergen where my daughter is currently being cared for, and bring her back to London to live with her.'" Mr. Churchward's voice was getting faster and faster as though by hurrying over the words he could somehow lessen their impact. He shot both Joanna and Alex a hunted glance like a rabbit trapped in the poacher's sights. "'I am aware,'" he continued, the letter shaking now in his hand, "'that Joanna will detest the strictures that I have placed upon her, but that her desire for a child is so strong she will have no choice other than to put herself into the greatest danger and discomfort imaginable in order to rescue my daughter—'"

He stopped as Joanna took a sharp breath. "Madam—" he said again.

Joanna had turned even paler, so deathly white that Alex thought she might faint. "He abandoned a baby girl in a monastery," she whispered. "How could he do such a thing?"

Alex got up and threw open the door into the outer office, calling for a glass of water. One of the clerks scurried away to fetch it.

"Fresh air," Churchward said, pushing open the window and causing a draft to blow in that scattered the papers on his desk, "burnt feathers, *sal volatile*—"

"Brandy," Alex said grimly, "would be more effective."

"I do not keep spirits in my place of work," Churchward said.

"I would have thought that you would need them sometimes," Alex said, "for the benefit of both yourself and your clients, Mr. Churchward."

"I am perfectly all right," Joanna interposed. She was sitting upright, still very pale but with a dignity drawn about her now like a cloak. Alex pressed the glass of water into her hand, holding it steady with his hand clasped about hers. She raised her eyes thoughtfully to his face before she drank obediently. A shade of color came back into her cheeks.

"So," she said after a moment, "my late husband manages to manipulate me from beyond the grave. It is quite an achievement." She met Alex's gaze. "Were you aware that David had an illegitimate daughter, Lord Grant?" She placed the glass gently on the table.

"No," Alex said. "I knew that he had a mistress but not that the woman bore him a child. She was a Russian girl who claimed she was Pomor nobility. I thought she had returned to the mainland, but she must have died shortly before Ware if the baby is now an orphan."

Joanna's gaze was cloudy and disillusioned. "A Russian noblewoman," she said slowly. "David would have loved that. How that would have enhanced his prestige!"

"The girl was young," Alex said, "and wild. Her family had cast her out, washed their hands of her, I believe." He looked at Joanna's tight expression and felt something shift inside him. "I am sorry," he said. He realized that he meant it. Whatever his opinion of Joanna Ware, he knew that this must be an immensely difficult issue for her to confront. He had to reluctantly admire her unflinching acceptance when most women would be having the vapors to have been bequeathed their husband's bastard child.

"I am not naive enough to think that David was not capable of such a thing," Joanna said slowly. "Indeed, perhaps I should be grateful that there are not more of his offspring scattered about the globe, or at least not as far as I am aware." She looked at him. "Are you aware of any more of his sideslips, Lord Grant?"

"No." Alex shifted. "I am truly sorry." Ware's profligate tendencies were the one aspect of his friend's character that Alex had always had difficulty accepting. Some had seen Ware's dissolute whoring as part of his heroic, charismatic persona. Alex had, in contrast, considered it the single weakness that David Ware had possessed, but a weakness he could condone because Ware's marriage bed had been so cold and his relationship with his wife so fraught with dislike.

He looked at Joanna. She did not look like a woman who would wither a man to nothing in her bed. She looked warm and tempting and eminently appealing. Whatever the quarrel with Ware had been, it must have been so bitter and deep that she had driven him away.

"You do not try to soften the blow." A faint smile touched Joanna's lips. "There is no comfort to be had from you, is there, Lord Grant?"

"Very little, I fear," Alex said. "But I am also sorry that Ware saw fit to do this."

"Well, that is something, I suppose," Mr. Churchward interposed huffily.

"Because," Alex finished, "I fear his judgment must have been severely lacking to leave the future of his daughter in Lady Joanna's hands."

He saw Joanna's eyes open very wide in shock. "You think me an unsuitable guardian?"

"How could I think otherwise?" Alex said. "Ware mistrusted you. He told me so. I cannot see why he would leave his daughter's upbringing to a woman he disliked so strongly."

Joanna chewed her lower lip hard. "Always you fall back on David's judgments, Lord Grant," she said. "Do you have no independent thoughts of your own?"

Alex brought his hand down flat on the table with a slap that made the piles of legal documents jump and flutter. He was furious—with Ware for involving him in his unpleasant personal vendetta against his wife, with Lady Joanna for forcing him to question his judgment and with himself for doubting his loyalties for even a second, for doubt them he did, the suspicions and misgivings wreathing his mind as unsubstantial as smoke and yet somehow impossible now to dismiss.

"Ware was my friend and colleague for over ten years," he said through his teeth. He wondered if he was trying to convince Joanna—or himself. "He was an inspirational leader to his men. He never let me down. He saved my *life* on more than one occasion. So, yes, I trust his word and his judgment."

They glared at one another until Mr. Churchward raised a pacifying hand.

"Lord Grant." Mr. Churchward's voice brought them back to the point. "Perhaps we could postpone the discussion until I have finished?" He polished his glasses, replaced them on his nose and resumed: "'Further, I hereby appoint my friend and colleague Alexander, Lord Grant, as joint guardian with my wife to my daughter, Nina, to share *all* the responsibilities and decisions relating to her upbringing.'" Mr. Churchward cleared his throat. "'Lord Grant will in addition be sole trustee, controlling all financial aspects relating to my daughter's rearing and education.'"

"What?" Alex exploded. He felt trapped, baffled and angry. He could barely believe what he was hearing. Ware had been his friend since childhood. Alex had thought they had known one another well. Yet despite knowing his history, his way of life and the demands of his profession, Ware had put him in this invidious position, burdened him with the responsibility for his child, her welfare and upbringing, a duty Alex would be obliged to share with the wife that David Ware had hated... Truly, Ware *had* lost his mind. Either that or he had embroiled Alex in his game of revenge against his

wife with a callous disregard for the feelings of everyone but himself, and Alex could not, would not believe that a man of Ware's honor would do such a thing.

He looked at Joanna. Her eyes burned as hard and bright as sapphires. "So," she said slowly, "I am to have the child reside with me but *you* will hold the purse strings for both of us, Lord Grant."

"So it seems," Alex said. He could feel Joanna's gaze riveted on his face with such intensity that he could sense the power of her fury and distress no matter how well she strove to hide it.

"You said at the start of this interview that you did not know the contents of this letter, Lord Grant." Her tone was dry, skeptical and hard. "I find that difficult to believe when you and David were evidently so deep in each other's confidence."

"Believe it," Alex said. He was struggling with his own response to Ware's outrageous behavior and was in no mood to be gentle. "I had no notion. I want this burden as little as you do."

"Then just as you think that David was mistaken to leave a child's welfare in my hands," Joanna said very politely but with the anger burning though the words as hot as a furnace, "so I cannot imagine why my late husband thought for *one moment* that *you* were the appropriate person to have care of a small child nor control of her fortune."

"At least I have proved that I can provide materially for my family," Alex said, giving her a contemptuous look that brought the color flying into her cheeks. "I do not shirk my responsibilities. In contrast, your rackety lifestyle in the ton is hardly suited to the stable existence Miss Ware will require, Lady Joanna."

Joanna's eyes were icy with outrage. "I *beg* your

pardon? Rackety? You know nothing of my way of life, Lord Grant, other than what is based on David's lies and your own arrogant assumptions!" Her tone dripped disdain. "If it comes to that, you are the one who *rackets* about the world like a poorly aimed cannonball. You may provide materially for your family but you have no interest in engaging with them in any emotional sense!"

Alex's anger and guilt kindled to a blaze at her words. He had inherited little in the way of fortune but had plowed every penny he had back into his estates and into ensuring his cousins were well provided for financially. It was enough. It *had* to be enough because it was all that he could give. Amelia had been the one who had been warm and loving. When she had died he had cut that emotion from his life. The thought of Amelia twisted a bitter knife in him again. He had failed once before; he could not fail Ware in this obligation. He was hog-tied, compelled by honor and his own guilty conscience to assist Ware's orphaned daughter.

"I am sure that your objections spring only from the fact that I am to be your treasurer," he said, venting a cold anger. "I imagine you would give a great deal to alter that situation, Lady Joanna, given that Ware apparently left you without the means to support your extravagant lifestyle."

Joanna's piquant face sharpened into contempt again. "I have no need of the money, Lord Grant. As I said, I earn sufficient for my needs and have inherited more. Besides, money is no substitute for love—the love that you so singularly fail to give to those who rely upon you and which David's daughter will also need in her life—"

"Lord Grant! Lady Joanna!" Churchward was remonstrating with them like a fussy governess. "Please! This is most unbecoming!"

There was a silence, a very long, deep and stormy silence, broken eventually by Churchward muttering "oh dear, oh dear" under his breath, a rather ineffectual remark, which Alex could not help but feel added little to the situation.

"Mr. Churchward is right," Joanna said. She made a visible effort to reassert her self-control. "Our being at daggers drawn does not help the situation, Lord Grant."

They looked at each other, locked in a baffled hostility.

"Why?" Alex said fiercely. "Why would Ware do this?"

Joanna shook her head. "I have no notion why David should encumber *you* with such a responsibility, Lord Grant." A bitter smile twisted her lips. "I understand well enough why he has done this to me. He wishes to punish me for being an unsatisfactory wife to him by forcing me to go to the ends of the earth to save his child." Alex caught the tiniest waver to her voice. "He seeks to exploit what he knew was my desperate desire for a baby of my own by telling me that I can have Nina, but only if I go to fetch her myself, a journey he knows will terrify and endanger me..." Her voice faded and she turned her face away for a moment so that Alex could not read her expression. When she resumed, her voice was calm again.

"I cannot imagine what possessed David to embroil you in his revenge upon me, though. Perhaps he knew we would inevitably dislike one another, and so being obliged to share the upbringing of a child would keep us at each other's throats and make my life as difficult as possible." She looked at him. "I am sorry he involved you in this, Lord Grant."

She got to her feet, and Max the dog made a grumbling sound, struggled upright and shook himself, making the dust dance in the sunlight.

"If that is all, Mr. Churchward," Joanna said, turning courteously to the lawyer, "then you must excuse me. I have urgent arrangements to make for my journey."

Alex stood up, too. He was incredulous that Joanna could even consider leaving when so much was unresolved. "Wait a moment!" he said. He put out a hand to halt her. "You cannot simply walk away from this. We have to talk."

Joanna shot him a glance. "I do not wish to talk to you at the moment, Lord Grant," she said. "We will only quarrel further. I agree that we need to discuss arrangements, but I suggest that you make an appointment to see me."

"You make it sound as though we are organizing a rout," Alex snapped, "rather than ensuring the welfare of a defenseless child."

Joanna ignored him. She gave the lawyer her hand. "Please accept my apologies, Mr. Churchward, on behalf of my late husband for placing you in such difficult circumstances," she said. "I am always grateful for the service you have provided my family and I am so very sorry you have been drawn into this situation."

"Madam—" Churchward sounded shaken "—you know that if there is any way in which I may serve you…"

"Of course." Joanna took a deep breath and Alex

realized suddenly what it was costing her to maintain her innate dignity. "Be assured that I shall be in touch, Mr. Churchward, and thank you."

"Wait," Alex said again. He put out a hand to her as she started to walk toward the door. "I will escort you to your carriage, Lady Joanna."

Her blue gaze flickered up to meet his again. "I do not require your escort."

"I insist."

"Pray, do not." She turned on him fiercely and he saw how close she was to the edge now, how tightly stretched her control. "I know that you only wish to accompany me in order to speak with me," she said, "but I *cannot* talk about this now. Please excuse me."

The door closed behind her and for a moment there was a silence in the office. Alex realized that Churchward was watching him with an unreadable expression.

"Was there something else, Mr. Churchward?" Alex asked politely.

"No, my lord." Churchward shut his mouth like a trap.

"It seems," Alex said, "that you have a deal of sympathy for Lady Joanna."

The lawyer's eyes narrowed with disdain. He took off his spectacles and polished them violently on the edge of his coat. "I am impartial in my dealings with all my clients, Lord Grant," the lawyer said. "Lady Joanna has always treated me with the utmost courtesy and consideration and in return she has my absolute loyalty."

"Very commendable," Alex murmured. "And David Ware? Did he have your loyalty, too?"

There was an infinitesimal silence before Churchward answered.

"I served Commodore Ware well," he said.

"A lawyer's answer," Alex said. "You did not like Ware?"

Churchward inclined his head. "It is generally accepted that Commodore Ware was a hero."

"That," Alex said, "was not what I asked."

There was another silence. The door to the outer office was ajar; Alex could hear the sound of voices and the scrape of quills as the clerks worked, but in Mr. Churchward's inner sanctum there was a tense quiet.

"Perhaps," Churchward said, "you should be asking yourself why my answer matters to you, Lord Grant. Why do you question?" He looked up and met Alex's eyes very directly with a challenge in his own. "You were Commodore Ware's greatest friend," he said. "Surely your loyalty to him is unshakable. Good day, Lord Grant."

And he held open the door for Alex, leaving his question hanging in the air.

Chapter 4

JOANNA HAD PUT Max in the carriage, where he jumped up on the seat and went to sleep. She asked the coachman to wait for her and walked briskly along the crowded pavements to Lincoln's Inn Fields. She needed to be in the open air, needed space and time to think. She barely saw the crowds that passed her other than as a flash of color and a blur of faces. The babble of voices, the shouts of street vendors and the calls of coachmen and grooms broke over her like a wall of noise; the sun seemed too bright and hurt her eyes, the smells of unwashed bodies pressing close, of dung, of cut grass and flowers, sweet and sour, seemed to assault her. She walked almost blindly until she found a bench in the shade of an elm tree, and she sat down on it feeling suddenly old and tired.

It did not grieve her that David had been unfaithful to her. The thought left her hollow and unemotional. It had happened so many times before that she had no trust in him remaining to be betrayed. She had known from early on in their marriage that he simply could not keep his breeches buttoned. And yet it had never occurred to her that he might have fathered a child on another woman. When she had first heard Churchward mention David's daughter, she had felt shock and disbelief, a blind denial. Her whole world had seemed to shift and turn dark, blurring at the edges. She felt stupid and sick and naive to have assumed that just because she and David had no children, another woman had not borne him a son or daughter. In that moment all the desires and dreams of motherhood that she had secretly cherished and had fiercely repressed burst out. She was almost engulfed in anger and bitterness, and in a regret so poignant that it stole her breath.

"You are a barren, frigid bitch..."

She could still remember every last word of that last horrible quarrel she had had with David that had culminated in him leaving her lying unconscious and bleeding on the floor. He had been incandescent with fury that after five years of marriage she had failed to burnish his glory by providing him with a son and heir, a whole tribe of little explorers to follow in his footsteps around the globe. How he would have loved that...

David had been absent for the majority of their married life, which, as far as Joanna could see, was a big disadvantage in the production of progeny. He had seemed to believe, however, that he should merely have to look at her and she should be pregnant with triplets. When it had not happened, his pleasure in his young wife had turned to impatience and then to outright hostility and anger. Joanna had suffered his fury in silence, racked with guilt that she had not been able to perform a wife's duty.

Her courses had always been regular. To start with, that had been reassuring. It had made her think that surely a pregnancy was only a matter of time. But after a while it became a mockery. Her sexual relationship with David, initially no more than a mild disappointment to her, had turned to an obligation and then to something that she dreaded for its cold lack of love. She knew that many women disliked the enforced intimacy of the physical side of marriage, but she had stubbornly hoped for more pleasure than their meaningless coupling provided. Yet it seemed it was not to be. She told herself that a child would be a solace; it seemed that was not to be either.

Her aunt, superstitious as a witch in the last few years of her life, had sent potions and unguents and advice that had been quite shocking and inappropriate from the wife of a vicar. She had lectured her niece on a wife's submission in the marriage bed and Joanna had tried to obey. Neither the advice nor the potions had worked to produce the longed-for offspring. And then David, fueled by his rage and his frustration, had come to her bed one night and taken her once again with no care or consideration, and afterward had hit her, beaten her, and at last her guilt had turned to hatred for him.

Joanna wrapped her arms about her body and hugged herself tightly. Hideous visions, hideous memories filled her mind, blocking out the blue of the sky and the call of the birds. The searing pain, David's shouts of anger, the crop falling again and again on her naked body, merciless and harsh... She had known that David had been intent on demonstrating his absolute power over her, master in his home and of his wife, her body, her spirit. He thought he had claimed every facet of her life, but he had been mistaken. His viciousness had turned his biddable country wife into a different woman. Oh, how she had changed.

After the attack Joanna's courses had stopped completely and she had wondered if she was, at last, pregnant. She had longed for it desperately with every fiber of her being, hugging the hope to her like a secret. Yet even then her instinct had told her that there would be no baby. She tried to ignore the stubborn feeling, but over time it grew stronger and stronger. She started to believe that the hatred she felt for David was a canker that had killed all chance of a child. Superstitious as her aunt, she thought she had ill wished the baby and driven out all hope. And when her courses had started again a few months later, almost as though nothing had happened, she had felt empty and bereft, different in some way, as barren as David had taunted her she was. The doctors had shaken their heads and said that nothing was certain, but Joanna had known.

She opened her eyes. The sky, a little blurred but a beautiful clear, sweet blue, swam back into focus. She felt the breeze. Heard the sound of voices carry to her, saw the richness of spring color all around. She drew a deep breath.

She had told herself that it did not matter that she would always be childless, David's grass widow, abandoned as he sailed the world. She had carved out a life of her own in ton society. She loved her beautiful, stylish existence in her beautiful, stylish house. She had her work; she had her friends. And she had told herself that it was all she wanted.

She had lied.

David had known that she had lied to herself and to everyone else. He had exposed that falsehood in searing detail in his letter:

I am aware that my wife will detest the strictures that I have placed upon her but that her desire for a child is so strong that she will have no choice

*other than to put herself into the greatest danger
and discomfort imaginable in order to rescue my
daughter…*

Such cruel, heartless words revealing the true nature
of her desperation and lonely desire to be a mother! She
felt a tight, painful lump in the back of her throat. David
had stripped away the pretense that had protected her
and shown her weakness and her vulnerability. She wondered if Alex Grant had picked up on the implication of
David's words, if he had realized that her husband had
detested her for her childless state. Her insides curled
up at the thought of his scorn.

So now she could lie to herself no longer. She could
not pretend that her life gave her everything she wanted.
The truth hurt very much. It was more painful than
anything she had allowed herself to feel ever before.
But she had also been given a chance. She had to save
this child, little Nina Tatiana Ware, alone, unloved, an
orphan abandoned in a monastery somewhere in the
Arctic wastes. Her mind, her heart, fastened on to the
necessity of claiming the child with a tenacity that she
knew instantly could not, would not, be shifted. Come
hell or high water, she was rescuing Nina, bringing her
back and raising her as her own. The giving part of
her, the part that had been thwarted time and again
because she had never been able to find enough people
or animals or causes to love, almost exploded within her,
making her shake with longing and fear and newness
and excitement.

"Lady Joanna!"

It was not the moment that she wanted to be interrupted. Stifling a most unladylike curse and hastily

rubbing the tears from her cheeks, Joanna turned to see that Alex Grant was approaching her along the gravel path. She might have known that he would not accept his dismissal. He was not the sort of man to go tamely away when he wanted something. She found she could not speak. Her throat was stiff and dry. The words would not form. *If he tells me all this is my own fault because I drove David into the arms of another woman,* she thought viciously, *or if he demands to know again in that high-handed manner of his what I did to make David hate me, I think it very likely I will box his ears in public and damn the scandal of it.*

Alex Grant said nothing. He settled himself on the bench beside her and allowed his gaze to wander across the green swath of parkland to the buildings beyond. The silence fell between them. It felt strangely comforting. The breeze rustled the thick green leaves above their heads and cooled Joanna's hot cheeks. The sounds of the city were muted as though the heavy cares of the world were suddenly far away.

Joanna looked at Alex. His body was relaxed, long and lean and elegant in a casual jacket, breeches and boots. He looked comfortable inside his skin. She realized that she had not noticed earlier in Mr. Churchward's office. She had noticed him with the prickly sense of awareness and distrust that characterized their encounters, but she had not looked at him properly. When he had come to call on her in his dress uniform he had looked authoritative, powerful. Now the power was still there, but it was banked down. She felt a prickle of apprehension, the legacy of David's cruelty. Like David, Alex Grant was a very physical man, a man of great strength and force. Yet there was a difference and she struggled to define it. Perhaps it was that her instinct told her that Alex, unlike his late comrade, would never misuse that power. But instinct, she reminded herself, was a notoriously unreliable guide.

Nevertheless it felt oddly reassuring and peaceful to have him sitting beside her, his elbows resting casually on his knees, as his thoughtful dark gaze dwelled not on her for a change but on the far horizon.

"I will find which navy ships are traveling to the Arctic and will arrange with the Admiralty to go to Bellsund Monastery to bring Miss Ware back for you," Alex said.

Joanna's feeling of peacefulness fled. How typical of a man that he should be thinking of solutions to problems she had not even articulated when she had simply been sitting and feeling. She felt a quick flash of antagonism flare back into life.

"On the contrary," she said coldly, "I shall charter a ship and travel to Bellsund to bring Miss Ware home."

"That's impossible." Alex spoke flatly, but Joanna sensed some emotion behind the words. Was it shock, disapproval or something more complex? She could not be sure. His expression was unrevealing, but she was certain he was not as calm as he sounded.

"How so?" She could think of at least ten reasons why it was difficult—if not impossible—for her to travel to Spitsbergen, but she wanted to hear his.

"Ships do not sail regularly to the Arctic," Alex said. "You will not find anyone to take you."

"They will if I pay them enough."

Again she saw emotion flicker in his eyes. "You must make a great deal of money selling fashionable baubles

and trifles to the ton if you can afford to charter a ship."
He sounded contemptuous and again her skin prickled
with antagonism. "Although I am sure that you have no
real idea of the costs involved."

Joanna did not, but she was damned if she was going
to admit it. "I am touched by your concern," she said,
"but you need have no fears. I mentioned that in addition
to the income from my bauble selling I also inherited a
considerable legacy from my aunt a year ago."

It was not precisely true—the sum was adequate
rather than enormous and this trip would take all of it
and more—but Alex Grant did not need to know that.

Their eyes met, hers bright with defiant challenge,
his dark and stormy.

"You cannot sail off to the Arctic on your own." Alex
sounded angry now. "The idea is absurd. I have already
offered to escort Miss Ware back to London."

"No!" Joanna could not explain to him that as soon
as she had heard about David's daughter she had had
an overwhelming, tenacious urge to claim the child as
her own. She only knew that the thought of the child,
orphaned in a monastery so far away, had kindled in
her an emotion fiercer than any she had experienced
before—the urge to claim and defend and protect, to
take something for herself from the wreckage that
David had left behind and to shield that child against
all adversity.

"David laid that requirement on me," she argued. "I
must fulfill it."

"You have never before done what your husband required of you," Alex said, making her catch her breath
in outrage. "Why start now?"

"Because I wish to," Joanna said. She was damned

if she was going to explain. "The monks are far more likely to be persuaded to hand the child over to me, his widow, than to you, Lord Grant." She looked at him. "You have no arts of persuasion, have you? You are more inclined to direct action, from what I have seen."

"I can convince them to let me bring Nina home," Alex said. His face was dark and unyielding. "I know the Bellsund Monastery… The monks trust me." His dark gaze appraised her. "In truth I imagine that they will have considerable concerns about handing the child to you, Lady Joanna. A single woman, a widow, commands courtesy, but has little stature in their society, and a foreign one even less so."

This was another stumbling block that Joanna had not anticipated. She did not doubt Alex's assertion, for in the short time she had known him he had been brutally honest with her. David was another matter. Had he known that the monks would be reluctant to entrust Nina to her when he had written his extraordinary codicil? Was he trying to trick her, lead her on a wild-goose chase, tempting her with the promise of a child, her heart's desire, and then snatching it from beneath her nose? Surely not even he could be so cruel. Yet she had no way of knowing, and thinking of a little girl left alone in the confines of a monastery, she knew she had no choice other than to go to try to fetch her back.

She sighed. "I am sorry," she said. "I cannot permit you to act for me in this. And I do not see," she added, "why you are so anxious to offer me your help. I would have thought that another responsibility, another tie, would be the last thing that you would wish for." She looked at him. "And that I would be the last person you would help anyway."

"I am not in the least bit anxious to help you," Alex said with brutal candor. He sounded exasperated and angry. "The friendship I had for Ware means that I feel an obligation to the child, that is all. If I had known that he had left a daughter orphaned and in such dire straits—" He broke off. "Ware appointed me her guardian alongside you," he added. "I wish he had not, but I take that duty seriously and as such will do what I can to help her. If that means assisting you, then, against my will, I shall try."

"How very handsome of you!" Now Joanna felt exasperated, too. "Well, I do not require your unwilling assistance, Lord Grant! I am perfectly capable of traveling to Bellsund on my own."

She tried to sound confident but was aware of feeling woefully inadequate. She shivered at the thought of everything she had to accomplish. She was no explorer, fearlessly seeking out new lands and new adventures. David had never wanted her to travel with him and she had heard the most terrible stories of hardship and sickness and shipwreck. If she had her way she would go no farther than the shops in Bond Street, but that was not an option…

Alex was watching her and she thought she could see pity as well as irritation in his gaze. It stiffened her backbone.

"If you have nothing pertinent to add to our conversation," she said, "then I shall bid you good day. I have arrangements to make. I will contact you again when I return from Spitsbergen with Nina, so that we may make the financial arrangements for her upbringing. Though by then—" she allowed her gaze to travel over him "—I imagine that you will be long gone from London on your next adventure."

Alex's black gaze snapped at her. He ignored the jibe. "You are a complete fool even to think of doing this journey, Lady Joanna."

"Thank you," Joanna said. "I am aware of your opinion of me. And you are a boor."

She made to rise, but his hand snaked out and caught her wrist. "Are you really prepared to go all that way into the unknown, Lady Joanna?" His gaze burned into her. "I do not think you have the courage to be so foolhardy."

Joanna shook him off, incensed by both his taunts and even more by the incendiary power of his touch.

"You mistake, Lord Grant," she said icily. "I know you think me shallow and silly, but I will go to Spitsbergen and prove you wrong. I have no intention of succumbing to seasickness, or fever, like David did, or… or scurvy, or whatever it is your sailors suffer from! I will take fruit with me to eat and I have plenty of warm clothes to protect against the cold climate—"

She broke off as Alex gave a crack of laughter. "Fruit will perish within a few days, and I doubt very much that your London fashions are designed to withstand a polar winter, Lady Joanna."

"That is why I plan to set out at once," Jo said. "How bad can it be? People travel every week to far-flung destinations like India and the Americas!"

"You have no idea what you are talking about," Alex said brusquely, demolishing her optimism in one blow. "I'll wager you have never even been abroad in your life!"

"I have been to Paris," Joanna said defiantly. "I went after the Treaty of Amiens."

"Paris is scarcely comparable with the Arctic!" Alex expelled his breath in an exasperated sigh. "I might have known you would have followed the fashionable crowds to France."

"I did not follow," Joanna said. "I led."

Alex sighed again. He was rubbing his thigh in absentminded fashion, as though his leg was paining him.

"Lady Joanna, please…" He sounded frustrated, angry even. "You have absolutely no concept of the utter discomfort of such a trip." His gaze considered her from saucy hat to stylish shoes, his disapproval, his utter contempt, quite plain. Joanna's face burned under his scrutiny. "You would hate it," he said. "You would not be able to maintain even a quarter of your style without hot water and clean clothes and servants to wait on you."

Joanna's face burned even hotter. "Do you really think such things weigh with me?" she demanded.

"Yes," Alex said. "I do." His shoulder lifted in half a shrug. "Oh, I do not blame you for it—"

"How magnanimous of you!"

"But a woman who has had nothing important to do with her life, whose whole existence centers upon frivolity and idleness, will never be able to survive in so inhospitable a climate…"

Joanna did not hear the rest of his words. She was too angry. Idle, superficial? She supposed she had never been a bluestocking, writing intellectual tracts or holding philosophical salons. That was Merryn's interest. And it was also true that her existence in ton society was amusing and lighthearted for the most part. But that did not mean that she could be dismissed as no more than a giddy social butterfly, a woman with the emotional depth of a small puddle. How dare Alex Grant, with his juvenile bravado and high-handed manner, dismiss her as having no backbone? She felt a sheer, bloody-minded determination to prove him wrong.

"No," she interrupted. "You may save your breath, Lord Grant. I am going."

Alex got to his feet and took a few furious paces away from the bench. He was moving stiffly, as though once again his old injury was hurting. He turned back so sharply that Joanna almost flinched. He rested a hand on the arm of the seat, leaning in, trapping her against the hard wooden back. Once again, his physical presence engulfed her. She felt a tide of heat race through her body and retreat again to leave her shaking with a mixture of awareness and fear.

"You do not understand, Lady Joanna," he said between his teeth. His eyes were blazing. Joanna could feel his anger like a living force. "Women have died on less demanding journeys."

"And women have died at home," Joanna argued hotly, "from sickness or in child bed or even from their clothes catching alight from a candle." She spread her hands wide. "Men, too. Lord Rugby died of a chill he caught in Brighton. One cannot protect against every accident, Lord Grant."

"One can avoid actively seeking them out," Alex said. He looked as though he wanted to shake her. "Must you be so willfully foolish, Lady Joanna? If you insist on going then I shall do everything in my power to oppose you." He straightened. "No one will give you passage.

I will make it my business to see that you fail in this venture before you even begin."

His hands were on her upper arms. The sensation of his touch whipped through her, making her shiver. He pulled her to her feet. Suddenly they were very close together, so close that she could hear how hard he was breathing and smell the scent of his citrus cologne mingled with the fresh morning air. She looked up into his face and saw the anger there; saw also the moment it transmuted into something else, hot and primitive, stealing her breath. He bent his head. She knew he was going to kiss her.

Not like this. Not in anger.

She did not say the words aloud, but her feelings must have shown in her eyes, for his brows snapped together in another intimidating frown as though he, too, had realized how close they had come to a shocking—and very public—kiss. He lifted his hands from her shoulders with such care that it seemed he could no longer bear to touch her. Joanna's heart plummeted and she felt a little sick.

"Lady Joanna—" Now it sounded as though he could not bear to speak to her, let alone touch her.

"Lord Grant." She was sure she could outdo him in hauteur if she tried.

He smiled a little grimly. "We have an audience," he murmured. "Though if yesterday is anything to go by, that should encourage you to throw yourself into my arms."

"I shall try to restrain myself, difficult as it may be," Joanna said coldly. Inside she felt shaken. She had come so close to casting herself into his arms. The burn of his touch was still in her blood.

Turning away with deliberation, she saw that several ladies were scurrying across the grass toward them.

"Why are they dressed exactly like you?" Alex inquired.

"Because they wish to imitate my style." Joanna sighed. "I shall have to introduce a new fashion now. It does not do to look like everyone else."

"How demanding your life must be," Alex murmured. "I am surprised that you have the energy to contemplate a trip to the Arctic when there is so much to be done here."

"So many baubles and trifles to sell," Joanna said sweetly. "Excuse me, Lord Grant. I must take full advantage of the demand for my services. There are ships to be chartered. I am sure that you understand."

She had the satisfaction of seeing his black frown return. "We shall see," he said. With a muttered curse he turned on his heel and walked away.

Chapter 5

"OF COURSE LORD GRANT would not wish you to venture to the Arctic, Jo darling," Lottie Cummings said comfortably. "He has the most frightful prejudice against women traveling, and it is all to do with the death of his wife, poor creature." She poured tea into the Sevres porcelain cups that Joanna adored. They were sitting in Lottie's morning room, a room Joanna had decorated and furnished. It was as light and airy as Lottie herself.

"She died in some hideous accident," Lottie added, passing the plate of petits fours, "or from scarlet fever or smallpox, or from some other ghastly illness. I forget exactly, but apparently Lord Grant blamed himself because he had insisted on her accompanying him abroad."

"Poor man," Joanna said, surprised by an unexpected pang of compassion for Alex Grant losing his wife so horribly. "How dreadful for him." The loss must have hurt him deeply, she thought. For all his brusqueness and his almost brutal directness, Alex was a man of intense passions. She had felt that earlier, the volcanic emotion within him. She shivered, remembering.

"Well…" Lottie waved a vague hand and the pastries slid dangerously in the direction of Max's expectantly open mouth. "It is most generous of you to sympathize with him, Jo darling, when he has been so unhelpful to you. I always said that you are a nicer person than I by far. I will ask Julia Manbury what happened," she added. "She remembers all the old scandals."

Joanna stirred milk into her tea slowly. "Did you ever meet Lady Grant?" She was aware that her interest was not entirely objective. She felt an odd stirring of something that was remarkably like jealousy.

Lottie wrinkled up her nose. "I think I remember her vaguely. She was a winsome little chit as I recall. Not very clever, but pretty and biddable."

"Just the way Lord Grant likes his women to be," Joanna said dryly. "Obedient and quiet. David was the same," she added bitterly. "These adventurers are all cut from the same cloth when it comes to wanting a submissive wife."

"Oh, dear." Lottie's berry-dark eyes sparkled with malice. "You really are at daggers drawn with Lord Grant if you compare him to David."

"How could we not be opposed?" Joanna demanded. "Lord Grant promises to make sure that no one will offer me passage to Spitsbergen, though I hope I can still persuade someone to take me." She sighed. "I have a feeling it will be most expensive."

"Well, I know the very ship for you!" Lottie popped a sugared almond into her mouth and crunched it hard. "I am afraid that dear Mr. Cummings has refused to sponsor Lord Grant's delightful young cousin in his harebrained scheme to find lost gold in Mexico, which means that poor Devlin is knee-deep in debt. You know that he co-owns a cutter with the most gorgeous American captain called Owen Purchase who apparently fought at Trafalgar? Captain Purchase has the most delectable voice," Lottie said, diverted. "It is smooth and rich and I swear I could melt into a puddle just listening to him. But Cummings is not so susceptible as I am and turned them down flat, so now they are both in danger of the Fleet if they do not find someone to charter their ship!"

Joanna felt winded at the speed with which Lottie's mind jumped ahead. "I have met Captain Purchase," she said. "He sailed on one expedition with David. You say he has a cutter to charter? How big a ship is that?"

"Oh, medium size!" Lottie waved an airy hand. "With guns! Isn't that terribly exciting?" She patted Joanna's knee. "Leave it with me, darling. You know that I am a managing female! I should love to arrange your trip. We shall need lots of warm clothing. You must come with me to Oxford Street—I have seen the most darling little fur mantles in Sneider's. We shall take Max with us to the Pole, and Hanson, my butler, and my maid, Lester, for I shall be lost without her, and.,,"

"Wait!" Joanna put a hand to her spinning head. "You are coming, too?"

Lottie looked pained. "Well, of course I am, darling! I am hardly going to arrange all this for you and then stay behind, am I?"

"And you are suggesting that we take Max on a voyage to the North Pole?" Jo said faintly. "And your butler and maid?"

"We shall need servants," Lottie said calmly, "or how shall we manage? And Max would pine if you left him behind in London and anyway, he already has a fur coat of his own, though perhaps we could get him bootees in case his paws stick to the ice."

"But why on earth would you wish to go to Spitsbergen?" Joanna asked. "I am told," she added dryly, "that it is the most vastly uncomfortable place in the world."

"Oh, utterly disagreeable, I am sure," Lottie said, "but what a marvelous adventure, Jo darling! I have always wanted to travel but did not have the excuse before. We shall set a new fashion!"

Joanna looked at her suspiciously. There had to be more than mere boredom to prompt Lottie into leaving behind her home comforts—although it did seem she was intent on taking most of them with her. Could James Devlin be the draw? Lottie did seem surprisingly deep in his confidence.

"What on earth will Mr. Cummings think?" Joanna asked. "I cannot believe he would be happy to see his wife vanish off to the Arctic for months on end."

"Oh, Mr. Cummings will give me no trouble," Lottie said airily. "He has no use for me here other than to spend his money and I might as well do that in a good cause. I will not let luscious Lord Grant best you, Jo darling. He needs to be taught a lesson." She selected another bonbon from the silver dish. "Not that I understand this frightful desire of yours to claim David's little bastard for your own and lumber yourself with a child, of all things! It seems extraordinary to me."

"Please, Lottie," Joanna said. "It is hardly Nina's fault that David fathered her out of wedlock and please don't refer to her as though she were some sort of freakish pet I am adopting."

Lottie was completely uncrushed. It was one of the odd but endearing things about her friend, Joanna thought, that she was utterly irrepressible. "Oh, very well," Lottie said, shrugging. "I will not call her David's by-blow if you do not like it, but you must allow that it is most odd in you to wish to take her up."

Her bright, inquisitive gaze was resting on Joanna's face and for a moment Joanna hesitated on the edge of disclosure. Then she drew back. With Merryn she might have confided her dreams and desires of motherhood and how the need for a child had devoured her with a sudden and unexpected passion. But Lottie… She and Lottie had never had a friendship of any depth. Lottie was kind and generous, but she was also staggeringly indiscreet and utterly incapable of faithfulness, let alone keeping a secret. Joanna knew that there would be enough gossip about David's scandalous legacy without Lottie contributing to the *on dit*.

"David asked me to take care of Nina," she temporized a little awkwardly, knowing that whilst it was true it was not the reason.

"Well, I know, darling," Lottie said, insensitive as always to any undercurrents, "but David is dead. He could ask all manner of things of you and you need not comply. You could just leave the brat in Spitsbergen and forget about her. I would. Think of the whispers of scandal when everyone hears what is afoot." She frowned. "You are the darling of society, but I wonder if even you can carry this off, my love. Your cousin John Hagan will not care for it—"

Joanna made an impatient gesture. "I cannot bear that man! Do you think I shall be swayed by his opinion?"

"Maybe not," Lottie said shrewdly, "but he has influence. And sometimes I think you forget that he owns the house in Half Moon Street. If he chose, he could make matters very difficult for you, Jo darling. And you are alone and unprotected, with very little money."

"I earn several thousand pounds a year!" Joanna protested, "and there is my jointure and the legacy…"

"I know," Lottie said, munching. "As I said, very little money. Not enough to keep me in hats!" She looked her friend over with a critical eye. "It is a wonder you are so stylish on such a pittance."

Joanna was silent. She knew there was a grain of truth in what Lottie was saying. Sometimes she forgot just how precarious her place in society was. The ton had embraced her, but it could break her, too.

When she had first heard of Nina Ware's existence she had not for a moment considered leaving the child to her fate. Both her head and her heart recoiled at the thought. It was impossible. Alex might embrace his guardianship of Nina only out of a sense of responsibility but she was acting out of both integrity and love. Yet she also knew that David was asking far more of her than that she should simply take on his illegitimate child. He was exacting a high price from her. He was asking her to defend his child against the prejudice and cruelty of a society that would brand Nina a bastard without a place in the world. If Joanna took on that challenge she knew she might be condemned and cast out. The ton loved its favorites but it was a fickle mistress and could tear down as easily as it made. And her position was already insecure. She had no home other than the house in Half Moon Street, which she had almost forgotten belonged to John Hagan since David's death. Hagan had graciously allowed her to stay in it, but now that she had rejected his marriage proposal, would he be so generous in the future? And then there was fact that she had no income other than her legacy and the money she earned from her commissions. If no one chose to employ her on her return, if society froze her out, she would be ruined.

She shivered at the prospect and tried to push it from her mind, concentrating instead on the little girl, orphaned and alone in a monastery far away. Once again her heart cried out for someone to love and she felt her resolve stiffen to rescue Nina Ware and bring her home, no matter the odds against her.

"I shall be with you on our trip to chaperone you and give you my consequence," Lottie said comfortingly, ignoring the fact that she was at best flighty and at worst utterly unreliable. She did not wait for Joanna's response. Her butterfly mind had already skipped ahead. "I wonder if Merryn would like to accompany us on our journey. It might be good for her. We could bring her out of herself and introduce her to some young officers. She spends far too much time moping about."

"She is quiet," Joanna said. "I realize that you do not understand the concept, Lottie, but truly, Merryn is happy as she is."

"But she cannot stay here!" Lottie said, rather as though Merryn was a waif and stray. "She has no friends and nowhere to live. And we must be gone soon if we are to make the expedition this summer."

"I will ask Merryn what she wishes to do," Joanna said. "In the meantime there is the practical problem of chartering the ship."

"And the question of clothes," Lottie reminded her.

"Of course. But the ship is probably more important."

"Darling, how can anything be more important than

what to wear?" Lottie lay back on the sofa, raised her feet in the air and admired the scarlet slippers peeping out from beneath the hem of her gown. "I wonder whether Mr. Jackman could design me a fashionable overshoe for use in the snow."

"You will have to wear boots," Joanna said.

"Darling, only if they look elegant! I want none of those great clumping creations that the poor people wear!" Lottie reached again for the bonbon dish and smiled, a smile like a contented cat. "Anyway, you need not worry about the ship. Captain Purchase will be thrilled that you wish to charter the *Sea Witch* and keep him out of jail! And even better, he and Devlin may sail us there, or whatever the correct terminology is! I will send a message to Dev directly."

Alex Grant, Joanna reflected, was going to be mad as fire that she had not only disregarded his warnings about traveling to Spitsbergen but was actually recruiting both a friend of his and, even worse, his cousin, to convey them there. He could not stop her, she reassured herself. Even so, a traitorous feeling ran through her blood; the wish that Alex was on her side rather than against her.

"DID WE HAVE TO MEET here, Purchase?" Alex looked around the inn with a certain degree of disfavor. The small room was dark, hot and smoky, loud with voices and laughter, and thick with the scent of ale and cheap perfume. They were in the backstreets of Holborn and it was clear that the alehouse offered far more refreshment than mere drink. The exceptionally pretty light skirt who had greeted Alex on arrival had seemed disappointed when he had turned down her offer of companionship and had flounced off to find a more congenial and generous patron, muttering that it was not a coffeehouse, in and out with no deposit made. Alex appreciated the wit and ordered and paid for a pint of ale, but he was still disinclined to accept whatever extras were on offer. He did not want a quick tumble with a whore. That would bring no more than relief of the most fundamental kind and possibly a dose of clap into the bargain. He was too jaded to find the prospect even remotely appealing. He wanted Joanna Ware. Joanna, with her lovely lissome body, which admittedly he had not seen but had imagined in rather too much fevered detail… Joanna, whom he distrusted and yet wanted with a lust so intense he burned with it. Joanna, whom he wanted to shake for her willful insistence on traveling to the Arctic herself to fetch little Nina Ware because could she not see how dangerous it was?

But he would thwart that plan easily enough. That was what he was here for tonight.

"You're in a bad mood," Owen Purchase said in his rich southern drawl, tipping his chair back and raising his tankard to his lips. "It's a permanent state with you at the moment, I hear."

"I suppose Dev told you that." Alex eased himself onto a bench behind the rough wooden table. "And I suppose he's here, too, upstairs with some girl?"

Purchase grinned. "What are you now—his father?"

"I feel like it sometimes." Alex groaned. "I want to drag him out of there, warn him to be careful to avoid the pox—"

Purchase spluttered into his ale. "He's young, Grant. The young make their own mistakes. They never listen."

He put down the tankard, leaned his elbows on the table and surveyed his colleague with amusement in his bright green eyes. "Neither do their elders, I hear. David Ware?"

"You've heard the news, then," Alex said.

"I've heard Ware made you joint guardian to his bastard child along with his widow," Purchase said. He tilted his head to one side. "And that you're trying to stop her traveling to Spitsbergen to fetch the girl home."

"The word is that you were in Queer Street because Cummings and his fellow bankers had refused to sponsor your wild-goose chase to Mexico," Alex said, "so you plan to allow Lady Joanna to charter your ship for her foolish voyage to Spitsbergen."

Purchase laughed, his teeth a white flash in his tanned face. "Bad news travels fast. I'll make that Mexican fortune and prove you wrong yet, Grant."

"Maybe," Alex said. "In the meantime can I persuade you not to agree to a charter with Lady Joanna?"

Purchase was silent for a moment and then he shook his head slowly. "I am already committed. I signed the papers this afternoon."

Alex felt a sharp flash of surprise followed by an equally sharp stab of anger. Joanna, it seemed, had wasted no time.

"Damn her," he said through his teeth. "Ignorance combined with money is a fatal combination."

Purchase raised his brows. "You are mighty vehement, Grant. Why?"

Alex could feel his temper tightening intolerably as it had done in Lincoln's Inn Fields when Joanna had made it so plain that she intended to ignore his advice and travel to Spitsbergen.

"The Arctic is no place for a woman," he said abruptly, trying to control his anger. "You know that, Purchase."

Purchase shrugged elegantly. "I'll allow that it is a harsh climate."

"Harsh!" Alex exploded. "It's lethal! And this is a woman who cannot live without luxuries! She has no concept of privation or hunger or even of pitiless cold—"

"She'll soon learn," Purchase said dispassionately.

"She will soon die." Alex stopped, shocked by the violence of his feelings, struggling to wrench them back under control.

Owen Purchase was looking at him with an arrested expression on his face. "I didn't think you liked her, Grant."

"I don't," Alex snapped.

Purchase shrugged again. "If it is not concern for Lady Joanna that prompts your feelings, then what is it? Guilt about your wife?"

Alex felt his stomach drop.

Guilt.

Not to his closest friends had he ever expressed his sense of blame over Amelia's death, yet the shame stalked him every day. He had been the one who had forced Amelia to travel with him. His was the responsibility for her death.

In the early days his guilt had been all-consuming; it had been a ravenous beast that had almost swallowed him whole, almost destroyed him. Somehow over time he had found a way to live with it, to pacify it, almost to soothe it to sleep. And then Joanna Ware, in her naiveté, had expressed her determination to go to the Arctic and the beast had awoken and its claws were as sharp or sharper than before. All his memories had flooded back to haunt him. Amelia had traveled—and she had died as a result. And somehow, he did not know why or how, did not want to know why, that made him angrier than ever with Joanna.

"You read too much poetry, Purchase," he said shortly, turning away from confidences, turning away even from his thoughts and the implication of what they meant. "Your imagination gets the better of you."

Purchase laughed. "If you say so." He leaned forward. "Lady Joanna paid in full, in cash, in advance." He made an eloquent gesture. "What can I say? I am an adventurer these days, Grant, and I don't turn down offers like that. You'll know that Dev and I are crewing for her. We sail in a week."

"A week?" Alex exclaimed. "You'll never be ready in time. Provisioning alone would take you longer than that."

"Money talks," Purchase said, "and Lady Joanna's money is mighty persuasive."

"It's madness." Alex slumped back in his seat, aware of a mixture of exasperation, frustration and a certain very reluctant admiration that Lady Joanna Ware had proved that obstinacy was one of her finest qualities.

"I don't suppose," he added, "that your ship is reinforced to withstand the ice either."

"*Sea Witch* is no bomb ship," Purchase allowed. "Her decks aren't reinforced, but she's a tough little vessel for all that."

"Sea Witch," Alex said. "Are you trying to curse her?"

"I thought it was appropriate," Purchase said, grinning. "She handles like a woman in a temper." He laughed. "And she's all the more challenge for it."

Alex moved his tankard in slow circles on the tabletop. "You'll not reconsider the commission?" he asked.

Purchase shook his head. "Sorry, Grant."

"Then give me passage, too," Alex said.

"As crew?" Purchase smiled.

"As a guest," Alex said. "I'll pay my way."

"Why?"

"Because I am Nina Ware's guardian, too, and I feel an obligation to see her safe."

Purchase's clear gaze considered him thoughtfully. "Seems Ware chose well when he named you joint guardian, Grant. You may hate him for shackling you, but you will always do your duty."

"Quite," Alex said tightly. In the previous day, he thought bitterly, he had fought more battles between honor and inclination than ever before. "So?" he asked.

"You'll have to ask Lady Joanna if you can come," Purchase said, grinning hugely and clearly enjoying the moment. "She has the final word."

Alex swore. "Purchase—"

"Don't worry, you can always work your passage as cabin boy if she turns you down," Purchase said, his grin widening still more until Alex's face relaxed into a reluctant smile. "That's better. What the hell has happened to you to turn you into a bear with such a sore head?"

"Lady Joanna tries my patience," Alex said suc-cinctly. He thought of Joanna stating defiantly that she would take fruit to Spitsbergen with her to ward off the scurvy and maintaining that her clothes would be warm enough to keep out the Arctic cold, and was gripped by acute irritation. He had not known whether to shake her or kiss her and the fact that he wanted to kiss her at all was precisely the problem.

"Ah." Owen Purchase straightened in his seat. "Lady Joanna is a fine woman…"

Alex glared. "That's your lust talking, Purchase."

Purchase laughed. "I could call you out for that, Grant, but I like you too much to kill you. I'll admit to a certain partiality for Lady Joanna." He shifted on the bench, crossing his long legs at the ankle.

"You want her for yourself," Alex said sharply.

Purchase did not deny it. "She was too good for Ware," he said.

"I am surprised to hear you say that," Alex said stiffly. "You admired Ware as much as I did."

He was surprised. No one criticized David Ware. Ware had been a hero. Everyone knew it.

"Ah, come on, Grant," Purchase said, his drawl even more pronounced than normal. "Ware was a damned good captain but a damned poor husband." His mouth thinned. "You know that—you were the one forever dragging him out of whorehouses so that he didn't miss the boat."

"And in return," Alex said sharply, "he saved my life, Purchase. Not a bad bargain."

"Ah, well…" Purchase's cool gaze was thoughtful on him. "I understand your sense of obligation."

"I doubt that you do," Alex said. He rubbed the ache

in his leg, the constant reminder of his debt. "Ware could have left me to die in that crevasse, Purchase. He should have done, because he risked his life for mine instead of ensuring one of us survived to lead our men back to safety. So don't speak to me about his weaknesses."

"I've never denied that Ware had physical courage," Purchase said. "But don't you see he did it for his own glory? You're right—he should have left you. That would have been the responsible thing to do, but instead he had to play the hero."

"Enough," Alex said through shut teeth. He could see that Purchase's desire for Joanna was skewing his judgment. Perhaps they had been lovers and she had poisoned Purchase's mind against her husband. Perhaps they were still lovers. His bad temper tightened like a ratchet.

Purchase drained his tankard. "One more thing and then I'll stop pushing my luck. Did you never think Ware's discipline a little on the harsh side?" Over the rim of the beaker Alex saw that Purchase's eyes were bright and hard with contempt. "Sure, his men obeyed him, but they didn't love him like yours love you—if I can be so inappropriate as to speak of love to an Englishman."

"A Scotsman," Alex corrected, but with a faint smile.

"Even worse," Purchase drawled. "No wonder you're so dour. It's the iron in your soul."

"Dev says it is my Calvinistic upbringing," Alex said. He stopped, shook his head. "Let's not talk about this, Purchase. We'll only argue and I don't want to quarrel with you."

For a moment the tension hung on the air, but then the other man's face relaxed and he nodded.

"Another one?" Purchase asked, holding up his tankard inquiringly.

Alex shook his head. "I need to find Lady Joanna and persuade her to allow me to accompany her on this voyage of hers. For the child's sake."

"Try some charm, if you have it in you, Grant," Purchase advised. He cocked his head. "Anyway, you're in luck. Lady Joanna is currently around the corner at the Castle Tavern."

Alex peered out of the grimy window. The evening was well advanced and the spring light was fading now, leaving the sky streaked with pink and gold. Torches flared in the street outside and the lights of the inns and coffee shops and gaming hells dappled the cobbles. The evening crowd, raucous and rowdy, already three sheets to the wind on ale and gin, thronged the narrow alleyway. Holborn at night was the last place Alex would have expected to find Lady Joanna Ware.

"What the deuce is she doing there?" he asked.

Purchase gestured to one of the extremely pretty tavern girls to refill his tankard. "She's a Lady of the Fancy," he said.

"A what?"

"She supports the pugilistic club," Purchase said. "She is their mascot. I believe there is a match tonight."

"A mascot? Lady Joanna attends boxing matches?" Alex could hear the incredulity making his voice rise.

"It's a fashionable sport with the ton," Purchase said. "The Duke of York is one of the patrons attending tonight."

"I don't care if the King attends," Alex expostulated. "It simply isn't appropriate for a lady."

"By all means tell Lady Joanna that when you see her," Purchase said amiably, winking at the tavern girl as she slid into the seat Alex had vacated. "It should help your cause tremendously in persuading her to permit you to accompany us to Spitsbergen." He paused, then sighed and reached for his beer again. "Good luck, Grant," he added. "You're going to need it."

Chapter 6

"THERE IS A GENTLEMAN to see you, ma'am." Daniel Brooke, the extremely deferential ex-prizefighter who now worked as manager of Tom Belcher's inn, the Castle Tavern in Holborn, came into the small private parlor and bowed to Joanna. It looked extremely comical, for Brooke was a short, broad, bald and muscular man, who looked almost as wide as he was tall. He was the younger cousin of Jem Brooke, a man to whom Joanna had cause to be very grateful. Jem, also a prizefighter in his time, had for a short while protected her from David's wrath after their terrible quarrel over her failure to provide her husband with an heir. The morning after David's assault on her, Jem had mysteriously arrived on Joanna's doorstep saying only that a gentleman had sent him to help her. Joanna had had no inkling as to the identity of her knight errant or how he had known of her situation, but Jem was a tower of strength, his size, bulk and skill supremely reassuring when David had attempted to barge back into the house later that day, asserting his marital rights. Jem had thrown him out into the street with one hand.

Once David had returned to sea and she no longer needed a bodyguard, Joanna had helped set Jem up in a tavern of his own out at Wapping where he now served particularly tasty whitebait suppers. But somehow along the way she had become the toast of the prizefighters, patron and mascot, a Lady of the Fancy—and she did not have the heart to tell them that she abhorred fighting, abhorred violence of any kind, unsurprisingly enough.

That was why she was sitting here alone, nursing a glass of stout, whilst in the adjoining room an impromptu ring had been set up and a fight was in progress between the champion, Hen Pearce, and a young hopeful. It was her second glass and the rich malt taste of the beer was both warming and strong. Joanna seldom drank and then usually wine or champagne. This was earthier, but it relaxed her. It had been a week of shocking disclosures in which the worst elements of the past had been raked up and her feelings exposed mercilessly. Her emotions felt frayed and raw, but for a little while in this tavern with fifty men outside who would raucously defend her to the death, she felt obscurely safe.

The door opened and Joanna shuddered as a wall of noise washed through, the sound of flesh against flesh, the sympathetic groans of the crowd as the youngster took a hammering. Joanna put her fingers in her ears.

She became aware that Alex Grant was standing in front of her, immaculate in his casual evening attire. His lips were moving. She took her fingers out of her ears.

"What on earth are you doing in a prizefighting tavern if you dislike the sport?" he demanded.

How marvelous. Within the space of ten seconds he had managed to destroy all her feelings of relaxation and put her back up. The prickles of irritation jabbed her.

"How do you know I dislike it?" she countered.

"You are sitting in here alone with your fingers in your ears and an expression on your face as though you were sucking lemons," Alex said. "What are you doing here?"

"I came to try to find myself a bodyguard to accompany me to Spitsbergen," Joanna said. She gestured Brooke forward. "Lord Grant, this is Daniel Brooke, a former prizefighter. Brooke, Lord Grant."

Brooke bowed politely to Alex, but there was a steely light in his eyes, as though he was spoiling for a fight.

Just say the word, his demeanor seemed to suggest.

Joanna saw Alex's gaze sweep over Brooke with the same look of shrewd appraisal that the prizefighter was giving him. Many men would be intimidated by Brooke's raw aggression, Joanna thought, but Alex held his ground. He was at least half a foot taller than Brooke, leaner and less bulky, but in his own way he had a dangerous edge. Perhaps it came from having knocked about those corners of the world where only reckless adventurers chose to tread. A man had to be strong, resourceful and courageous to survive in such places. But this was perilous ground. Joanna gave herself a little shake. Those were the kind of thoughts she had had about David when first she had met him. David Ware, the hero…

The two men measured each other and Joanna felt something elemental in the air, then Brooke stepped back and nodded once, and the tension diminished.

"A bodyguard," Alex said, and he, too, nodded, and Joanna saw the tight muscles in Brooke's shoulders ease a little more.

"Good gracious, Lord Grant," she said. "Do I discern approval from you?"

A smile lifted the corners of Alex's mouth. "A journey of the type you plan to undertake is full of surprises, Lady Joanna," he said, "and not all of them pleasant."

"So I thought," Joanna said. "Unfortunately, Brooke has turned me down because he does not like the cold. It is bad for his joints."

"A hazard of the profession, I suppose," Alex said.

"May I offer you a drink, sir?" Brooke inquired courteously.

"Thank you, but no," Alex said. "I am here only to speak with Lady Joanna." He turned to her. "You are aware that prizefighting is illegal, my lady?"

"The Dukes of York and Clarence are watching, as are three London magistrates," Joanna said. "I do not think we shall be troubled by the law."

Alex gestured to the armchair across from hers. "May I?" His gaze fell on the glass of stout. "Is that beer?"

"Stout," Joanna said. "I enjoy a glass of malt beer." She waited for the inevitable condemnation.

Alex turned to Brooke. "Perhaps I shall take a drink after all, thank you, Brooke. Brandy, please."

Brooke bowed and went out.

"You are extremely polite tonight," Joanna said.

"No sane man would be otherwise with a prizefighter in attendance," Alex said. He looked at the glass of stout again. "Are you foxed, Lady Joanna? Dark beer is the strongest."

"I know," Joanna said. "It is delightful."

"You *are* foxed."

"There are so many things about me that you can disapprove of," Joanna said sweetly. She slewed around in her seat to look at him. "Why are you here, Lord

Grant? And how did you know where to find me, for that matter?"

"Owen Purchase told me," Alex said.

"Ah. Then he will also have told you that Lottie and I have commissioned him to take us to Spitsbergen."

"He did." Alex frowned. "Mrs. Cummings plans to go, too?"

She thinks it will be an adventure," Joanna said. She sighed. "I suppose that you tried to dissuade Captain Purchase from accepting our offer?"

"I did. I failed."

Joanna smiled a little at his honesty. She was beginning to see that one would never get Spanish coin from Alex Grant, no matter how uncomfortable the truth. It was a quality that would have made her like him under normal circumstances, but his mistrust of her, those poisonous seeds that David had sowed, would always stand between them.

"Captain Purchase is very loyal," she said. "Or perhaps it is just the money I offered him."

Alex laughed. "Purchase is, as you so rightly point out, an adventurer." His look changed, became keen. "Though he does appear to hold you in esteem. Do you know him well?"

"Not in the way that you are implying," Joanna snapped, sensitive to the implication in his voice. "Lord Grant, your opinions are offensive. I can see that to you it is unaccountable that anyone might think well of me if they are not my lover!"

"I beg your pardon," Alex said mildly, taking the wind out of her sails. "I meant to imply no such thing. Brooke appears to hold you in esteem, too."

"The prizefighters are devoted to me," Joanna said.

"I am a Lady of the Fancy." She laughed as she saw his expression. "Oh, dear, Lord Grant—that moment of approval really was brief, was it not?"

"I do not care for prizefighting," Alex said stiffly, "nor for the sort of celebrity it bestows on you, Lady Joanna. To be acclaimed by the boxing fraternity is not my idea of success."

"Of course it is not," Joanna said, her temper fraying. "One would have to paddle up the Ganges in a canoe to gain your appreciation, Lord Grant. Oh, but I forgot—" Her tone was scornful. "That does not apply if one is a woman."

She saw that his face had set into its customary stern lines. "It is true," Alex said, "that I prefer women to stay at home."

"In their place," Joanna said. "Of course."

There was a cold silence between them whilst Brooke delivered Alex's glass of brandy and slipped out of the room again as discreetly as the best-trained butler. Joanna could feel Alex's gaze on her face, intense and thoughtful. Despite the friction between them it made her feel prickly and hot. There was something about Alex's quiet appraisal that stripped away all pretense and defense and left her emotions naked. She wished it were not so. Alex Grant was a man who distrusted and disliked her and as such he was the last person for whom she wanted to feel this disturbing current of attraction. It pulled and pushed her in contrary directions, provoking her, arousing her against her will.

"You have not answered my question," she said abruptly, breaking the sharp sense of awareness between them. "Why are you here?"

"To beg you to allow me to accompany you to

Spitsbergen," Alex said. His tone was ironic. "Purchase tells me you have the final word. If you turn me down I shall have to work my passage as a cabin boy."

Joanna gave a spontaneous burst of laughter. "A cabin boy? You?"

"Indeed. Even Devlin would be giving me orders."

"That would be a terrible waste of your experience and expertise." Joanna considered him. "You offered to pay Captain Purchase for your passage?"

"I did. He still maintained that it was your decision."

"How very gratifying that he cannot be bought," Joanna said. "The answer is no."

She saw a faint smile touch Alex's lips and knew he had been expecting her blunt refusal.

"Let me try to persuade you to change your mind," Alex said. He shifted. "It is not too late."

"Change my mind about going to Spitsbergen?" Joanna said.

"About the entire business," Alex said. His dark gaze slid over her thoughtfully. "You live very much at the whim of society, Lady Joanna. There will be those who not only disapprove of you going to Spitsbergen but of you rearing your husband's bastard child. I suspect that John Hagan, for example, will be appalled. What happens to you if the ton withdraws its favor from you?"

There was a hush in the room. Outside the door the tumultuous roar of the boxing crowd swelled and fell like the flowing tide.

"Then I starve," Joanna said lightly. She had confronted those fears earlier. She refused to let him frighten her. "But fortunately, Nina will not, will she,

Lord Grant? I assume that David has left you the means to support his child since you are to be our trustee?"

There was a rather odd silence. Joanna raised a questioning brow. For once, she thought, Alex Grant was actually looking a little… What was it? Embarrassed? Discomfited?

"Ware left a treasure map," he said gruffly.

Joanna blinked. "I beg your pardon? A treasure map?"

Alex put a hand into his jacket and extracted a flimsy piece of paper, yellow with age. He unfolded it and handed it to her. Joanna gaped. It was a very rough drawing of an island with inlets, bays and coves, crudely executed but with a large X marking a spot close to a beach on a long peninsula. There was, for good measure, the sign of the skull and crossbones.

"Well, really," Joanna said. "Why could David not deposit money in a bank like normal people?"

There was a hint of color along Alex's cheekbones. She wondered if he had thought the same thing. He did not strike her as the sort of man to have much truck with buried treasure. She found that she was smiling. It was so gratifying to see Alex Grant at a disadvantage for once.

"Did you bring this back from Spitsbergen along with the letter?" she queried.

"No!" Alex practically snapped the word. "Churchward gave it to me. It was with Ware's will."

"It looks all a hum to me," Joanna said. She shook her head. "How typical of David to be so mysterious."

"It is all rather unsatisfactory," Alex said stiffly.

"Well, that was David all over," Joanna said. "He was most unsatisfactory in so many ways." She glanced at Alex. His dark gaze was fathomless. "But I forget," she said, unable to erase the bitterness from her voice. "David could do no wrong in your eyes, could he, Lord Grant? He was above reproach even if he expected you to dig up Nina's fortune as well as everything else." She shifted in her chair. "And for that reason I repeat that I cannot permit you to accompany me to Spitsbergen. You neither like me nor trust me and the journey will be uncomfortable enough without turning around and falling over your disapproval at every turn. If you wish to take ship to find this so-called treasure then that is your choice—and your responsibility, but you are not coming with us."

Alex's frown had deepened. "It makes absolutely no sense to sail separately, Lady Joanna."

Privately, Joanna acknowledged that. It did not, however, change her feeling that the last person she wanted on her ship was this disapproving stranger.

"We need not be enemies," Alex continued. "For the sake of the child we could try to be friends."

"You aim too high," Joanna said. "Let us keep our expectations within reason. We could try to be civil." She shook her head. "The answer is still no. You are forceful by nature... You would be forever trying to tell me what to do and then we would quarrel. Simply being near you makes me feel—"

"Makes you feel what?" Alex raised one dark, quizzical brow.

"Makes me feel infuriated!" Joanna exclaimed, jumping to her feet. It was true. The room felt too small, airless and close, dominated by Alex's presence, the antagonism simmering between them like a kettle coming to the boil.

Alex got to his feet, too. "So," he said, "you swore that you would do everything in your power to bring Nina safely home and even in that you lied."

Joanna stared at him, flayed by his contemptuous tone. "What do you mean by that?"

"Only that anyone with any sense would see that it is in Nina's interests for you to accept my escort," Alex said. "But you are so headstrong that you will not agree to it."

"Don't speak of me as though you are referring to a horse," Joanna said furiously. "I am not headstrong, I am the one with sense here! We have been talking for all of ten minutes and already we are arguing. What Nina will need is reassurance and stability, not a pair of guardians who fight like cat and dog!"

She turned away from him and wiped away the errant tears that insisted on escaping from the corners of her eyes. She did not want to cry in front of Alex Grant. He already made her feel so vulnerable, so emotionally exposed. Her feelings felt as though they had been rubbed raw, stinging. David, she thought bitterly, had chosen well when he had sent this man to torment her.

"You must excuse me," she said rapidly. "It is late and my business here is concluded—"

She turned to find Alex very close to her.

"You're crying," he said, his voice rough with some emotion she could not place.

"Of course I'm crying!" Joanna exclaimed. "I have had a very bad week!" She flashed him a look. "Go away, Lord Grant. Can you not take a hint? I really do not want to cry in front of you!"

Alex ignored her words. His hand was on her waist, the gentle warmth of his touch searing her through the silk bodice of her gown. How had that happened? He was drawing her closer, as though he wanted to comfort her. Joanna had never equated a man's physical proximity with reassurance before; David had only ever touched her when he wanted to bed her. And surely Alex, of all people, cared nothing for whether she was distressed or not. She felt confused, disturbed. She was not sure what was showing on her face. Alex raised a hand and brushed away the smudges of her tears with the pad of his thumb. Her heart ached at the tenderness of the gesture. She looked up to meet the dazzling intensity of those gray eyes and then he was kissing her, his mouth gentle and persuasive, and the sheer surprise of it ripped through her and set her trembling.

"Open your mouth," he whispered and her mind reeled shock whilst her lips parted in instinctive response to the command and to the pressure of his. Alex coaxed them farther apart with sensual deliberation and she felt the slow sweep of his tongue against hers. She could taste brandy mingled with the salt of her tears. The heat consumed her then, fierce, scalding her, leaving her shaking and breathless. They fell apart and stood staring at one another.

"What was that?" Jo found her voice first. "Comfort?"

"Scarcely that." For a moment Alex looked as stunned as she felt, his expression taut and astonished, his gray eyes mirroring her shock and confusion. Joanna felt a violent wash of pleasure to see how shaken he was.

"That was not what I intended to do," he said slowly.

"I imagine not." Joanna bit her lip. She felt dazed and heated, her stomach burning with wicked excitement.

The air between them felt alive. From the room next door came the roar of the boxing crowd as atavistic as a beat in the blood. There was something equally primitive in Alex's eyes, but it did not scare her. It called to her.

"But now that I have..." He was drawing her close again, his voice so low that she could barely hear it, "I confess I have been wanting this for a long time. In Lincoln's Inn Fields, and even earlier..."

She could have stopped him. She thought she should have done, knew she should have done. She did not like Alex Grant, yet for some reason that very aversion seemed to make his appeal even more powerful. It added an undertow of raw passion that simultaneously seduced and appalled her. There was a dark current of attraction between them that tempted her with its wicked sweetness, drawing her in so that she clung to him instead of pushing him away. She did not understand it and when Alex held her she did not care.

This time it was not so gentle. Alex's lips captured hers and took them with all the passion she had always sensed was in him. Joanna yielded to the danger and the excitement, sliding her arms about his neck, pulling him closer. The kiss was so urgent and primitive that she shook with the power of it. It called to an answering need in her. Gone was the ice maiden, the woman David Ware had scorned as barren and frigid. Her mind spun as she realized that she had never felt like this before, never experienced this intensity, this utter desire. It was what she had searched for and never found. She made a small, surrendering noise deep in her throat and felt the harsh need surge in him as he gathered her closer, every hard line of his body taut against hers. There was a tense, heated spiral of desire tightening within her. She wanted him to make love to her here, in this inn parlor with the wild noise of the crowd in her ears.

When he finally released her Joanna pressed her fingers to her mouth in disbelief and felt her lips swollen and moist from the demand of their kisses.

"Well," Alex said, "that was interesting."

Interesting? Was that what he called it? Joanna stared at him in outrage. He had kissed her with lust and sweetness and a fiery heat that had her body still humming and he thought it was interesting? Really, she thought, he only needed to speak to annoy her.

"I am glad that you thought so," she said frostily, trying to damp down her feelings.

His grin was pure wickedness. He looked damnably pleased with himself. Joanna's annoyance grew.

"I suppose it was a little more than that," he said.

"You flatter me," Joanna said. "I should like to know how you can kiss me like that when you profess to dislike me so heartily."

"It seems that I do not need to like you to kiss you," Alex said. His gaze was dark and hot. "Nor do you need to like me to kiss me back."

She felt color flare into her face. "It is unaccountable, is it not," she said, "for I do not like you at all."

"And yet…" Alex ran his finger down the curve of her cheek. Her skin seemed to warm to his touch; she resisted a powerful impulse to turn her face against his hand, seeking further caresses. She was simultaneously mortified and fascinated by her response to him. She could feel the arousal building deep inside her again, tight as a knot.

"And yet you want me," Alex said.

"I want a carriage with matching grays and a diamond necklace from Hatton Garden," Joanna said, "but it is not going to happen, just as any sort of *affaire* between us is not going to happen."

"Is it not?" His voice was dangerously soft. His hand fell to the hollow at the base of her throat, his touch as gentle as the brush of a butterfly's wing. Joanna could feel her breathing catch. She knew that the pulse there would be pounding; her heart was racing so fast now that she could feel the beat of it against the silk of her bodice. Alex ran a finger along her collarbone, dipping his hand beneath the ruffled neckline of her gown to caress the upper curve of her breast in a touch that was fleeting and yet wrenched so deep a sensation from Joanna that her knees almost buckled beneath her. Her nipples hardened instantly and a tiny gasp broke from her lips. Alex's gaze was intent, dark, focused, utterly consumed with desire. He slid the slippery silk from her shoulder and his lips replaced his fingers, drifting down across the tender skin of her neck and the delicious line of her breasts to dip into the hollow between them, his tongue flicking, hot and shocking against her skin.

Joanna's mind spun with dark, erotic images, her body melting into slow, luxuriant pleasure. It was like a game, a dare, a test of how far he could push her, and she knew she should stop it, stop him, but she did not want to because she was trapped in a web of sensual delight.

She felt his palm against her breast, warm through the silk of her chemise. The spread of his fingers against the slippery richness of the silk made her gasp again, the thought of his hands on her body with only the thin material between setting her shaking. She reached out to steady herself and her hand brushed the edge of the table, her wedding ring catching on the wood. It was a tiny thing and yet it caught her attention, not because she felt that she was in any way being unfaithful to David's memory—such a thought was laughable given their estrangement—but because it reminded her who Alex was. Her late husband's best friend, a man who disliked her and yet could make such exquisite love to her that her body hummed and sang under his touch.

Wrenched by a spasm of self-disgust, she pulled back and he let her go. He was breathing as hard as she was. His gray eyes were smoky dark.

For a moment neither of them spoke and then Alex smiled. "So," he said, his voice very soft, flagrantly seductive. "Have you changed your mind? Can I come with you?"

Joanna was so disoriented that for a split second she wondered what he was talking about. Then she remembered. Spitsbergen, the Arctic, the voyage…

She stared. "Did you kiss me simply to try to seduce me into consenting?"

Alex looked amused at the chagrin she could not keep from her voice. "No," he said. "I would not have stopped there if I was trying to seduce you."

"I stopped," Joanna said. "You did not."

He shrugged. "I might have known that we would quarrel about that, as we do about all things." He shot her a challenging glance. "You enjoyed it."

Her chin came up. "So did you."

"On that we do agree then."

Again there was a taut silence.

"How vexing you are," Joanna said. "How maddening it is that I can find you so utterly infuriating and yet—"

"And yet you wish to tear my clothes off and make love to me?" He smiled at her evident outrage. "Forgive me, you know how very direct I can be."

"What I wish to do or do not wish to do makes no odds," Joanna said. "You still cannot come with me to Spitsbergen."

The words came out with stark finality and Alex looked taken aback.

"You refuse me—after that?"

"That was a mistake, Lord Grant." She stepped back to try to gain some breathing space. "David's daughter is the only thing that brings us together, Lord Grant. I am going to fetch her from Spitsbergen. You will be going wherever the Admiralty posts you, I imagine." She held his gaze. "And since you have always made it so clear that you desire no emotional ties or responsibilities, perhaps you will wish to exercise your guardianship via the lawyers in future?"

Alex looked angry now. There was an ominous stillness about him. "Are you still trying to imply that I shirk my duty?"

"No," Joanna said. She pressed her damp palms together. "No, of course not. Not in any material sense at least."

"And I do not intend to evade my responsibility to Nina either." Alex moved restlessly. "So I will accompany you on the journey and keep you safe. You can scarcely offer her a good home if you are sick or injured or dead."

"But I do not want you with me," Joanna argued, feeling her temper rising again, irritated by his stubbornness. "I have told you! Can you not see—"

"I can see that you are afraid of our attraction," Alex said bluntly, "and that is why you are denying me." His eyes were an intense dark gray. "You are afraid that if we spend time in one another's company we will become lovers because that is what we both want."

Joanna's throat dried at his words. That was precisely what she was afraid of.

"We might, of course, kill one another first," she said politely.

Alex smiled again, that adventurer's smile. "We might. It is a risk worth taking."

"No, it is not."

"You are trying to pretend that nothing happened between us."

"No," Joanna said. "I am not. I cannot deny our inconvenient attraction." She made a helpless gesture. "But I do not wish for an *affaire* with you."

Alex stepped closer to her.

"Yes, you do," he said. "I can tell you do. Whatever is between us burns you as fiercely as it does me, Joanna."

Overwhelmed by his physical proximity, Joanna could only shrug helplessly. "You see—we always disagree." She tilted her face up to meet the intensity of his gaze. "I don't deny that I want you," she said honestly. "I do not like it, nor do I understand it, but—" She broke off. His hand was on her wrist again, his touch warm, compulsive, drawing her closer. She stepped away, swept by fragile, turbulent emotion. She did not for a moment believe that this man was like her late husband. Alex might be direct and even harsh, but he was never untrustworthy or dishonest. She felt it. She knew it instinctively. He would never physically hurt her. Yet indulging in an *affaire* with him would be madness. Once their desire burned out there would be nothing left but reproach and dislike.

"I will not do it," she said. "You think me shallow, and as light with my reputation as many other ladies of the ton, but I am not, and even if I were, you are the very last man I would take as a lover. I would never give myself to a man who has no respect for me."

Alex's dark gaze was hooded. "You damn near did."

"Which is why I do not intend to see you ever again," Joanna said.

The temperature in the room fell as swiftly as though a door had opened to allow in the coldest winter night.

"You will see plenty of me," Alex said. "I fully intend to be on that ship."

"I don't want you there," Joanna said, holding fast to her temper.

"Your wishes count for nothing in this," Alex said. "I cannot in all conscience as Nina's guardian allow you to wander into danger through your own stupidity."

Joanna gritted her teeth. "How arrogant you are! I do not need a hero to protect me. I can think of nothing worse."

She broke from his grip, grabbed her cloak and bonnet from the chair and flung open the door.

"Brooke," she said, throwing Alex a defiant look. "Lord Grant is leaving."

"My lord." The prizefighter bowed to Alex with an exquisite courtesy that barely masked his hostility and stood to one side to allow Alex to exit. Alex ignored him. He took Joanna's hand and pressed a kiss on it. She felt the brush of his lips on her skin and repressed the response that flared through her.

Brooke rocked back on his heels, spoiling for a fight. "My lady?" he said, but Joanna shook her head. Alex stood back courteously for her to pass and they went out.

In the street the night was dark and hot. The pugilist club members were spilling out of the inn now that the bout was over, raucous and full of ale and good humor with the money they had won. When they saw Joanna, a ragged cheer broke over the crowd. They surrounded her, pressing close, bowing, wanting to kiss her hand. She saw Alex watching, his expression darkly disapproving in the glow of the lamplight and she felt reckless and defiant and blew kisses to all her admirers. The riotous mood of the crowd swelled; Alex's frown correspondingly deepened. Two pinks of the ton made an elaborate leg to Joanna, competing to quote sonnets in her praise whilst the more disorderly elements in the throng booed so loudly that Joanna felt obliged to intervene before there was a breach of the peace.

"Go home and sleep it off, Lord Selsey," she said when one sprig of nobility tried to kiss her and almost took a tumble in the gutter. "You are foxed."

"Devil a bit, ma'am," Selsey said. "Still sober enough to offer you my hand and my heart—"

"Again," Joanna said, sighing. "Your guardian would never allow it, I fear."

"We could elope," Selsey said hopefully, rebounding

off a lamppost and seeming only slightly cast down as Brooke picked him up by the scruff of the neck and deposited him in the road.

"I need hardly worry for your safety at present," Alex said, forcing his way through the mob to her side, "since I perceive you have more than a hundred men devoted to your service."

Joanna smiled. "Yes. Are they not delightful?"

"They are drunk and rough," Alex said.

"And totally dedicated to me," Joanna pointed out. "I love them."

"We love you, too, ma'am!" one pugilist shouted, whilst the crowd whooped and cheered.

Selsey, who was being steadied by his almost equally drunk friend, was blinking at Alex like an owl. "I say!" he exclaimed. "But surely… My God, it is you! Lord Grant, a tremendous honor to meet you, sir!" He attempted another bow and almost overbalanced. "I say, chaps…" He addressed the crowd at large, "It's Alex Grant, the explorer, you know, the one who wrestled a puma to the ground to save the life of his friend and discovered the ruins of Azer…Azerban… Discovered some ruins in the desert anyway, and—"

Within seconds, it seemed to Joanna, Alex was besieged by well-wishers. The boxing crowd, full of bonhomie, were ready to laud this latest hero who had crossed their path.

"A kiss!" someone shouted. "A kiss from our Lady of the Fancy for Lord Grant!"

Alex turned, the wicked challenge flaring in his eyes. "Lady Joanna? Surely you would not disappoint your admirers."

"Of course not," Joanna said recklessly. She stood on tiptoe, intending to give him a peck on the cheek, but Alex cupped her face in his hands and brought his mouth down on hers and the night faded away and the sound of the excited crowd rang in her ears and the stars wheeled and spun overhead.

"I thought," she said as Alex released her and steadied her with a hand on her arm, "that you had no desire for celebrity, Lord Grant?"

"I do not," Alex said, "but I did have a great desire to kiss you again."

"Hypocrite," Joanna said and heard him laugh.

She watched the crowd submerge him and carry him off. "Totally eclipsed, I fear," she said, smoothing her gloves. "I have lost all my admirers to Lord Grant and he does not even want them!"

"He shows well to advantage," Brooke said with a sly sideways glance at her. "I'd like to see him in a fight."

"You almost did tonight," Joanna said. "I thought you were going to start a mill earlier."

Brooke shrugged. "Wouldn't do that, milady, not when you have a fancy for him."

"I do not!" Joanna said. She blushed. "Brooke—"

"Just let me know when you don't like him anymore," Brooke said, "and I'll plant him a facer." He held the door of a hackney carriage for her. "Here you are, milady. It's Tom Finn—" He nodded to the driver. "He'll see you home all right and tight."

As Joanna glanced back, she could see the Duke of Clarence wading his way through the crowd about Alex and clapping him on the back. The two of them were practically being carried along the pavement by a riotous mob in search of the next alehouse. And it served

Alex Grant right, she thought, if he had become the unwilling hero of the boxing fraternity. He needed to lose some of that stern disapproval.

She shut the door of the carriage with a decisive click and sat back with a sigh. She knew that Alex had not conceded on the matter of escorting her to Spitsbergen. He was like a burr against her skin, an irritation that she wanted to be free of but which also fascinated her. Joanna shifted uncomfortably on the seat of the hackney carriage. She could not explain her attraction to him. She wanted to break it. Yet if she was honest, she had to admit that she also wanted him.

"I would never give myself to a man who has no respect for me."

"You damn near did..."

David Ware had ridden roughshod over her feelings and her self-respect and she had learned the hard way never to let that happen to her ever again. She would not give herself to another adventurer, to a man who would stay only long enough to enjoy the pleasures of her bed and would then be gone on the next expedition, the next challenge, the next adventure. No woman would ever be able to hold Alex Grant because his first love would always be to travel and explore. With Alex it would be a brief taste of delicious pleasure—and she was sure it would be utter bliss to take him as a lover—and then it would be the bitter taste of loss and that would last a lot longer. And Alex could never trust her, never like her, for David's shadow would always come between them. Even if she told him the whole truth of David's cruelty, she doubted that he would believe her. He had been David's friend since childhood, David had saved his life, she could see that it was a point of honor for Alex to keep faith with his friend's memory.

She reminded herself of that as she went upstairs to try to sleep.

The night seemed long and the bed empty.

Chapter 7

THE ROOM WAS HOT and stuffy. It smelled of beeswax polish and dust and it was as far from the fresh salt air and open horizons of the sea as Alex could imagine. As soon as he stepped inside he had felt trapped and on edge. Despite his being a sailor, a most superstitious breed of men, Alex had never considered himself irrational. Yet now he had a strong conviction that something bad was about to happen and as he looked at the men sitting around the table his stomach roiled with tension.

The week had already been extremely trying as a result of David Ware's inexplicably cavalier behavior in dragooning him into wardship of his daughter. Alex wanted to forgive Ware and to understand why his friend had acted in this manner, but he could not come up with a rational explanation other than that Ware had wanted to do the best thing for the child and had thought that he would be a reliable guardian. That did not really fit with the facts. It left unanswered questions that were starting to torment Alex through his sleepless nights. If Ware had wanted what was best for Nina, why had he never mentioned her before or taken an interest in her welfare? Why, when he had known that he was dying, had he not told Alex of the baby and entrusted her to his care, instead of requiring that Joanna make this perilous journey to the Arctic to rescue her instead? There seemed to be no satisfactory answers and it was becoming more and more difficult to explain away or close his eyes to the less-than-admirable aspects of Ware's behavior—his infidelities, his lack of care for those who depended on him, his harshness when opposed.

Alex's encounter with Joanna the previous night had not helped, fueling both his anger and his sexual frustration until he was boiling with it. He had been utterly determined to accompany her to Spitsbergen and was thwarted by her refusal. They were at an impasse. He was even more irritable over the lamentable lack of control he appeared to have over his physical desires, wanting Joanna but distrusting her, aching for her at the same time as wanting to shake some sense into her.

As though that were not bad enough, he had felt a completely unexpected and unwelcome urge to comfort her in the tavern parlor. He wished he could attribute her tears to female manipulation, but he instinctively knew she had not been pretending. Her distress was all too real. She had been pushed to the edge of control by the shocking revelations of the week and he had wanted to shield her with a powerful desire that owed nothing to lust and was more about protection. Now, *that* was particularly worrying.

Alex ran a hand over the back of his neck, trying to ease the tension in his muscles. The entire situation was maddening. Joanna Ware infuriated him.

He felt bewitched.

He had also been surprised in Joanna. He acknowledged it. He had made judgments, assumed that she would be as inclined to indulge in a love affair as were many fast widows of the ton. But when she had refused him she had spoken with a passion and sincerity he could not doubt. It was a different Joanna Ware he had seen in that moment, a woman quite contrary to the superficial, confident society hostess.

That morning he had tried to burn off his bad temper and his bodily frustrations with a bout of fencing at Henry Angelo's academy. It had probably been a mistake, for his leg ached like the devil now and he hated the fact that more and more he was beginning to notice the restrictions the old injury was placing on him. At the back of his mind was a fear, faint but persistent, that one day it would prevent him from exploring and would confine him to "home," wherever that might be, like a caged animal pacing the rest of its life out in captivity. The thought appalled him. And then when he had arrived back at Grillon's, Frazer had greeted him with the news that word had come at last from the Admiralty about his next posting.

"They wanted to see you immediately, my lord," Frazer had said, his mouth turning down at the corners. "I had to tell them you were out attending to some pressing business matters. That was two hours ago. I'm guessing they are not best pleased to be kept waiting."

ALEX HAD BEEN EXPECTING a frosty welcome for his tardiness and had been most taken aback to be greeted with great bonhomie. Contrarily, this was making him suspicious. He shifted surreptitiously in his chair and rubbed his bad leg, which was throbbing unpleasantly.

"Good of you to join us, Grant! Splendid to see you, old fellow!" Charles Yorke, the First Lord of the Admiralty, shook him warmly by the hand. Yorke was not a man for whom Alex had ever had a great deal of respect. He disliked the fact that the First Sea Lord was a politician rather than a sailor. For how was a man like that ever to understand the challenges facing a serving officer, let alone the experiences of his men? Even worse was the fact that Yorke's brother Joseph also sat on the Admiralty Board. At least Joseph Yorke had served in the navy, but his appointment looked unpleasantly like nepotism to Alex. He understood that that was the manner in which such business was often conducted, but that did not mean that he liked it. He took the chair that Charles Yorke indicated and tried not to let his antagonism show.

Alex reminded himself that all he was here for was to discover what his next commission would be. Since Joanna Ware had summarily turned down his offer to accompany her to Bellsund he had no need to beg his masters to allow him to undertake another trip to the Pole. In fact, he had no responsibilities to keep him in London at all. He could be in and out of this office in moments and back to his ship where he belonged. He could escape from the stifling heat and airlessness of this room and be out in the fresh air again. He felt oppressed, as though all the monstrous piles of paper on the table before him might rise up and smother the life out of him. He had never been content to sit indoors. Ever since his boyhood on Speyside, he had lived to be out in the fresh air.

"Delighted to have you back in London, Grant," Charles Yorke was saying. "Delighted, what! His Grace of Clarence tells me you were a tremendous hit with the boxing crowd at Cribbs's last night."

Alex tried not to grimace. He had spent the best part

of the night trying to escape from an overexcited mob that had kept toasting him and buying him drinks until he had almost slid off his chair with excess.

Fortunately Yorke did not appear to require an answer. "It will be a great pleasure to have you working here at the Admiralty for a space," he continued. He waved an expansive hand around. "Promotion, don't you know... Maybe a rear admiral's position in a year or two—" Alex saw Joseph Yorke smile through gritted teeth and there were nods around the table. "You're a hero, Grant, an idol of the people and no mistake."

Alex felt a pang of shock. Working at the Admiralty? He found his voice. "Gratified as I am, gentlemen," he said, "I do not quite understand..."

"Of course not, of course not!" Yorke boomed magnanimously. "Just a simple sailor, eh, Grant?" He inclined his head toward another of the navy board, James Buller, a career politician.

"The government is pleased with you, Grant," Buller said in his high-pitched voice, brushing snuff off his sleeve as he spoke. "Need a hero now Nelson's gone. Cochrane's too showy, don't you know, and too insubordinate. Explorers are all the rage in society now—"

"I see," Alex said grimly. He caught the eye of Sir Richard Bickerton, onetime colleague of Nelson, who cast him the ghost of a wink.

"You're famous, Grant," Bickerton said dryly. "I know how much you will relish that."

"Quite, sir," Alex said. He took a deep breath. "Gentlemen, you do me too much honor. All I wish is to be assigned another commission and rejoin my ship."

There was a sudden hush about the table. Alex

looked at Charles Yorke, who was fidgeting with his quill pen.

"Sir?" he said very politely but with an undertone of steel.

"That's the thing, Grant," Yorke said, tapping his fingers uncomfortably on the polished surface of the table. "No money for further exploration at the moment, y'see. Can't be done."

"Government can't afford it," Buller confirmed with gloomy relish.

"Tide might turn in a few years, of course," Yorke continued, "but for now we need you here in London, Grant, pressing the flesh, you know. You're famous, like Bickerton says. You'll be the most splendid ambassador for the navy in ton society. Guest of honor, what! Dinners, balls, marvelous stuff!"

Alex expelled his breath very slowly. This was starting to look very, very bad. He could see his future stretching ahead, desk-bound in some pointless Admiralty job during the day, his evenings an endless whirl of dinners and social events until society tired of him or some new sensation came along to displace him. He felt the walls close in on him, felt trapped, felt his blood turn cold at the prospect of never being given another command.

He could see Joseph Yorke looking at him with dislike and a spurt of powerful envy. Ironic, Alex thought, to be envied for something he had not even sought in the first place, for fame and popularity and the love of the people, when all he wanted was to escape from all that celebrity.

"Gentlemen," he said, setting his jaw, aware of anger and a strange sense of desperation jetting up within him, "might I ask you to reconsider? I am a sailor. I am not cut out to be some sort of ambassador in society."

"Exactly what I said, Grant," Joseph Yorke agreed. "You have no social graces at all."

"Nonsense, Grant!" Charles Yorke interrupted his brother. "Society adores you!"

"I do not adore society," Alex said, sitting forward urgently, trying to find a way through this thicket of unwanted approval. "Please—I beg you to give me another role." He was aware that diplomacy was not his strong suit. He had never been a politician nor had he cultivated the connections needed to prosper. Until now it had not mattered. He had been a sailor, an explorer. His men were like Devlin and Purchase, young, anxious for adventure and promotion, efficient and daring. They had charm and courage. The Admiralty had wanted them at sea—until now. Now it seemed that the politicians and financiers were in charge, there was no money for exploration anymore and he was about to be promoted to some role he was woefully inadequate to fulfill, his only duties charming the ton and acting the role of heroic explorer in the ballrooms of London. The thought revolted him. He knew that he would rather resign than have this job. He swallowed hard. He was older and wiser than Devlin—he could not simply turn in his commission on a whim. Yet what choice would he have if the only alternative was being chained to a desk, London's least enthusiastic celebrity, paraded about like a lion at the Tower of London menagerie for the entertainment of the crowd?

Most members of the Admiralty Board were looking at him with baffled incomprehension. Joseph Yorke looked mulish and envious. Only Bickerton had a spark of sympathy in his eyes.

"Understand your need to be at sea, old fellow," Bickerton said, "but…" His shrug indicated that he was in a minority of one and that the argument was already lost.

"Gentlemen," Alex repeated, suddenly seeing a glimmer of light and grasping after it, "I wonder if you would consider an alternative?"

Charles Yorke was frowning now, displeased that his largesse had not received the response he had been expecting. "An alternative, Grant? An alternative to cultivating the support and approval of the Prince Regent and the leaders of society?"

"I think," Alex said gravely, "that you will like this."

There was silence. Everyone was staring at him.

"There is a mission of mercy," Alex said, "that I feel I simply must fulfill."

Charles Yorke sat forward, his frown easing a little. "Go on, Grant. A mission of mercy, eh? I do like the sound of this."

"When David Ware died," Alex said carefully, "he left behind an illegitimate daughter. The matter came to light only a couple of days ago. I am named one of the child's guardians, along with Ware's widow, Lady Joanna."

There was a rustle of speculation and comment about the table.

"Disgraceful," whispered one of the board members. "What could Ware have been thinking?"

"How very ramshackle of Ware to put his wife in

such a situation," Joseph Yorke said coldly. "And how very out of character."

"Indeed," Alex agreed smoothly. "Ware was… an original. He left the child in the care of an Eastern Orthodox monastery in Spitsbergen, scarcely ideal for a baby girl. I feel it my duty to assist Lady Joanna Ware by accompanying her on her journey to rescue the child and bring her back to London. So you see, gentlemen—" he spread his hands in a gesture of appeal "—this is why I feel I must return to the Arctic as soon as possible…"

He saw Bickerton's lips twist into an appreciative smile at his strategy. "Nice work, Grant," he said.

Buller was looking cautious. "There's no money to sponsor such an expedition," he began.

"But what a marvelous, marvelous venture!" Charles Yorke threw up his hands, a broad smile splitting his face. "I can see the news sheets now—dashing naval adventurer in Arctic rescue! Polar hero comes to the aid of grieving widow and orphaned child… Absolutely splendid, Grant! The prince will love it. The papers will love it! The people will love it!"

The rustle of comment about the table swelled to a roar of approval once the First Lord of the Admiralty had given his agreement. Alex sat back in his chair feeling a rush of relief.

"Splendid!" Buller echoed, rubbing his hands. "I must go at once to acquaint the prime minister with the news!"

"I'll tell the prime minister," Joseph Yorke said, glaring at him. "And the Prince Regent."

"Those were fine tactics, Grant," Sir Richard Bickerton said as he and Alex strode out of the Admiralty and Alex drew in a deep, appreciative breath of fresh air.

"Used the Admiralty's desire for a hero to work in your favor, eh? Didn't think you could pull it off, old fellow, but I have to hand it to you—masterly stratagem." He laughed. "And by the time you return they will probably have changed their minds and decided to post you somewhere exciting, like the South Americas, especially if you cover yourself with glory on this trip."

"Thank you, sir," Alex said. "That is exactly what I was hoping."

"Rum business about David Ware's sideslip," Bickerton said, rubbing his chin doubtfully. "You do realize that the story will be all round the ton within the hour? It'll be the *on dit* in every ballroom in London. Yorke will lose no time in turning it to his advantage." He looked at Alex. "Dashed bad form of Ware to leave Lady Joanna in such a situation. I'm surprised at him."

"Indeed," Alex agreed.

"What does Lady Joanna think of your plan to escort her to Spitsbergen?" Bickerton pursued.

"She does not wish for my escort," Alex said, "but now she will have no choice in the matter."

Bickerton pursed his lips on a soundless whistle. "Well, rather you than me, Grant. I would not choose to incur Lady Joanna's disapproval." He frowned. "Mind you, I do not think this escapade of hers will play well in society. All very well for you to go off to the Arctic on some mission of mercy—you're a damned explorer, a hero, it's what you do! But for a woman alone, a widow, to go to the ends of the earth to rescue her husband's bastard child…" He shook his head. "Some will consider it eccentric and others a downright disgrace."

Alex drove his hands into his pockets. "Lady Joanna

is stubborn," he said. "She will not change her mind about going."

"Then it is good that she has you to protect her," Bickerton said gruffly. "Damned fine woman. Plenty of mettle."

"So everyone keeps telling me," Alex said. He hesitated. "Did you know David Ware, sir?"

Bickerton gave him a shrewd look from his blue eyes. "Not well," he said. "Why do you ask?"

"I wondered what you thought of him," Alex admitted. He was not really sure why he was asking. Perhaps, he thought wryly, he wanted to reassure himself that David Ware had been a good man so that the disloyal doubts that he was starting to harbor could be put to flight.

"Splendid fellow, by all accounts," Bickerton said. "Absolute hero, which makes this business with the bastard brat all the more surprising. But then—" He shrugged. "Great men must be allowed their weaknesses and Ware's was most certainly women."

He shook Alex's hand and went back inside Somerset House, and Alex walked along the Strand, and turned down Adam Street toward the Thames. The fresh breeze from the river was cold and clean and cutting even in the warmth of a London spring. Alex watched the ships on the river and felt relief and pleasure to be out in the open air and to have escaped the gilded trap the Admiralty had prepared for him. He wondered what would happen when Lady Joanna Ware learned that he had set himself up as Nina's savior, the dashing explorer who had selflessly offered to travel back to Spitsbergen to rescue Ware's baby daughter. Bickerton was right; Yorke would milk this for all it was worth and use it to boost both Alex's popularity and that of the navy itself.

Alex's lips twisted into a parody of a smile. He had done it to save himself from the disaster of the Admiralty grounding him in London. He had done it out of a need to escape the impossible, unbearable role of celebrity explorer, lionized by society, fawned over by the Prince Regent himself.

He knew that Lady Joanna Ware would despise him for using her.

IT WAS A PERFECT AFTERNOON for a drive in Hyde Park.

"Shopping is such an exhausting business." Lottie sighed, flinging herself back in abandoned pose on the plush green cushions of her landau and smiling flirtatiously at the footmen in their livery. "I would go home to rest before the ball tonight were it not for the fact that I simply cannot miss being here to see and be seen!" A tiny frown marred her brow as she looked from them to Joanna, who was sitting opposite her, a frothy pink parasol tilted against the sun. "Darling Joanna, are you sure I cannot buy your twin footmen from you? These two are all very fine, but they do not look the same and I have asked and asked at the employment agency but they cannot seem to find twins for me." Her mouth turned down at the corners. "It is most disappointing."

"I am sorry, Lottie," Joanna said, smiling. "I don't want to sell. It gives me too much pleasure to excite so much envy over them!"

"Oh, well, I can understand that." Lottie pouted. She smoothed her fingers over the heraldic embroidery on the hammer cloth. "I thought I might try to persuade you, for what else is there for me to do in life? You know that I live to spend!"

Joanna sighed. She knew that Lottie was bored, bored by her life in the ton with its emptiness and extravagance, bored with the entertainments and events even as she grasped greedily after some new experience to fulfill her. Joanna loved the social whirl of the season—it was familiar, distracting, safe in some odd way because it occupied her and kept her thoughts from dwelling too much on the failure of her marriage and her failure to have a family of her own—but deep down she also knew that life in the ton was shallow and empty. Unlike Lottie, though, she had her work, her drawings and designs. Alex Grant might disparage them, but they gave her a purpose as well as an income. Though whether she would still have a clientele when she returned from Spitsbergen remained to be seen. Already that morning she had had to tell Lady Ansell that the redecoration of her dining room would be delayed by at least six months. Her ladyship had not been pleased and had scurried away to complain to her bosom bows in the ton.

"My dears!" Lady O'Hara, an inveterate society gossip, brought her barouche alongside them. "I have just heard the news!" She put one gloved hand on the edge of Lottie's landau in a confiding gesture. "How noble you are, Lady Joanna, how truly courageous to rescue your husband's bastard child and bring her home!" She leaned closer to Jo, her gray eyes sharp and not in the least friendly. "Of course, it is difficult to travel abroad—especially to so far-flung a place as the Pole—and to maintain your reputation as a lady of quality."

"I shall do my poor best," Joanna said. She glanced at Lottie. "Word has spread fast," she added dryly. "I only heard the news of David's daughter myself yesterday morning."

"Well, you cannot blame me," Lottie said with a toss of the head. "You have been shopping in my company the entire day today, so you know I have not had the chance to gossip about you! More is the pity," she added, "for I love to be first with the *on dit* and I see I have been pipped to the post now. Perhaps the servants were listening at the keyhole when we talked yesterday, or Mr. Jackman has passed on word that we have ordered very special Esquimaux boots for our trip—"

Lady O'Hara, whose carriage was now being jostled out of the way by those of Mrs. Milton and Lord and Lady Ayres, gave a little shriek. "Esquimaux boots? Oh, how marvelous! They will be all the rage this winter!"

"How gratifying it will be to bring them into fashion," Joanna agreed, "for they are the most elegantly cozy footwear imaginable."

"I shall tell everyone to order some," Lady O'Hara promised.

Lottie's dark eyes were sparkling as she looked around the park. "No wonder there is such a crush today," she said. "Evidently we are the talk of the town, Jo darling! How splendid this is!"

"I am not sure that everyone approves," Joanna murmured. A little shiver ran down her spine as she remembered Lottie's prophetic words the day before:

"You are the darling of society, but I wonder if even you can carry this off... Think of the whispers of scandal..."

How infuriating it was that the qualities of daredevil risk taking, of adventure and exploration, were lauded in men like Alex Grant and yet were considered utterly unbecoming in a woman.

"Lady Joanna!" Now it was Lord Ayres hailing them. He was a thin, dyspeptic man who looked as though he spent his life disapproving of things. "Surely the gossip cannot be true," he said plaintively. "Curiosity about travel is a most ill-bred trait in a woman."

"And in a man?" Joanna queried gently.

"It is not to be encouraged," Lord Ayres said, "unless the traveler is a heroic explorer such as Lord Grant. Now, *he* is equipped to deal with all manner of peril." He shuddered. "But indeed, travel in general is a fearful and fearfully vulgar business. I would not like you to encourage people to try it, Lady Joanna. God forbid that you should set a new fashion."

"But you travel to Brighton and Bath every year, my lord," Joanna protested as Lady Ayres nodded to reinforce her husband's view.

"Brighton is not abroad," Lady Ayres pointed out. "It is far more difficult to uphold one's standards abroad. For a start, there is an unfortunate preponderance of foreigners—"

"Ghastly accommodation and utterly inedible food," Lord Ayres added with gloomy relish. "What do they eat at the Pole anyway? Fish?"

"Pickled eider-duck eggs," Joanna said, "or so I believe. My late husband claimed them to be a great delicacy."

Lady Ayres was so pale at the thought of a pickled egg that she looked in danger of swooning. Lottie was finding it difficult to keep a straight face. "How marvelous that there will be eiders," she said. "We may use the duck down in our mattresses and then our accommodations shall not be so ghastly."

"They are probably correct that it will be very uncomfortable," Joanna said as Lord and Lady Ayres moved away to make space for more gossipmongers beside the carriage. "Lord Grant was right, you know, Lottie. We shall detest it. No hot water and no proper food and we shall probably freeze until our fingers drop off…"

"Faint heart!" Lottie was looking excited at the prospect of adventure, even a frozen one. "You will have to ask lovely Captain Purchase to keep you warm whilst I will cozy up to Lord Grant's adorable cousin! Or perhaps I will have Captain Purchase, too," she added on an afterthought. "I have not quite decided which one of them to favor yet."

The crowd of people had been growing whilst they talked and now the press of riders and carriages about them was already becoming so close that the horses were in danger of taking fright. Joanna's heart sank to see John Hagan pushing his way through the throng. She had hoped that after he had seen her with Alex a couple of days before, he might take the hint and remove himself and his unwanted attentions, but it seemed he was more persistent than she had given him credit. As David Ware's cousin he had the spurious excuse of being concerned for her welfare, but Joanna knew this was no more than a ruse. Hagan had been making advances to her since before David's death, which argued a complete disregard for propriety. It was only after she was widowed that his slimy suggestions had included marriage rather than a mere *affaire*.

"The Ring is more blocked than Bond Street today," Hagan said disagreeably, clinging tenaciously to the side of Lottie's landau. "Dear coz," he addressed himself melodramatically to Joanna, "what is this new scandal I hear? You are to visit the Pole? It cannot be! As a woman you are too precious and too poorly designed to travel. And as head of the family I simply cannot permit it."

"Doing it too brown, Hagan." Joanna's head whipped round at the sound of Alex Grant's sardonic voice. "There is nothing poorly designed about Lady Joanna." Their eyes met and Joanna saw the gleam of wicked amusement in his. "Besides," Alex continued, "she will have me to protect her on her journey." He bowed. "Your servant, Lady Joanna."

"Lord Grant." Joanna inclined her head with frosty disdain as he brought his horse alongside. He had a magnificent seat; he looked as though he had been born in the saddle. She realized that she had not expected him to ride and now she wondered why on earth not. He had been born and raised in the Highlands of Scotland after all and had probably ridden all his life.

"I believe I must have missed that part of our discussions where I agreed to your accompanying me to Spitsbergen," she said sarcastically. "Remind me."

"Oh, but you cannot refuse Lord Grant's generous offer to assist you on your quest!" Lady O'Hara put in eagerly. "I heard from Lord Barrow, who had it from Charles Yorke himself, that Lord Grant had begged the Admiralty Board to be permitted to offer himself as your protector!" She flashed Alex a sycophantic smile. "What a true hero! So good! So noble!"

"I beg your pardon, ma'am?" Joanna looked at Lady O'Hara in some confusion. "Lord Grant did what?"

"He begged the Navy Board to post him back to the Arctic," another lady put in, pushing to the front of the crowd. "I heard it, too! Is that not so, Lord Grant?" She looked appealingly at Alex. "Lord Yorke said that you were so moved by the thought of Lord David's orphaned daughter and so touched by Lady Joanna's plight that you urged them to support your case!" She pressed her hands together. "I agree with Lady O'Hara, my lord—your nobility is astounding!"

There was a rustle of approval and agreement at this and shouts of "Good show, Grant!" from some of the gentlemen in the crowd. Joanna looked at Alex with growing incredulity.

"I am not sure that I quite understand," she said slowly. "Can it be that you have expressly ignored my wishes in this, my lord?"

"I have," Alex said. "You are outmaneuvered, I fear, Lady Joanna."

"Well, what a hypocrite you have turned out to be, Lord Grant!" Joanna looked at the crowds of admirers and hangers-on trailing Alex along the Ring and felt a rush of fury. "So you were the one who made public the terms of David's will! You pretend to be uninterested in fame and public adoration and then you use a dead man and an innocent child to boost your own reputation and to thwart my plans as well!" She found she was shaking with rage at his deceit. "You knew that I did not want you with me on this trip. I could not have made it plainer! Upon my word, I thought I had seen every trick that a self-aggrandizing adventurer might pull to pursue fame, but this crowns it all!"

Alex looked furious. "It was not like that—" he began, but then a group of excited young bucks grabbed his attention, begging him to tell them about his most recent expedition.

"Lottie," Joanna said, taking advantage of the fact that Alex was distracted and slewing around on her seat, "pray give the coachman the order to move off. I would like to go home now."

Lottie, who had been deep in conversation with John Hagan, made a moue. "But, Jo darling, we are the *on dit!* Don't spoil my fun!"

"No," Alex said, shaking off the youths and leaning over to put his hand on Joanna's arm. "Lady Joanna, we must speak—"

"As always, you choose precisely the wrong moment, Lord Grant," Joanna snapped. "We have nothing to say to each other apart from goodbye!"

She was not entirely sure what happened next. One minute she was sitting in the landau and the next, Alex had leaned down from his horse, put an arm about her waist and scooped her up out of the seat to ride before him on the big black hunter. He turned the horse and cut a path through the milling crowd, leaving them almost delirious with excitement. One lady screamed, a debutante swooned with shock and another had the vapors out of what Joanna suspected was pure envy.

"What the devil was that?" Joanna was flustered and annoyed as Alex reined in a considerable distance from their rowdy audience.

"An old Russian Pomor trick." Alex sounded grim. "Very showy and easier to do when you are moving than standing still."

"You seemed to manage it just fine," Joanna said, "damnation take it."

Alex threw her a glance. "Your language is most unbecoming to a lady. I noticed it before."

"Oh, did you?" Joanna still felt ruffled. Alex's proximity was not helping. She could feel the hardness of chest against her back and the strength of his thighs cradling her. His breath stirred the hair at the nape of her neck. She shivered, feeling the goose bumps rise all over her body. "I learned my language from my uncle," she added. Her voice sounded slightly husky. "He was a clergyman with a vast vocabulary for hellfire." She sighed. "What do you want with me that you have to abduct me in front of a crowd?"

"I want to talk to you," Alex said. "Without an audience. I want to explain."

"There is nothing to explain," Joanna said. She half turned toward him. It proved to be a mistake for they were very close together, his arms holding her like steel bands, his face set and hard. There was a frown between his brows. The line of his mouth was grim.

"You exploited the situation for your own gain," she said. "You used your celebrity to try to force me to accept your escort." She felt angry, but more than that, she felt betrayed. She and Alex might always disagree, but she had believed him to be straightforward and above this sort of duplicity. Now she felt a naive fool, confused by her physical attraction to him, deceived into thinking him a good man.

"I said that it wasn't like that." Alex's tone was fierce, his Scots accent suddenly strong. Joanna's heart skipped a beat to hear the passion in his voice.

"Lady Joanna—" He stopped. "They were going to

give me a desk job at the Admiralty," he said bluntly. "Parade me about the ton as their pet hero and explorer. I will not be their tame celebrity. I'd rather resign my commission."

It was the truth, stark and unvarnished. Joanna knew that as soon as she heard it. There was so much in his voice, so much he was not putting into words. He did not beg; he would not. He simply looked at her and she felt as though her entire world was shifting. All her senses seemed acutely aware of him. She could feel his gaze like a physical touch caressing her face. She could hear the sound of his breathing.

"Joanna," he said, and she had to repress a shiver.

"Don't," she said. "Don't take advantage of my damnable susceptibility to you to try to get what you want."

She saw him smile, his teeth a white slash in the tan of his face. "Devil take it, you read me so well."

"I want to refuse you again," Joanna said. "I really want to."

"I know." She felt him shift, felt his arms hold her a little closer, a little tighter. She knew he could sense the conflict raging inside her. Awareness swirled in her, sharp, sweet lust underpinned with the desire for his strength and protection.

"Damn it to the pits of hell and back," she said feelingly. Why could she not simply refuse him, dismiss him to that future that he had so tellingly described? Surely he deserved it. She hated her own weakness, but she could not deny the strange sense of affinity she felt for him.

"Very picturesque," Alex said. "Another of your uncle's epithets?"

"Yes." She half turned to look at him. "You know that I do not like you?"

"I could hardly be more aware of it."

"There would have to be certain rules between us."

She felt him go very still as he realized that she was about to capitulate.

"Very well." He sounded cautious.

"Neither of us will ever speak of David to the other one," Joanna said. "Not ever. This agreement of ours is for Nina's sake only."

She felt his surprise. She knew he thought she had been about to make quite a different demand.

"I thought," he said slowly, "that you would one day wish to tell me your side of the story in relation to Ware."

"Well, I do not." Joanna spoke emphatically. "There would not be the slightest point in that, Lord Grant. If you agree to adhere to that stipulation, then you may accompany me to Spitsbergen."

She saw the expression leap in his eyes and he smiled, that wicked adventurer's smile, and she felt as dizzy as a pea-brained debutante.

"Thank you." His voice was smooth, all trace of his previous emotion banished. If she had not seen and heard for herself how passionate he had felt at the prospect of being trapped in London, she would not have believed it. Once again that inscrutable reserve was in place.

"I think that as we are in agreement, we should put on a show of unity," Alex added.

Joanna glanced over her shoulder at the indiscreet tidal wave of people who were variously running or riding across the park toward them, anxious to be the first with the next celebrity *on dit*.

Alex followed her gaze, a frown between his brows. "You will permit me to escort you to Lady Bryanstone's ball tonight," he said.

He did not appear to anticipate a rejection, Joanna thought. How quickly he took control.

"I am already promised to Lord Lewisham for this evening," she said haughtily. "And I think you should let me down now."

Alex swung from the saddle and lifted her down with as much ease as he had originally picked her up. For a moment Joanna felt the press of his body against hers, hard, muscular. Her feet touched the ground but he did not let her go.

"Lewisham, is it?" He spoke low in her ear. His hand tightened on hers. "Do you always choose escorts who are so old and harmless?"

Joanna looked at him. She knew that she did choose gentlemen who were safe, inoffensive and practically sexless. Held tight in Alex Grant's anything-but-safe embrace she could recognize that she had chosen them because they were not a threat to her. They were the opposite of Alex, who possessed the infinite enticement of the dangerous adventurer.

"Tell Lewisham you have a better offer," Alex pressed softly. "Tell him you will be attending with me."

Joanna shivered. After the encounter she and Alex had had at the boxing club she knew it would be madness to allow him to escort her that night. Alone together in the intimate dark, in the heat of a London night, she might forget those scruples that had driven her to refuse him. She swallowed hard.

"When I do have a better offer," she said, "then I shall dismiss Lord Lewisham." She stepped out of the circle of his arms. She wanted to regain control and step away from this tumult of emotion that Alex evoked in her. Now that she had accepted his escort to Spitsbergen the most difficult thing would be keeping him at arm's length.

"I do not need an explorer to help me find my way to Lady Bryanstone's ball, my lord," she said. "Your protection is not required. Good day."

Chapter 8

TWO HOURS INTO HER preparations for Lady Bryanstone's ball, Joanna was still in her negligee and was
discussing different hair arrangements with Drury, her
personal maid—should it be the psyche knot or ringlets
that night?—when John Hagan burst into her dressing
room without so much as a knock. He was very red in
the face and was brandishing a piece of paper.

"It is too much!" he proclaimed. "Look!" He thrust
the sheet under Joanna's nose so that she had little alternative. "You have made the family name a laughing-
stock, madam, and it has to stop!"

Joanna dismissed her maid, who scurried out as
though her skirts were on fire. "What on earth can be
so serious that you burst in here with so little courtesy?"
she demanded of Hagan. "This is shocking conduct,
sir!"

"*My* conduct is shocking?" Hagan spluttered. "You
speak to me of my conduct when you are sprawled all
over the scandal sheets like an abandoned whore in a
brothel?" He gave the papers another shake. "Never in
all my born days has a Ware so besmirched the family
name!"

Joanna calmly took the paper from him and spread
it out on her dressing table. It was true that it was one
of the more outrageous of the scandal sheets and the

cartoon in the center was not designed to soothe the ire of an acerbic man such as John Hagan. In the middle of the picture was Alex bestriding the earth like a colossus and wielding his flag in one hand and his sword in the other very much in the style of the ice sculpture at Lottie's ball. Joanna wondered fleetingly whether the satirist had been present at that event. Alex was looking stern and distant, an adventurer surveying the far horizon. At his feet scurried various tiny figures in naval uniform; she could recognize Charles Yorke's fair hair and rounded face and his brother's lantern jaw and envious expression. There was a grandstand stuffed with cheering supporters who included the Prince Regent and his brothers, and a number of boxers and Pinks of the Fancy. And there was she, her hair tumbled, her clothing sliding off, hanging on to Alex's leg and begging to be taken with him on his travels. It was a witty, clever and very cruel caricature.

"Oh, dear." Joanna pressed her hand to her mouth.

"Precisely," Hagan said, rocking back on his heels, hands behind his back and his favorite look of self-righteous smugness firmly on his face. "Oh, dear, indeed."

"It *is* very funny," Joanna ventured.

Hagan gave her a black look. "You can say that? And you looking like a strumpet?"

"The Prince Regent is depicted as Humpty Dumpty," Joanna pointed out. "And Lord Yorke as a gnome. I think I have got away relatively lightly."

Hagan looked disdainful. "It does not surprise me that you should say that. It is all of a piece with your behavior. You make a fool of me and of your late husband's memory and you think that it is funny." He snatched the paper from out of her hands. "This flighty life of yours is over, madam. You will go to Maybole."

"I beg your pardon?" Joanna said. Shock clutched at her.

"A period of rustication in the country is just the thing for you," Hagan said. "You will retire from town."

Joanna's heart started to race. "I will go to the Arctic and fetch my late husband's child," she corrected carefully. "You have no jurisdiction over my behavior, Cousin John. I regret that I cannot do as you request, but Nina's welfare must be my priority now."

Hagan's face was a mottled red. "You do not behave as a respectable lady should," he said. "It is a disgrace. You will cease this ridiculous plan to go to the Pole and rescue Ware's bastard child. You will not adopt her." He caught her wrist in a grip that made her wince. "If you persist with this fool's errand, madam, I shall have no option but to wash my hands of you. You will have no home to return to in London. I shall make sure that no one will receive you, even less employ you."

He let go of her with an exclamation of disgust and paced away from her. In his fussy evening dress he looked hunched and malignant.

Joanna's nails dug into her palms. She tried to keep calm, tried to find a way out of this tangle. Hagan was, she knew, a man who was happy only if the proprieties were observed. Until Alex Grant had arrived in London, until David's letter had dropped like a pebble into a calm pond, he had been content enough with her way of life. He had in fact viewed her as a decoration to the Ware name with her style and elegance, her following in society and her popularity. Joanna was sure that those were the reasons that had prompted John Hagan to propose to her in the first place. He was not a man driven by strong passion other than for matters to be conventional and tidy. He had seen David Ware's elegant widow and thought she could be an ornament for his home, perhaps. He had buried two wives already, he had his heir, now he had Maybole and wanted a fashionable hostess to put in it.

That had all changed now, of course. Joanna knew that there would be no more marriage proposals from John Hagan, not now she had proved herself to be a disappointment rather than an asset. He would try to force her to conform and when she refused he would disown her.

"Cousin John, please!" she said. "You know that I have nowhere else to go and that Merryn depends upon living here as much as I do, as will Nina once we return from Spitsbergen. We depend upon your charity."

Hagan turned. There was an expression on his face compounded of calculation and lust. Joanna's stomach tightened when she saw it. She should have known, she thought bitterly, that there was no point in appealing to his better nature when he had none.

"Perhaps," he said slowly, his tone so unctuous it felt to Joanna as though oil was seeping out of his pores, "we may come to an agreement about the child—and about your home."

"An agreement," Joanna echoed. She felt a little sick. She did not need to ask what sort of arrangement Hagan had in mind. She could see it in his eyes. He had come across to her now and was toying with the fastenings of her negligee. Joanna felt despairing. She could feel Hagan's breath hot and rapid on her neck. She thought of

David, and the way he had taken her with cold cruelty, and felt her stomach curl up with revulsion.

"Cousin John—" she began.

"My dear." Hagan's smile was vulpine.

"I really do not want—" Joanna began.

"You do not want to lose your home, do you?" Hagan murmured. "Or to be destitute. And you will be, my dear, if you do not see the sense in pleasing me."

Joanna froze. If she refused him she would lose her home, her place in society. She would be shunned and turned out, she would have no money and no means to make any. David's relatives were mostly dead and they had thought he was marrying beneath him anyway. There was no help there. And her remaining family were poorer than she was. Lottie might give her and Merryn a home if Hagan threw her out, but she would be less eager to have Nina to live with her. The first time the child put her little sticky fingers on the Exeter carpet or the Indian-print wall hanging, Lottie would surely have a fit of the vapors. It would not serve.

While she had been thinking, Hagan had slipped his hand inside her negligee and his hot, sweaty fingers were now rubbing over her nipple with disgusting intimacy. Joanna felt his wet mouth against the side of her neck. She screwed her eyes tight shut as he pulled the negligee open. She was doing this, she reminded herself urgently, so that she could not only save Nina but also give her a good home and defend her from those who would denounce her as a bastard throughout her life. The desperate maternal need twisted inside her. She simply had to claim and protect this child. David had already deserted Nina; she could not do the same.

Yet the price was so very high. A shudder racked

her body. What guarantee did she have anyway that Hagan would not double-cross her once he had taken her? Could she really succumb to his blackmail and do this? And if she refused, might he force himself on her anyway, as David had done? The thought paralyzed her. She remembered David's viciousness and her limbs felt weighted with lead.

Hagan was urging her toward the bed now. Joanna tried to absent herself from her body and fixed her gaze on the splendid Chinese silk of the cover as Hagan's busy hands moved over her body. The Chinese silk really was a beautiful piece of work. She felt a sudden pang of loss. She loved beautiful things. She did not want to give up her elegant home and all her collection of paintings and china and her matching footmen and be thrown out on the street. Nor could she live as a governess or a servant of some kind. A different sort of shudder shook her. Of course she could not be a governess or servant. She had no intellectual accomplishments and she did not want to have to do manual work for a living. She knew it was shallow of her, but at least it was honest.

But deeper, far deeper than that, was the knowledge that there would be no possible way she could claim Nina without a home to offer her. That was the truth that cut her to the bone; that would be the inconsolable loss.

Hagan was breathing so hard now that she was afraid he might be ill. His moist lips were trailing down her neck to her breast. Oh, this was a very, very high price to pay to keep all the things that she valued. She had only ever slept with one man in her life and she had not wanted the second one to be John Hagan. She had wanted...

She had wanted Alex.

The thought burst into her head with the power of an explosion. She could well imagine what Alex would say if he were to see her now; she could almost hear his denunciation, feel his blistering contempt for her lack of moral fiber. Alex was strong. He would not compromise as she was compromising, so desperately, so cravenly.

That thought was followed by one that was even more extreme. She would ask Alex to give his protection to her and to Nina. He had persuaded her to accept his escort to Spitsbergen—she would trump his suggestion with an even more outrageous one of her own. She would ask him to marry her. That would protect her from Hagan's venom and mean that she could offer Nina a safe home into the bargain. It was her only hope, for once she had rejected John Hagan's advances he would see her ruined.

She wrenched herself out of Hagan's grip, grasping for her tattered robe. "I am sorry, Cousin John," she said. "I cannot do this."

Hagan gave a roar of rage and thwarted lust and grabbed at her. "Oh, yes, you can, you little whore! You're not getting away from me now!"

Joanna scooped up a vase from the windowsill and hit him over the head with it. The vase broke and Hagan staggered like a wounded beast, swearing with words Joanna had never heard before, even after nine years of marriage to a sailor.

The bedroom door burst open. Merryn stood in the doorway holding another blue porcelain vase, this time with a dolphin motif on it. She had such a fierce expression on her face that Joanna almost quailed to see it.

"Don't break that one as well!" Joanna called, securing her negligee around her as Hagan lurched past Merryn and down the stairs. "I have already smashed one piece of Worcester porcelain and it is frightfully expensive." She looked at the shards on the floor and shook her head. "What a waste!"

"Drury said that Mr. Hagan burst in and was going to rape or murder you," Merryn said, lowering the vase. She looked at Joanna's rumpled hair and skewed robe. "I hope I was not too late," she added.

"Not at all," Joanna said. "I am still alive, as you see, and he wasn't really going to rape me." She hesitated. "Well, perhaps he might have done. He suggested an…arrangement, but at the last moment I could not go through with it and I fear that my refusal angered him."

"An arrangement?" Merryn wrinkled up her face. "Is that what you call it?" She placed the vase carefully on the dresser. "Surely your virtue is worth more than a piece of china."

Joanna laughed. "I am not sure. I have never had to make the comparison before. It all depends upon what one wants and I do love my porcelain collection." She saw Merryn's expression and pulled a face. "I know. You think me shallow."

"No," Merryn said. "I think you are making light of this on purpose because you do not wish to alarm me. It sounds to me as though Mr. Hagan tried to blackmail you into sleeping with him, the insufferable toad!"

"Indeed," Joanna said. "And as I have both refused

him and offended his pride, I need to act quickly before he throws us out into the gutter."

Merryn sat down heavily on the bed, crushing the exquisite Chinese-silk cover. Joanna, touched that her sister had rushed to her rescue, managed not to protest.

"Is that what he threatened?" Merryn asked.

"He did," Joanna said a little bleakly.

"Toad," Merryn said again. "What are we going to do?"

"I am going to persuade Lord Grant to marry me," Joanna said. Her heart was beating hard, but she knew she sounded confident. Of course she did—she had had years of practice at perfecting her social facade when beneath it any number of emotions might be running riot. At the moment her chief feeling was one of terror; ever since the idea of marrying Alex had popped into her head she had been vacillating between fear and… well, an even greater fear.

Merryn had given a little gasp at her words. "Marriage? But you do not even like him!"

"That is nothing to the purpose," Joanna said. She hurried on, as much to repress her own doubts as to convince her sister. "Look at all the alliances that are forged for convenience. All I have to do is marry Lord Grant for the protection of his name and for that, my love, I do not need to like him at all."

Merryn stared. "But you swore never to remarry! You said it was the last thing you wanted."

"I lied," Joanna said. "The last thing I want is to lose all this." She gestured around the opulent room with its rich red carpet and exquisite decoration. "I am very superficial," she explained, seeing Merryn's uncomprehending look, "and this makes me happy."

"Having a child is what will make you happy," Merryn said incontrovertibly. "You pretend to be frivolous, Jo, but you are not really."

"Yes, I am," Joanna corrected. She smiled at her sister. "Oh, I concede that being able to care for Nina and giving her a good home will make me very happy, but I am not prepared to do it on a pittance. I have a certain style to maintain."

Merryn stuck out her bottom lip in the stubborn gesture Joanna remembered from their childhood. "I know that you claim to be selfish, Jo," Merryn said, "but the truth is that you are doing this for Nina and for me, too, so that we will have a roof over our heads and be safe and protected."

"You have me all wrong," Joanna said dryly. "I am doing it for myself." Nevertheless, she returned Merryn's hug, holding her tightly for a brief moment.

"I foresee a stumbling block," Merryn said, pushing back the fair hair from about her face and rubbing eyes that were suspiciously red with tears.

"Oh?" Joanna frowned. "What have I forgotten?"

"That you have nothing to offer Lord Grant," Merryn said. "It is expecting a great deal of him to ask him to do this purely out of honor and a responsibility toward Nina."

There was a pause. Merryn was sitting with her hands clasped in her lap, looking earnestly at her sister. Not for the first time, Joanna wondered how she had grown so cynical and Merryn had managed to stay so naive. It was the wicked influence of the ton upon her, she supposed, and the disillusionment of her marriage to David. For most certainly she could not say to Merryn:

"You mistake. I can offer Lord Grant myself…"

No indeed, she could not say that. Merryn would be shocked to the core. And truth to tell, there was a little—a very little—of her vicarage upbringing still within her that meant that she was shocked, too. But Alex could give her something that she needed—the means by which she could both provide for Nina and remain in the comfort to which she had become accustomed—and this time she was prepared to barter herself for it. Her uncle would probably have denounced her as a whore, but Joanna could not see that it was much different from a marriage of convenience with cold-blooded bargaining over money and land.

"Well," she temporized, "if I put it to Lord Grant as a business proposition—that I will care for all aspects of Nina's welfare and perhaps offer to take his young cousin Chessie under my wing for a season as well so that he is free of all family obligations…"

"That is still not my idea of an ideal marriage," Merryn protested.

Joanna laughed. "I hope that you never make the kind of match," she said, "where you discover that the less you see of your husband, the better."

"I suppose," Merryn said doubtfully, "that Lord Grant might be persuaded to help. He is not a rich man, but we could live cheaply, somewhere small, a village in the country perhaps—" She broke off. "But I do not suppose you would like that," she finished a little sadly.

"I would hate it," Joanna said frankly. "You know I detest the country. I find it dull and slow and dirty."

She remembered the long, monotonous hours in her

uncle's country vicarage measured out by nothing more than the chiming of the long case clock in the hall. That dreary boredom had been one of the reasons why she had practically thrown herself into David Ware's arms when she had met him at a local assembly. He had seemed so vivid and dashing in comparison to her drab existence. And of course he had been, but he had also been a complete cad and in throwing herself at him she had made a dreadful mistake. But she would not allow herself to think about the disaster of her first marriage. This time she would have her eyes wide-open and would be marrying Alex to secure the things that were important to her.

"It was fun growing up in the country," Merryn was saying. "It is far more friendly than London and there were places to play and quiet corners where I could go to read."

"I sometimes think," Joanna said, smiling to take the sting out of her words, "that you were growing up somewhere completely different from me."

"But you did not read," Merryn said.

"No, I found it boring."

"Nor did you explore outdoors—"

"In case I spoiled my clothes."

"So it is not surprising that you prefer London, where you may be entertained all the time," Merryn finished. She glanced at the clock and stood up.

"Are you going out this evening?" Joanna asked.

For a split second Merryn looked suspiciously guilty, but then she shook her head. "It is already ten o'clock, Jo. You know I still keep country hours. No, I am going to bed."

"Good night then," Joanna said, giving her a kiss on

the cheek. "Please, would you send Drury to me? I need her help to dress."

Merryn closed the door behind her and Joanna sat for a moment staring at her reflection in the pier glass. Was she really going to do this? She had told Alex that night at the boxing inn that she was not careless of her reputation and it must be true or she would not be sitting here agonizing about her actions. This would be a bargain, her choice, struck to gain the things that she wanted most. It would not be the same as David's careless, cruel claiming of her. She closed her eyes briefly. Best not to think of David when she was planning to seduce his best friend.

She went over to her wardrobe and started to sift through the scores of gown that hung there. The red silk was too fussy. The gold brocade was too formal. The purple velvet was simply too last season.

An hour and a half later, dressed in her most becoming silver gauze gown, Joanna thought she looked every inch the sophisticated society matron. The gown skimmed her hips and clung lovingly to her curves. It rustled when she moved, the shades of silver shifting like opalescence in the light. It was a seductress's gown, a costume, a disguise. She tried to draw confidence from it, to become the person who was looking back at her from the mirror. It was surprisingly difficult. She felt terrified, for the first time in her life wishing that she were like Lottie with the experience of dozens of lovers to draw on.

She drew herself up. So she did not have much idea of how to seduce Alex, but really, how difficult could it be?

She picked up a matching gauze scarf and wrapped it about her shoulders. The hackney carriage was waiting outside. There was no going back.

LOTTIE WAS DRAWING. It was not one of the female accomplishments that she possessed—in fact, had anyone asked her she would probably have said that the only feminine gifts she had were unmentionable ones—and as a result, the map was coming out extremely lopsided. John Hagan, looking over her shoulder, seemed unimpressed. He adjusted the candles to throw more light on the writing desk.

"Are you sure that is what it looked like?" he demanded.

Lottie gave a pettish little shrug. "Near enough. There was a long peninsula and the treasure was buried near the beach and it was called—" She stopped. She could not for the life of her remember the name of the place she had seen on Ware's hand-drawn Spitsbergen map.

"You will have to go back for another look," Hagan said. "I am not setting off on some wild-goose chase without knowing the name of the place at the very least."

Lottie gave an exaggerated sigh. "Darling, much as I enjoy debauching James Devlin, he is going to get a little suspicious if I seem more interested in the treasure map his cousin gave him than in his cock."

There was a pause. Lottie saw Hagan flush darkly and knew that in that moment he was thinking more about her locked in flagrant immorality with Devlin than he was about David Ware's hidden treasure. Men, Lottie thought. They were all the same, led by their pricks. She knew that given half a chance he would have her across the desk. She had no intention of giving him that chance. She did have some standards. And besides, Hagan was looking particularly unattractive tonight with a huge reddish bruise on his forehead and a cut above his eye. She'd asked him what had happened and he'd refused to tell her.

"I am sure," Hagan said, clearing his throat, "that you will think of a way to distract Mr. Devlin's attention. You seem a most…imaginative…creature." His voice lingered over the last few words.

Lottie gave him her little catlike smile and leaned forward so that Hagan could see right down the generously cut neck of her gown. "It will cost you, darling," she warned. "If I get you more information I shall want a bigger share of that lovely, lovely treasure."

"You are greedy, madam," Hagan said, staring at her cleavage as though transfixed. "It is not as though you have a need of the money."

"No," Lottie said, draining her brandy and making sure she did not offer him another glass, "but I do feel very strongly that you should pay for my help in some way, darling. After all, Joanna is my dearest friend and I am being a teensy bit disloyal to her in assisting you like this, am I not?"

Hagan grunted. "It sounds to me as though you are not finding the process too onerous, madam."

"Oh, Devlin is a very talented lover," Lottie said blithely, "but he is a young man, you know. I fear his sexual demands might well exhaust me." She gave a heavy sigh. "I need to be…reassured…that my efforts are in a worthy cause." She fluttered her eyelashes at Hagan. "Mr. Cummings refuses to buy me the stunning diamond bracelet that Lady Peters is obliged to auction to cover her gambling debts. He says that I have too many diamonds already. As though one could ever have too many diamonds!" She looked appealingly at Hagan. "So you see…"

Hagan toyed with his empty brandy glass. "I am sure," he said, "that we might come to some…accommodation, madam."

"Well, that is excellent, darling," Lottie murmured, getting to her feet and gathering up her drawings so quickly that Hagan pulled back. "I shall allow Mr. Devlin to shaft me with great vigor until he reveals all his secrets." She saw Hagan's look of barely controlled lust and gave him a dazzling smile. How she adored shocking people. "The servants will show you out," she added. "Good night."

Chapter 9

THE NIGHT HAD BEEN long and hot and Alex was tired and, he thought, as the cool night air made his head spin, more than a little cast away. Truth to tell, it had been the only way to get through an interminable evening. Charles Yorke had arranged a dinner at the Admiralty at which the Prince Regent was the honored guest, and as he was not escorting Lady Joanna Ware to Lady Bryanstone's ball, Alex had run out of reasons for refusing to attend. Indeed, it had been made very plain to him that he could not refuse, not if he wished the Admiralty to maintain their support for his trip to Spitsbergen and provide him with supplies and a ship to accompany the *Sea Witch* in case of any difficulties.

As he entered the doors of Grillon's and made his way to his room, Frazer came out to meet him, his long dour face even longer and more dour than ever in the candlelight.

"There is a lady waiting to see you, my lord."

Alex swore. Dodging invitations from overamorous ladies had become something of an occupational hazard in the past week, but none of them had previously had the temerity to invade his bedroom, least of all with the connivance of his steward.

"Frazer," he said, "it is three o'clock in the morning."

"Aye, my lord."

"And I wish to sleep."

"Aye, my lord."

"And I am foxed."

Frazer sniffed. "You do indeed smell like a rough night in a taproom in Aberdeen, my lord." He paused. "It is Lady Joanna Ware, my lord."

"I don't care if it is the pope," Alex said irritably. Joanna Ware was here, in his bedchamber, at three in the morning? He must be fantasizing now.

"You should have sent her away," he said.

"He tried to. I refused to go."

Alex spun around. The door to his chamber had opened and Joanna was standing in the aperture. There was one candle burning on the nightstand behind her. It cast a halo of light around her head, burnishing her hair to bronze and gold. She came forward, her skirts making the softest, most sensual rustling sound. Alex caught a breath of her perfume, honey and roses mingled with her warmth, so sweet and seductive it went straight to his head—and his groin. She was wearing a confection in silver lace that clung in all the appropriate—or was that inappropriate?—places and was so opaque that it was almost transparent. Alex found himself staring.

Behind her stretched the unruffled cover of Alex's bed. A minute ago he had been longing for sleep. Now it represented quite a different temptation.

"What the devil are you doing here?" he demanded. "How did you know I was staying here?" He knew that he sounded ungracious, but it was either that or grabbing her and kissing the life out of her. He had no real wish to do that in front of Frazer, but it was a close-run thing.

"Brooke found you," Joanna said. "He can find anyone. I need to speak with you."

"Could it not wait?"

"Naturally not, or I would not be here." She wrinkled up her nose as the smell of taproom reached her. "Oh, you are foxed!"

"Just a little."

"I am sorry, madam," Frazer said.

"Don't apologize for me, Frazer," Alex said. "I am quite capable of apologizing myself if I feel the situation warrants it." He turned to Joanna. "Lady Joanna, go home. I'll call on you in the morning."

"In the morning I may not be there for you to call upon." There was just the tiniest catch in her voice and befuddled as he was, Alex caught it. Looking at her face, he saw determination there as well as anxiety in the way that she pressed her hands together. He felt something shift inside him, a stir of compassion mixed with something else, an emotion he thought long lost. He swore.

"My lord!" Frazer sounded like an outraged uncle now. "Not in front of the lady!"

"Frazer, fetch me some cold water, if you please," Alex said, ignoring the remonstrance. "Lady Joanna, what may I offer you? Other than a hackney carriage home."

"I came here to seduce you," Joanna said in a rush.

"Excuse me, my lord," Frazer said into the silence that followed. "I do not believe that I should be present at a moment like this."

"Damn right you shouldn't," Alex said. "Pray excuse us." He caught Joanna's arm and steered her back into the room, closing the door behind them and leaning his shoulders against it.

"You came here to seduce me?" he repeated.

"Yes." She looked annoyed.

"Then why didn't you?"

"I beg your pardon?"

"Why didn't you do it?" Alex repeated. "Good God, you don't announce something like that!" He cast his hands up. "You do it!"

He saw Joanna bite her lip. "I couldn't do it!" she protested. "Frazer was there and I did not want to shock him. I like him—he brought me a glass of wine whilst I waited for you and we were talking about his home—" She stopped, as though the reality of the situation was suddenly catching up with her. For a second she looked tragic. She also looked seventeen rather than twenty-seven; despite the sophistication of her silver gown she looked bewildered, a little lost, as unhappy as a virgin bride whose mother had just scared her with tales of men's uncontrollable lusts.

A feeling of tenderness stirred within Alex. He recognized it with incredulity and wondered if it was the drink addling his head. Could Joanna Ware really induce such an emotion in him when he did not care for her? It seemed insane. Just for a second he was afraid he *was* insane.

"You have made a spectacular muddle of this, have you not?" he said a little more roughly than he had intended.

Her eyes flashed, magnificent lavender blue. "Well, thank you! Forgive me if I do not have any experience to draw upon!"

"I cannot imagine what you were thinking."

She blushed a deeper rose. "Neither can I!"

There was a tentative knock at the door. Frazer stuck his head around on Alex's summons and looked mightily relieved to see that they were both still respectably dressed. He handed Alex a ewer of water.

"I was not sure if you were…um…negotiating terms," he said.

"Not in the sense in which you mean," Alex said, glaring at Joanna. He emptied the ewer of water over his head. Joanna looked scandalized.

"What a frightful mess!" she said. "That is an Aubusson carpet, you know, though what they are doing putting it in a hotel room where it is abused by people like you, I cannot imagine."

"At least I can think now," Alex said. Frazer went out, taking the ewer with him, and Alex rubbed a towel around the back of his neck. "So, what the hell is all this about?"

He saw Joanna's lips tighten into a very cross, very tight bow and felt once again the urge to kiss her.

"I need you to marry me," she said.

Alex rocked back on his heels. "Why on earth?" he said.

"Because I am desperate."

"Thank you," Alex said dryly. "I am still waiting to understand where the element of seduction comes into this."

Joanna sighed sharply. She took a few steps away from him. Her skirts swished like the hiss of an angry cat. "I was thinking that the only time we do not argue is when we are kissing," she said crossly. "So it seemed logical to approach you in that way."

"I might have slept with you," Alex said, following his own logic, "but why imagine that I would marry you?"

Now she looked even more infuriated. He supposed that he might have put it in a more chivalrous way, but his head was aching.

"Because you are supposed to be a gentleman," she snapped, "and that is what a gentleman does!"

"Your logic," Alex said, "is hopelessly at fault."

"As are your manners." She sounded exasperated. He saw the pink color run up under her skin, saw her shake her head in defeat. "I am sorry," she said abruptly. "I am tired, and evidently I was not thinking straight at all, and I can see I have made a fool of myself—"

"Joanna." Alex found that he had taken her hands in his. He felt her tremble, felt, too, an urge to comfort her that was unfamiliar and disquieting. The contrast between the sophisticated façade conjured by the silver gown and the real emotion beneath her brittle exterior was extremely confusing.

"Tell me what this is really about," he said.

She freed herself and went and sat on the side of the bed. Alex's body responded to the vision of her, hair escaping from its knot, silken skirts spread about her. Hell. Did she not realize what she was doing to him, here in his bedchamber in the dead of night? For a widow she was exceptionally naive. She had boldly stated her decision to seduce him and seemed to think that because he had turned her down she was now as sexless as Frazer. He certainly was not going to sit down beside her. That would present him with an excess of temptation. He drove his hands into his pockets and strode across to the other side of the room.

"It is John Hagan," Joanna said. She spoke in a rush. "He said—" Her breath hitched despite her valiant attempts to keep it steady. "He said that if I went to the Arctic I would have no home to come back to and that he would make sure no one received me." She made a despairing gesture. "He said he did not want Nina in the family, that she was David's bastard brat and should be left to rot unless—" Her voice quivered. "He wanted—" She stopped, met his eyes. "Well, he suggested an arrangement…"

"I see," Alex said. He felt a tight, possessive fury. "And you refused him."

"Not exactly." Joanna's blue gaze was defiant. Alex felt her words like a kick in the gut. "I need a home to offer Nina," she said, "and I could see no other way. I cannot work as a servant or live in penury—I have to be comfortable! So I thought—"

"Bloody hell, Joanna!" Alex thought he was going to explode. He grabbed her shoulders. "You refuse to have an *affaire* with me because of your so-called moral principles and then you sleep with John Hagan because you wish to preserve your standard of living!" He let her go. He was seething with anger and a primitive possessiveness that felt white-hot.

"I should have known," he said bitterly, "that had I offered you that carriage and four you mentioned, you would have changed your mind."

"It was not like that," Joanna said. She had her hands on her hips. Her eyes were as vivid as stars. "Hagan was blackmailing me, but I could see no other way!" Her voice faltered. "I really do want to help Nina and to keep her safe, Alex. And anyway—" her tone strengthened "—I could not go through with it. He was too unattractive and I thought he might cheat me."

Alex gave a short laugh. "You were probably right." He looked at her. He was astounded at how angry he felt; he was furious with her for even considering succumbing to John Hagan's blackmail and he was even more enraged with Hagan for his intolerable behavior. He could see why Joanna had come to him. She needed not only somewhere for herself and Nina to live, but, more important, the protection of his name against Hagan's mean-spirited revenge. The man had influence and would turn the ton against her. Joanna, a widow with no fortune of her own, had survived as society's darling because she had pleased those who had power and influence. Now, though, they might bring her down simply to prove that she was their creation.

He realized that Joanna was gathering up her gauze wrap and preparing to leave.

"It was a mistake for me to come here," she said abruptly. "I can see that. If Hagan really does throw me from my house I suppose I can always find another gentleman to wed me—"

Alex's head still hurt and his thought processes were taking longer than usual, but the one thing he did know was that no one else was going to marry Joanna Ware. That seemed crystal clear.

"Lewisham, or Belfort or Preston?" he suggested softly. "They are not men, my dear, they are barely alive."

"I know." Once again she gave him a look of challenge. "But they are safe. And so would I be, Merryn and Nina, too."

"None of them would wish to take on another man's illegitimate daughter," Alex pointed out.

"I suppose not." She fidgeted with the fringing on the gauze scarf, pleating it between her fingers. "I know that you do not wish to wed any more that I do, Alex, but you at least might do it for the sake of the child." She let the material slip from between her fingers. "David made you Nina's guardian for a reason and I think that reason was because he knew you would not let him down. No matter how much you hated the responsibility he placed on you, you would still do your duty…" Her voice faded away. "You do hate it, don't you?" she added softly. "I feel that anger and reluctance in you all the time."

The bitterness and fury twisted in Alex again. How much could he tell her, here in this shadowy room, how much of his guilt about Amelia's death, how much of the way that he chafed against responsibility and obligation and yet would never shirk it? It was almost as though it was his penance, his punishment. Oh, yes, David Ware had chosen his daughter's guardians well, for neither of them would ever desert the child. Joanna, with her tenacious desire to help Nina, and he with his appalling sense of culpability from which he could never be free, a sense of guilt that meant he could never again fail an innocent child…

"Yes," he said gruffly. "I hate it."

"Why?"

He had never lied to her before. They had, he realized with a sense of surprise, been utterly open and direct with one another. But this was different. This canker in him, this blame, the guilt he felt about Amelia's death, was not something he ever spoke of and he would not start now. No, a partial truth would have to suffice.

"Because I hate to be tied down," he said. "I want no responsibilities. I am an explorer." He shrugged. "It is a compulsion, hard to explain…"

She nodded. Her gaze was cloudy. "I understand."

If Ware had had the same compulsion, he imagined that she would understand very well, more than any woman he knew. But…

"You do not want that in a man," he said.

"Of course not." There was bitterness in her voice now. "But I want the child, Alex. I feel a moral obligation to care for her, but more than that I have to help her. I cannot leave her, so far away, unloved and abandoned… And I am shallow enough to want to keep my style of life as well. I admit it freely." She drew a deep breath, got to her feet. "So I am offering you a bargain. I know I have little to offer you in return, but all I ask is that you give us the protection of your name and somewhere to live—" she smiled slightly "—myself and Merryn and Nina. Perhaps your cousin Francesca could come to stay with us, too. I could sponsor her come-out, if anyone in society will still speak to me." She stopped again. "Anyway, I ask nothing else of you. I will raise Nina and care for her and you will be free to travel as you please, no obligations, no ties. What do you say?"

Alex thought about it. On one level it seemed an obvious solution to all their difficulties. In giving Joanna his name and a roof over her head he would not only protect her from Hagan and from the censure of society, but he would also ensure that Nina was well cared for and provided for in every material sense. He would have a great deal more control over Nina's future than if she lived with Joanna and he was only their paymaster. He would also have fulfilled his duty. Joanna would provide the child with the emotional care that he so manifestly could not and she could also take Chessie under her wing as well. Best of all he would be free—free to go where he pleased, to pursue his dreams to the ends of the earth if he wished. It seemed ideal. True, he had not looked for further responsibilities, he would prefer not to be encumbered by them, but he already had Chessie to provide for and he would not shun his duty to Nina either. He could not. His honor was engaged even if he was not.

And then at the back of his mind came the whisper of Devlin's voice and the thought that he had been pushing away ever since he had returned to London:

"Balvenie needs an heir..."

He had been ignoring that whisper, ignoring that necessity, because his appalling guilt over Amelia's death would not permit him to put someone else in her place.

He looked at Joanna. She was very pale. Her face looked carved from marble. Her breathing was shallow, nervous. He remembered the words of David Ware's codicil, the taunting lines that made it clear how greatly Joanna wanted a child. It was borne out by her utter determination, her desperation even, to claim Nina. But was there any reason why she could not have a child of her own? It was true that in nine years of marriage she had not given Ware a child, but that was probably merely chance. She thought she had little to offer him, but in fact she might give him a very great deal. An heir for Balvenie... It would be another obligation discharged, another responsibility fulfilled. It would be perfect. He would be marrying Joanna for sound practical reasons and they both understood that. He desired her, but he would never love her and so he would not be betraying Amelia in any way. He would not be replacing her.

Joanna met his eyes and he was shocked to see that she still looked nervous. "You're afraid," he said abruptly, seeing the way that her fingers trembled and she locked them together to try to quell it.

"Of course I am afraid!" She turned on him with a flutter of silk. "I swore never to wed again. It is no secret that my marriage to David was unhappy. And I don't want another adventurer who blazes across my life, promises everything and then walks out and leaves me with nothing!" She sounded despairing.

"At least this time we would both know the terms of our agreement and we would adhere to them," Alex said roughly. It was the first real insight Joanna had ever given him into her estrangement from Ware and he knew she had done it unconsciously, under stress.

"Yes." She let out her breath on a sigh. "I am not as young and foolish as I was when I wed David. So I ask for nothing more than your name and a home." She straightened her spine. "What do you say?"

"No," Alex said. "I don't want a glorified house-keeper turned nursemaid."

Her chin came up. "I am told they are cheaper than a wife."

"Perhaps." He caught her by the shoulders and felt the heat of her through the thin silk of her gown. His desire for her burned as hot as a furnace now. "I don't want a marriage in name only," he said. He thought of Balvenie and his need for an heir.

"You came here to seduce me," he said. "So do it."

THE BREATH LEFT JOANNA'S lungs in a rush. Intentions, she thought, even bad ones, were all very well in theory. She searched his face, so stern, so dark. Seduce him? It felt impossible when he looked so unapproachable. In fact, it had always been impossible, hopeless, utter madness, even to imagine she could do it… Her confidence had always been woefully short, hiding behind the temptress image of the silver gauze gown.

"Are you telling me you will not marry me unless I seduce you?" she demanded. She felt outraged, unbelieving. "You are even less of a gentleman than I had thought!"

He laughed. Damn him. In the candlelight he looked disheveled and reckless, suddenly every inch the adventurer he was. "Had you more experience," he said, "you would know that very few men are true gentlemen at a time like this." He shifted. "Some would be, perhaps. I am honest enough to admit that I am not one of them." He was watching her and the look in his eyes made her feel very, very hot. "You made the original suggestion, if you recall," Alex continued. "So, yes, that is correct. I will not wed you unless you seduce me. Seal the deal."

"Seal the deal?" Joanna wrinkled up her nose. "What an uncommonly vulgar expression."

He took a step closer to her. "I do not want any misunderstandings about our marriage, Joanna. If we wed it will not be in name only. I desire you and I would not wish to wed you and then take my pleasure in another's bed because yours is denied to me."

Well, there was some honor in that, Joanna thought. She remembered David and his utter inability to be faithful, and felt, oddly, precious and cherished. And

Alex was right, of course—it had been her idea in the first place, what seemed like a hundred years before. Now it seemed impossible yet strangely intriguing at the same time.

"Pleasure," she whispered, and could not quite suppress a little quiver of anticipation.

"Yes." Again that wicked smile lit Alex's gray eyes. He tilted his head. "Do I infer that you are not accustomed to it?"

She was not, of course. David Ware had cared for no one's pleasure but his own. There had been little space in his universe for anything other than himself.

"I…" There was no way of talking about such things without mentioning David and she really did not want to think about him now.

"For an aspiring seductress you are strangely reticent," Alex said.

For a seductress she was hopeless. She knew it, but she did not need him to point it out. Nor could she go through with this outrageous dare, not now it came to the point. It was, she thought, the natural conclusion of the dark, dangerous game they had been playing, simultaneously distrusting one another, goading each other and yet captured by this strange, potent attraction that would not ease its grip. And now Alex had thrown down the ultimate challenge and she had proved too weak-willed to accept it. She thought of a future without home or money or anyplace in the world. For a terrifying few seconds her mind was completely blank; it simply could not provide her with any pictures of what such an existence might look like. But the alternative was standing in front of her and he looked dangerous.

"You can never forbear to criticize," she said. "I have changed my mind. The entire agreement is off—"

Alex made an exasperated sound, put out a hand and grabbed her. He tangled one hand in her hair, tilted up her face and kissed her. Immediately their lips touched, the desire engulfed her, hotter, sweeter and more intense than before. She drew back before she drowned in it and opened her eyes. "I'll not kiss a man who smells of brandy, thank you."

"Live dangerously," Alex said. He was smiling. He was so close that she felt dizzy with the effect of his nearness. "It is not any brandy," he added. "It is the Prince Regent's best brandy." He looked at her. The expression in his eyes was dark and concentrated. "Your choice," he said. "It's either on—or it's off."

Much as her clothes would soon be if she did not get out of there fast. Joanna trembled.

"Off."

He did not move. He was standing between her and the door.

"Coward," he said. "You're willing to risk an uncertain future for Nina and Merryn—and for yourself—because you dare not sleep with me?"

The heat in the room seemed to rise. The candle flames danced, bright and hot.

"Blackmailer. You are no better than Hagan." Joanna raised a hand to slap him. She felt a shocking welter of emotions: anger, desire, shame and furious arousal all mixed into one.

He caught her wrist negligently and dropped it as though it was of no account. "It was your idea," he said. "A good one, for once. But—" he shrugged "—by all means go if you wish." He turned away.

"No." Something snapped inside her. "I can't. I want Nina." She did want the child, desperately. She also had less worthy aims. She looked down at the silver gauze gown. "And I want to live in London and wear beautiful gowns."

Alex laughed. "So in the end you'll make love with me for the sake of your wardrobe? That sounds about right."

He picked her up and tossed her on the bed. It was so sudden and shocking that she lay there, winded for a moment. He was kneeling above her and he looked huge and powerful and shockingly masculine and she felt her heart race with a mixture of apprehension and fascination and the most wicked, wicked delight. The sensation curled in her belly, tightening to unbearable tension. She felt tormented by the most excruciating need, simultaneously furious with him and yet frantic to feel him inside her. She had never felt such intolerable desire; even thinking of it caused her whole body to tighten still further with shock and desperation.

Alex bent down until his mouth covered hers, trapping her between his body and the bed. Her hands were spread against the coverlet and she could feel the rough brocade against her palms. The kiss was a clear statement of intent and her body instantly recognized it as such. His lips were insistent, demanding, his tongue tangling with hers and inciting a heated response she could barely control. She could feel his arousal against her belly; feel, too, the way her body rose to meet his, the way her breasts peaked against her silken chemise and her hips arched to press closer. Then one thought pierced the sensual haze.

"Please don't squash my gown," she murmured,

remembering the shocking price she had paid for it at Madame Ermine's shop.

Alex drew back with an exasperated sigh. "Take it off, then," he said. "Before I do it myself but with less finesse."

"I am not able to take off my gown without the help of a maid," Joanna said.

Alex sighed again and before she knew what was happening he had rolled her over so that she was lying on her stomach on the bed. She gave a little squeak of protest as she felt his impatient fingers at the nape of her neck, brushing her hair aside, starting on the tiny mother-of-pearl buttons that ran down the back of her gown. She felt his fingers slip and heard him swear.

"Please don't damage it," she entreated again.

He made a sort of growling sound in his throat. "You need something else to think about." His lips touched her nape, spreading heat and shivers across her skin. His teeth nipped the naked skin of her shoulder and neck as his fingers continued their downward path. He worked on the fastenings of her gown with a concentrated efficiency that offended her but also hotly, shockingly, aroused her. His fingers were steady on the buttons, whereas she was shaking all over.

He pulled the gown from her. She heard something rip and started to protest, but he rolled her over onto her back and covered her mouth with his, and then his tongue was dancing with hers and he tasted so delicious, of raw spirit and equally potent masculinity, that she forgot her objections. His mouth was hot and hard, the demand explicit, and she writhed beneath its command and beneath the touch of his hands. Apprehension fluttered briefly and then died within her. No, this was not

David, selfish in his need. She had known from the beginning that Alex was not a man who used his strength to frighten others. Though his hands and mouth plundered, they gave pleasure, too, such exquisite pleasure as he rolled the silk chemise from her shoulders, and down to expose her breasts to his gaze. His touch was light, caressing and infinitely sweet as it drew out her response. She shifted restlessly, wanting him, arching her breasts to his lips. He paused, his breath just brushing one tight pink peak, and she ached for him to take her in his mouth.

"You have the most delicious…"

She waited, her body tense as a bow.

"Underwear." His hand was splayed across her stomach, hot on the rumpled silk of her petticoats. "Do you buy it in Bond Street?"

"As if you care." She grabbed his head and brought it down to her breast, and heard him laugh as he licked and tugged at her nipple. She almost screamed as the sensation seared through her, then remembered that she was in a hotel room and that Frazer was nearby, and felt wicked shock and endless pleasure cascade through her at the wantonness of it all. She pulled Alex to her, digging her nails into the hard muscles of his shoulders, and ripped his shirt off him with absolutely no regard for whether she damaged the material or not. It was not as though he prided himself on his appearance as she did.

It was her last logical thought before he kissed her again and she tumbled into that dark, erotic place from which she never wanted to escape. His tongue slid against hers and she reached for him with absolute demand. He had taken all her clothes off now and it was

her hands, not his, that went to the band of his pantaloons, feverish to remove this last barrier between them.
She heard him catch his breath, saw in the candlelight
the dark intensity of his expression and could not help
the flicker of apprehension twist inside her, the last dark
remnants of David's cruelty. This time, though, Alex felt
her withdraw, and he drew back. His eyes glittered with
the same need she could feel within herself, a desire at
war with the last shreds of her fear.

"Don't be afraid…"

How had he known? Her tense muscles eased as he
lightly kissed her brow and her collarbone, the hollow
beneath her ear and the line of her neck. His hands
were soothing now, lulling her into relaxation even as
they trailed the sweetest, most gentle excitement in their
wake.

"Trust me."

She did. She acknowledged it, felt relief. He would
never hurt her. She knew that.

Alex slid down the bed and eased her legs apart.
Joanna froze as he lowered his head to her. She gave a
little moan of denial and tried to move, but now he was
holding her firmly, ruthlessly possessive, and his tongue
had an erotic mastery that made her cry out. She was
caught in a spiraling whirl of feeling, and then a raining
tumult of sensation took her entirely by surprise, raising
her up and tumbling her over the edge of an abyss to
lie spent and shattered below. She gasped and opened
her eyes and the room spun and rocked and her body
clenched tight again and again in a torrent of bliss.

"I've never… I didn't know…" She lay stunned and
breathless on the bed. Those feelings of anticipation,

she thought. The sense of fulfillment that had never been satisfied…

She looked at Alex. He was propped on one elbow beside her. He looked supremely pleased with himself.

"You didn't know," he murmured, "how extraordinary."

Joanna rolled over on her side and reached for the sheet. She was suddenly anxious to cover herself up and retreat from such open vulnerability.

"I didn't mean—" she started to say, but he took the sheet from her and pulled it down so that she was once again exposed to his eyes.

"I know what you meant," he said. He smiled. "But we haven't finished yet."

Joanna gave a little moan as he covered her, sliding between her legs, driving deep into her sleek heat in one smooth thrust. It had been so long for her and never, ever like this. Before, she had endured, waiting for the end. With Alex she was immediately swept up in the same storm of sensation as before, the pleasure thrumming through her body, hot and strong. He felt so big and she felt impossibly full and yet desperate to draw him deeper still. She felt herself twitch and writhe beneath him, caught her breath on a gasp and curled her fingers tightly into the sheets.

"Alex…"

He kissed her again, gently biting down on her lower lip, then salving it with his tongue, easing himself out of her and back with strong fluid strokes that drove her straight back into that tumult of pleasure. She raised her hips to meet him and heard him groan as he thrust harder, long and deep. He paused and she hung on the edge for what felt like agonizing moments and then he bent his lips to her breast, sucking, nipping and teasing her, and the fire licked hotter and she thought she would be consumed. She reached for him in desperation and he slid deep again and she splintered apart at last, more violently than before, the pleasure bursting through her mind in a scatter of blinding white light. She heard Alex gasp her name in a dark whisper and it seemed the sweetest thing she had ever heard, and then he emptied his seed into her body and they lay still, intimately entwined, and all she could hear was the harshness of their breathing. Their bodies were slick against each other, hot with sweat, the roughness of his thigh against the smoothness of hers. He brushed the hair away from her face, running his hands through its softness, holding her head still as he kissed her mouth gently. It was the tenderest thing she had ever experienced. She felt her body consumed with total satisfaction, felt it slipping and sliding toward sleep. She knew that she should get up, leave, go home, but for now she was too content to move. Sleep claimed her before she had any further thought.

Joanna woke after a few hours. The candles had burned out and the air smelled of tallow. Her body felt lush and ripe and complete and for a moment her mind drifted, uncertain of where she was and not really caring. Then she remembered and she sat bolt upright.

She glanced at Alex. He looked young and tousled and vulnerable, so different from his usual hard-edged sternness that her heart missed a beat and a feeling of tenderness stole through her. The covers were about his waist, revealing his hard, muscular chest. The stubble was darkening his chin, and his eyelashes lay thick and black against the line of his cheek. Joanna sat still, unable to breathe properly past the strange, smothering feeling in her chest. It did not feel like shock, or shame, or any of the other emotions she might have expected to feel waking naked in the bed of a man she had known for barely a week. It did not feel like fear for the future, or regret, or loss of the past. She did not know what it was, but she felt it for Alex Grant, of all people, and it scared her. It scared her to death.

It was not the infatuation she had felt for David Ware before they had wed. Never for one moment had she felt for Alex that blind and unquestioning devotion she had given so openly and in the end so pointlessly to David.

She knew what Lottie would say if only she knew. She could almost hear Lottie's voice:

"What you are feeling is gratitude, darling, because unlike David, Alex actually devoted himself to your pleasure in bed! You have found a new hobby and you are in lust…"

Lottie, she was sure, would be light and irreverent and very probably jealous. But mere gratitude, the shock of discovery, did not entirely account for her feelings and it was surely best not to examine them too closely. Sometimes there were benefits in being superficial.

Joanna tried to ease herself surreptitiously from beneath the covers. She could see her clothing scattered across the floor. That silver gown would never be the same again, but if she collected up the pearl buttons then perhaps Madame Ermine could salvage something from the wreck. She would have to make up some excuse, of course, as to how they had come to be ripped off…

Alex had felt her move and put out a lazy arm to draw

her back down beside him in the bed. She felt suddenly panicky, her feelings smothering her, prompting her to get away. She struggled a little but he held her firmly.

"So…" he said. His voice was amused, gentle and warm. Joanna felt an odd pang of longing, wanting the intimacy and yet knowing it was illusory. "Do we have a bargain?"

"I don't know," Joanna said. "Do we?"

She saw the corner of his mouth curl up in a smile. "I believe that we do. I will marry you and give you—and Nina—the protection of my name. In return, you will make a home for her and for Merryn and Chessie, too, if you so wish—and—" his hand drifted across her stomach, sending little ripples of awareness skittering over her skin "—you will give me an heir to Balvenie."

For a moment Joanna thought she had misheard him. Then she went utterly still beneath Alex's hands. In a moment she remembered Devlin's words in Lottie's ballroom that Alex's Scottish estates lacked an heir. In all her plans and calculations she had completely overlooked it. Disbelief rocked her, followed swiftly by a rush of despair so great that she felt almost physically sick with it.

Alex was asking of her the one thing that she could not give.

The harsh irony of it mocked her. It was something that almost any woman could do for him, but not her. It was the only thing he asked, it was the bargain that he was prepared to strike, and she was incapable of meeting his requirements.

And he did not know.

He knew that she and David had quarreled irreparably and he knew David had hated her. He even knew that she and David had been childless, but he did not know that was the reason for their estrangement. She had almost blurted it out to him that very first night in the ballroom when he had asked her what she had done to incur her husband's hatred:

"In five years of marriage I failed to give him the heir he wanted so he beat me until he had surely made it impossible that I would ever carry a child…"

But she had not told Alex any of that. It was still her secret.

"You did not mention an heir before," she said. Her voice sounded strained, and his hands, which had been stroking her in the slyest, most seductive of caresses along the line of her hip and down her thigh, stilled for a moment.

"Did I not?" He sounded genuinely surprised. "But you do wish for children?"

"I…" She opened her mouth to tell him the truth. Then she thought of Nina, the only child she had a chance of claiming, and the desperation tightened inside her with the painful cruelty of a vise. If she agreed to Alex's terms now she would knowingly be denying him the chance of the heir he craved. She would be deceiving him, tricking him, lying to him in the most fundamental way there was in order to fulfill her own needs and those of her late husband's child. The fierce maternal need that burned within her was so powerful it scorched out all other feelings.

"Of course," she said. "I have always wanted children." Her voice sounded rough to her own ears, rusty with betrayal even though she spoke the literal truth. "But no one can guarantee to provide an heir," she continued. "That is in God's hands."

Alex will never know…

"True." Alex smiled. "But we can make sure we do our best to try to conceive one."

His hand slid over the curve of her hip, pinning her to the bed, and he bent his lips to the arch of her throat. Joanna was shaking now both as a result of what he was doing and the enormity of the lie that she had, by omission, told him.

"So," he whispered, against her hot skin, "it is agreed."

Still time to change your mind…

Her conflict, her need, her desperate desire for a child, tortured her. It would take one word.

"Yes." The whisper left her lips and seemed to hang on the air.

Then Alex lowered his head to her breast and her mind spun away to somewhere dark and hot and wickedly fierce, and Alex took her again. The betrayal was complete.

Part 2
Spitsbergen, The Arctic,
June 1811

Chapter 10

Definition: An adventurer is a person who enjoys taking risks; someone who travels into little-known regions; someone engaged in a dangerous but potentially rewarding adventure; daredevil, swashbuckler, hothead, lunatic.

JOANNA WAS FEELING SEASICK, horribly, disgustingly and intolerably ill. It was vile, worse than her worst imaginings, and those had been pretty bad. She had been feeling sick for almost a month nonstop and all she wanted to do was die, but unfortunately it seemed that death was not interested in claiming her.

The ship lurched again. Joanna groaned. Her wedding, by special license on the morning on which they had sailed, had started so well. She flattered herself that she had looked absolutely divine in the most gorgeous pink gown with mameluke sleeves and a huge matching bonnet. Alex had looked handsome in his navy dress uniform. Lottie had been matron of honor, Merryn a bridesmaid and Dev and Owen Purchase had acted as groomsmen. And then they had boarded the *Sea Witch* and the nightmare had begun.

Joanna had been blithely sure on the basis of no evidence whatsoever that she would be a good sailor. Alas, they had only been three hours out of Chatham when the weather had deteriorated and a storm had blown up in the North Sea, tossing the *Sea Witch* about like a cork.

"We may be in for a little motion," Captain Purchase had said in his lazy, southern drawl, his green eyes narrowed on a far horizon that was suddenly as gray as pewter with curtains of rain sweeping across the sea. "I suggest that you go below, ma'am."

Joanna had gone and had not reemerged since. She had no idea now how many days had passed or what progress they had made in their voyage. She lay in her cabin whilst the world heaved and plunged around her and her stomach heaved and plunged with it. She could not move without a wave of dizzying nausea threatening to cut her down. She had taken to her bed and prayed for the world to end. It had not. Instead, her world had been reduced to the sound of the creaks and groans of the ship, the reek of tar and oil and a feeling of abject misery.

She rolled over and faced the wall. She felt wretched and lonely. Alex had not been to see her for several days. That was probably something to do with the fact that she had forbidden him from coming near her whilst she looked so grotesque. On that first night he had been extremely kind. She had not known he had it in him. He had stroked the hair away from her sweaty forehead, he had passed her the bucket when she had needed it and he had tried to get her to eat something to settle her stomach. She had been mortified that he should see her looking like a ghost with a face pasty white and hair in rattails, as sick as a drunkard in the street. It made her feel vulnerable and unprotected. She prided herself on her poise and her fashion and without it she felt almost naked, especially before Alex's perceptive gaze. For her pride's sake she had banished him, so she supposed she could hardly blame him for not coming back except to leave bowls of greasy broth for her which she refused to eat.

Joanna rolled over again as the nausea tumbled over her like a wave. It seemed that Lord and Lady Ayres had been right. It really was impossible to maintain one's style whilst traveling.

She remembered the piles of luggage on the quay that afternoon in London—Lottie had brought a hip bath and boxes of herb-scented soaps, her china tea set and a crate of tea, twenty pounds of bonbons, a writing desk and footstool, seven portmanteaux, a butler and a maidservant. Joanna had tried to be more practical, with a crate of apples and oranges, several bags of firewood, a big fur-lined basket for Max, a box of toys for Nina and only five portmanteaux. She thought that she would never forget the look of utter incredulity on Alex's face as he had seen the vast array of their baggage. Dev and Owen Purchase had been doubled up with laughter. Alex had looked from the luggage to Joanna and Lottie in their sealskin capes and Esquimaux boots and had shaken his head.

"You look like a bear," he had said to Joanna.

"Not the most charming compliment I have ever received on my sense of style," Joanna had said, "but precisely what I would have expected from you, my lord."

"The food will rot within days and if we have a storm we shall all be swimming in tea," Alex had added. "The writing desk will be useful for firewood, however. I should have asked the Admiralty for two additional ships instead of one to carry all your luggage."

At that point the band that the Admiralty had sent to give them a grand send-off had burst into music, the crowd had cheered and Lord Yorke had started to make a speech. Alex had grabbed Joanna's arm and hustled her belowdecks to their cabin, a minuscule, dark, poky space that Joanna had assumed at first to be a cupboard.

"We are expected to share this?" she had queried incredulously. "It is smaller than a single one of my wardrobes at home."

"You do not surprise me," Alex had said.

"And the bunk is like a coffin," Joanna had complained. She had seen the look of resignation harden on Alex's face. He had predicted that she would not deal well with the voyage and she realized that she was fulfilling his expectations even before they were under way.

"Be grateful that you do not have to swing around in a hammock like most of the crew," he had said coldly and had left her there.

As far as Joanna was concerned, that had been the high point of the voyage.

She missed Merryn, who had chosen to stay in London with her bluestocking friend Miss Drayton. As a parting gift, Merryn had given her copies of Dr. Von Buch's travel memoir and Constantine Phipps's record of his 1774 voyage to the North Pole.

"They are frightfully interesting," Merryn had assured her earnestly. "I know you will love them."

"I'm sure I shall," Joanna had said, placing them at the bottom of her trunk.

Early on in the journey, Lottie had been to see her, looking as smart as paint and chattering on about how marvelous Captain Purchase was, how entertaining the crew, how comfortable her quarters and what an absolutely wonderful time she was having aboard. Joanna had wondered if they were on the same ship.

"You missed the Shetland Islands," Lottie said, "though truth to tell that does not mean you missed much. They looked dreary and it was raining. We lost Captain Hallows's ship in the storm as well, though Captain Purchase is sure he will catch us up in the end." She cheered up a little. "The true enjoyment of the voyage for me lies in the company of so many handsome and strapping young officers. One is spoiled for choice!" She frowned at Joanna. "'Tis lucky I have their attentions to distract me, for you are becoming the most tedious bore, my love, lying down here in the dark. Could you not make more of an effort, Jo darling? I am sure that this seasickness business is all in your mind!"

Joanna had reached for the bucket at that point and Lottie had shrieked and run away and had not been back since. In fact, Max was the only one who had been with her the entire voyage, curled up on her bunk, snoring, oblivious to everything and proving to Joanna once more that dogs were so much easier and more reliable than people ever could be.

Joanna opened her eyes and stared at the oil lamp that swayed on its chain from the wooden ceiling, swinging rhythmically with the ebb and flow of the waves. The bright sunlight dappled the paneled walls. Suddenly she wanted to be out of the noisome dark and in the fresh air. She was so, so tired of feeling ill.

There was a knock at the cabin door. Joanna rolled

over, her stomach roiling with the familiar sickness, and prayed that it was not going to be Lottie gabbling on about her latest conquest amongst the crew.

"You did not give me leave to enter, but I am here anyway."

Alex.

Her first emotion was an odd sort of embarrassment to see him again, as though he were a stranger who had invaded her bedroom. Her second was simple horror. She had not washed for two days—or was it three? Her nightgown was stained, her hair knotted and she probably smelled. In fact, she was sure that she did.

"I've already told you that you cannot come in." Her voice came out as a croak. "I look dreadful, far too dreadful to be seen."

He laughed. Damn him to hell and back. "Yes," he said, "that is absolutely true. You do. In fact, I did not know you had it in you to look so bad."

Joanna turned over and peered crossly at him. In contrast to her state of disarray, he looked extremely well, fit, vital, tanned from the wind, his dark hair ruffled, his entire body radiating health. He brought with him the scent of the sea, of fresh air, sun and salt winds.

She buried her face in the pillow. "You could have lied and said I looked well to a pass," she said, muffled.

"I never lie." The bunk gave as Alex sat down. Joanna froze. Why was he staying? She did not want him to stay. She wanted him to go away and talk about shipping tonnage with Devlin, or navigation with Owen Purchase, or whatever it was that sailors talked about on a voyage, subjects in which she had absolutely no interest at all.

"I've brought you some porridge," Alex said.

Porridge. How disgusting. Her stomach churned.

"Please take it away again."

"No." He shifted. The cabin seemed full of his presence, the air buzzing. "You are going to eat it. Enough is enough. Frazer has been making you all those bowls of broth and you have hurt his feelings turning them down. Besides, if you do not eat soon you will become genuinely ill."

"Genuinely ill?" Joanna shot up in the bunk without thinking, the frowsty blankets slipping about her. "Do you think I am pretending?"

She saw Alex grin and almost hated him. "No, of course not. Some people are very prone to seasickness, and it is debilitating, but once you are back on dry land the effects vanish like magic."

Joanna hunkered down again. "Then pray wake me up again only when we reach land."

"No." With incredulity she realized that Alex was actually pulling the blankets off her now. She clung to them for dear life. "I have had enough of this," he said. "You are going to eat and then you will get up. We are sailing up the west coast of Spitsbergen. You must start to get ready for when we disembark. Besides—" a new note came into his voice that sounded like pride or pleasure or both "—you will want to see the view. It is very beautiful."

"The only view I want to see is of dry land when I am about to step onto it," Joanna said.

"Stop being so spoiled and sorry for yourself." Alex's voice had a thread of steel in it now. "You are behaving like a child."

Joanna threw the pillow at him. Alex laughed, catching it without dropping the bowl of porridge. She sat glaring at him.

"Get up, Joanna," Alex said, the wicked smile still tilting his lips. "Do you wish me to bring you a mirror to show you how urgent it is that you make yourself presentable?"

"No!" Joanna knew she was vain, but she had always thought that there were worse sins than wishing to look her best. Now, though, she not only felt disheveled, she also felt painfully self-conscious. There was something in Alex's eyes as he sat looking at her—looking at her in all her hideous disarray—that made her body flush hot all over. It reminded her of the night they had spent together at Grillon's Hotel. It was odd, Joanna thought, that now she was respectably married to Alex she should feel this constraint in his company. They had been so close, so intimate on that one illicit night, but the time they had subsequently spent apart had reminded her that they barely knew one another. She felt gauche with him. She felt as though she barely knew him.

"Oh, give me the bowl," she snapped, capitulating. She saw the look of satisfaction on Alex's face and started to eat in quick spoonfuls. The food tasted surprisingly good. Her stomach steadied and suddenly she was starving hungry. She wolfed down the rest and looked up to see that Alex's gaze was fixed on her.

"It was good," she said grudgingly. "Thank you." She sighed. "I am sorry if I have upset Frazer."

Alex inclined his head. "I'm sure he will forgive you if you sample his boiled gannet stew." He saw her blench and added, "Though I was the one who made your porridge today."

Joanna stared. "You did?"

"Of course. Sailors are taught to be resourceful." Alex cocked his head to one side. "I do not suppose that you can cook?"

Joanna felt a spurt of annoyance at the way in which he had phrased the question, as though he was already anticipating her denial. "Of course not," she said. "Why would I wish to cook? I am an Earl's daughter." Her aunt had tried to instill in her the housewifely skills suited to a vicar's niece—baking, preserving fruit and something she vaguely thought involved vinegar and had been called pickling—but sadly, the only skill she had been set on learning was how to use her looks to escape the vicarage.

"There is no need to look so disapproving," she added defensively. "Did you really expect me to have such talents? You knew what I was like when you married me."

There was a pause. For some reason Joanna felt small and miserable. She had never regretted her lack of culinary skills before.

"That is true, I did know." Alex's words hardly gave her the reassurance she craved. He stood up. Joanna gave a sigh of relief as though the space in the cabin was once more expanding and there was air to breathe again. Having Alex so close did odd things to her equilibrium. "I will send Frazer with some hot water for you," Alex said. "You will feel better after you have washed."

In the cabin doorway he paused. "Joanna…"

An odd shiver passed through Joanna at his tone of voice.

"Yes?" She kept her own quite steady.

"If you do not get up then I shall come and dress you

myself," Alex said pleasantly but with a glint in his eyes that was dangerous. "And I do not think you would like that. I have no skill as a lady's maid."

No skill as a lady's maid...

A long slow shiver brushed over Joanna's skin like a cobweb. He had been adept enough at getting her out of her clothes that night at Grillon's.

"And Joanna—" He was still looking at her with that disturbing light in his eyes. "I shall be sharing your cabin again tonight." He nodded toward Max. "The dog will have to find other quarters. I refuse to share your bed with that piece of fluff."

He went out and Joanna sat staring blankly at the door. She was not sure what appalled her more: Max's eviction or the thought that Alex would be living with her in the ridiculously cramped quarters of the cabin, even if it was only for a week or so until they landed. A week could be a frightfully long time. Alex would see her in a state of dishabille, before her gowns were chosen, her hair curled and her toilette complete. She had thought it appalling that he had already seen her when she was ill, but at least she had had an excuse for her grotesque appearance. She had never imagined that Alex would insist on invading her cabin like this and forcing an intimacy between them that she really did not want.

She drew her knees up to her chest and hugged them tight. She did not wish for intimacy with Alex. Each time he touched her it would be a reminder that he wanted an heir and that she could never provide one for him. It would remind her of her betrayal and her empty promises. She rested her forehead on her knees. Such hateful deception, but what else could she have done? Nina, abandoned and unloved, needed her, and in return she desperately wanted the child. She had done what she had to do to secure a future for both of them, but the guilt felt like a leaden weight inside her.

She thought again of that night she had spent with Alex. It seemed so long ago and so distant now that it was almost no more than a heated dream. It had awoken all her senses and opened her up to the possibilities of what could be between a man and a woman. It had been tempting and dangerous because it had made her want more than Alex was prepared to give. And it was painful, too, because it had made her see how different her life might have been if she had not fallen in love with David and taken a wrong turn so far back. All she had ever wanted was a loving husband and a family. It had been such an apparently simple aim and yet it had gone painfully wrong and now her second marriage was poisoned, too, based on an appalling lie.

Joanna closed her eyes, took a deep breath and opened them again. It was best not to think of it. Alex would never know the truth. She would simply have to act her part, give herself to him in the marriage bed and hope that his yearning for travel would take him away soon and for a very long time. Alex was an adventurer, after all. He lived to travel and explore. Like David, he was unlikely to want to spend much time in her company. And she would have Nina, and Merryn and Chessie, to provide the family she desired. The thought should have reassured her. Instead it left her feeling cold and lonely.

Joanna eased herself from the bunk and stood up. Miraculously the world remained steady. With hot water, clean clothes and the ministrations of a maid, she thought, all would soon be well again. It had to be. She had to go forward both with her journey and with this marriage, go forward into the unknown, for she had no other choice.

Chapter 11

ALEX STOOD ON THE quarterdeck looking out toward the coast of Spitsbergen. Sailing these seas never failed to stir him. They were the greatest challenge he had ever known, quixotic, changing with a sudden backing of the wind, flat glassy blue giving way to angry gray. Then the seabirds would follow the ship, hanging on the edge of the wind and calling like the spirits of sailors lost in the deep. The mountainous coastline, cut by the vast scars of the fjords, plunged deep into the waters with rocks so razor sharp they could cut a ship in two.

He had sailed to Spitsbergen twice before. On the first occasion it had been directly after Amelia had died and he had found in the bleak landscape some echo of his own grief and guilt. His first marriage had been very much a love match. He and Amelia had wed when she was barely out of the schoolroom. This second marriage of his was a vastly different affair. He had only himself to blame that far from being a marriage of convenience, it was proving to be very inconvenient indeed.

Not for the first time in the past weeks, Alex asked himself savagely what he had expected. He had chosen to marry Joanna Ware knowing full well just how flighty, superficial and shallow she could be. He had gone into this without illusions, only asking in return that Joanna do her best to furnish him with the heir Balvenie lacked.

He had hoped that the incendiary passion that had flared between them in London, which had both taken him aback and pleased him, would still be burning between them. He had never imagined that Joanna would respond to him with such unbridled desire. He had expected her to be as superficial in bed as she appeared to be out of it. Instead he had uncovered a woman of unexpectedly deep passions, a woman he wanted to make love to with a fierce desire.

He had not been able to fulfill that desire because Joanna had been seasick, and in the meantime the passion that had burned between them seemed to have dwindled to ashes. Now there was an uncomfortable sense of distance between them, a reserve like a barrier that would require the will of both of them to break down. For the sake of their marriage he hoped that Joanna was willing to try. He did not want a distant, cold relationship with a virtual stranger. A marriage in name only would not provide him with the heir he wanted.

He drummed his fingers on the rail. He doubted very much that he would die of thwarted lust, though it was intensely frustrating, and the fact that Devlin and Lottie Cummings were indulging in a very indiscreet *affaire* right under everyone's nose only served to make him feel more irritated. More concerning at the present, however, were his doubts about how Joanna would deal with the privations of the journey to Bellsund Monastery and how she would cope emotionally with whatever she found there. Alex had the feeling that it was going to be very difficult. Joanna's behavior an hour ago in the cabin had not set a good precedent. She had been as willful and spoiled as a child and it had annoyed him even as he had tried to be tolerant. It was not that he was unsympathetic of her plight; seasickness was deeply unpleasant and she had suffered with it badly indeed. They had been unfortunate that the summer seas had proved so stormy, but he had hoped that now it was calmer Joanna would get up, eat and make ready for landfall.

He had been hoping that for the past two hours. Now he was resigned to the fact that she would not be joining him on deck. He felt disappointed in her and angry as well. She had assured him that she would do whatever it took to secure Nina and take her to safety. She had fallen at the first hurdle. But again, he had to ask himself what he had expected. Joanna was as she was, unused to hardship and privation. He had simply hoped for better.

He heard the sound of voices on the poop deck and turned abruptly to see Joanna approaching, escorted by an eager phalanx of the ship's young officers, including Dev. Alex stared. It was Joanna, no doubt about it, but a Joanna restored to all her London glory, dressed in a glowing red pelisse with matching bonnet and gloves, neat boots on her feet, her hair pinned up, glossy and brown, beneath the brim of her hat, her face bright and with a hint of pink color in her cheeks rather than the wan ghostly image of two hours before. She was carrying Max and he was wearing a matching red coat.

"I feel marvelous," she said as she reached Alex's side. She smiled up at him, a brilliant, charming smile that Alex knew was as much for the benefit of their audience as it was for him. She put a small, gloved hand on his arm. "I do not know what was in that porridge, Alex darling, but it worked miracles! And who would have thought that Frazer would prove so adept as a lady's maid?"

Her posse of admirers laughed. Alex felt his throat turn dry.

"Alex darling…"

One thing he would not tolerate was that she address him with that casual, meaningless endearment which she and her friends seemed to scatter at whim. That teasing little smile on her lips reminded Alex of the woman he had made love to in London. It made him want to scoop her up into his arms and kiss the life out of her, audience or not. Suddenly he wanted to rip apart the superficial facade and rediscover the woman who had been warm and sensual and responsive in his arms that night.

"Gentlemen—" He dismissed the officers with a sharp jerk of the head and they suddenly recalled that they had work to do. Alex and Joanna were left alone.

"I did not think you were going to join me," Alex said. "You took so long."

Joanna arched her brows. "I was less than two hours." A mischievous smile curved her lips. Alex felt his senses jolt. "If you think that is a long time you should see how long it takes me to get ready for a ball." Her smile faded a little. "But of course you will not have to endure that," she said. "I forgot that as soon as we return to London you will no doubt be able to persuade the Admiralty to give you another posting and you will be gone. Doubtless we shall barely see one another after that."

Alex found he was stung by the lack of regret in her tone, even though he knew it was only what they had agreed as part of their pact.

"You will not be rid of me so easily," he said

smoothly. "We shall still share the responsibility of Nina's upbringing and I am of a mind to stay in England until you are all settled in your new home—and you are enceinte with my heir, of course."

He saw the color sting Joanna's cheeks. Her lashes swept down, hiding her expression.

"It is most indelicate of you to speak openly of such matters," she said frostily. "Anyone could overhear you when we are in public."

"My dear Joanna," Alex said, "I fear you will have to adapt your notions of decorum. I do not merely intend to speak of such matters—I intend to make love to you at every available occasion. I would not wish you to be in any doubt as to my intentions."

He heard her sigh sharply, an indication that his amorous approaches would be about as welcome as the plague. She flicked him a glance. "You may find yourself ashore for longer than you wish if you are waiting on my pregnancy," she said.

Alex smiled at her, determined not to concede. "There will be compensations," he said. "I doubt I shall grow bored of occupying your bed."

Joanna set her lips in a mulish expression. It was clear that she did not wish to pursue the conversation. She had turned away from Alex so that he could not see her face. She seemed to be studying the view with a fierce attention. Alex waited. What should he expect now? That she would denigrate the stark beauty of the scenery the way that Lottie Cummings had criticized Shetland? He was well aware that Spitsbergen was too wintry and too empty to please many people. It frightened them, especially those who had never seen anything but the soft, rolling green fields of southern England. As a Scotsman he was accustomed to scenery that daunted other men; he loved it, found his inspiration and his peace in it. But he knew he could hardly expect Joanna to feel the same way.

He waited, braced, for her to tell him that the place looked like hell on earth.

Joanna's face was tilted upward now and suddenly Alex remembered that she had not seen the sun for several weeks. She had not been outside at all. He realized that she was lapping up the heat sensually, as a cat would, luxuriating in it, eyes closed, a small smile on her lips, her body soft and pliant in the warmth. Alex felt a sudden tightening in his groin. Her lips were soft, pink and parted in frank appreciation. He wanted to kiss her. He ached to kiss her.

The sea breeze plastered the feathers in her hat against her lips and she opened her eyes and brushed them away.

"How wonderful to be in the open air again," she said. "I had almost forgotten what it was like."

"It was not quite so wonderful when the weather was bad," Alex said. He was intrigued by this quicksilver change in her, from stubborn and petulant to open and appealing. Perhaps she was not quite such a hothouse flower as he had imagined. "The only good thing that can be said about the storms that we endured was that the wind was behind us and so lessened our journey time considerably," he said. "I have known it to take two months or more to make this journey."

"Then I count myself most fortunate." Joanna pirouetted on her heel and ran across to the starboard side of the ship, gripping the rail in her hands.

"I had no notion it would be so warm," she called to him over her shoulder.

Alex laughed. Merryn, he thought, would have been quizzing him about weather patterns, average temperatures and barometric-pressure readings. Joanna, in contrast, seemed quite happy to take at face value the fact that today it was relatively warm for the Arctic. She had no intellectual curiosity, unlike her sister.

"It will probably be snowing in an hour," he said.

Joanna looked at him dubiously. "Truly?"

"Possibly." Alex raised a shoulder in a shrug. "Predicting the weather is not an exact science, particularly here where matters can change dramatically in the space of a half hour."

"Oh, well…" Joanna smiled at him, an open and uncomplicated smile this time. "I shall simply have to enjoy this for as long as it lasts, then."

It was not, Alex realized with surprise, a bad philosophy. Perhaps, he thought, there was something to be said for living in the moment after all.

Joanna walked across the deck again, turning slowly to take in all aspects of the view. The sky was a perfect clear blue, the color of a duck egg.

"There is no smoke here to obscure the view," she said, "not like the London fogs. It is so light it almost hurts my eyes and the air is so clear and fresh it cuts like a knife. Everything sparkles!" There was an expression of astonishment on her face as she took in the jagged peaks of the mountains cut by glacier streams and the long white folds of snow on their flanks, as pale and soft as a blanket.

"So much snow," she whispered, "and so white it is

almost blue… I have never seen anything like it, not even when I was a child in the country and it snowed every winter."

She spun away from Alex again as though she could not keep still. "Where are the icebergs?" she demanded.

"There are no icebergs here," Alex said. "They do not form in the same way that they do to the northwest. No one knows why."

Joanna pouted with disappointment. "No icebergs? But there must be sea ice."

"Farther to the north," Alex said.

Her face lit up. "Oh, I would love to see it!"

"Perhaps you will," Alex said. "A ship from the Greenland fisheries came alongside this morning and told us the ice stretches a long way south this summer." He came to stand beside her at the rail. Her eyes were alight with excitement and so blue that they seemed to reflect the sky.

"I have never seen anywhere so empty," she whispered. She turned to him spontaneously. "It is very beautiful."

Alex felt his heart leap. He looked down into her face, so vivid and excited, more animated than he had ever seen her.

"Do you truly think so?" he said.

"Oh, yes…" He saw her shiver and wrap her arms about herself like a child hugging a treat to its heart. "I had no idea. I thought it would be dark and cold and miserable, or foggy and wet and miserable, or simply miserable. " She was laughing.

"It can be every one of those things," Alex said.

"I suppose so." The sparkle did not die from her eyes. "But on a day like this it is enchanted."

"And yet you hate the countryside in England," Alex said.

Joanna laughed. "So I do. I am very fickle."

They looked at one another for a long, long moment and Alex felt something warm unfurl inside him. "You are full of surprises, Joanna," he said slowly. "I thought that you would hate it here."

"I thought that I would, too," Joanna said. "I probably shall when it rains. And I detest the cold. But for now it is like paradise." She tilted her head to look at him. "I wondered why you became an explorer." Her voice was soft. "You said once that you felt a compulsion to travel and I did not understand it, but now…" She placed a hand on the rail and looked out across the water. "It is as though there is something out there, something hidden that calls to you and draws you on, and it gives you no rest…"

Alex felt the hairs rise on the back of his neck. Never in his life had anyone put into words the passion and the elemental mystery that he felt as an adventurer in distant lands. And now this woman, who did not share his passion, whom he would have sworn had absolutely no depth to her character, had spelled out more precisely than he could have done himself exactly how he felt… He had never shared such ideas with anyone, never spoken of them to Amelia or even to Ware and the others he had traveled with. They were locked inside him, a secret, the essence of his soul.

He stared at Joanna and her eyes widened in bewilderment to see the passion in his.

"That is it precisely," he said. He realized that his voice was a little rough. "That is exactly how I feel."

"Then I am sorry for it," Joanna said, turning away, "for I imagine it gives you no peace."

"But how did you know?" Alex put a hand out and caught hers. He felt disturbed, vulnerable in some odd way that he could not place, as though she had seen too much. "Did Ware tell you?"

"David?" She looked startled and then she laughed. "Hardly. I do not think David explored because he felt a compulsion to do so. He realized early on that it was a route to riches and fame and he exploited it as such. But you—" A smile had slipped into her eyes like the sun on the water. "You are different, are you not?"

"Yes," Alex said. "I am not like Ware."

He felt shock as soon as he had said it, as though he had in some way been disloyal, and yet he knew it to be true. He had seen the way in which David Ware had embraced his celebrity. He had understood Ware's values but they had not been his own.

He held Joanna's gaze with his own. For a long moment the emotion spun out between them and it felt sweet and fragile, but then the withdrawal came into her eyes and she freed herself from his touch. "I beg your pardon," she said with a hint of restraint. "We swore never to speak of David and I know it is very bad form to discuss a previous spouse with a current one."

"Joanna," Alex began. He was not sure what he wanted to say. All he was aware of was that for a moment they had shared a powerful affinity and he wanted it back. He was astonished by how much he wanted it. But Joanna had turned away from him and, following her gaze, he saw that Lottie Cummings was hurrying toward them across the deck. She was wrapped in furs to the neck, looking comically like a man dressed as a bear in a theatrical performance. Alex stifled a curse. The moment was broken.

"Lottie," Joanna called, "what do you think of Spitsbergen so far?"

"It is utterly ghastly, Jo darling," Lottie said. She gave an exaggerated shudder. "I am beginning to wish I had not come!"

The rest of the party, Alex thought dryly, had been thinking much the same thing for several weeks. Everyone, that was, with the exception of Devlin. It was impossible to keep secrets on a ship and Lottie's rapacious appetite for young men was much debated by the crew, and with ribald hilarity.

Joanna's face was registering vivid disappointment as she took in her friend's displeasure. "But you told me only a week ago that you were having an absolutely marvelous time!" she protested.

"Was it only a week?" Lottie said crossly. "It feels like years! I thought that the Arctic Circle would be more congenial once we got here. It sounds as though it should be interesting, but what do I find? Nothing! Where are all the people, where are the towns?" She flung out an arm. "Where are the trees? God knows, I never expected to feel the need of a tree until I was without one!"

For a moment Joanna's eyes met Alex's in a half-shy glance of shared amusement. He raised his brows and smiled at her.

"You did not comment on the lack of trees when we were speaking just now, Joanna," he murmured. He wondered whether she had the independence to express her own different views of the scenery when confronted by Mrs. Cummings's disapproval.

"No, I did not," Joanna agreed. "I do think it is a pity there is little greenery to soften the view." She took a breath. "But you must admit, Lottie, that it is spectacular. It is magnificent in its bleakness."

Alex smiled at her and saw her blush. That was Joanna, he thought suddenly, quick to smooth matters over, wanting to keep people happy. He remembered the way in which she had reassured Mr. Churchward over the matter of the will and felt a strange tug of emotion deep inside.

Lottie was giving her a look of extreme disapproval. "I think that your recent sickness has turned your mind, Jo darling! It is the most barren and unappealing place that I have seen in my life."

"Which rather begs the question of why you came," Joanna murmured. She slipped her hand through her friend's arm. "Come, let us go below and Hudson can make us a nice pot of tea to cheer you up—"

"Darling," Lottie said dramatically, "Hudson jumped ship in Shetland. He was the one who ran away with Lester, my maid! Do you not remember my complaining of it to you at the time?"

"I must have been too sick to hear you," Joanna said with a look of apology. "I did wonder why it was Frazer who came to me to act as lady's maid rather than Lester."

"Oh, Frazer has proved the most marvelous general factotum," Lottie said, waving an expressive hand. "He is as skilled at helping me dress and arranging my hair as any maid could possibly be."

"He is certainly very adept with the curling tongs," Joanna agreed.

"Surely it is most improper for Frazer to see a lady in a state of dishabille?" Alex queried. "I am surprised that his straitlaced soul can cope with it."

"Oh, Frazer tells me that he has seen many ladies in a state of undress," Joanna said with a wicked smile. "Before he joined the navy he worked as a tailor," she added, seeing Alex's look of blank astonishment. A little frown creased her brow. "Did he never tell you?"

"No," Alex said. "Frazer's past has always been shrouded in mystery." He wondered what else his dour steward had confided in his wife. "I hope," he said, unable to prevent himself, "that he has not been talking about me as well?"

"Why should he do that?" Joanna inquired lightly. "He is the soul of discretion."

"Of course," Alex said quickly. "Of course he is. It delights me to see you so restored to health that you wish to take some refreshment, Joanna," he continued, "but I am sorry to have to tell you that the china tea service broke in the storms. You will have to use a metal beaker. And," he added, "you had better make sure that the cook has not disinfected it with vinegar to get rid of the biscuit weevils."

Joanna shuddered. "Could this voyage be any more unpleasant, Alex darling?"

"A great deal more," Alex said a little grimly. His wife, it seemed, was slipping away from him again, back to her London persona, changing before his very eyes. He was determined to claim her back.

"Joanna—" he caught her hand as she made to sweep past him and drew her close "—a moment of your time…"

He dismissed Lottie with a polite nod and kept his gazed fixed on her when she seemed reluctant to depart. Eventually she flounced away, the bearskin coat flapping in the breeze.

"Alex?" Joanna said interrogatively.

"Yes," Alex said, his fingers tightening on hers. "Don't call me darling," he added. "Unless you mean it."

Her eyes narrowed. "It is only a form of words," she said defensively. "It means nothing."

"Precisely," Alex said. He looked down to where Max in his bright red coat was squashed between them. "And don't use that dog as a shield," he added. "He is too small to be an active combatant."

He leaned forward and kissed her. He sensed her surprise, but she made no move to withdraw from him and he felt fiercely glad. She parted her lips beneath his and she tasted delicious, sweet as honey, fresh and cold as snow. After a moment he took Max from her arms, placed the dog firmly on the deck and drew Joanna closer so that he could kiss her properly, long and deep, his arms tight around her. The huge red bonnet was getting in his way, so he unfastened the ribbons and cast it aside, running his fingers into Joanna's hair, undoing all of Frazer's careful pinning and curling. He heard Joanna give a muffled protest beneath his mouth and kissed her all the more insistently until he felt her yield again, her body softening against his, her fingers clutching his lapels to keep him close. His world contracted until it comprised Joanna and nothing else: her touch, her scent, her taste and his own driving need. He felt as though he could never get enough of her.

A gust of wind caught the ship, sending it heeling to starboard and shaking them apart. Alex caught Joanna's arms to steady her. She was breathless, her cheeks stung pink and bright by the cold northern wind, her eyes alight, her hair in blown curls wild about her shoulders. They stared at one another and Alex saw in Joanna's face stunned surprise and something else, something passionate and elemental that made his heart race. He felt a surge of power and possession so intense it shocked him. He raised his hand and touched her cheek tenderly and then he saw that they were not alone and allowed his hand to fall back to his side.

"There is no privacy on a ship," he said regretfully, smiling at her.

Dev had come up the companionway and had caught the red bonnet, which had bowled along the deck and almost gone flying over the side. He presented it to Joanna with an elaborate bow.

"Lady Grant…"

Joanna took the hat with a gracious word of thanks and a smile. She seemed to have recovered her poise, but when she gave Alex a quick, sideways glance of farewell he thought she still looked shy and a little stunned. She picked up Max and hurried away down the steps to join Lottie.

"I came to let you know that I will be traveling with you as far as Bellsund," Dev said, "and will take a party of men from there to Odden Bay to hunt for Ware's so-called treasure. It is only a short distance across the sound."

Alex nodded. He studied his cousin's face keenly. "You have told no one about the map, I hope," he said.

DEV LOOKED SHIFTY. "Of course not!" He sighed as gales of laughter wafted up from the deck below. "I had best go and remind the crew that it is not part of their duties to entertain Lady Grant. They are so charmed by her that they have quite forgotten that it is supposed to be bad luck to have a woman aboard." He laughed. "You're a lucky fellow, Alex. There isn't a man on this boat who doesn't envy you."

"Except you, I imagine," Alex said dryly.

Dev pulled a face. "Oh, Mrs. Cummings is very… accommodating…but Lady Grant is…" He paused, and Alex was astonished to see his cousin was actually blushing.

"Lady Grant is—what?" he inquired.

"Don't ask me to put it into words," Dev said, blushing harder and stumbling over his thoughts like a youth suffering the pangs of calf-love. "You know I'm not good at expressing myself." He frowned. "There is something untouched about Lady Grant, for all that she was a widow before she wed you." His frown deepened. "Perhaps I mean something unawakened." He shook his head. "Just now she looked like a princess in a fairy tale. And don't tell me not to be fanciful," he added as Alex opened his mouth to speak, "because I know you feel it, too. I saw the expression on your face."

"You see too damned much," Alex said. He did not particularly want to share that moment with anyone else. He was still trying to work it out himself. He had never felt like that before in his life.

"You know Purchase cares for her, don't you?" Dev continued. He shot Alex a look. "By which I mean that he is genuinely in love with her."

Alex narrowed his eyes. He thought back to the conversation that he had had with Owen Purchase in London. He was certain now that his friend had never been Joanna's lover, but that did not mean Purchase might not wish it to be so. Alex found that he did not like the idea. He did not like it at all, and his feelings had nothing to do with the need to be certain that his heir would be his own flesh and blood.

"Purchase would never play me false," he said, trying to ignore the primal instinct that made him want to go and find the man and kick him over the side of his own ship. "He's been my friend for years. And Joanna—" He thought of his wife, so warm and passionate in his arms, and of the look of shock on her face after they had kissed, as though she could not quite believe that what she was feeling was real. He had recognized that emotion—for he had felt it, too. "Joanna would not deceive me," he said slowly.

Dev was looking at him quizzically. "Why did you marry Lady Joanna, Alex?"

"From anyone else," Alex growled, "I would take that as an impertinent question."

"I'm curious," Dev said, unabashed. "You do not strike me as the sort of man to covet either Ware's fame or his wife, so…" He let the sentence hang.

"Is that what people think?" Alex was startled. "That I wish to take Ware's place?" He never paid attention to the *on dit,* but now he could see that the gossip might be that he wanted to step into Ware's shoes as society's hero explorer—and into his bed, too.

"This isn't about Joanna," he said, "Or about Ware, for that matter. It is about providing for Ware's child and giving Balvenie an heir."

He saw an odd expression come into Dev's eyes. "An heir?" his cousin said, and there was a note in his voice Alex could not quite place.

"You advised me to it yourself when I first returned to London," he said, frowning.

"So I did," Dev said. He avoided Alex's eyes. "Excuse me, Alex," he said abruptly. "Purchase will be needing me." And he walked off, leaving Alex wondering what on earth it was that he had said.

Chapter 12

"I AM NOT PRECISELY SURE," Joanna said after supper, sipping her tea from a metal beaker, "what one does on a ship to pass the time?" She and Alex were alone in the mess room, for Dev and Owen Purchase were up on deck and Lottie had disappeared to sort some clothes that required laundering. Joanna had been surprised to discover that she had developed an appetite again after so many days subsisting on a few mouthfuls of gruel and dry biscuits. That was until she had seen the meal that the cook had prepared for them, which had apparently been a beef and pease stew that resembled no meat Joanna had ever seen before. Mindful of Alex's gaze on her she had forced down a few mouthfuls without complaint and washed it down with some of the ship's beer. The drink had tasted vile, but something was needed to take away the flavor of the food.

"You could read," Alex said. "What about those books your sister gave you?"

"I find Dr. Von Buch's travel memoirs very dry," Joanna said. She had already started to use the pages as curling papers.

"And Captain Phipps's account of his expedition?" Alex asked.

"Full of tedious detail on ship's rations and information on reinforcement with beams and scantlings, whatever they may be," Joanna said. "I expect that you found it riveting, my lord?"

"Not in the least," Alex said. "Alas, poor Phipps should have stuck to sailing and left the writing to someone else." He toyed with his brandy glass, watching her with a keen look that made her skin prickle. "We could play chess if you wish," he murmured. "Or we could talk."

Talk.

Alex's sudden interest in her company outside of the marital bed seemed extraordinary, Joanna thought. Earlier on that day he had as good as told her that his only interest was in producing an heir. She had assumed that he would be extremely attentive to her in bed and practically ignore her out of it. And indeed, she knew plenty of couples whose marriages subsisted on the basis of the less conversation, the better. Yet now it seemed that Alex wanted to talk to her as well as make love to her.

"I expect that you would prefer to be working," she said, watching him set up the chessboard. "You do not strike me as a man who likes to be idle."

He smiled at her and she felt warmed by it. "You are correct, of course. I dislike inaction. But this evening I would rather be with you."

Extraordinary. Joanna could not imagine why he would wish for such a thing. She could feel herself blushing. She picked up one of the carved chess pieces in an attempt to cover her confusion. It was a deep cream color, smooth against her fingers. "Are these carved from bone?" she asked incredulously.

"Only whalebone, not human bones," Alex said. "Spitsbergen is a hunting ground for whalers." He looked up. "Where did you think all those fashionable accessories you love came from, Joanna?"

"I didn't think about it," Joanna admitted. "You mean things like handles for umbrellas and parasols, and stiffening for gowns—"

"And oil, and soap," Alex agreed.

Joanna shuddered. "I shall refuse to wear stays from now on."

Alex looked at her, a smile glinting in his eyes. "You shall not hear me complaining." He sat back, looking at her. "Wait until you see a whale, Joanna," he said, and once again Joanna heard in his voice the same pride and pleasure with which he had spoken of Spitsbergen itself. "They are the most magnificent and awe-inspiring creatures in the universe. A blue whale could overturn a ship with a flick of its tail if it chose."

"And who could blame it," Joanna said, "if man hunts whales to turn them into umbrella handles? Will we see blue whales here?" she asked.

"Rarely," Alex said. "Bowhead whales are hunted in these waters. You are a country girl," he added. "Surely you grew up accustomed to hunting."

"I did not care for it," Joanna said. "It is willfully cruel." She put the chess piece down. "It was not an opinion that found any favor with my uncle, I fear. He was a hunting parson of the old school."

Alex laughed. "Hunting, fishing, swearing and sermonizing?"

"Something of the sort." Joanna opened the play, advancing her pawn. "I learned to play chess because the alternative was to read his books of sermons."

The mess room settled down to quiet as they started the game. Joanna watched Alex's fingers as he moved the chess pieces around the board, long, strong, tanned fingers that she remembered against her skin with a little shiver. She forced herself to concentrate on the game. She did not want him to beat her. The light in the cabin had changed now from the bright white of day to the softer light of evening. Owen Purchase had told her that in these northern latitudes the sun never set in the summer. The paler light cast Alex's face into shadow, emphasizing the line of his cheekbone and jaw and the dent of frowning concentration between his brows.

Joanna won the game and she could see from the look in Alex's eyes that he was surprised.

"Another game?" she asked, smiling demurely. "I should like to give you the chance to even the score."

Alex sat up straight and moved his chair closer to the table as she reordered the board.

"You are competitive," Joanna said, giving him a sideways look. "You did not expect me to win."

Alex laughed reluctantly. "All right. I'll admit that I did not think chess would be your forte."

"Because you think that I am stupid." Joanna gestured to him to open, then moved her knights to flank his pawn.

"An aggressive ploy," Alex said. He looked up from the board. "And no, I have never thought you stupid."

"Shallow, extravagant and irresponsible," Joanna said. She took the pawn.

"I thought you all of those," Alex agreed, "but then I was judgmental."

"And arrogant," Joanna said sweetly.

The shadow of a smile touched his mouth. "I'll give you that."

This time she noticed that Alex paid her the

compliment of concentrating very hard on the game. When she castled, he narrowed his gaze on the board and renewed his attack.

"Check," he said, moving a bishop to take her king. His hand captured hers and she looked up to meet the brilliant gray of his eyes. She shook her head; freed herself.

"Checkmate," she said, taking his king with her queen and enjoying his look of complete confusion.

"Devil take it," he said. "What move was that?"

"The Queen's Triumph," Joanna said. "My uncle invented it. There was a great deal of fuss at first and correspondence flying back and forth, but in the end it was agreed that it is quite within the rules."

Alex was retracing the moves on the board. His gaze rested on her thoughtfully. There was admiration in it. "I should have seen it coming," he said.

"Indeed you should," Joanna said. The look in his eyes was making her feel breathless. "Would you like a chance to win back some pride at least?"

"No, thank you." Alex put his head on one side as he watched her stack the set away. "I can accept when I am bested."

"Then you are a very unusual man," Joanna said.

"I hope so."

The silence washed between them, taut and alive with sudden possibilities.

"I think I shall go up on deck for some fresh air before I retire," Joanna said abruptly, standing up. She knew what was going to happen between them and she was shocked at how nervous it was making her feel. She had slept with him before, she reminded herself desperately. It had been nice. In fact it had been more than nice. Nice did not do justice to the experience. There really was no need to be afraid…

Alex eased himself from his seat. "An excellent idea," he said. "I shall join you."

Panic gripped Joanna tightly. "You cannot retire when I do," she said. "I shall take at least two hours to get ready for bed and shall require Frazer's help—"

"It will be more fun to have mine." Alex held the mess-room door open for her most courteously. "I am sure that anything Frazer can do, I can do better."

"I require my sheets to be warmed," Joanna said, feeling even more nervous.

"I can do that," Alex said promptly.

"With a hot-water bottle," Joanna corrected. "And someone to unfasten my gown and brush my hair…" She stopped.

Alex spread his hand. "Again, I am most adept."

"At brushing hair?"

"At helping you out of your clothes," Alex said. His hand was warm on hers as he guided her up the companionway. "Accept it, Joanna." His breath brushed over her skin, raising goose bumps in its path. "You are my wife and I want you and if you had not been sick for the whole voyage, I would have been in your bed for the entire time. That is how to pass one's time on a ship and playing chess be damned."

The blunt assertion stole Joanna's breath. "You would have been in my bunk." Her voice sounded strained, even to her own ears. "That…that box downstairs cannot be dignified by the word *bed*."

"The precise description does not matter," Alex said. "I don't care what you call it, but I am your husband and I will occupy your cabin. With you." He paused.

"How singular. You have not argued with me yet. Can it be that for once we are in agreement?"

Joanna fidgeted. "You are asking this because…?"

"You are answering a question with a question. And you must be aware of the reason. I am asking it because I have a strong physical attraction to you and a desire to make love to you again." Alex sounded impatient, Joanna thought. Even, possibly, slightly annoyed. Her own feelings of annoyance prickled in return.

"Well, that is very like you," she said. "You admit to liking me—"

"No, I admit to finding you very attractive. Mere liking does not cover the situation at all."

"You admit to finding me attractive and then you make it sound like an insult." Joanna stamped up the steps to the sloop deck. "For about five minutes whilst we were playing chess I actually felt quite…quite in charity with you, Alex, but that is all gone now!" She threw out a hand in exasperation.

Alex trapped her body between him and the sloop-deck rail. "Give in to it," he said. "You know you want me, too." He kissed her, all heat and Arctic cold until the contrast made her head spin. "You are my wife and I want an heir," he whispered against her lips. "We had an agreement."

His words were like a shower of cold water over Joanna's burning skin. In an instant she remembered that Alex's need for an heir was his sole concern. It was why he had agreed to wed her and the reason that their marriage was built on sand. She and Alex had made a bargain. It was time for her to start paying.

Joanna took a deep breath. Frighteningly, treacherously, she found that she wanted to tell Alex the truth.

There had been a fragile truce between them that evening that could never grow to more if it was stunted by lies and deception. She could not make love with him again knowing that she was deliberately misleading him about their chances of conceiving an heir. Already she hated the dishonesty.

"Alex," she said again, "there is something I must tell you—"

"Darlings!" Lottie swooped down on them out of the shadows like an enormous moth and Joanna heard Alex swear under his breath. A feeling of relief overwhelmed her. Already her pitifully small stock of courage was fading and the moment for truth had passed.

"There really is no privacy on a ship," Alex said ruefully, releasing her. "Mrs. Cummings—" he bowed abruptly "—what may we do for you?"

"No one can sleep because it is so light," Lottie said, "and so I decided that we should have a little party instead." She gestured to a ragtag-and-bobtail group of the crew who were following her carrying a variety of musical instruments. "Mr. Davy tells me the crew are all prodigious musicians."

"Good gracious," Joanna said, glancing at Alex. "I had no idea sailors had so many talents."

Alex laughed. "Purchase's crew are all former navy men and they are trained to be competent in sewing, carpentry, sail-making, net-making, shoemaking and barbering, as well as proficiency on three musical instruments," he said. "And they have to be able to haul sledges and navigate by the stars."

"Goodness," Joanna murmured, wincing as the impromptu band started to tune up. "I had no notion.

I expect that their sewing is a deal neater than mine as well."

Alex drew her to one side of the deck as the band struck up a jig. Lottie was already dancing with the quartermaster. The crew were laughing and clapping and the music hung on the night air and the lanterns flared and the rum rations were passed around and the spirit burned Joanna's throat with its hot, sweet power and the night suddenly seemed brighter and more vivid still. Someone snatched her from the circle of Alex's arms and whirled her away and she spun across the deck in a wild dance, passed from hand to hand, the blue arch of the sky overhead, the cool night breeze on her face, the laughter ringing in her ears. Alex caught her and they twirled back into the dance and he refused Dev's laughing request to cut in, holding her close so Joanna could feel the beat of his heart thundering against hers. The rum came around again and she took some more and saw Alex shaking his head, but he was smiling. Eventually she was exhausted and Alex spread a rug on the deck in a quiet corner away from the melee and he drew her down to sit beside him. The wood was hard at her back, but Alex's arm was around her and his body warmed hers. She rested her head on his shoulder and felt the sky whirl overhead.

"I do not imagine it is always like this," she said dreamily. "In the winter it must be bleak beyond belief."

"Yes," Alex said. "One winter that I spent in Spitsbergen was as a very young midshipman on one of Phipps's expeditions. We became trapped in the ice and we thought the ship would be crushed. We managed to cut away the ice around the ship so that it sat in a pond of water, but there was no way in which we could escape." He gave a short laugh. "Tempers became very frayed that year."

"What happened?" Joanna asked. Sitting here on this balmy night within the protection of Alex's arms it was so difficult to believe that this land could kill as well as delight, even though she knew that David himself had died here.

"Our senior officers kept us all very, very busy," Alex said. "We were roused by a bugle call for breakfast and then obliged to run around the ship for two hours on the ice. We measured out a track and marked it with posts and lighted it with lanterns. We called it Rotten Row."

Joanna laughed. "Did you all survive?"

"The food almost killed us even though the ice did not," Alex said. "We were lucky to escape with our lives."

Joanna shivered, as though David's shadow had fallen between them. Alex did not speak, but she knew that he, too, was thinking of his friend. Joanna snuggled closer to him, trying to banish the ghosts. For a moment he did not respond and there was a stiffness in his body, as though he was resisting the intimacy, but then he sighed and drew her close, his cheek against her hair. The night was getting cooler. She shivered a little.

"Are you cold?" Alex asked.

"No," Joanna said. "I am afraid."

"Of the journey?"

"Of what is waiting at the end of it," Joanna said. "There is so much that is unknown." She tilted her head so that she could look at him. She did not know why she was confiding in him. Perhaps it was the rum loosening her tongue. He was not a man who invited confidences, she thought. He was too reserved, too well defended to approach. The sun had dipped behind the mountains now and the polar dusk was full of long shadows. It was impossible to see Alex's expression.

"You have set so much store by finding Nina and giving her a good home," he said. "It would be strange if you did not have some anxiety now that you are so close."

"Anxiety!" Joanna said before she could help herself. "I am terrified!"

She thought he was smiling. "There is no shame in being afraid," he said. "You are venturing into the unknown. You are very brave, Joanna."

Joanna was so startled that for a moment she was silent. "Do you think so?" she said slowly. "I thought that venturing into the unknown was to sail the seven seas and trek through uninhabited lands and that courage was to shoot dangerous wild beasts."

Alex laughed. "You mistake. Courage is facing the things that frighten us, the things that we do not want to do. Courage is mastering that fear, not allowing it to dictate to us." He shifted. "You did not want to have to come here, but you came. You did not let your fear dictate your actions. That is true bravery."

Joanna shivered at his words. She was feeling anything but brave. Alex took his coat off and placed it about her shoulders. Immediately she felt enclosed, protected in some mysterious way by his presence. The coat smelled of him, of cedar cologne and cold Arctic air and she wanted to draw it close about her even as she made a feeble attempt to give it back.

"Oh, no!" she said as she saw him in the crisp white

of his shirtsleeves. "You will literally freeze out here without a jacket!"

"We shall go below shortly," Alex said. He bent his head to kiss her again and this time the warmth unfurled in her stomach in a slow curl of sensual pleasure. Navy rum rations, she thought hazily, were a wonderful thing. They lulled her fears and smoothed the hard edges from the guilt that stabbed her each time she thought of her deceitful bargain with Alex.

"I am glad that you came with me," she whispered.

She felt him go very still for a moment and then he rubbed his cheek against her hair. "Truly?" he said. There was an odd note in his voice.

"Truly." She felt very warm and grateful and happy. "Thank you. You're prickly," she added sleepily, irrelevantly, raising a hand experimentally to rub the stubble on his lean cheek. "A gentleman always shaves, no matter the situation."

She thought she heard him groan at the soft touch of her fingers on his skin.

"Enough," he said, capturing her hand in his and kissing her fingers. "It is not my style to make love to a woman who is three sheets to the wind, but you do tempt me."

"I am not so very foxed," Joanna whispered.

"Then you give me no choice." He had swept her up in his arms even before she had caught her breath and was carrying her away from the light and the laughter and the noise, down the companionway into the secret darkness below. Joanna's world rocked with the gentle shift of the ship on the swell. There was hot excitement inside her and Alex's arms about her were like steel, sure and hard. He placed her gently on her feet outside the cabin and pressed her back against the door, kissing her, his tongue stroking deeply. The pleasure rippled through Joanna and she made a soft sound of need in her throat. Alex held her trapped against the door and kissed her long and lingeringly until they were both gasping for breath.

He flung open the cabin door and they tumbled inside. Joanna looked at the tiny box bunk.

"How do we—" she started to say.

Alex silenced her with a finger against her lips. He slid his hand into her hair, tilting her head up so that he could kiss her throat. Joanna could feel his smile against her skin as his lips grazed the hollow behind her ear. His teeth nipped the tender line of her neck and she squirmed. She wanted to tell him to be careful he didn't tear the Gothic-style ruffles on her bodice—and God forbid that he rip one of the flounces on the hem of her gown—but the worry was lost in a tide of sensation so sweet and fierce that she shook with it.

Alex pushed the bodice of her gown down to free one of her breasts and held it in his palm, tugging gently on the nipple, rolling her between his finger and thumb until she groaned. In all her twenty-seven years, Joanna thought faintly, she had had no idea that her body could provide her with such exquisite delight. It was a shocking revelation. She was afraid that her legs were going to give way completely.

Alex bent down and slowly circled the nipple with his tongue. Joanna gasped and he drew her into his mouth, biting gently down, sucking and teasing until she moaned. It was such delicious torture. She could feel her muscles jump and quiver, feel a heat in the pit of her stomach that built and burned. And then she felt him lift her until she was sitting on the high edge of the bunk, and he fell to his knees and his hands were beneath her petticoats, hot on her skin through the silk of her drawers. He tugged the ribbon at her waist and Joanna felt the material ease and then he was pulling them down. He pushed up her skirts with all their ruffles and flounces so that they foamed over the white skin of her thighs, leaving her silk stockings with their pretty red ribbons exposed and above that the pale expanse of her naked skin.

It was too much. Joanna's body felt hot and tight and ready to explode. She grabbed Alex's shoulders, her fingers digging into him through the material of his shirt, and dragged him to her so she could kiss him again, her mouth slanted against his, her nipples pressed hard and tight against the barrier of his chest. Without breaking the kiss Alex stood and Joanna stretched up, raising herself to keep her mouth beneath his and keep that sweet, demanding contact. The bunk was high and she was straining to maintain the connection between them, bracing her hands behind her on the bed, her muscles taut as she tilted her head back to take Alex's kiss.

"Don't move." His whisper was laced with wickedness. He eased back and Joanna opened her eyes to see that he was looking at her and his gaze was intent and hot. In a flash she knew what she must look like, her hair spread about her bare shoulders, one breast cupped by the neckline of her gown and thrust forward by the position she was in, as though begging for his hands and his mouth on her. She gave a little moan and Alex lowered his head and kissed the underside of her breast, running his tongue up to the nipple and making her catch her breath on a scream. The skin all over her body rose instantly into goose bumps, sensitive to the slightest touch.

She felt Alex's hands move, heard something give, then felt him pull her forward so that she was sitting on the very edge of the bunk. His fingers were against the softness of her inner thigh, parting her to his touch, drifting over her hip and her stomach, returning to her cleft to torment and tease. She shifted forward instinctively and then he was pressing inside her slick heat and she gasped in relief. She strained forward wanting all of him, but he held back. Each gentle sway of the ship against the tide eased him a little deeper inside her then out, until Joanna started to wish they were in the teeth of a gale again. She wanted more than this gentle torment. She wanted all of him. She squirmed, but the position he was holding her in made it impossible to drive him deeper. His hands were on her bare thighs above the stockings, forcing her legs wide apart, and she had to keep herself braced against the bunk in order not to tumble backward. She was shaking all over, the muscles in her stomach tightening and jumping with intolerable need.

"Alex! No, no more!" She almost felt like crying. It was too much. The shimmer of intense desire and the force of such overwhelming emotion threatened to overcome her.

"Please," she begged. "I cannot bear it."

Alex leaned forward and kissed her lightly and the movement brought his body more tightly into hers and she whimpered with dazed pleasure. He slid his hands beneath her hips and lifted her, forcing her at last to take all of him, driving in and pulling out, hurling her body into a tender, terrifying climax. She was conquered, mastered, and yet she felt powerful and triumphant and shaken to the core by the strength of the emotion within her. Tears prickled behind her eyelids and she did not understand why. Her body felt soft, satiated. She felt Alex's hands move over her, undressing her, easing her onto the bunk where he lay curved behind her, his chest against her back.

"We can sleep like this," he said. His arms were about her. It felt astonishingly comfortable. She had not felt so safe in a very long time.

Chapter 13

THE BUGLE CALL AT SIX O'CLOCK in the morning almost split Alex's head in two. "Goddamn Purchase," he muttered under his breath. He rubbed his face. Joanna had been right last night. He was in dire need of a shave.

Alex rolled over. Joanna was lying beside him in a tangle of honey-brown hair, and the bugle call had not even caused her to stir. She felt so warm and soft and smelled so sweet that for the first time in his navy career Alex was tempted to ignore reveille and stay exactly where he was. For a few moments he simply lay watching her. There was something so trusting and vulnerable about Joanna in sleep, so different from the guarded woman who hid beneath that superficial carapace. He kept getting glimpses of a different Joanna, but the more he grasped after them, the more they seemed to slip from his reach. He was not even sure why he wanted to know her better. He had gone into this arrangement asking nothing of her except that she provide him with an heir and make no emotional demands upon him, but it was proving impossible to remain so detached. Last night, he thought, he had not even been thinking about conceiving his heir. Good old-fashioned lust had driven such thoughts from his mind and it had been Joanna he had wanted, not the son she would give him. And yet it was not even as simple as lust. He was committed somehow when he had sworn he would not be. He had thought the extent of his obligation would be no more than a practical matter, ensuring Joanna's physical safety on the journey, but from the moment he had kissed her the day before, it had turned into something far greater than that.

"I am glad that you came with me," she had whispered the previous night and he had felt as though all the breath had been knocked from his body when he had heard those words. After she had spoken he had waited to feel the familiar chafing of responsibility and the urge to be free. It had not happened. Hell, he was even beginning to like the thought of being with Joanna, and that was more frightening than the most dangerous physical adversity he had ever been in.

His body tightened with something that felt like tenderness. Slowly, almost reluctantly, he put out a hand to touch Joanna's cheek.

He touched fur instead. Recoiling, Alex saw that Max had at some point insinuated himself between their bodies and was curled up in a warm, happy, snoring ball. The dog opened one eye, gave Alex a look of profound triumph and went back to sleep.

The bugle call sounded again, its note sharp and urgent. Something was wrong, Alex thought. He rolled out of the bunk and stood up, grabbing his clothes and dressing haphazardly. He could hear shouts from above now and the pounding of feet. Joanna had woken and was sitting up in the bunk, the covers clutched to her breast. She looked confused and sleepy and scared.

"Alex?" Her voice was blurred with sleep. "What is happening? Is something wrong?"

"No," Alex said. "Don't worry. I'll be back soon."

He bent to give her a hasty kiss. Remembering that it took her about two hours to dress, he added, "Perhaps you should get up, though."

He staggered up on deck and emptied a pail of cold water over his head. Dev, looking as fresh as a daisy, Alex thought sourly, pressed a beaker of cocoa into his hands.

"You're too old to drink so much rum," his cousin said unsympathetically. "You look like death. Or perhaps it is that you are too old to indulge in other excesses—"

"Enough," Alex snapped. He looked across to where Owen Purchase was deep in conversation with the coxswain. "What's the emergency?"

"Sea ice," Dev said succinctly. "The wind turned a half hour ago and the ice is forcing us in to the shore."

Alex walked across to the side. The wind was cold and keen today and the sky gray. He could see the difficulty; the northwesterly was forcing the slabs of ice ahead of it, pushing them toward the ship, fencing *Sea Witch* in against the rocky shoreline. A mere fifty yards to the west the water was clear, a mocking, shining path away from danger. But they could not reach it and within a half hour, he thought, they would either be completely trapped in the ice or they would be wrecked on the rocks.

"What do you think?" Purchase spoke urgently to him from close by.

"We don't have any choice," Alex said grimly. "If we wait, we'll either run aground or be crushed." He glanced across to the open sea. "We'll have to cut our way through to open water and we'll have to do it now."

He heard the captain draw a sharp breath. "I've never

done that before," Purchase said. "It's bloody dangerous. The ice is unstable—"

"I've done it before," Alex said, "and it isn't as dangerous as sitting here waiting to be shipwrecked." He nodded to Dev. "Bring the saws."

As Dev sped away, Alex turned to see that Joanna had come up on deck. He stifled a groan, wishing he had told her to stay in the cabin rather than get up and get dressed. He had no wish to deal with female hysterics at a time like this.

"Alex!" Joanna came across to him and put a hand on his arm. Her face was pale. "What is going on?"

"Nothing," Alex said. "Go back below."

He spoke abruptly and he saw Joanna's chin come up and her face set into stubborn lines. There was a spark of anger and obstinacy in her blue eyes.

"No," she said. "I shall not. Not until you tell me what is happening."

"The ship is trapped in the ice, Lady Grant," Purchase said. "Lord Grant is going to cut us a path through to the open sea."

Joanna flicked a look at him then focused back on Alex's face.

"Isn't that rather dangerous?" she whispered.

"Yes," Alex said. "It is. But if I don't do it we will all perish." He heard Purchase give a murmur of protest, not at the truth of his words but at the brutal way he had expressed himself.

Joanna's face paled even further. Her eyes burned as bright blue as sapphires now. Alex watched her, waited.

"You might drown," she said, and it was not a question. She looked again from him to Purchase and beyond them to the waiting crew: Dev with the ice saws, men with ropes and ladders. Alex saw her shiver as she picked up on the tension in the air. His blood beat hard with anticipation and the need to be gone, to get the job done.

"I had not thought that I would be a widow again so soon," Joanna said. "It is not to my liking." She grabbed Alex by the coat and pulled him close. Her breath warmed his lips.

"Be careful," she said in a fierce whisper. There was something in her eyes that made his heart leap. She pressed a kiss on his cheek, released him and moved over to the rail, making it plain that she was prepared to stay there all day.

The men were grinning and Purchase gave him the ghost of a wink. "Seems you have something to come back for, Grant," he said.

"Yes," Alex said. He glanced across at Joanna. Someone had brought her a blanket and a cup of cocoa and she sat huddled up in a corner of the deck, a small but dignified figure. She was watching him. Something caught and burned inside him.

Something to live for…

For too long he had not believed there was anything truly worth living for.

Dev threw the rope ladder down and he went over the side.

JOANNA WAS COLDER THAN she had ever been in her life. She felt as though her hands, despite their fur-lined gloves, had been frozen to the ship's rail like a bird on a twig. The chill was bone deep, enough to turn the blood cold.

She could not believe that the beautiful country she had fallen in love with the day before had turned into this spiteful, gray wilderness with a lowering sky and a biting wind edged with snow. Their progress out of the ice field had been tortuously slow. She had watched, her heart in her mouth, as Alex and Devlin had balanced on the ice floes, cutting what looked like a tiny clear path through the slabs that imprisoned them. As the water opened up, Owen Purchase eased the *Sea Witch* forward inch by slow inch, the sails trimmed to catch a breeze to help them whilst at the same time trying to make sure the wind did not drive them farther into a frozen wasteland. Every creak, every groan of the ship seemed magnified as the ice scored along their sides and closed in behind them as they passed. And always out of reach, the tantalizing clear blue ribbon of water that would see them to freedom.

"You have been out here all day," Lottie scolded, appearing at one point in three layers of sealskin and with a bowl of hot broth for Joanna clasped firmly in her hands. "Come belowdecks before you catch an ague."

"I cannot," Joanna said, teeth chattering. "I need to know that Alex is safe."

Lottie had gone away and Joanna had drunk the broth and tried to warm her hands on the bowl, and then, despite the cold, she thought she must have fallen into a doze, for she was not sure how much time passed. She was awoken by a grinding, splintering crash; the ship shuddered and then lurched forward as the wind cracked in the sails overhead, pulling them at last into the open sea. There was a shout from the bows, men were running, the rope ladder went down again and then Alex and Devlin were pulling themselves back over the side, and the crew were laughing and slapping them on the back as the ship turned into the wind and set a course north.

Joanna took a step forward, stumbling a little with cold and stiffness. Across the wide deck Alex saw her and stood quite still for a moment. Then he was beside her, grabbing her by the arms, fury in his eyes, but beneath it puzzlement and another emotion that made her heart miss a beat.

"Have you been out here all day?" he snapped.

His coat was soaking wet and ice-cold beneath Joanna's fingers. There were snowflakes on his eyelashes.

"Yes," Joanna said.

"You could have frozen to death!" Alex roared. A muscle was working in his jaw. "Have you no sense?"

"About as much as you," Joanna said, "standing here berating me when you should be belowdecks getting out of those wet clothes."

They stood staring at one another for a second in bafflement and anger, and then Alex grabbed her and kissed her so hard her head spun, then more gently, tenderly, the kiss melting into a conversation without words that made Joanna unutterably glad that she had not broken faith with him. When he let her go Alex kept hold of her hand, turning it against his heart. He did not say anything and he was still frowning, but he did not let her go.

Joanna felt icy cold and burning hot both at the same time, vibrantly alive, her emotions in turmoil. She knew she was falling in love with Alex. Her head had warned her against it but her heart had not been listening and had taken the leap. Even as she felt his fingers entwine with hers and watched the snowflakes melt against his cheek she felt herself sliding deeper, more helplessly in love.

He is another adventurer, whispered the voice in her head, and even though she knew Alex was not like David, she shivered. Not so long ago she had wanted him gone so that she could forget the wicked deception she was practicing on him. Now she ached for him to stay with her even though she was haunted each day by the knowledge that their marriage was based on a sham. She was trapped.

TWO DAYS LATER THEY SAILED into the shelter of Isfjorden.

"We shall be starting at seven tomorrow morning," Alex said, drawing Joanna to one side after the customary evening dinner of stewed beef and biscuits. "The ice is too thick at present for us to sail into Bellsund Sound, so we will drop anchor here and travel overland."

Joanna, he thought, looked distinctly displeased. "Seven o'clock?" she said, sighing. "To think that in London I rarely set foot out of bed before eleven!"

"I'm afraid that you will have to be a great deal more prompt than that tomorrow," Alex said. "And you and Mrs. Cummings will have to travel in the supply cart. It will not be what you are accustomed to, but there are no carriages—and barely any roads—in Spitsbergen."

"I shall ride," Joanna contradicted him. "I have had the most perfect habit made for me in London and I do not intend to waste it. There are breeches so I can ride astride, and a fitted military-style jacket—" The rest of her description was totally lost on Alex, banished by the vision that her words had conjured up.

Joanna was going to be wearing breeches and riding astride?

In all his plans and thoughts about this trip and the difficulties he would encounter along the way, Alex had not calculated that there would be any fashion-induced ones. He looked at Joanna and tried to imagine the effect that her figure in a pair of breeches and tight jacket might have on Purchase's crew. He was all too aware of the effect that the mere thought was having on him. For three nights he had slaked his lust in his wife's bed and yet the desire he felt for her was not diminishing in any way. In fact, since the day she had stubbornly insisted on keeping watch whilst he and Dev had freed the ship from the ice, his need for her had been edged with something far deeper and more complicated. Even before that he had felt himself slipping into uncharted waters and had been powerless to prevent it. Now his need for her drove him to seek out her company even if it was only to take a turn about the deck together in fine weather, or to talk, or to play chess. She always beat him. He was resigned to it by now.

"I had better ask Purchase to send only those men with us who are old or infirm," he said now. He looked at her and shook his head. "We shall see how long you can endure being in the saddle," he added. "This isn't like riding in Hyde Park, you know."

Joanna arched her brows at him in a look of challenge he was beginning to know. "You said yourself that I was a country girl," she said. "I'll wager I can last as long in the saddle as you."

"Fifty guineas says you shall not," Alex said.

She turned and put both hands against his chest. "I'll win," she promised, smiling. "Again. You'll see."

The following morning Alex wished he had wagered on how long it would take Joanna to get ready rather than on whether she would be able to ride for the entire day. Purchase sounded reveille at six; an hour later there was no sign of either Joanna or Lottie Cummings.

"I do not suppose," Alex said grimly to Dev, "that there is the slightest chance of Mrs. Cummings being ready to travel within another hour?"

"Not the slightest," Dev said, grinning. "You had best call up reinforcements and send Frazer in."

Lottie appeared within an hour and a half, and after waiting a further thirty minutes, Alex stormed down the companionway and into Joanna's cabin without knocking.

And stopped dead.

His wife, her hair in one long thick plait, was sitting on the edge of the bunk wearing the most provocative outfit he had ever seen her in. Merely the sight of her perched there was sufficient to bring back heated images of every night they had spent together, enhanced now by her outrageous riding habit. Buff-colored pantaloons were molded to her shapely thighs. The navy-blue jacket was nipped in at the waist and seemed to strain over the curve of her breasts. Alex's mouth went dry. His mind went completely blank. His body clenched.

"Am I late?" Joanna said anxiously, misreading his expression. "I am so sorry. I cannot get the boots on."

She gestured toward a pair of shiny black hussar boots with jaunty tassels.

"It's like trying to force a greased pig into a rabbit hutch," Frazer said sourly from his place on the floor. "Cannot be done, my lord."

Shaking his head, Alex got down on one knee and

with much pushing and pulling he and his steward finally inserted Joanna into her boots.

"Even Mrs. Cummings was ready before you," Alex said as he helped her to her feet. He looked at her. Now she was standing up, the outfit seemed even more outrageous than before, for the jacket was short and the pantaloons skimmed over the curve of her bottom. Rolling his eyes at Frazer and resisting the urge to cover her up with a blanket, Alex ushered her out of the cabin.

By the time Joanna had mounted the steps to the deck and then climbed down the side of the rope ladder into the longboat, it seemed that every sailor on the *Sea Witch* had found a reason to pause in their work and watch the disembarkation. It was fortunate, Alex thought grimly, that the sea was calm and the ladder was not rocking too violently, because at least the exercise was over relatively quickly even if it did leave him wishing to plant several men a facer for the way in which they were staring at his wife. Owen Purchase and Dev, barely able to hide their appreciation, rowed the longboat across to shore. Lottie, clearly envious of the attention Joanna was drawing, was pointedly ignoring Dev and made a big fuss about having to climb out on the shingle. She insisted that Purchase carry her up the beach to where the horses were waiting so that she did not splash her riding habit.

"What on earth is that?" she asked disagreeably, pointing at one of the shaggy ponies that the Russian Pomor guide had brought down to the beach for them. "It certainly isn't a horse!"

"Highly bred horses would break their legs in this terrain," Alex said, "whereas these tough little ponies are bred to it. Have you changed your mind about riding now, Mrs. Cummings?"

"No," Lottie said hastily, giving Purchase a charming smile and pressing her body blatantly against his as he lifted her into the sidesaddle. "I want to see the country."

"You will only see half the country if you ride side-saddle, Lottie," Joanna pointed out as Alex bent to give her a leg up. "Would you not prefer to try to ride astride?"

"Not on a horse, I thank you," Lottie said, making Dev blush.

Joanna swung expertly up into the saddle, leaving Alex looking at Dev in blank astonishment. She took the reins from the guide and thanked him very prettily in Russian. Alex's jaw almost hit the floor and the man's face cracked into an appreciative smile.

Catching her husband's look of utter incredulity, Joanna blushed. "Merryn taught me a few phrases of Russian before we left England," she said. "I thought it would help. Though I'm not very good," she added. "They probably will not understand me at all."

Alex felt stunned. He also felt a little ashamed of himself that he had assumed Joanna to be so wrapped up in herself that she would not even think of learning the language. He saw Owen Purchase give Joanna a smile and a strange possessive pride and an equally strong jealousy gripped him like a vise. He brought his pony alongside hers, cutting the other man out.

They rode all day. The weather was fair, Spitsbergen looking as beautiful as Alex had ever seen it. The breeze was soft and from the south. Tiny yellow poppies grew through the black rocks.

"There is crowfoot," Alex said. "It is prolific here in the summer."

"How charming," Joanna said. "Look, Lottie!"

"Darling," Lottie said, "I really cannot get excited over a plant that is so small and green."

They saw no one all day. Joanna was at first talkative, exclaiming over the view, asking questions, but as the day went on she fell silent and as the afternoon progressed Alex could see that she was swaying with tiredness in the saddle. He tried to persuade her to ride in the provisions cart, but she set her lips mulishly and said she would carry on. Alex admired her determination, but wanted to shake her for her stubbornness.

"You have nothing to prove," he argued when they stopped to water the horses. "Devil take it, you have already bested me at chess and shown that you have the stamina to ride across rough terrain for hours!" He gestured toward the cart, where Lottie was sitting looking bad-tempered amidst the packing cases. "For pity's sake, take a rest!"

"It would not be a rest if I was obliged to listen to Lottie's complaints," Joanna said, hauling herself up into the saddle again. "Nor is a cart a mode of transport I could bring myself to use." She smiled suddenly. "Lottie's reputation for style would never recover, you know, if it were noised about the ton that she had traveled alongside a sack of dry biscuits."

By the time Alex called a halt to the day's journey, on the edge of a small inlet, he could see that Joanna was almost asleep in the saddle. He lifted her down, holding her gently, feeling tenderness and compassion for her, mixed with exasperation. She was white with fatigue by now.

"You have only yourself to blame," he said more roughly than he had intended, strangely moved by her spirit and determination.

"I know." She smiled at him. "You are right, as always."

Alex's lips twitched. "I suppose you think I am being judgmental again."

"You can safely leave me to make my own mistakes," Joanna said, "though I appreciate your concern." She looked around. "Where are we to stay tonight?"

Alex nodded in the direction of the shore. "We stay in that trappers' hut."

It was a long, low building, scarcely more than a box that looked as though it had been tossed onto the beach by an angry sea. Around it were scattered bones bleached white by the sun and the tides. Seeing them, Lottie gave a theatrical shriek and threw herself into Owen Purchase's arms.

"Darling, where on earth have you brought us?"

The guide was laughing and Alex translated for them.

"He says it was the home of a Norwegian trapper who hunted bears and Arctic foxes and eider duck last winter."

"He left enough bits of them behind," Lottie grumbled.

"Oh…" Joanna's gasp was a half laugh, half groan. "I suppose there is no hot water?"

"Not until we find some and heat it up," Alex said.

"Food?"

Alex nodded toward the cart. "We will make some porridge and cocoa once the fire is lit."

Joanna pulled a face. Alex waited for her to complain

at the paucity of their supplies, but she was silent. Lottie, on the other hand, was voicing sufficient grumbles for two.

"What can I do to help?" Joanna asked after a moment.

"You can collect birch wood for the fire," Alex said. "It burns well. You'll find some washed up on the beach. But don't venture out of sight," he added. "There is always a danger from the bears."

Joanna nodded. Alex watched her walk over to Lottie. He saw Lottie shake her head, saw Joanna say something to her and saw Lottie shake her head again.

"Darling." Lottie's voice floated to him across the still Arctic air. "What is the point of being surrounded by so many strapping young men if we have to lift a finger ourselves? No, indeed, I intend to wait here until someone fetches me food and drink. I have paid for this trip, you know."

"Remind me," Owen Purchase said a little grimly in Alex's ear, "why I allowed that woman to join us on this trip."

"Because she is rich and Dev wanted to sleep with her," Alex said, equally grimly.

Purchase laughed. "She is behaving exactly as I imagined she would," he said. He shook his head. "It's the devil of a thing to be proved right."

"Whereas Joanna," Alex said, his eyes following the slim figure of his wife as she walked along the beach, bending every so often to pick up pieces of flotsam, "is the reverse."

"Not at all," Purchase said. His eyes met Alex's and held them for a long moment. "Lady Grant is behaving exactly as I knew she would," Purchase said. "You are the one whose expectations were all wrong, Grant." He nodded briskly and walked away, leaving Alex staring after him.

JOANNA LAY BACK AGAINST the soft furs of the dogsled, Max curled up by her side. Alex had been quite right; it was a deal more comfortable than riding. She had ached all over last night. Waking up in the morning had been worse, though. She was covered in dust, her skin felt gritty and rough and her hair was dull and lifeless. She had found a tin plate and had peered at her appearance in it and then she had wished she had not bothered, for she looked appalling, worse even than she had when she was sick on the ship. She had not thought that possible. Now she could see it was.

Breakfast consisted of strips of the most disgusting meat that Joanna had ever tasted washed down with cold water. The weather had changed and in the thick damp mist the fire had refused to light, spitting and hissing, so there had been no cocoa.

"This is salted seal meat," Dev had confided in her as he passed her a plate of what had looked like boiled leather. "Pray do not tell Mrs. Cummings, though. She thinks it is salt beef."

They ate largely in silence, even Lottie, who, extraordinarily, seemed to have run out of things to complain about. But at least today, Joanna thought, stretching luxuriously against the rich warmth of the fur-lined sledge, with Max's little body pressed cozily against her, they were crossing the mountain passes and so would be traveling over snow not the rocky terrain that lay lower down the mountains.

There was absolutely nothing to see. The mist pressed

closer than a smothering blanket, lifting only occasionally to reveal mountains as black as coal. The snow hissed beneath the blades of the sledge. Joanna could not believe that a country that had looked so beautiful the day before could now seem so comfortless, pewter from horizon to horizon, dark, stony and disheartening.

"Everything is so gray," she had complained when they set out.

"Most quelling," Lottie had agreed as she had scrambled in beside Joanna into the fur-lined interior of the sledge. She had at first refused to ride in it, claiming that she had never seen dogs with such mad blue eyes and that she did not trust them not to overturn the sled. "Gray has never been one of my favorite colors," she had added. "It is too draining for my complexion."

"Alex tells me that this is good weather and that sometimes it can rain for twenty days on end," Joanna said glumly. "That is when it is not snowing. So perhaps we should count ourselves lucky."

"Darling," Lottie said, "there is nothing in the least to be grateful for in this godforsaken country. Are you regretting coming?" she added, fixing Joanna with her bright dark gaze. "I cannot believe that David's little bastard can possibly be worth all this trouble when we could be strolling in the park now or trying hats at Mrs. Piggott's shop." She did not wait for a reply but chattered on: "Did you hear that the Parisian bonnet will be all the rage this winter? It is Lady Cholmondeley who sponsors the trend and says that it should be decorated with flowers, but I have in mind to thwart her by announcing that I prefer fruit on mine. I intend to have the sweetest little beaver hat made especially and adorned with plums and apricots. What do you think?"

Joannà, whose mind had drifted away to fret over her first meeting with Nina, jumped.

"I beg your pardon, Lottie," she said. "I was not attending."

"Why on earth not?" Lottie looked affronted.

"I was thinking about Nina," Joanna confessed, "and whether she will like the toys that I have brought for her."

"Darling!" Lottie's face cleared. "Of course she will! They are from Hamleys! She will love them! She has probably never even seen a toy before, locked up in that ghastly place with a bunch of monks!"

Joanna frowned. "I suppose not. It is true that I can give her plenty of things that she will never have had before—"

"Toys, and pretty clothes." Lottie nodded sagely. "Only think what fun we will have back in London, darling, dressing a little girl in miniature versions of all the latest fashions. Why, she will be just like a doll!" Lottie's face fell. "At least she will be if she is pretty. I am not sure what we shall do with her if she is not."

"Lottie," Joanna said, "Nina is not a toy herself."

Her head was aching. Suddenly she wanted to cry and she was not entirely certain why. Surely Nina would be delighted to have so many gifts and presents showered on her. What child would not? And yet… Joanna thought of the box of balls and spinning tops and dolls that was bouncing about in the provisions cart and anxiety clutched at her and she was not quite sure why. She wanted to talk to Alex, draw comfort somehow from sharing her fears with him, but he was riding with Dev and Owen and their guide up ahead.

Late in the afternoon they drove into a tiny settlement of huts on the edge of another wide fjord. Karl, the Pomor guide, was bursting with pride.

"This is his home, is it not?" Joanna said as Alex helped them out of the sleigh. "That much Russian I do understand."

She looked about her. The village was no more than a bunch of cabins grouped along the edge of the strand, but it looked sturdy and was built of brick rather than the driftwood of the trappers' hut the previous night. There was a forge and a couple of storage barns and a long low building that looked like a hall. On a little hill overlooking the ocean stood a large wooden cross.

"The Pomors are a very spiritual people," Alex said. "They use the crosses for navigation as well as worship. The monastery at Bellsund is only a day's ride from here and there have always been strong links between the village and the abbey."

The villagers were coming out to greet them now, hunters in leather jerkins and women in white aprons with children hiding behind their skirts.

"I did not realize that people lived her all year round," Joanna said. "Merryn's book implied that the settlements were mainly used for overwintering."

"So you did read it!" Alex said, smiling at her. "I thought that books bored you."

"I flicked through a few chapters," Joanna murmured.

"It is the Norwegians who tend to visit just for the hunting and trapping," Alex said. "Some of the Pomors have lived here for many years and as you see, they bring their families with them."

"They must be very hardy," Joanna said.

Lottie, she saw, was looking about her with her customary disdain.

"What a primitive and ghastly place—" she started to say, but Joanna kicked her firmly in the ankle.

"What a delightful village," Joanna said, smiling at Karl. "We are very grateful to be staying here."

"They are holding a feast in our honor tonight," Alex said. He nodded toward Owen Purchase, who was shouldering his rifle and chatting to a couple of the Pomor hunters. "Purchase is going to shoot some ptarmigan for us."

"Ptarmigan?" Lottie wrinkled up her nose. "Isn't that a bird? What are we to do, gnaw on the bones? This isn't the Middle Ages, you know."

"A pity," Alex whispered to Joanna, "for if it were we could duck her for being a witch." He raised his voice. "I am sure," he said smoothly, "that you will feel a great deal better after you have had a hot bath, Mrs. Cummings." He gestured to the women who were crowding about them. "They are waiting to show you to the sweat baths so that you may wash and relax."

"A sweat bath!" Lottie exclaimed. "How utterly disgusting! You will not tempt me into sweating!" She snatched the skirts of her gown away from the fingers of one small child, who started to wail.

Alex turned to Joanna. "Then it would appear," he said, "that it is just you and I, my lady."

The idea of a bath, sweat or otherwise, sounded extraordinarily tempting to Joanna. The idea of a bath with Alex in it as well, however, was rather more disturbing. She eyed him cautiously.

"You are to accompany me?"

Alex's expression was suspiciously bland. "It is the custom here in the North."

"Is it indeed?" Joanna challenged.

He took her hand. "It is perfectly respectable for a married couple to bathe together, Joanna. I assure you that I would do nothing to offend the sensibilities of our hosts, and anyway—" he lowered his voice "—we have been very intimate these past few days. There is no need to be shy now."

Joanna's face flamed. "I am not shy!"

"Yes, you are." Alex's smile said that he knew better. "You have been shy with me from the start." He touched her cheek. "I like it—but you don't have to feel like that anymore."

Joanna closed her eyes for a moment. She felt hot and stirred up by the expression in his eyes but at the same time helplessly adrift. The feelings that Alex was starting to conjure in her seemed too complex and difficult to control. At the beginning it had been about claiming Nina, but when she had started to fall in love with him that had all changed. She remembered once telling Merryn that adventurers were the worst type of man to fall in love with because they would always care more for traveling and exploring than for any woman. She thought of those words with a shiver.

Their hosts were helping to unload their baggage from the cart now and taking it toward one of the living huts. The women swept Joanna up in a laughing, chattering group and carried her away toward the nearest cabin.

"They will fetch me when they have made you ready,"

Alex said, smiling at her as she cast him a look of apprehension. "I have told them that we are but recently wed," he added. "They wish to give us the bridal *bania*, the bridal bath."

It seemed to Joanna that the news of her wedding had indeed sent the village women into a fever of excitement. As they drew her into the warm shadowy interior of the bathing hut they plucked at her clothes and at her hair, exclaiming and smiling. Her meager words of Russian seemed totally inadequate now. All she could do was smile and nod as they gestured to her to sit on a cushioned bench and started to unpin her plait, which felt stiff with dust.

The hut was extraordinarily hot after the clinging chill of the mist outside and it smelled absolutely wonderful with the scent of birch and pine. What light there was filtered in through one small window and the tiny gaps between the wooden logs that made up the wall. Joanna started to relax as the warmth seeped into her veins. One of the girls brought her a cup of wine spiced with nutmeg. It was strong and delicious. They were brushing out her hair now, exclaiming over the length and the thickness of it. The long strokes of the brush were very soothing, as was the sweet tide of wine. Joanna, who had spent most of the day warding off frightened thoughts about meeting Nina on the morrow and how she might start to build the foundations of a relationship with a little girl who must be lonely and abandoned, allowed her mind to rest for a while. In the sweet-scented darkness of the bathing hut her fears were lulled, her anxieties about the future banished. Even when the women started to ease her from her riding habit, she barely noticed. There was a great deal of hilarity about the boots, which needed three of them to pull off.

It was only when they started to peel away her underclothes that Joanna realized with a rush of astonishment that they intended her to be completely naked. She sat up abruptly and her head spun with the wine and the heat. The women were around her like a flock of birds, chattering and plucking and seemingly taking no notice of her puny efforts to resist them. One of the girls, who could not have been more than sixteen, smiled at her and put a reassuring hand on her arm.

"Please do not worry, my lady. It is part of the bridal preparations."

"You speak English!" Joanna said. She felt hugely relieved, less alone. "What is your name?"

"I am Anya and I learned your language at the monastery school at Bellsund," the girl said. She had laughing brown eyes and the widest smile that Joanna had ever seen. "The bridal *bania* is very special," she confided. "We were all so happy when we learned that you and the stern lord were newly wed."

"The stern lord." Joanna laughed. "Yes, that is a good description of Alex."

"So we make you beautiful for him," the girl said as someone else whipped away Joanna's last shreds of underwear before she could even protest. "There is soap here to wash, and almond oils for your hair—"

"Thank you," Joanna said hastily, gesturing them to step back. "If you please, I shall do the washing myself and…um…do you have a robe I could borrow?"

There was some grumbling at this. Clearly, her

British reserve puzzled her hosts. However, they backed away good-naturedly, leaving her with cool springwater to wash and, more important to Joanna, her privacy. She lathered her hair slowly, enjoying the rich scent of the almond oil after so many weeks on the ship and the past few days of rough traveling. The soap was gentle and smelled of herbs and she reveled in washing herself all over. After what seemed like a very long time, Anya knocked gently at the door and brought her a robe of the softest wool to wrap about herself, and then gestured to her that she should enter the inner baths. Joanna stood up and felt so dizzy and disorientated in the heat and darkness that she almost fell.

Her head spun even more when she went into the inner room and Anya shut the door softly behind her. Here it was fiendishly hot, like the fires of hell. She had never experienced anything like it. There were no windows and one long wooden bench along the wall—and Alex was sitting on it. He was, as far as Joanna could see, utterly naked apart from a cloth across his lap. His chest already gleamed with sweat.

"How did you get in here?" she asked foolishly, backing toward the door, her fingers rough against the hardness of the wood.

"There is another entrance," Alex said. He put out a negligent hand and pulled her down beside him, and because of her utter confusion she collapsed onto the bench beside him like a rag doll folding up. He steadied her. In the near dark she saw his teeth gleam in a smile.

"Are you quite well, Joanna?"

"I feel very odd," Joanna admitted. "I fear these unusual customs are rather unfamiliar to me."

"Of course," Alex said. He brushed the hair back from her face and she flinched from his touch, for it sent such awareness skittering across her skin that her entire body tingled.

"Relax," Alex murmured. "You feel very tense. I had hoped that the bath would refresh you. It is renowned for its medicinal properties, you know."

"Medicinal," Joanna murmured. That sounded most reassuring.

"Would you like me to tell you a little of the history of the baths?" Alex asked. "It might help you to feel a little more calm."

Well, Joanna thought, a little history seemed unexceptional. As a subject it had never particularly interested her, but anything that helped to distract her from the potency of Alex's presence beside her must surely be a good thing. The heat was building now. Alex leaned forward and poured water on the pile of stones in the center of the room, and the steam rose hissing into the air and wreathed about them and it felt almost too hot to breathe. Then he tipped a bottle of clear liquid into the center of the column of steam, and the scent and the fumes made Jo's head feel so heavy she wanted to lie down. The room was spinning slowly, pleasantly, and her blood beat hard in her veins.

"Vodka," Alex said. "A terrible waste, but it is part of the ritual."

"What is vodka?" Jo asked.

"A spirit so strong it would make last night's rum taste like lemonade at Gunter's," Alex said, smiling.

"I do feel foxed again," Joanna admitted.

"It is merely the scents, and the intensity of the

heat," Alex said. He slid a little closer to her along the bench.

"All the Scandinavians have a bathing custom." Alex spoke softly after a moment. "It goes back many hundreds of years. In countries with climates as harsh as this the glowing heat relaxes the muscles and soothes the soul."

"Delightful," Joanna murmured. She was starting to adjust to the intensity of the heat now. Her skin felt as though it was shimmering with it and a strange new consciousness of her body was creeping through her. It was as though every part of her was alive.

"After they have experienced the heat of the sweat baths," Alex continued, "they beat themselves with a birch switch to improve the circulation of the blood."

Joanna gave a little gasp. Her mind filled with deep, dark images. Her body burned. "Birch switch?" she said faintly. "Beating?"

"It is the custom," Alex said smoothly. "For medicinal purposes."

"Oh, of course."

How decadent was she, Joanna wondered, to have put quite a different emphasis on his words?

"And then," Alex finished, "they run outside completely naked and either roll in the snow or plunge into the waters of the fjord."

"How extraordinary." Joanna shifted on the bench. Never had she felt so aware of her physical body. The wooden bench was so hot it stung her skin. She was rosy all over, the sweat rolling from her and the woolen gown intolerably sticky as it clung to her damp body. Her abdomen felt tight with pleasure, her nipples were hard where they rubbed against the wool of the gown.

This, she reminded herself sternly, was supposed to be a relaxing but medicinal experience, not a sensual one.

"You look most uncomfortable," Alex said. There was amusement in his voice. "You would surely be more at ease if you removed that robe."

Joanna realized that she was clutching the neck of the gown very tightly at her throat. Alex rested his head against the wooden slats behind him and closed his eyes, for all the world, she thought crossly, as though he was as thoroughly relaxed as he claimed she should be. She eased her grip a little. It was true that to lose the robe would be a great deal more comfortable. And it was practically dark in the bathhouse. Alex would not be able to see anything if she did… And what did it matter anyway, for he was her husband…

Stealthily, she eased the robe away from her body and dropped it to the floor with a sigh of relief. The swaths of steam curled up around her naked body and she felt hot and tight and excited and not one whit more relaxed.

"Traditionally," Alex said without opening his eyes, "the sweat of the bride is baked into the wedding bread and cakes when she is covered in milk and dough in the sweat baths."

"I know that I sound like Lottie," Joanna said, "but it really does not sound very pleasant for everyone else to have to eat me."

Alex shifted and opened his eyes suddenly. His gaze swept down her body. He touched the curl that nestled in the hollow of her throat then leaned forward and licked up the drops of water there.

"I will taste you," he said. "That will suffice for us."

Joanna's heart leaped and started to race with a deep, harsh beat that seemed to fill her whole body.

"Hmm." Alex's voice was deep and rough. "Salty."

Joanna shivered despite the intense heat. Her senses were bewitched. The darkness, the scent, the warmth... She felt drowsy and languid yet somehow more awake and alive than she had ever felt before. She lay back on the hot wooden bench and felt Alex's hands and his lips on her body, and she was so heated and so wet and so open to him that she cried out in longing. It was like a feverish dream as he sank inside her and her mind tumbled over and over into the dark and she gave herself up to him and felt as though he possessed her soul.

Later Alex wrapped her in the woolen robe and carried her back to their hut and she dressed for the feast and they ate roast ptarmigan and freshly baked bread and fruit and honey. The villagers danced and sang the bridal songs of their homeland and gave Joanna a shirt, which they said was for her to wrap her firstborn child in for it would bring good luck. Joanna felt a pang of grief but folded the gift away carefully at the bottom of her trunk.

The bridal feasting became wilder. Joanna saw Lottie slope off outside with a particularly well-set-up young Pomor hunter and wondered what Dev would think of that, but he was surrounded by three beautiful Pomor girls and did not even appear to notice. Later still, Alex took her back to their hut and made love to her again. Afterward Joanna lay awake and looked at the soft midnight light. Alex's hand was resting lightly on her stomach as he slept and it felt like a gesture of possession. He would be asking soon when she would know if she was enceinte. Suddenly the pain ripped through her as viciously as it had done in the past and she knew she was grieving not only for the deceit that lay between them but also for the bitter truth that she would never be able to give Alex a child when it was becoming something she longed for very deeply.

Chapter 14

JOANNA WOKE WRAPPED in Alex's arms. She felt cramped and stiff. The magic of the night before had gone and the morning was damp and gray and her heart felt cold and sad, too. Today it was not so easy to keep the world at bay. Today they would go to Bellsund to find Nina and she was afraid. And remembering Alex's tenderness of the night before, she felt a fraud as well—a deceiver, the wife who had betrayed him. She despised herself.

She felt the sting of tears in her throat and eased herself from Alex's embrace. He made a soft sound of protest, but he did not wake, and after a moment she slipped from the hut and went out into the morning air. Max, yawning, jumped from his basket and followed her outside. She walked down to the inlet to wash her face and hands. The water was so cold and crisp that it stole her breath. She wondered what on earth it must be like to run from the intense heat of the bathhouse and plunge into the icy waters of the fjord. Surely only the most mad and hardy could survive that. But then, she had thought herself a delicate lady, yet had done things on this trip that would send the matrons of the ton run screeching for their smelling salts.

There was a crunch of shingle on the beach before her and she looked up from the stream and her heart almost froze in her chest. She had forgotten Alex's strictures about safety, forgotten that in this land there was more than one way to meet a swift death. For there it was, not the pure white that she had always imagined but a sort of rich cream color, gleaming in the morning sun. The bear sniffed the air, turned its head and looked directly at her.

It was beautiful. It was also enormous and terrifying—but somehow quite enchanting in its power and strength and grace.

Joanna's heart stuttered in her chest and then began to race. She straightened up and stood still, watching it come. It moved slowly, deliberately, without taking its gaze from her. She felt transfixed, her legs as weak as water, fascinated, terrified. She knew that she should move, run for cover and raise the alarm in the village, but her legs did not seem to want to obey her. She opened her mouth and no sound came except a dry gasp as her breath caught in her throat.

There was a noise behind her, the rattle of stones on the scree slope and she turned her head. Alex was standing above her on the hillside and he had a rifle in his hands. His face was white and his eyes burned dark. Max was with him, running in circles, barking and barking, the sound bouncing off the high walls of the mountains and echoing back.

And still the bear came on.

Alex did not move. The bear was a mere two hundred feet away now. It looked enormous. It raised its head and seemed to dance for a moment on the balls of its feet like a boxer.

Terror swept through Joanna in a hot tide. She tried to scramble away, up the slope, slipping and sliding as the stones ran beneath her boots. The bear was so close now that she could almost feel its breath on her face. She was shaking so hard that she felt faint and sick.

Alex was not going to help her.

A scream trapped in her throat. Her mind tumbled with despair. And then Alex raised the rifle and fired over the bear's head.

The smack of the shot echoed around the mountain like the roar of a cannon. The bear stopped and stared at Joanna for what seemed like forever and then it turned and ambled slowly away.

Joanna lay still for a moment, shaking, her hair in her eyes, her pulse drumming in her ears so loudly that for a moment it was all she could hear. She rolled over, sat up and looked at Alex. He was stark white. He put the rifle down and she could see he was shaking.

"I couldn't kill it," Alex said. His voice sounded strange, remote. "I should have shot it down much sooner."

Joanna looked at him, arrested by the note in his voice. "Alex—" she said uncertainly. Reaction was setting in now, making her shiver and shiver with shock. She wanted to rail at him for risking her life, but she could not find her voice. She wanted to shake him for leaving it so late; she wanted to cry. Yet there was something in Alex's stillness and the stunned way in which he stood staring in the direction that the bear had gone that held her quiet.

"I failed," Alex said quietly. His gaze came back and focused on her hard and fast. "I failed again." He dropped to his knees beside her and grabbed her shoulders, his fingers biting into her flesh. Joanna gave a gasp.

"You should never have come," Alex said. "I knew you should never have come. I could not protect you properly when it mattered." He released her abruptly, stood up and walked away.

"Where are you going?" Joanna demanded. But he did not answer. He did not even turn.

The others, alerted by Max's barking and the sound of the shot, were coming out to meet her now, Dev running faster than Joanna had ever seen a man move, Owen Purchase with a rifle, Lottie grabbing her cloak about her. Behind them the villagers crowded from their huts.

Joanna scrambled stiffly to her feet and started to brush the dirt from her skirts with hands that shook.

"Jo!" Lottie's voice had lost all its usual assurance. She grabbed Joanna's hands. "We heard the shot. What happened?"

"I came out on my own," Joanna said. "So stupid, when we were told to be careful. I forgot…" She gave a convulsive shudder. "There was a bear, Lottie. It…it was so beautiful. Alex said he couldn't kill it and truly I would not have wished him to, but I was so terrified—" Her voice broke.

Dev, who was bending to pick up the rifle, gave her a sharp look. "Alex did not shoot it?"

"He fired over its head," Joanna said. She shuddered again and Lottie put an arm about her, steering her back toward the hut.

"Where's Grant now?" Purchase demanded. There was a white line about his mouth and a hard look in his eyes.

"He's gone." Joanna's teeth were chattering so

much she could barely form the words. "I don't know where—"

"Don't say any more," Lottie scolded. "Not until we get you inside."

They wrapped her in blankets and gave her brandy to drink even though Joanna protested that she would rather have something hot. Lottie knelt before her, rubbing her cold hands. Owen Purchase had a poker face on, as though he should have been there to protect her, as though he wanted to kill Alex for failing in his duty.

"Nobody died," Joanna pointed out as she swallowed the spirit and felt it make its fiery way down her throat and curl into her stomach.

"I don't understand," Lottie said. She still looked shocked, as real as Joanna had ever seen her, all her shallow pretense stripped away. "Why didn't Alex fire sooner? Why didn't he kill it?"

"I don't know," Joanna said. She shivered inside the rough blankets, feeling the scratch of them against her skin. "I don't know," she said again. "He said he had failed me in some way and then—" she made a slight gesture "—he just walked away."

Out of the corner of her eye she saw Dev and Purchase exchange a glance. She looked up, wanting to defend Alex from their censure. For all her anger with him earlier, she could not bear for them to blame him.

"I didn't want him to kill it," she said defiantly. "It was too beautiful to kill."

"And it would have made a terrible mess," Lottie said, recovering some of her sangfroid.

"But a good meal," Dev said regretfully.

Joanna edged toward the fire, trying to get warm.

"Alex said that he had failed, Dev," she repeated. "What did he mean by that?"

She saw the two men exchange another look. "I don't know," Dev said slowly.

"Yes, you do," Owen Purchase said. He sounded grim. "We both know, Devlin. He meant that Amelia died because of him, and now—" he made a gesture that was full of repressed anger "—he fails to protect Joanna properly, too."

Dev's mouth set in an ugly line. "Amelia's death wasn't Alex's fault in any way," he said. "He was badly injured trying to save her. Her loss almost destroyed him—"

"Well, he almost lost a second wife just now," Owen said contemptuously. "He took an appalling risk. He should have shot it at two hundred yards."

Dev's hands balled into fists. "Don't you dare accuse Alex of cowardice and failure, Purchase—"

"Gentlemen." Joanna scrambled up and placed herself between them. The atmosphere was as taut and ugly as at a dogfight. "This isn't the time or the place for a mill," she said. "We need to find Alex." She looked appealingly at Dev. "Do you know where he will be, Devlin?"

"He will probably have gone to Wijde Bay," Dev murmured, turning away, his shoulders slumping. "There's a place there he once told me about. It's called the Villa Raven. It's not far."

"A villa!" Lottie had brightened immeasurably, like the sun coming out. "Why did no one tell me there was a villa here? How marvelous! Let us all go!"

"Mrs. Cummings," Purchase said dryly, "this isn't like the villas on the Thames in London. The Villa

Raven is no better than this hut, indeed probably far worse. It is in the most beautiful setting, but is said to bring misfortune on all who stay there."

"One of Sprague's crew lost his big toe to frostbite and left it there," Dev agreed. "And then there was Fletcher, who died there from scurvy—"

"It sounds charming," Joanna said. She picked up her cloak. "I shall go. I need to talk to Alex."

"No!" Lottie caught her arm. "Jo darling, you've almost been eaten by a mad, rampant polar bear! How could you possibly even think of venturing out into the vast wastes of Spitsbergen alone?"

"I'll take a rifle," Joanna said. "Papa showed me how to shoot when I was young. I used to hate the noise and the smell and everything about it, but I do know how to use it."

"I'll come with you, ma'am." Owen Purchase stepped forward. "There are a few things I want to say to Grant."

"No," Joanna said firmly. All she knew was that it was imperative that she find Alex. The look she had seen in his eyes when he had walked away had shaken her to her soul. "Thank you," she added, "but calling Alex out will not solve this particular problem, Captain Purchase."

Dev grinned and handed her his gun. "I won't try to stop you," he said. "I'll just give you some advice. Take Karl as your guide and send him back when you find Alex. We will wait for you both here. Oh, and if you need to shoot anything, try lying down to do it. You won't get as much recoil if you do."

"I'll remember that when there's a polar bear charging me," Joanna said dryly. Lottie passed her a satchel.

"I am told that there is something that passes for food and water in here," she said. "Try to make sure that you are not the meal, Jo darling."

"Thank you," Joanna said. She hugged Lottie and went out to where the horses were tethered. Karl was lounging in the sun, smoking some extremely potent and smelly tobacco, but he straightened up when he saw her and gave her a little bow and his gap-toothed smile.

"Please take me to the Villa Raven," Joanna said, and saw Karl's smile fade. He muttered something, crossed himself and spat on the ground for good measure.

"He says that place is haunted by bad spirits," Purchase said helpfully.

"Please tell him he does not need to accompany me all the way, only show me where it is," Joanna said.

A brief, tense interchange took place between the men and then Karl nodded with clear reluctance.

Purchase turned back to her. "All right," he said. "He'll take you down to the strand and watch to make sure you reach the hut safely and then he'll leave you." He shook his head. "I wish to hell you'd let me come with you, Lady Grant. I don't like this at all."

"I need to see Alex alone," Joanna said. "Captain Purchase—Owen—surely you understand—"

She saw a flash of something in Owen Purchase's eyes. "Oh, I understand, all right," Purchase said. He straightened. "And Devlin was right," he added reluctantly. "Grant is a fine man. I only said what I did because I was angry."

Joanna felt the prickle of tears at the back of her throat. "Thank you," she said.

She remembered the fierce objections Alex had made back in London when she had first outlined her plan to

travel to Spitsbergen. She thought of Lottie's idle speculation that Amelia Grant's death had been the cause of
Alex's determination to prevent her from taking the
journey and she shivered.

"I failed," Alex had said, "I could not protect
you…"

She put her foot in the stirrup and pulled herself up
into the saddle. "Let's go," she said.

"WHAT ARE YOU DOING HERE?"

Alex had known someone would come after him. He
had assumed that it would be either Dev or Owen Purchase and he would have had absolutely no compunction
about telling them to go to hell.

He had not for a moment imagined that it would be
Joanna.

He watched her dismount, tie her horse to the post
outside the Villa Raven and come up the rotting wooden
steps toward him. She was looking around with the
greatest of distaste as her gaze took in the desolate
spit of land and the rickety hut, one wall of which was
almost flattened by drifting sand.

The anger seethed inside him. He knew that it was
not fair to vent it on Joanna, but he was beyond fairness
now. All the memories he had repressed for so long, all
the guilt, all the horror, had come rushing back like a
poisoned tide. He had loved Amelia and he had failed
her. He had started to care for Joanna against all sense
and against all reason—and he had failed her, too. The
bitterness twisted in his gut like a rusted knife.

"Were you not content with almost getting yourself
eaten by a bear?" he inquired with deadly politeness.

"Did you really feel the need to venture abroad again so soon with no one to protect you?"

Joanna swung the rifle over her shoulder and placed it carefully against the wall.

"I can shoot," she said.

From the look in her blue eyes Alex thought she would very much like to shoot him. Excellent. It would put him out of his misery.

"I don't want you here," he said brutally. The guilt and grief lashed him again, as it had been doing from the moment he had walked away from her. Anger, with her, with him, pain, blame, hideous remorse… He felt sick with it. He grabbed her shoulders and felt her flinch.

"Why are you here?" he repeated.

She looked up at him and her eyes were that same clear candid blue that he remembered from the meeting in Churchward's office. It seemed so long ago.

"I came to find you," she said simply. She held his gaze fearlessly. "I thought that you might need me."

He squeezed his eyes tight shut. Her words hurt and it was his turn to flinch.

"I don't. I do not need you."

"Yes, you do." She spoke very calmly.

He shook his head. "Blame me. Argue with me." He ran a hand over his hair. "We always argue."

"Not this time." She moved from beneath his hands and went to sit down on the villa steps.

He had wanted to see the real Joanna Ware, the woman he had glimpsed beneath the facade of dashing society hostess. Here she was. And he realized that he had made a fundamental mistake; there was no facade. The darling of the ton, the Lady of the Fancy and this woman were one and the same. The style, the clothes, the balls and parties were simply aspects of a character that could also embrace a warmth and generosity toward those she cared for. He had not seen it before because he had been determined to believe her to be fickle and shallow. Ware's hatred of her and his own obstinacy had blinded him.

I thought you might need me…

She had cared about him, about how he might be feeling, putting aside her own pride and anger to offer him comfort. He felt humbled. He looked at Joanna. She was staring out across the bay with a fierce concentration and a very stubborn set to her chin. Alex felt a pang of emotion so poignant and powerful that he rocked back on his heels.

His wife. With a shock he realized that that had been what he had thought of as Amelia's role, not Joanna's. Although Amelia had died five years before, she had still been enshrined in his heart as his wife. It did not matter that he had married Joanna, that he had made love to her, that he wanted her to be the mother of his heir. Somehow he had still thought of Amelia as his real wife.

Until now…

He sat down next to Joanna. She cast him a sideways glance but she did not speak. After a moment he took her hand. He saw a little smile touch her lips. He wanted to kiss her.

"I want to tell you about Amelia," he said abruptly.

He heard the tiny catch of her breath and thought he saw a fleeting look of fear in her eyes.

"You never speak of her," she said.

"Well, I am doing so now."

She avoided his eyes. "You loved her?"

"Yes," Alex said. "Yes, I did. I loved her very much. We had known one another since we were young. I wanted her to travel with me where and when she could. She was not anxious to do so, but I insisted. I thought, in my arrogance, that it was a wife's place always to be by her husband's side."

Joanna's bright blue gaze was fixed on his face now. "What happened?" she said softly.

"We had been married five years when I was posted to India," Alex said. "The ship came under attack from a French squadron under Admiral Linois. We were escorting a couple of merchant ships that were anchored out of Vizagapatam." He paused. "There was an accident with some loose gunpowder in the magazine. It had not been doused down. There was a spark—" Alex stopped. He could still hear the explosion echo through his head, still taste the smoke and gunpowder gritty on his tongue, still smell the blood. He shuddered. Joanna's fingers tightened on his, her hand, small and warm, lying within his.

"There was a terrible fire that ravaged the ship," he said tonelessly. "I fought my way below to find Amelia. I found her, but…" He hesitated. "She was horribly burned. I knew she was going to die. With almost her last breath she asked me to forgive her for failing me." His voice roughened. "She kept apologizing to me, over and over again, because she had not been able to escape the flames. But I was the one who failed. I had insisted that she come with me. If she had stayed at home in England she would not have died."

There was silence. The wind was starting to rise, whistling through the spars of the ancient hut.

"She was pregnant with my child," Alex finished. "And I never wanted another wife nor another child until you came to me that night in London to make your bargain."

For a moment he saw vivid emotion in Joanna's face. Her fingers trembled in his. A moment later she bent her head and her bright hair fell forward, shielding her expression.

"You lost a child as well," she said. "Oh, Alex..." Her voice was so soft he had to strain to hear it. "I am so sorry. So very sorry."

"I never told anyone about the child," Alex said. The memory of Amelia had always been strong within him. He had clung to it, he realized, because he had felt in some way that if he started to forget her that would mean that he had started to feel less guilty, less responsible for her death. For years he had not wanted anyone else in her place. Balvenie could not have an heir because he had lost the wife and the child who should have stood beside him. But then Joanna had come to him and everything had started to change.

"Amelia was very gentle and sweet," he said. "She had no core of steel. She was not like you." He realized that until very recently he would have thought Joanna to be the weak one. He had been very mistaken in her.

"She would never have ridden all the way here to find me," he said. "She would have waited until I came back to her."

"She sounds like a woman of great good sense," Joanna said. She glanced down at her Esquimaux boots. "What sane woman would choose to ride out here, ruining her boots and her riding habit in the process?"

Alex heard the briskness in her words but underneath

it some strong emotion. He put a hand against her cheek and tilted her face up to his. Her skin was warm beneath his touch and so soft he wanted to kiss her. Suddenly, fiercely, the impulse gripped him. He wanted to reassure her, to tell her that he admired her for what she had done.

"I am glad you came," he said gently.

Her gaze clung to his. He pulled her close, his arms going around her. She felt so warm and so strong that again he was startled. How could Joanna Ware, who had seemed so brittle, instead prove to be so resilient? He rested his chin against her hair. It smelled of earth and felt dusty against his lips.

"Today," he said slowly, "when I saw the bear coming, I could not move. It was the most damnable thing." His hands tightened on her, she winced, and he eased back a little. He did not want to let her go completely, though. The need to keep her very close to him was strong.

"I knew what I had to do," he said. "I wanted to fire, but somehow I could not seem to move. I cannot explain it. All I seemed to be able to think was that I had failed before and now it was going to happen again in a different way…"

Joanna turned her face against his jacket in a little caress. "You did not fail Amelia, Alex," she said quietly. "You did your very best to save her. Dev said that you almost died, yourself, as a result. And today, well, you did not fail me either."

"I left it too late," Alex said. "I should have killed it." The anger swept through him again, but the hot, shaming tide seemed less powerful than it had before. Something was easing inside him, loosening its grip, starting to let go.

"Then I would have been really angry with you," Joanna said. "How could you kill something so magnificent?" She sighed, shivering a little in the wind from the sea. "We should go back. The others will be worried about us."

"Soon," Alex said. "I just want you to myself a little longer. Not only is there no privacy on the ship, there is no privacy on this expedition."

Joanna gave him a smile. "We managed well enough yesterday," she said demurely. Then, as he moved to kiss her: "However, I do draw the line at making love in this disgusting villa. I am certain it must be infected with fleas."

"It is too cold for them," Alex said. He kissed her again. Her lips clung to his for a brief moment, soft and sweet, and then she pushed him away.

"No," she said. "Absolutely not."

"Oh, very well," Alex said. He stood up and helped her to her feet. He stood still, looking down into her face for a moment.

"Joanna Grant," he said slowly, "you are the most surprising woman I have ever met."

Once again, for a fleeting second, he saw that shadow touch her eyes again and then she smiled. "I am glad that you realize it," she said lightly. She looked down at her feet, where the sole of the Esquimaux boot flapped. "You mentioned before that sailors were talented at shoe-making," she said. "Do you think any of them could fix my boot?"

Chapter 15

IT WAS ON THE MORNING of the following day that they rode along the coast toward the settlement of Bellsund. Alex had insisted that Joanna rest when they returned to the village and given the soreness and bruising of her body she had not argued with him. She had sat in a sheltered spot in the sunshine and listened to the women chattering as they washed the clothes, and she had cradled the babies and played with the children and had thought about the tragedy of Alex losing not only Amelia but also his unborn child as well. She had not thought it possible to feel worse about her betrayal of Alex's trust, but now the remorse hammered at her with no respite. He did not deserve such deceit.

He had asked her, the previous day, why she had come to find him and she had told him that it was because she had thought that he might need her and it had been true, but it had not been the whole truth. She had gone to him because instinct had driven her to do so. She had known that something terrible was paining him. She had wanted to ease that hurt because she loved him.

She was in love with him, utterly and completely.

She was in love with Alex Grant, the explorer, the adventurer, the man who wanted no ties and no responsibilities, who had offered her a bargain and whom she was cheating every step of the way.

"You can see now why Purchase could not bring the ship this far," Alex said, breaking into her unhappy thoughts. They were cantering along the shingle toward Bellsund. The cart, with Lottie and the luggage, was lurching along behind, and Lottie's squawks of complaint rose in the air to mingle with the cries of the seabirds.

"When the wind is from the east it blows the ice into the inlet and then it piles up and blocks the way through," Alex said.

Joanna reined in for a moment to study the view, glad of the distraction. Huge blocks of ice were heaped up higgledy-piggledy against one another as though thrown there by monstrous hands. She had never seen anything like it, not even in the harshest English winters when the rivers sometimes froze. It was easy to see how a ship might be crushed, the timbers creaking with strain and eventually cracking under the enormous pressure. She shuddered.

"That is what would have happened to us if you had not cut the *Sea Witch* out of the ice, isn't it?" she said. "We would have been trapped in the middle of something like that and crushed to death."

"Either that or driven onto the rocks and broken up," Alex said. "These are dangerous seas. The power of nature here is profound."

Joanna nodded. "When will it clear?" she asked.

"It could be any time," Alex said. "In the summer months the ice can shift and change within hours. You saw that yourself. When the wind veers, the current will sweep the ice away. You can see Bellsund

Monastery now," he added. "Over there, on the edge of the promontory."

Joanna turned in the saddle. "It looks like a fortress rather than a monastery," she whispered, staring across the bleak, barren ground. "I had no notion it would be like this."

The sprawling monastery had gray walls built of huge boulders that looked to be at least forty feet high and ten feet thick. There were squat round towers with pointed roofs, massive gates and behind the wall a jumble of other roofs, spires and buildings. Stumbling over such an enormous community in so empty and desolate a land was breathtaking and extraordinary, and yet the forbidding dark walls seemed almost to spring from the landscape like the natural rock.

Joanna shivered. Now that she was almost at the end of her journey she felt sick and scared, exhausted with longing to see Nina at last, fearful of finally stepping up and claiming David's daughter as her own. She straightened in the saddle and saw that Alex was watching her.

"Are you quite well?" His voice was soft. He put a hand over hers as they lay on the reins. "You do not have to do this, you know. I could go for you—"

"Thank you," Joanna said, "but I do have to do this." She dug her heels into the horse's sides and set off at a gallop, suddenly desperate to reach their destination. After a second she heard Alex follow her, the horses thundering along the strand toward the monastery gates. The cart and its outriders were left far behind.

The gates swung open onto a wide cobbled courtyard surrounded by buildings. A groom came forward to take their horses. Alex jumped down and held out his arms to help Joanna dismount. She slid down to the ground, suddenly aware of how stiff and tired she was, so grateful for his support that for a moment she clung to his arms before she dredged up the strength to release him and stand straight and alone.

Alex was talking in Russian to a young monk who had emerged from the gatehouse to greet them and Joanna stood by feeling both self-conscious and humble. She could see now how much Alex had smoothed this process for her, shepherding her safely across this empty and alien land, protecting her, guiding her and now dealing with the monks. Despite Merryn's tutoring, she could speak so little Russian. Caught up in all the emotional turmoil of David's legacy to her, she had overlooked so many matters—matters that Alex had made easy for her. For a moment her throat closed with tears as she realized how much she owed him.

"They are going to take us to see Father Starostin," Alex said. "He is the archmandrite, the chief abbot, of the monastery. He is a great man and a great scholar. I believe he has lived here at Bellsund for almost forty years."

Joanna nodded. "Thank you." She could feel the monk's gaze resting on her. Though he was young, he had an old man's face, wise and contemplative. His scrutiny made her feel vulnerable. He seemed to see too much, all her hopes and her fears. But she was tired now, too tired to keep her feelings from showing.

The monk led them along a series of roofed and arched passageways between the buildings, past a magnificent church, a bell tower and a set of gates that opened onto a lush botanical garden.

"The climate is mild here because we are in a valley,"

Alex murmured as he saw her gaze take in the verdant trees and plants. "They also have a most cunning system of hot-water pipes that run underground and heat the soil."

"Lottie will be pleased," Joanna said. "She will see trees at last."

"She will also be able to have a hot bath," Alex said, "which will no doubt please her even more, since she spurned the sweat baths. The guesthouse is most comfortably appointed."

Joanna's bones ached for a hot bath, too. *Soon,* she thought, *we can have warmth and clean clothes and soft beds, and all will be well.*

They turned a corner, ducked under a magnificently carved stone gateway and then the young monk was knocking on a huge wooden door and with a murmured word slipped inside, leaving them standing on the threshold.

"He will only be a moment," Alex said. "He has gone to tell the abbot that we are here."

Joanna's heart was beating in her throat. Her thoughts were tumbling over themselves like butterflies trapped in a net. For the first time she wondered what Nina would look like. Would she be fair like David, or would she resemble her Russian mother? She wondered suddenly how Nina would feel, being taken from this environment that she knew, a child who was barely more than a baby and had already lost her mother, being taken so far from home to a new life. Why had she not thought of that before? Another wave of anxiety took her and she pressed her hands together and felt the slippery dampness of her palms.

The door opened.

"Abbot Starostin will see you now," the young monk said.

Joanna hesitated, and Alex took her arm and drew her forward. "Courage," he whispered.

They were standing in a study. It had wide glass windows looking out across the gardens to the sea. A huge fire blazed in the hearth. There were richly colored rugs scattered across the stone floor and a desk with a vast book upon it open to show illuminated writing and pictures of men and sea monsters, whales and mermaids. There was such a profound sense of peace about the room that for a moment even the excited pounding of Joanna's pulse eased and she drank in the tranquillity.

A man rose from a chair beside the fire and came toward them. He was old and a little bent. In his hand was a letter and Joanna recognized David's writing on it with a leap of her heart. So it was true. Up until that moment she was not sure she had really believed it. But her late husband had left instructions at the monastery as to the arrangements he had made for his daughter. He had told the monks that one day his wife would come for the child. And now she was here.

The excitement burst within her like an explosion of light. A shiver went through her and she knew that Alex had felt it, for he looked sharply at her. She started forward, no longer able to wait.

"Father Abbot—"

But the monk's grave old face did not change to show a matching pleasure. His gray eyes, pale and shrewd, searched her face. He gave her his hand and his skin felt cool and papery and dry against her feverishly hot fingers.

"You are welcome at Bellsund, Lady Grant," he said

in perfect English. He turned to Alex and gave a little bow. "Lord Grant, a pleasure to see you again." A tiny frown marred his brow. "I understand, Lady Grant, that you have come from England to fetch Nina Ware, your late husband's child, and take her home?"

"That is correct." Joanna could barely form the words. Her heartbeats echoed in her ears and it almost felt as though they were audible, bouncing off the stone walls. She was shaking.

The abbot nodded slowly. "It is as Commodore Ware's letter decrees," he said. There was something hard to define in his tone. "I will take you to Nina at once since you have traveled so far and I can tell—" he smiled faintly "—that you are most anxious to see her."

They followed him down the endless stone corridors again and out into the bright, cold air. Joanna, who had thought she would have so many questions, so many things that she wanted to ask, found herself silent as she walked beside the abbot. Her apprehension had a different quality now. It stemmed from the abbot's quiet acceptance of what had happened. There had been no censure in his tone. It was not that he had forbidden her to see Nina or to take her away. But there was something else, something that she could not understand. Joanna could feel it and it breathed fear along her nerves and she knew Alex felt it, too, because he drew closer to her, offering her wordless comfort through the strength of his presence.

They turned a corner and then they were alongside a long low building and there was a garden and the sound of children's voices on the air. Joanna blinked. It seemed so unexpected.

"We have a school here," Abbot Starostin said, and Joanna remembered Anya telling her that she had learned her letters and her English at the monastery school. "The hunters and trappers come and go," the abbot continued, "but there is always a place here for their children."

The children were playing. There were ten or eleven of them, and they had hoops, bats and balls, shiny marbles made from the pebbles on the beach and painted spinning tops that shone brightly in the sun. Joanna thought of the crate of toys from Hamleys. They were so much shinier, newer and more expensive than these handmade playthings, so much better. She could give Nina lots and lots of games and dolls and spoil her with gifts and trinkets.

"That is Nina," Abbot Starostin said, pointing to a little girl who was sitting with two other children, chattering as they threaded bright stones onto a leather strip. "She is almost six years old now."

Dark, like her mother, Joanna thought, not fair like David…

She was a dainty child, with black hair and black eyes. She was wearing a faded pink dress with a tiny version of an embroidered white apron over it. Old clothes, Joanna thought.

I will buy her new ones, whatever she wants, dresses with sashes in every color of the rainbow and bonnets with ribbons to match…

She wanted to run to the child, gather her up and hold her close. The urge to do so, the consuming strength of it, stole her breath.

"The other boy and girl are her cousins," the abbot was saying. "They are called Toren and Galina."

Joanna looked at him sharply. "Cousins? But I thought that Nina was an orphan."

"She is," the abbot said, "but her mother came to Spitsbergen originally with a brother. He, too, has family here in the village and when Nina was orphaned and left with us they came to ask if they might take her in. Nina does not live here," he added. "She lives with her family."

Joanna watched as Nina held one of the perfectly round pebbles up to the sun, laughing as the light sparked colors of gold and russet and deep red in the stone. The other little girl, Galina, looked a solemn child. She placed another stone in Nina's palm and their dark heads bent together as they looked at it.

Something hard and sharp lodged itself in Joanna's chest and stuck there.

Cousins, playmates, friends... Family in the village, a school, a community, people who loved her...

It was so very different from all that she had imagined.

Nina looked well cared for, well fed. Happy.

The abbot was still talking, quietly, explaining about Nina's family and the school and the sorts of lessons they offered there when the children were older. Joanna tried to imagine Nina in quite a different setting, walking with her governess in the park in London, riding in Joanna's carriage, playing with Max. Nina would make new friends, Joanna thought. Perhaps she might even go to school, to one of the Bath seminaries. The horizons were wide, the possibilities endless, with a little money and a place in the world.

I will love her, too, Joanna thought violently, watching the two little girls laughing together. *I want her. I will give her everything that she needs.*

But something inside her was cracking and breaking. She tried to shore it up, but the split grew wider and wider until it yawned with a despair that threatened to consume her.

In all her thoughts and plans she had never once considered what Nina would want. She had never imagined that Nina might have other relatives and that there were people who loved her and who would miss her when she was gone.

I have been so selfish, Joanna thought. *I only ever thought of what I wanted.* She could feel her heart breaking piece by little piece.

The abbot was watching her with his perceptive gaze. She said, "I can see that Nina is very happy here, Father Abbot. We must talk about her future and how Lord Grant and I may help ensure that she may stay with her family for as long as she wishes. Now, will you please excuse me?"

And then she turned and walked away before she started to cry.

"JOANNA!" ALEX WAS almost running by the time he reached the inner courtyard of the monastery. He was desperately worried. He had heard in Joanna's voice that brittle tone that he was starting to know. It did not mean that she did not care; quite the contrary. It was her defense, her protection. He knew that she must be hurting terribly and the thought made him feel sick.

He had been about to follow her when Father Starostin had put a hand on his arm to detain him and Alex had been obliged to stop.

"Your wife is an extraordinary woman," the abbot said. "Such generosity and selflessness, to think of the child's happiness before her own wishes and desires."

"Yes," Alex said. He shook his head. He could not believe what Joanna had done, not when he knew how deeply, how desperately, she had wanted Nina. "There are matters that we must discuss, of course," he said. "Formalities…finances…"

Father Starostin patted his arm. "We have managed very well without those until now. There is no financial obligation, Lord Grant." He looked back at Nina, engrossed in her play. "I will make sure that when she is old enough, she knows the truth," he said softly. "About her father—and about Lady Grant's generosity. She may wish to write, to visit…"

"Of course," Alex said.

"Bring your wife to see me when she is recovered, Lord Grant," the abbot said, "and we shall talk on it. You are, of course, welcome to stay at Bellsund for as long as you wish."

Alex had thanked him and had gone out, impatience and the need to find Joanna thrumming in his veins, but she had already disappeared. The sky above the monastery had turned heavy and gray with the onset of snow. The wind had turned to the north, spiteful and biting cold.

Lottie was supervising the bringing in of her luggage when Alex reached the guesthouse door, and for once she seemed in a good mood.

"Hot water!" she said to Alex, beaming. "Warmth! Young men! I think I might decide to live here."

"The young men are monks, Mrs. Cummings," Alex said. "I do beg you not to corrupt them." He ran an impatient hand over his hair. "Have you seen Joanna? We are just this minute come from the abbot and I need to find her urgently—"

"Oh, she went out!" Lottie said, waving a vague hand toward the door. "She said that she might be gone some time…"

Alex was out of the door before she had finished speaking.

He could not find Joanna in the lush beauty of the botanical gardens and he stopped, frustrated, trying to think what she would do, where she would go, if she felt so raw and despairing that she wanted to hide from the world. Certainly she would seek out solitude and in Spitsbergen there were plenty of places she might find it. But she was on foot and in her second-best pair of boots at that, so she could not have walked far. For once he blessed the utter inadequacy of her fashionable wardrobe. He slipped out of the monastery gate, turned away from the village and walked out onto the strand.

A hundred yards along the beach he found her. She was standing staring out to sea. She had her back to him. No cloak, no hat. She must have taken them off in the guesthouse and wandered out just as she was. The snow was swirling about her. Her long dark hair tangled in the wind.

"Joanna." Alex stopped a few feet away from her and she turned to look at him and his heart stuttered when he saw her face. Her blue eyes were terrifyingly blank. He doubted she even saw him, let alone knew who he was. She had turned inside herself and he did not know how to reach her. Her gown clung to her body, soaked through already by the snow. There were flakes in her hair and on her lips. Alex looked at her and felt a violent surge of emotion.

"We must get into shelter." He spoke above the rising howl of the wind. Already it was too late to return to the monastery. The snow had thickened to a blizzard and he had seen storms like this blow up time and again. If they did not reach a trappers' hut soon they would lose their way in the white wilderness and very probably freeze to death even though they were so close to the village.

Alex put an arm about her, wrapping them both in his cloak, guiding her along the shore toward the nearest dwelling. She felt stiff, but she came with him docilely enough and he had no difficulty drawing her in through the door into the meager shelter within. Unlike some of the trappers' huts it was snug and well cared for, ready for overwintering once the long dark Spitsbergen nights came. Alex sent up a silent prayer that it was proof against the storm.

Joanna sat down on the edge of the bed. Her arms were locked about her body, but she was not even shivering with the cold. It was as though she was not really conscious of either herself or her surroundings. Alex wished he had some way to light the fire, something hot to give her, but there was nothing they could do but sit out the storm and hope that it would be of short duration, no more than a squall.

"You have to get out of those wet clothes." The words came out more roughly than Alex had intended. "Come on. I cannot have you taking a fever."

She allowed him to undress her, passive beneath his ministering hands and it was only when she was sitting there in her shift that suddenly she looked up and her eyes met his. There was such a blind anger and such terrible hurt there that Alex flinched.

"Alex," she said. Her arms went about him in desperate need and he drew her closer so that her head was resting against his chest. He found himself cradling her, whispering endearments, pressing his lips to her hair. She clung to him, soft and pliant in his arms. He felt her body shake with the sudden onset of tears; they soaked his shirt, hot against his cold skin. She was crying so hard now that the shudders were racking her entire body. He held her tighter until she stopped at last.

"I had to do it," she said.

"I understand." His heart felt so full that he could hardly speak. "You were so generous. More generous than I could ever have imagined."

"I did not want to be." She sounded angry, vicious even. "I wanted to take her away. I wanted her to be mine…" Another sob racked her. "But she never was…"

"Hush…" Alex gentled her with his hands. Her face was streaked with tears and her eyes were swollen and red and he felt the most enormous compassion for her. He touched her cheek, tilted her chin up in his hand and then she was leaning into his touch, linking her hands behind his neck and their lips met and his world exploded.

There was neither love nor tenderness in the kiss. It was deeply physical, a desperate cry from Joanna for relief from intolerable strain. Alex knew she only wanted him as an escape from the pain, but she was holding nothing back and every desire he had ever had leaped into full and shocking life. If he thought she had been responsive before, now she was as fierce and elemental as the storm. He kissed her back, his hands hard on her slender frame, his palms tingling from the rub of her silk chemise and the warmth of her skin beneath it.

She opened her lips to him, nestling closer now, and his mind went blank of everything except the innocent scent of her, almond and herbs, and the taste of her on his tongue and the tightening spiral of his lust. He responded to her by taking her mouth with a growing demand, pressing deeper and closer, and whatever claim he made she met and pushed him further. Her tongue tangled with his now, tempting him, intimate, provocative, the kiss delicious in its intensity. She pulled him down to lie beside her on the bed, running her hands over the muscles of his shoulders and chest, pressing herself against the whole hard length of him. He felt the swell of her breasts through the thin silk of her shift and his body tightened and heated to feverish proportions. But though his desire drove him he grabbed the last shreds of self-control and eased back, feathering kisses across the curve of her cheek and the line of her throat, tracing his fingertips lightly across her skin even as he drew away from her.

Her face was flushed now, her breathing had quickened and her eyes were glittering deep blue with desire.

"Joanna," he whispered. "Wait—"

"I want you." She grabbed a handful of his shirt and pulled him back down to her so that their lips were touching. "Oh, please…" Her tone had changed. There was something desperate in it now even as she kissed him again with heat and need and longing. She slid a hand beneath his shirt and his skin jumped and quivered at her touch. She tugged the shirt up and pressed her lips where her hands had been and he groaned aloud.

"Please, Alex…" Her lips were grazing his belly now. He could feel her breath brushing against him even as the tip of her tongue traced a tantalizing path lower and lower to the band of his breeches. "Please make love to me."

How many men would refuse such a plea? Alex wondered dazedly. He felt he ought to—that if he was a gentleman he would offer her comfort in other ways that were not so deeply physical. He should talk to her, listen and allow her to pour out her feelings. And yet, if all she wanted in this moment was to escape from the intolerable loss of giving Nina up then he would not refuse her that comfort.

Then all thoughts were lost in the hot darkness conjured by her lips and her hands. She was easing open his breeches now and her breath caught on a sigh of satisfaction as she found him so primed and hard for her. She rose to her knees and shed her shift and in the pale light of the hut she was naked and beautiful. He pulled her roughly down beside him and looked at her and his heart ached because she was so lovely and she tasted so sweet and yet she looked so impossibly wanton with her hair spread about her and her limbs pale and tumbled in abandonment.

"Now," she said. The dark blue glitter of her gaze challenged him.

"No." If he was going to do this he was damned if it would be no more than a swift coupling to wipe out her misery. He was not going to allow her to use him to that extent. He would make sure she could not forget this. He would bring her back to him.

He would show her he loved her…

He touched her cheek again then ran his fingers over her lush lower lip, seeing her eyes darken still further with lust. She moved restlessly on the bed and reached for him, but he resisted, bending to kiss her again, a kiss that began gently and deepened into rich sensuality and sweet demand. He felt her sigh against his mouth and he prolonged the kiss until the tension and haste left her at last, replaced with a different sort of eagerness that was soft and tender. Her whole body seemed to relax beneath his hands, melting into pleasure.

Only then did he let her touch him at will, her hands smoothing and roaming with caresses that brought him to wicked pleasure all too quickly. Fire roared through his veins and he forced it back down, controlling it so that he did not simply plunge inside her and take what he wanted. Outside, the storm was driving itself to a whirling, frenzied rage that threatened to lift the hut from its foundations.

Alex groaned as Joanna slid down on top of him, hot and silken. He could not keep still and rose to meet the glide of her body on his. She gasped and he raised a hand to bring her head down to meet his, kissing her hot, open mouth, feeling the press of her breasts against his chest, lowering his hands to her hips to anchor her hard and deep above him.

"I love you," she whispered.

Alex heard the words and felt them like a breath across his soul. Something inside him, the last defenses he had been keeping against her, snapped once and for all.

I love you, too…

He felt her teeter on the edge and then she cried out

and drew him in deeper still, and he fell with her into a void so bright and light and consuming he had never known anything like it.

JOANNA WOKE TO THE WARMTH of the sun. Opening her eyes, she saw that it was filtering through the shutters and lying across her body in bars of light and shadow. For a moment she was aware of a feeling of sublime well-being and happiness, and then she remembered everything that had happened and something inside her chilled and shriveled like a flower left out in the frost. She could see her clothes lying in pools on the floor. Alex's cloak was still wrapped about her and beneath it she was naked. Alex had gone.

Shivering, resolutely refusing to think about the fact that Alex was no longer there, she reached for her clothes and dressed as best she could. Her shift felt cold against her chilled skin. The temperature in the hut could be barely above freezing and she was starting to feel icy both inside and out. Her limbs were stiff and she moved slowly, almost painfully.

She opened the door of the hut and the sunlight struck across her eyes, almost blinding her. The sun was high in the sky. She must have slept through the night and the entire morning. The air, cutting and fresh, teased her hair. She wrapped the cloak about her and wandered down the beach toward the shore. The sea was calm again now. Mist rose from its surface like wraiths. Joanna sat down on a boulder and drew her knees up to her chest.

The anger and grief that had possessed her the day before had gone, leaving her feelings hurt and battered, but no longer aching with pain. It was interesting, she thought, that David had not lied to her. His daughter had indeed been waiting for her at the end of her journey. Probably David never thought that she would have the tenacity to make the trip to Spitsbergen to claim Nina and so would never know one way or the other. He had laid out the temptation before her to cause her emotional misery, but she had been stronger than he had imagined, for she had undertaken the trip and she had survived the physical hardship. And in the end she had done the right thing, the only thing that she could do, in letting Nina go.

Well, it was over now. Joanna brushed a strand of hair away from her eyes. Her feelings for David felt remote and cold. It was as though she had been scoured clean of all emotion for him. He no longer had the power to hurt her because the worst had happened and she had survived it and that was because she had changed, become stronger and braver than she could ever have imagined, and Alex had been by her side.

Her heart did a giddy little swoop as she finally allowed herself to acknowledge how completely she had turned to Alex in her unhappiness. She had given herself to him wholly and without reservation. At first it had sprung from her need to blot out the pain, to forget. But Alex had refused to allow her to use him. He had made her see him as he truly was, a man she loved for his integrity and his directness and his honesty. She loved him for being a man of principle and honor, the hero she had wanted when she had been young, a man who had sworn to protect her and had been true to his word.

For a moment Joanna was filled with elation, excitement and hope. And then the truth of her situation hit her like a flood tide and she wanted to cry, for she knew that falling in love with Alex was probably the single most foolish thing she could have done. Alex had all those admirable qualities and more, but he was at heart still an adventurer; exploring was his lifeblood and he had never made any secret of the fact. He did not want a settled home or any emotional ties. He had been scrupulously honest in making that clear to her from the start. And now the original reason for their marriage—to rescue Nina and provide her with a secure home—was gone, but she and Alex were still shackled together. And worse, his one demand of her, that she give him a child, would never be fulfilled.

She had deceived him. That was the biggest betrayal of all.

She had to tell him. She could not bear it any longer and now that everything else was at an end it was only right to end this, too.

The crunch of footsteps on shingle drew her back to the present. She raised her head and saw that Alex was standing a few feet away from her. He was in his shirtsleeves. The wind stirred his dark hair. And looking at him it was as though every fiber of Joanna's being caught alight and burned. Alex, who had possessed her body with such heart-stopping passion and tenderness from the first… Alex, the husband who had become her lover in every sense of the word…

Alex, the husband she had cheated.

She knew she had to end it. She looked away, overcome with emotion, unable to find the words.

"I am sorry I was not back before you woke," Alex said. "I went to the village to get some food and to send word to the monastery that we were safe."

Joanna felt a lurch of guilt. She had not spared a thought for any of their companions, who would probably have been beside themselves with worry. She looked from Alex's face to the rather unappetizing food in his hands.

"Thank you," she said. She took a deep breath and made what felt like a monumental effort. "I am sorry," she said. "So sorry that it was all for nothing."

Alex was frowning at her. "Joanna," he said, and his gentleness smashed her heart, "you made the right decision about Nina. I cannot reproach you for it. You have been very brave." He took her hand. "I understand that giving up Nina is desperately hard for you to bear," he said. "You had built so much upon saving her and caring for her as your own. But in time we will have children of our own. I know you may not want to talk about that now, but once your sorrow has eased—"

Something broke within Joanna. "Don't," she said. Her voice shook. "Please don't say anything else. We will not have children of our own."

Alex had gone very still. Joanna freed her hand from his. It felt wrong to touch him now. She linked her fingers together to stop them from shaking.

"When we were in London you asked me why David and I had quarreled," she said. Her voice trembled. "The reason was because I failed to give him an heir. In five years of marriage I was never once pregnant. David and I quarreled because I was barren."

The word, so harsh and cold, seemed to hang between them in the air.

Alex was staring at her. "But surely," he said, "that was no more than mere chance. You said yourself—" his voice warmed into hope "—that conceiving a child was in God's hands. Unless you are certain that you cannot conceive, unless there is good reason to believe it to be so—"

He stopped. Joanna knew that he must have seen the change in her expression, the guilt she could not hide.

"There is good reason to believe it," she said.

Alex was shaking his head. His eyes had gone blank with shock. "But when I said I wanted an heir for Balvenie you said nothing!" He was looking at her with incredulity and dawning distaste, and when she did not contradict him he got to his feet and turned away from her.

"Am I to understand," he said in a tight tone she barely recognized, "that you knowingly deceived me? That when you came to me asking me to wed you and we made our bargain, you knew I was asking for something that you would never be able to give me?"

"Yes," Joanna said. "Yes, I did."

Alex rubbed a hand over the back of his neck. "And you did this—"

"For Nina's sake." Joanna's voice faltered. "And for my own, I admit. Alex, it was my only chance to have a child!" She looked at him beseechingly. "You know how desperate I was—"

"And you knew that in taking what you wanted you would deprive me of a child of my own, the very thing that I wanted." Alex gave a harsh laugh. "Oh, I do not pretend to understand what it must feel like to be a woman denied of the chance to have a child." He shook his head. "But now I know what it is like to be a man deprived of the heir he desires." He looked down at her. "I pity your loss," he said roughly. "I might even go so far as to say that I understand your motives. But the dishonesty of your behavior—" He stopped. "You lied to me," he said, and the words fell like stones into the quietness. "Ware warned me that you were selfish and manipulative. How ironic it is, when I had at last come to believe that he was the unprincipled one, that he should have been right about you after all."

"Divorce me," Joanna said helplessly. It broke her heart to say the words, but it was the only thing she could do to set him free. "You could remarry and beget an heir—" she began.

"No," Alex interrupted fiercely. "You stay as my wife."

Joanna stared at him. "But you cannot want that! Why would you do that?"

She held her breath as Alex turned away and paced a little way away along the beach. She knew the words she wanted to hear him say; knew, too, that she had forfeit any right to his love through her deception.

"You will remain as my wife because I pity you, Joanna," Alex said over his shoulder, and the word made her shrivel inside. "I can see you must have been desperate to do what you did. I will not make that worse by causing a monstrous scandal that will ruin you." He turned to look at her and his face was as hard as granite. "You may return to London. I will give you a letter for the lawyers. You will have my name and an allowance and you can take up your life as it was before. I shall travel." He turned away to stare out across the cold gray bay. "I will take ship from here. The Admiralty will probably court-martial me for desertion, but at this moment I find I do not care."

He walked away and Joanna watched him go. She had thought she had lost everything when she had given up Nina, but that had not been true. This was more painful, to know that she loved Alex and to see him walk away from her. It was worse still to know that he despised her for her deceit and that very probably he wished never to see her again but that they would be locked together forever in a loveless marriage.

She sat for a time on the cold shore and then, when there was nothing else to do, she started to walk back to the monastery to pack her bags.

Chapter 16

THERE WAS NO SIGN of Alex when Joanna returned to the monastery and she was fiercely glad that she did not have to face him again until she felt a little less raw and could conceal her emotions better. In a little while, perhaps, they would have to meet and speak, and she was not sure she could bear it. They had become strangers again in the most painful way possible, ripped apart by her deception after the sweetest and most tender night spent together. It seemed too cruel.

With a heavy heart Joanna dragged herself to the monastery guesthouse, trying to prepare herself to face Lottie's blatant curiosity and tactless questions. When she walked in, however, it was to find that no one was there. No one except Frazer and Devlin, whose clothes were streaked with white dust and who was wearing a grim expression that sat oddly on his good-humored face. He was pacing the floor whilst Frazer poured huge jugs of water into a steaming hip bath.

"The treacherous, deceitful, conniving bitch," Dev was saying, and for one terrible moment Joanna thought that Alex had told his cousin everything that had happened, that it was common knowledge, and now everybody hated her. Her heart shrank, but then Dev turned, saw her in the doorway and blushed.

"I beg your pardon, Lady Grant," he said. "I know she is your friend."

"You are speaking of Lottie, I assume," Joanna said, pushing away her own preoccupations. "What on earth has happened? Where is she?"

"She is down in the harbor," Dev said.

"Good Lord," Joanna said. "Has she run off with one of the sailors?"

"She's run off with John Hagan," Dev said gloomily. "And he has run off with Ware's treasure." He ran a hand over his fair hair, making it stand up in spikes. "Damnation take it," he added a little sadly, "I never thought that she loved me. I was the one who told her that it was over! And now it seems she has taken me for a fool!"

"No swearing in front of the lady, Mr. Devlin," Frazer said disapprovingly. "Not that Mrs Cummings isn't as brazen a piece as ever lived," he added.

"You are going to have to explain this to me," Joanna said, sitting down. "What is John Hagan doing here? How did he get here? And how," she added, frowning, "did he know about the treasure?"

Dev blushed an even deeper red. "Lottie must have told him," he muttered, rubbing a towel over his face. "She…persuaded…me to show her the treasure map when we were back in London."

"You're a fool, laddie," Frazer said dourly.

"I know," Dev said. "Damn it—sorry, dash it—I went across to Odden Bay yesterday afternoon and dug the thing up myself and brought it back here and did all the dashed work, and then Hagan walks in calm as you please this morning and says that it was Ware's treasure and since he is Ware's heir, it should belong to him!"

"I still don't understand how he got here," Joanna said.

"He bought passage with Captain Hallows on the *Raison*," Dev said. "We lost them early on in the storm off Shetland and they only arrived this morning." He gestured to the wide circular window in the guest-room tower. "The ice vanished in the night. The wind changed and the ice broke up and the ships could get in. Mr. Davy has brought *Sea Witch* round from the Isfjord."

Joanna went across to the window embrasure with its wide, bright view. All of Bellsund Bay and the mountains beyond were bright and white and clear in the afternoon sun. There were two ships now lying at anchor out in the bay. The diminutive *Sea Witch* looked completely dwarfed by a Royal Navy frigate.

"Purchase has gone to see to the provisioning of *Sea Witch*," Dev said. "We shall be ready to sail for home tomorrow."

He looked a little embarrassed and Joanna realized that he knew Alex would not be traveling with them. Frazer, too, was busying himself with towels and hot water and did not meet her eyes.

"I'm sorry," Dev said in a rush. "I had hoped that Alex might—" He stopped; started again. "I cannot understand why he is abandoning his commission, or indeed, abandoning you—" He broke off, looking awkward. Frazer was shaking his head and muttering something under his breath that sounded to Joanna like "bloody fool," no matter how much the steward apparently deplored swearing.

"Alex is not abandoning me," she said lightly. The least that she could do, she thought, was to shield her husband from the censure of his friends when none of this was his fault. "I knew when we wed that Alex would always wish to travel," she said. "It was agreed between us from the first." She leaned against the wide stone sill of the window and stared fixedly at the view, blinking to drive away the tears. She knew her voice sounded brittle and unconvincing. She knew that neither of them believed her.

She turned back to the room. Both Dev and Frazer were staring at her with identical expressions of pity.

"You did not tell me," she said quickly, "what sort of treasure it was."

"Oh…" Dev's face cleared a little. "It was not quite as we had imagined."

Joanna shook her head. "Why does that not surprise me? I suppose this is another of David's unwelcome jests?"

"It is, in a way," Dev said, sounding puzzled. "The treasure is a piece of marble. I think Ware must have found a seam of it in the rock here and thought to mine it. Hagan seems delighted at the prospect. He says it is of quality as fine as can be found in Italy and that it will make him a fortune in London." He set his jaw. "Purchase and I tried to show him the error of his ways, but the abbot prevented us from giving him a drubbing."

"The abbot is a man of sound good sense," Frazer said. "Are you going to take this bath or not, Mr. Devlin?"

"I shall leave you to it," Joanna said, smiling. She looked at the hip bath. "At least you have Lottie's bath to provide some comfort even if she has betrayed us."

"I am sorry," Dev said. "She is your friend."

"I fear Lottie was always monstrously indiscreet," Joanna said.

"And monstrously disloyal," Dev said bitterly.

Joanna shrugged. She found she did not really care for much today. Finding Nina, giving her up and losing Alex were all so immense that she had no time for Lottie Cummings's perfidy.

She plucked Max from his basket and tucked him beneath one arm. The dog made a grumbling sound to be disturbed. "I am going down to the harbor," she said. "I need to find Captain Purchase and make a few arrangements." She went out into the courtyard. She felt enormous relief that the ice had gone and they would be able to return to England soon. She could not stay here in Bellsund with David's daughter so close by and yet forever out of reach.

As for Alex, she thought, she would make it easy for him. She had chartered *Sea Witch* for the journey home, but she would not be on the ship. Instead, she would take passage with Captain Hallows on the *Raison*. It would be an uncomfortable journey with Lottie and John Hagan on board, too, but she did not care. She could not feel anything now beyond a numb misery that she had lost Alex forever. With the last of her money she would pay Owen Purchase to take Alex wherever he wished to travel. She would be the one to give him the freedom to go wherever he chose. Small recompense, perhaps, for her betrayal of him, but it was the only thing she could do.

She walked out of the huge monastery gates and stood on the bluff above Bellsund Bay. It was another soft summer day like the one that had greeted her arrival in Spitsbergen. A breeze from the south tugged at her hair and danced with her skirts. She could feel the sun on her back and it was warm. The sky was a perfect clear-washed blue with the mountains so sharp against it that they looked like cutout shapes. The snow was so white it hurt her eyes.

She was going home. It was time to say goodbye.

She looked down on the ships anchored in the fjord below. She was going back now, back to London, back to the same life she had known before. It was odd that in the end nothing had really changed. She and Merryn would live in town and she would design beautiful interiors for people and attend fashionable events and smile and dance and skate across the surface of her life as she had before. She would be Lady Grant rather than Lady Joanna Ware, but it would make little difference because Alex would be in India or the Amazon Basin or Samarkand, wherever that was. She would have to ask Merryn for an atlas or buy a globe, perhaps, so that she might learn where all these places were.

Or perhaps she would not, for following Alex's journeys across the globe would only serve to remind her how far he was from her.

She heard a step behind her and spun around, her heart lifting with hope, only for it to swoop down into her boots a moment later when she saw it was not Alex but Owen Purchase who was standing there. He came to stand beside her and for a moment neither of them spoke.

"You're going to run away, aren't you?" Purchase said. "You're going to go with Hallows on the *Raison*."

Joanna shook her head. "I'm not running away," she said. "I am going home."

"Come with me," Purchase said. Then, as Joanna gazed at him incredulously: "We'll take *Sea Witch*. We can go wherever we choose. Anywhere in the world."

Joanna looked into his eyes and her heart stuttered with shock at what she saw there.

"Owen—" she began, but he shook his head.

"Don't say anything. Not yet." He half turned from her and stood looking out across the fjord. "I never thought I'd do this," he said, "never thought I would play a friend false by running off with his wife." He took a breath, looked at her. "But the truth is that you're too good for him, Joanna. He doesn't deserve you and it near enough drives me insane." He laughed harshly. "It sounds so trite to say the words, but they're true."

"No," Joanna said. "No, they are not. Owen, if you knew—"

"All I can see," Purchase said fiercely, "is that you are here and you are sad, and that Grant is nowhere to be seen and anyway, he is the bastard who has made you sad in the first place and I cannot watch that anymore."

Joanna struggled to find the right words. "Owen," she said, "you were the one who told me that Alex was a fine man, and you were right." She sighed. "I am not better than Alex. It's simply that he and I are wrong for one another. Something happened, and it can never be put right, and that is why I am leaving."

Owen took her hand. His eyes were a dazzling blue-green, the color of the summer sea. He looked so handsome that Joanna smiled ruefully, for how many women would have given all that they owned to be standing in her place? Yet she could never go with him, for she loved Alex too much. She would not compound her betrayal of him with another.

She freed herself gently and saw Purchase smile, too,

in wry recognition that she was going to refuse him. She did not say anything. She did not need to.

"Devil take it," Purchase said after a moment, and there was true, deep bitterness in his voice. "The only time in my life that a woman turns me down and it is the only time that it matters."

He raised a hand to her in farewell and walked away, his boots crunching on the gravel.

ALEX HAD SPENT AN HOUR that afternoon with Captain Hallows, of the frigate *Raison,* a man whom he had always deplored as a stuffed shirt and whom he disliked even more on this occasion.

"I'm anxious to be gone from this godforsaken place, Grant," Hallows had snapped when they met in the monastery library. "The forecast is bad and the ice could close in again at any moment. We're reprovisioning now and I intend to sail on tomorrow morning's tide."

"Of course," Alex had said. "Spitsbergen is no place for the timid sailor." He watched Hallows's indignant face grow redder and more indignant still before the man marched off toward the harbor to rejoin his ship.

Alex then called for pen and ink, and spent a second hour composing a letter to his London lawyers concerning the arrangements for his wife's allowance. Joanna, he thought, could take the letter with her on *Sea Witch* when she left. For a moment his thoughts veered, dark and angry, toward his wife, and then he pushed them away, for what was there to think about? Joanna had betrayed him in the most fundamental way possible, with deliberate deceit from the first. He could hardly bear to acknowledge that her perfidiousness hurt all the more because he was in love with her. That was a weakness he fully intended to exorcise. The hard angry slashes of his pen on the parchment helped express his feelings, but he ruined three perfectly good quills and a number of sheets of paper in the process.

He spent the rest of the afternoon and evening occupied in discussions with Abbot Starostin on the practical and financial arrangements for Nina Ware's future, for although the abbot had said there was no obligation to fulfill, Alex had insisted that there should be a formal settlement. He was still one of Nina Ware's trustees alongside his wife and he was determined to meet his responsibilities. In terms of Ware's so-called fortune, Alex, too, had seen the marble that Dev had brought back from Odden Bay and knew that John Hagan had claimed it as his inheritance. After a few minutes—and a conversation with the abbot—they had agreed that it would be of no practical use to Nina and therefore Alex would not oppose Hagan's insistence on taking it back to England. Privately Alex thought that Hagan was mad to imagine that he could ever mine the stone in sufficient quantity to make a fortune, for the harsh Spitsbergen climate made a mockery of the plan. Well, Alex thought sourly, let the greedy, unprincipled bastard find that out for himself.

The discussion of business matters soothed Alex, rational and unemotional as it was, but at the back of his mind he was aware that there burned something more dangerous, hot and strong, a feeling of detestation of what Joanna had done to him and a disbelief and dismay at her betrayal of him. Yet his feelings for his wife were anything but simple. He had to accept that Joanna had shown courage and resilience on this journey beyond anything that he had expected of her. She had proved herself truly generous in leaving Nina with her family. She was kind and loving and giving and he ached for the Joanna he had thought he was starting to know and love. He wanted to find that woman again—wanted it violently, far more than he had ever thought possible.

When the discussions were complete, Starostin ordered food for them, and wine spiced with herbs, and they talked of Alex's travels and of Spitsbergen and Russia and the future, whilst the light turned from bright white to the softer blue that heralded night. Eventually Starostin went to a small wooden cabinet in a corner of the study and took out two glasses and a thick green bottle.

"You will join me in a glass of vodka, Lord Grant?" he asked. "I should warn you, it is strong."

Alex laughed. "I have drunk some strong spirits on my travels."

"Of course." The abbot poured, came across to the long windows where Alex was standing and handed the glass to him. "You know that it is bad luck not to drink it in one go?"

They toasted one another and then Alex downed the spirit in one mouthful in the traditional way—and almost choked. Drinking with the abbot, he thought, might well prove the most demanding ordeal of his journey so far.

Several hours and eight measures of vodka later, Alex was feeling considerably mellower than he had all day and staggered back to the monastery guesthouse where he collapsed on the sealskin rugs on his bunk and promptly fell asleep. He woke to find himself lying in exactly the same position. His boots were still on. Clearly Frazer had despaired of him and Alex could hardly blame the man. He knew that he stank of spirits and it felt as though a furnace was hammering in his head.

The building was very quiet. Accustomed to waking to the sounds of his fellow travelers, in particular to Lottie Cummings's grumbling, Alex lay and reveled for a moment in the peace. Then he realized that it was probably too quiet. It was suspiciously quiet. He struggled up, glanced once at the clock, looked at it a second time in horror to see how much time had elapsed and levered himself from the bed, shouting for Frazer.

The steward appeared immediately in the doorway, a razor in his hand, a towel over his arm and with a bowl of steaming hot water, which he placed on the dresser behind him.

"About time, my lord," he said, his mouth turning down at the corners.

Alex rubbed a hand across the back of his neck. "Where is everyone?"

He walked past Frazer into the room beyond. The guest chambers opened off a central stone-floored room; the other doors were ajar. He could see Dev and Owen Purchase's spartan room with two small kit bags. The next room was empty. It should have been full to overflowing with Joanna's luggage. Fear, sudden and sharp, pierced Alex's aching head.

He looked at Frazer, who looked back at him with what Alex had no difficulty interpreting as gigantic disapproval.

"Frazer," he said. "Where is Lady Grant?"

"Gone, my lord," Frazer said, and closed his mouth like a trap.

Alex waited. When nothing further was forthcoming,

he added, "Do you have any more information for me, Frazer?"

"Captain Hallows took on supplies yesterday, my lord," Frazer said. "Whilst you were asleep, he sailed for England." His mouth shut again with an audible snap that promised no further words would voluntarily be forthcoming.

"Lady Grant went with Hallows on the *Raison?*" Alex checked the clock again. "How long ago?"

There was a silence.

"How long?" Alex bellowed.

"Four hours, my lord," Frazer said reluctantly. "Maybe five."

"Why the hell didn't you wake me?" Alex said.

Frazer glared. "Lady Grant asked that I should not," he said.

Alex rubbed his temples. Joanna's absence, the emptiness of the rooms, the silence, mocked him. He was the one who had told Joanna to go back to London, he remembered. He had told her that he would take ship from Spitsbergen. He had as good as told her that he never wanted to see her again. Mired in bitterness at her betrayal, he had thought that he did not. Yet now that she had gone he realized how much disillusion and anger had blinded him to what he truly wanted.

He grabbed his coat.

"Pack my bags, please, Frazer," he said over his shoulder, "and have them ready with the others to take down to the harbor. Where is Captain Purchase?"

"Captain Purchase is finishing provisioning *Sea Witch,* my lord," Frazer said.

Alex hurried down the guesthouse steps and out of the gate. He could see *Sea Witch* alone again within the curve of the bay, a tiny ship on a blue sea, dwarfed by the sharp black peaks of the mountains. The sea was quiet today, dazzling sparks of sunlight leaping from the surface.

He found Purchase in the middle of his men, helping the crew roll barrels of pickled eider eggs and salted herring on board the ship. The sight made him think how much Joanna would hate such a diet—and then he realized that she would not be eating it and he felt his stomach drop and the dread of loss choke his throat.

"Is it true?" he asked urgently. "Has she gone?"

"I assume that you mean Lady Grant?" Purchase said. His expression was hard. "Yes, it's quite true. They sailed on the tide this morning." A faint, cold smile tugged at the corners of his mouth as he and Alex stood side by side watching the provisioning of *Sea Witch*.

"She paid me another six months' charter," Purchase said. "It was for you." The look he gave Alex was hard with dislike. "She made it easy for you, Grant," he said. "She gave you *Sea Witch*." He paused. "So where do you want to go?"

His tone implied that hell might be his favored option.

Alex looked at the trim little vessel. She was no ship of the line, but she had proved her worth. And it had been their contract, his and Joanna's, in the beginning. He had given her his name and his protection and she had promised him the freedom to pursue his dreams.

But now his dreams had changed.

He thought of the bargain that they had made. He had demanded that Joanna make no emotional claim on him. He had insisted that she give him leave to continue to pursue his life as an explorer, to make no compromises or concessions, to be free to travel as he wished without responsibility or constraint.

He had been irredeemably selfish.

What could an adventurer offer the woman who loved him? he wondered. He could offer his heart, perhaps. He could give his love in return for hers.

He thought of Dev, telling him in London that it was not money that Chessie needed but company and love. He thought of Joanna upbraiding him for giving everything to his family in a material sense but nothing in an emotional one. He thought of the bargain that he had offered her and the fact that she had deceived him because she was so desperate for a child to love that she had been prepared to do anything to gain one. He thought of the way she had come to find him at the Villa Raven and how she had broken through the defenses he had put around his heart after Amelia died. Most of all he thought of her sacrifice in giving up Nina Ware for the sake of those who loved her. And what had he offered her in return? He had given her material protection, perhaps, but with it a life as hollow and empty of love as it could be.

But that could change.

Alex's heart started to race, the blood beating in hard urgent strokes through his body. "Can you catch the *Raison?*" he asked Purchase abruptly.

A brilliant light leaped in Purchase's eyes. "You're going after her?"

"I'd be a fool not to," Alex said.

"You've been a fool a long time," Purchase said. "Why break the habit now?"

"Because I love her," Alex said. He looked his

friend straight in the eye. "You know that. You love her, too."

Purchase did not deny it. "I know she's too good for you," he said bitterly, "but you are the one she loves." He shook his head. "She loves you, and in return you treated her as badly as Ware did. You hurt her." He moved away and spoke with his back to Alex. His shoulders were tensed, muscles bunched. "I could kill you, Grant," he said. "You may not have hurt her physically like Ware did, but in your own way you are just as cruel as he—"

"What?" Alex said.

Purchase turned. His face was tense. "I said you are just as cruel—"

"Yes, I heard you," Alex said. "Not that bit. The bit about Ware hurting Joanna physically." He waited. Purchase was silent and Alex felt the fear creep up his spine until he could not stand it. "For God's sake, Purchase," he burst out, "just tell me."

Purchase ran a hand over his fair hair. "I tried to tell you before but you'd hear no word against him, would you, Grant?" The look that flared in Purchase's eyes was murderous. "Ware told me about it himself, one night when he was in his cups. He boasted of it, the bastard, about how they had quarreled because she'd failed to give him a son, and how he'd beaten her. Said he'd left her lying on the floor that very night..." Purchase's fists balled. "I nearly killed him there and then with my bare hands."

"You should have told me." Alex felt sick and cold and furiously angry. He thought of Churchward and his devotion to Joanna, of the loyalty—and the love—she commanded, of Daniel Brooke and the boxing crowds swearing to protect her, and of Purchase keeping her secrets. And he thought of David Ware, the hero… He felt incredulous, ripped with disbelief and disillusion.

"Ah, Grant," Purchase said, "it was Joanna's place to tell you if anyone did. I should not have said anything, but I was too angry to keep quiet." He sighed. "In the interests of our friendship I should also tell you that I asked Joanna to run away with me."

Alex rocked back. "What?" he said again. "When?"

"Last night," Purchase said. "You can call me out if you like." His lips twisted. "I don't really care at the moment."

"She turned you down," Alex said. He felt hope flare inside him. "She wouldn't go with you."

Purchase's sardonic smile deepened. "No need to rub it in." He held Alex's gaze fiercely. "She's a fine woman. You'd better not make a mess of this again."

"I won't," Alex said. "I swear it."

"So what are you waiting for?" Purchase gestured to the ship. "Go!"

"Not me," Alex said. "You. Much as it pains me to admit it, you are the better sailor. I couldn't catch the *Raison*. You can." He hesitated. "Or am I asking too much of our friendship?"

Purchase grinned. "You're pushing it, for sure. But—" he laughed "—you're not wrong. I am the better sailor." He slapped his friend on the shoulder. "Come on. You can crew for me this time."

"Send a man up to tell Frazer and to bring the bags," Alex said. "And where is Devlin?"

His question was answered as Dev arrived at a run. "Lady Grant has gone!" he said.

"I know," Alex said, not slackening his pace toward the ship.

"You bloody idiot," Devlin said with blistering scorn.

"Everything you say is true," Alex said, "but we don't have time for it now. We have to catch the tide."

Dev grabbed his arm. "You're going after the *Raison?*"

"We are."

Dev looked dubious for a second. "Who's captaining *Sea Witch?*"

"Purchase."

Dev's brow cleared. "Oh, good. I mean—"

"You mean that way we have a chance," Alex said. "Does no one rate my skill as a captain around here?"

"It's not that," Dev said, blushing. "You're the best, Alex. But Purchase is reckless and that's what you need now."

"Thank you," Purchase said. He bowed ironically. "I'll say it again. What are we waiting for?"

Chapter 17

"Jo, DARLING!" Lottie Cummings said, slipping into Joanna's cabin on the *Raison* and closing the door softly behind her. "I am so desperately sorry! Please tell me that you forgive me!"

"For what, Lottie?" Joanna was not in the mood for forgiveness. "Are you apologizing for conspiring with John Hagan to steal David's so-called treasure, or for something else that I do not yet know about?" She raised a brow. "Did you try to seduce Alex on the voyage out when I was sick? The whole of the ton knew that you slept with David the last time he was in London, so I suppose you would only be adding to your tally of my husbands." She sighed. "It's an odd thing, Lottie, but you have so much and yet it seems to me you always want what other people have."

"It isn't like that," Lottie said, putting on her best repentant pout. "And I was incredibly discreet with David." She met Joanna's scathing gaze and made a little fluttering gesture with her hands. "I am sorry," she said, "but you know David was the most ghastly lecher, darling—I was only one of many, so you can hardly blame me for that! And as for John Hagan, if I had known what a dreadful common little man he really was I would never have agreed to help him, but I was curious about the treasure, darling—it seemed so romantic, if you know what I mean…" She broke off, downcast, as she saw Joanna's skeptically raised eyebrows. "I was unhappy," she murmured. "I knew Devlin was only toying with me and sure enough he broke off our *affaire* yesterday. He said he was bored." She sounded outraged. "Bored with me—can you imagine? And lovely, lovely Owen Purchase is in love with you, Jo darling, so there was really no one else to play with…" Lottie could not quite erase the envy from her tone.

Joanna sighed again. "It feels like a Shakespearean comedy where everyone is in love with the wrong person, except that there is nothing humorous about it."

Lottie threw up her hands. "Nonsense, darling! You are in love with Alex and he is most certainly in love with you and he has been for ages, because he would never have turned me down otherwise. I made a pass at him in London," she added helpfully, "but I fear he was not interested in me."

Joanna looked at her former friend in all the immaculate finery of her striped pink-and-cream morning gown, the traces of lines and wrinkles just starting to show about her eyes and in her plump cheeks. Lottie had used cosmetics as her defense today, for her face was perfectly painted and only the unnatural hardness in her brown eyes betrayed her unhappiness. And it was a genuine unhappiness. Joanna recognized that. Perhaps she had truly cared for James Devlin and when he had ended their affair he had hurt more than her pride. Perhaps Lottie knew that age was creeping up on her and that she would not always have young men clamoring for her attention. Perhaps she was simply not happy in her pampered life with Mr. Cummings no matter how materially indulged she was, and she was searching for something else. Joanna was not sure. *One day, she thought, we may repair our friendship and I will ask Lottie these questions and maybe I can help her. But not today...* Today her feelings were too raw. Lottie's betrayal was nothing, a mere pinprick, beside the pain of losing Alex, but she felt so tired and so empty that she had no resources left on which to draw.

Lottie, with the sharp social antenna that had served her so well in the past, sensed that this was the moment to leave matters for now and stood up with a rustle of scented silk.

"I will stop pestering you now," she said, "but I am glad that we are friends again, Jo darling, and I swear we shall have no secrets from now on and that I will never ever attempt to seduce one of your husbands ever again..."

"I appreciate that, Lottie," Joanna said tiredly as Lottie swept from the cabin. "I will see you at dinner." Since they were to be trapped on the same ship for several weeks, she thought, it was sensible to try to mend fences. She was not inclined to offer the same generosity to John Hagan, though. That was asking too much. He had had his servants carry the marble blocks onto the ship, carefully wrapped in blankets, and stowed the stone in the hold. He was full of plans for the mining of the marble seam, plans that Joanna simply did not wish to hear.

The sea was calm. Joanna sat in the cabin with Max—a much more luxuriously appointed cabin than *Sea Witch* had to offer—and wondered how she was going to pass the days of the journey since it did not appear that she was going to be sick this time. *It is true,* Joanna thought with a sigh. *I am shallow. I have no resources for solitude. I shall sit here and feel sorry for myself and it will be ghastly.*

It was considerably short of dinnertime when Joanna heard the pounding of footsteps in the passage outside and Lottie's voice raised in excited clamor:

"Jo darling, come quickly! Oh, you must come quickly and see this!"

The cabin door burst open and Lottie stood there, her face alight with a strange sort of excitement. She came into the cabin and caught Joanna's hands.

"It's the *Sea Witch!*" she said. "He's come for you, Jo darling! Oh, I knew he would!"

Joanna felt as though something had hit her hard in the solar plexus. She did not want to hope, did not dare. "He—who?"

"Alex, of course!" Lottie was squeezing her hands excitedly. "They came up on us very fast and I think they mean to board! They haven't even put the boat out—they have come alongside with ropes, just like pirates! Captain Hallows is furious…" She pulled Joanna's hand. "Come and see!"

Up on deck there was almost as much mayhem as Joanna imagined they would find in a sea battle. *Sea Witch* had come alongside the *Raison* so close that there was barely a gap between the decks. Ropes were snaking over from the smaller ship to the frigate. Alex leaped across, tightening them, binding the ships together. Dev was helping him.

Captain Hallows looked furious, red in the face, shouting, "You're a damned pirate, Purchase! You're bloody dangerous! I'll see you hang for this!" He turned on Alex. "As for you, Grant, you cannot board my ship! The Admiralty will hear of this—they'll never give you another commission! They'll court-martial you!" He glared at Dev, who was laughing so much that he almost fell off the rope. "Nor you, Devlin. No bloody discipline, that's your trouble! You're a bunch of pirates and you'll all hang!"

"Then I'd better take what I came for and not trouble you any further, Hallows," Alex said. He turned and his gaze met Joanna's and her heart started to race. He took one purposeful step toward her.

"What are you doing here?" Joanna demanded. Her voice shook. "I am supposed to be running away from you. You cannot come after me!"

"I can and I have," Alex said. He smiled suddenly and Joanna felt a tiny flare of hope catch inside her. "I came to ask you if you still love me," Alex said.

There was a concerted intake of breath from all those around them. Joanna gasped, too.

"You cannot expect me to declare my love for you in front of all these people," she objected faintly. "That is very bad ton."

"I do expect it," Alex said. He was poised, waiting. Everyone was watching her. She felt faint.

"Joanna," Alex said, "I love you. I will always love you. I would go to the ends of the earth for you." He smiled and her heart tumbled over. "Just so that we are clear," he said.

There was a smattering of applause.

"Nicely done, Alex," Dev said.

"Thank you," Alex said. He grinned, the devil-may-care adventurer Joanna remembered. Her heart did another painful little flip.

"Now, you are coming with me," Alex said, "before Hallows shoots us all."

He scooped her up. Joanna felt the heat of his body, heard the beat of his heart. She clung to him, not quite believing that he was real, that he was here, that he had come for her.

"Wait!" she said. She put a hand against his chest. "My luggage! My clothes! Alex—"

"You won't need them," Alex said.

"I cannot be without all my luggage!" Joanna argued.

"Joanna," Alex said, his voice so firm she abandoned all thought of protest. "I am not waiting two hours whilst you pack a portmanteau. Hallows will have had me clapped in irons by then."

"Oh, very well," Joanna said, bowing to the inevitable. "Max!" she added suddenly as Alex was about to swing her over the side into Purchase's arms. "Oh, Alex, I cannot leave Max behind!"

Alex swore. "Get the damned dog, Devlin," he shouted, but Max had already found his way up on deck and with one bound he was over the side and onto the *Sea Witch*.

"You see," Joanna said, laughing. "I told you he had plenty of energy. He simply does not choose to exert himself."

There was a strange banshee wail behind them and for a second time Alex stopped. A figure was emerging up the companionway, a man apparently oblivious to all the commotion on deck, covered in dust, and holding what looked like a small piece of stone in his hands.

"Cousin John!" Joanna said. "What on earth…"

Even as they watched, the stone in John Hagan's

hands seemed to crumble and slip through his fingers. Alex took one look at the pile of white dust and shook his head.

"I do believe," he said, "that Mr. Hagan has just discovered that his so-called fortune is worthless."

"You knew that would happen!" Joanna accused, looking at his face. "You knew that David's treasure had no value?"

"As soon as I heard it was marble I knew," Alex said. "It freezes in the ground and when it warms up it cracks and crumbles to dust."

The wind blew along the deck, scattering the white powder until there was nothing left.

"How like David," Joanna said, sighing, "to leave his daughter an empty legacy."

"A legacy his cousin stole," Alex said, "and all for nothing." He smiled down at her. "Meanwhile, you and I, my love, have much to talk about."

He strode to the side of the ship and tossed Joanna across into Owen Purchase's arms. Purchase set her on her feet.

"Much as I would like to hold on to you, Lady Grant," he said, "I fear I have renounced my claim."

"Before you abandon me entirely," Joanna said, "I believe that I owe you my thanks." She reached up and kissed his cheek. "You were the one who sent Jem Brooke to protect me against David's violence, weren't you? " she whispered. "It puzzled me for a long time until I remembered that you had been on the same expedition as David that winter and returned to London with him. You must have known what happened even though he tried to keep it a secret."

For a long, long moment Owen Purchase looked into

her eyes and then he smiled. "I don't know what you are talking about," he said, and walked away, back to join Mr. Davy at the wheel.

Alex leaped down onto the deck beside her. Devlin was releasing the ropes and *Sea Witch* seemed to leap forward, leaving the larger frigate floundering in her wake.

"If I were Hallows," Alex said, looking back at the *Raison,* "I would hate Purchase, too."

They stood looking at one another. Suddenly everything seemed still and quiet. The very mountains were holding their breath.

"You gave me *Sea Witch,*" Alex said, "and the freedom to go where I wished." He smiled suddenly. "That was very generous of you, Joanna, but I do not want your gift. I want you."

Joanna swallowed hard. "I do love you," she whispered, "but I could not believe that you might forgive me."

Alex took her hands in his. "Joanna, I love you, too," he said again. "I understand why you did what you did. I was very angry, but I do understand. So, yes, I have forgiven you. And I swear those things I said just now are not merely pretty words and empty promises."

Joanna was shaking. "But I lied to you, Alex," she said. "I tricked you, deceived you."

"And then you told me the truth," Alex said. He held her gaze. His own was very steady. "There are lots of things I want to say, Joanna," he said, his voice rough with emotion, "but first I must tell you that I know about Ware." She heard him take a deep breath. "I know what he did to you."

Joanna's heart gave a lurch of dread. There was a

feral light in Alex's eyes. It scared her even though she knew his fury was not for her. If David were not already dead, she thought, he would be meeting his maker very swiftly indeed.

"Who told you?" she said. She let out her breath on a soft sigh. "Owen, I suppose. It was a secret. Not many people knew."

"Why?" Alex said fiercely. His hands tightened on hers. His touch was warm and strong. "Why did you never tell me, Joanna? Did you not trust me enough?"

"No, I did not," Joanna said. "Not at the beginning." She looked up at him, her gaze begging him to understand. "I knew you would not believe me," she said. "Why would you, when David had poisoned you against me?" She sighed. "Later on I wanted to tell you, but I knew that you thought David a hero." She cast a look down at their entwined hands. "It would have been a terrible betrayal of all you believed of him."

"He was a damnable scoundrel," Alex said violently.

Joanna raised her hand and pressed her fingers against his lips. "No, Alex. He was just a man. He could be harsh—he had faults, but he had virtues as well—" She broke off as Alex gave a hard, disbelieving laugh, and she smiled, a wobbly smile. "They were a few, very small virtues," she added, "such as having the courage to save your life."

"It astounds me that you have the generosity to say that," Alex said gruffly. He drew her close and put his arms about her, resting his cheek against hers. Joanna wanted to sink into the warmth and intimacy of the embrace, but she dared not. Alex knew the whole truth now, but it changed nothing. Even though he had forgiven her for the deceit, it could not change his need for an heir.

"That was why you believed that you could not have children," Alex said. His voice was still harsh, the anger palpable. "You quarreled with Ware because he accused you of being barren and then the insufferable bastard assaulted you and made your fears a reality." His hands were gentle on her even though his tone was vicious. "For that alone," Alex said, "I could kill him."

Joanna started to shake. "As the months of our marriage went by and I did not conceive he grew more and more angry," she whispered. "There was no reason, no explanation, but I started to believe that it must be my fault. And then we quarreled and he hurt me and—" She stopped. Huge tears were rolling silently down her cheeks.

Alex drew her close. "Joanna, we need never speak of Ware again, except this one thing—" He hesitated. "After he hurt you—" Joanna shivered and felt his arms tighten about her " when the doctors came, did they tell you that you would never bear a child?"

Joanna rested her cheek against his jacket. She felt frightened to open up her mind to those memories again, but she knew she had to do it. She had to let the light in and trust that this time Alex would be there to help her. "N-no," she said. "You know what doctors are. They could not be certain. It was just that I felt it." She drew away from him. "I felt different," she said. "I felt empty. It is difficult to explain. I had lost all hope, I suppose, all belief that it might happen."

"But now," Alex said, his tone so gentle that she marveled at his tenderness, "could you begin to hope again and see what happens?"

Joanna looked across the blue, dancing sea. "I do not know," she said honestly. Then, with a rush of feeling: "Alex, I am afraid to hope, afraid to allow those dreams and desires back in. I don't want to give them the power to hurt me again."

"Yes," Alex said, "I understand." He kissed her hair. "But if you love me, Joanna, as I love you, then the worst that can happen is that we shall never have a child—but we shall still have each other. That is enough for me. Is it enough for you?"

Joanna smiled. "A little while ago I thought that I had lost you, too, lost all hope." She sighed. "But I am afraid, Alex. You are an adventurer, an explorer. Your first love will always be to travel."

"That was what I told you, was it not?" Alex said. "I was unconscionably selfish, offering nothing of myself to you or to Devlin or Chessie or to any of the people who cared about me." He sighed. "It is true that I shall always wish to travel. It is a passion, but I do not think it is my first love anymore. You changed that the day you came to find me at the Villa Raven." He shifted a little, raising a hand to Joanna's face, where the strands of hair danced in the breeze. "I was already half in love with you then," he said. "I had been even in London, I think, though I pretended it was only lust not love."

He touched her cheek. "It would be dishonest of me to say that I will stay in one place for the rest of my life," he said. "But I thought that to start with, we might go back to London—I have my peace to make with the Admiralty—and then perhaps to Balvenie and Edinburgh, and I can show you my home…"

He released her and made no further attempt to touch her and Joanna knew that he was waiting for her to make her decision. She looked at his face, the dark, stern face of the man she had once thought of as her enemy, and felt submerged by the force of her love for him.

"I have heard that Edinburgh is a very fair city," she said. "I believe the shops are almost as good as London's." The fear brushed her again. She could not help it. "Oh, Alex," she said, her breath catching, "we are all wrong for one another, you know."

"No," Alex said. "We are different from each other, that is all. Don't be frightened of it," he added. "If a marriage is worth having then it is worth the fight."

Joanna leaned on the rail and felt the spray against her face and tasted the salty tang of it on her lips. It should not work, of course. She was the darling of the ton and she needed the lights and the diversions of town. Alex loved traveling the world. And yet neither of them was that straightforward. Alex had shown her wide horizons and taught her how it felt to be truly alive. He had shown her that there was far more to see, far more to experience, than she had once thought. And for her sake, Alex was prepared to go back to England and build a home. That, surely, was a measure of his love for her.

"Well," she said, "I am not sure that I am prepared to follow you to the ends of the earth, but I will come with you to Scotland." She touched his cheek lightly, feeling the stubble rough against her fingers, reveling in the intimacy at last. "I have a small taste for travel now," she continued demurely. "Perhaps I might like to see other lands if you are with me. Or we could come back to the Arctic in winter and our boat will get trapped in the ice and we will lie in the snow and watch the northern lights. Alex darling," she added, and smiled, "and this time I do mean it."

Alex's arms went about her gently and he drew her to him so that she could hear his heart beating strongly against her ear.

"The shirt that they gave you at our wedding breakfast," he said softly, "the one we are to wrap our first-born child in for luck. Do you still have it?"

Joanna nestled closer to him. "I do," she said. "I could not destroy it, or leave it behind. It felt…" She hesitated. "It felt like the tiniest ray of hope."

Alex turned her face up to his. "Then," he said, "let us go and stake our claim on that future." He kissed her with sweetness and promise, and the hope unfurled in Joanna's heart and she felt the spark of it catch and grow, never to be extinguished again.

"Since you have left all your clothes behind," Alex whispered, against her lips, "I fear there is only one way in which we may pass the voyage home."

* * * * *